The Chocolate Is The Life

Kerri Thomson

This novel is a work of fiction.

Names, characters, businesses, places, events and incidents are either the products of the author's imagination or used in a fictitious manner.
Any resemblance to actual events or persons living, dead, or otherwise is purely coincidental.

ACKNOWLEDGMENTS

I guess I should thank my own misspent youth, with its somewhat misguided choices in body art, and my husband for being so tolerant of my elaborate fantasy life, love of vampires and chocolate.

I must also thank my besties Stephanie, Samantha and Danielle, all of my other female friends and the classic movie *Clueless* for teaching me everything I ever needed to know about the intricacies of friendship. A simple Bitch Please can often say more than a whole litany of other words ever could. Thanks also to my oldest childhood friend Sandi for her diligent chapter-by-chapter reading at the start of this whole process. It seemed fitting, seeing as she played a starring role in my earliest writing attempts: *Sweet Sandra, A Tale of Terror*. Coming to a bookstore near you never.

A big thank you to Jeff Harrison for his excellent work at editing this beast as well as Stacy King for spotting some things we had missed, and Kate MacIver for taking my amateurish attempts at cover design and helping turn them into something beautiful. Without judgment.

And finally, I must also thank Bram Stoker for *Dracula* and in turn Francis Ford Coppola for his 1992 film version of the novel. A special shout-out to Gary Oldman for telling Winona Ryder that he had crossed oceans of time to find her. And with that, I fear I've said too much.

On with the show.

I have tried to keep an open mind,
and it is not the ordinary things of life that could close it,
but the strange things, the extraordinary things,
the things that make one doubt if they be mad or sane.

- Bram Stoker, *Dracula*

ONE

Frankie MacSweeney stood in front of the full length mirror that dominated an entire wall of her best friend's spacious bedroom, dressed in Victorian evening wear, wondering how the hell she managed to get herself into this situation. It had started innocently enough; these things often did.

But I will admit, she thought to herself, *I do look pretty damn good.*

Her best friend Louise had been known to astound her on the rare occasion with excellent taste and superb attention to detail. The room she was standing in, even the house itself, stood as testament. Once a humble carriage house on her family's sprawling seaside estate, Louise would proudly announce that she had made it into a real home all by herself to anyone who'd listen. She had single-handedly transformed both floors of the dark timbered structure into a symphony of texture with soft cream-coloured walls offset by carefully chosen accent pieces in vibrant hues of red and pink, and the resurfaced oak floorboards shared space with plush ornate carpets. And the dress that Louise had selected was definitely another example of her discerning eye.

The shade of purple of the velvet gown was, without

question, perfect; its depth and richness gave Frankie's usual deathly pale skin the illusion of fine porcelain. Louise had then somehow managed to coax her pin-straight ginger hair into soft waves that swept over the front of one shoulder, and lightly rimmed her hazel eyes with a smoky grey pencil and some matching shadow. She then stained Frankie's lips a deep plum, just a shade darker than what she was wearing, which seemed to put even more colour into her skin.

Apparently, Frankie noted, Louise had drawn the line at makeup when it came to faithfully recreating a proper Victorian look. Not that anyone would be paying much attention to her face.

The dress was an architectural masterpiece, its sole purpose to intensify those most feminine of attributes. Or, put more simply, in this dress Frankie had some serious tits and ass. A small miracle, considering she considered her own physique much more boyish than bombshell. She had always been too tall, too thin. A pasty Yin to Louise's far more exotic Yang.

Louise sauntered back into the room just then, catching Frankie admiring herself.

"Ooh, looks like Pinocchio's become a real girl after all," she cooed. Frankie glared at Louise's reflection as she stood behind her, smirking in triumph.

"Don't try to be clever, Lou. It doesn't suit you. Stick with what you know."

Louise faked a wince before hip-checking Frankie out of the way so that she could take her place in front of the mirror.

"Soooo… which one of my boys will be first to fall tonight, do you think: Alex, Quinn or Dr. Jared?" She mused aloud as she turned from side to side, checking her dress from all angles.

Frankie sighed, failing to disguise her eyeroll. *Here we go again.* For as long as she had known her – nearly the better

2

part of a decade, in fact, since they had met at the tender age of fourteen - Louise had kept an array of hapless blokes strung along, each one more utterly smitten with her than the next. And, seeing as the party fell on the eve of her friend's twenty-third birthday, Frankie was relieved that some things never changes.

"I've lost track of which one's which. Please, do enlighten me," she replied dryly. Louise huffed at her in annoyance.

"God Frankie, don't you *ever* listen to me? Let's see… well first, there's Dr. Jared. He's this hot nerd at Daddy's factory, a chemist or doctor or something. He's on contract while they do some product testing and other stuff but more importantly Daddy's had him over for dinner a few times and he's been panting after me ever since. Not really my type – way too intellectual – but he totally worships me."

"Umhmm," Frankie was back at the mirror, fiddling absentmindedly with her hair. She really did listen…sometimes. Fortunately, though, Louise hadn't taken much notice – she was on a roll.

"Then there's Quinn, from the American office. He's VP of marketing strategy or something. I don't know what exactly, but who cares? He's beautiful and *completely* obsessed with me. Absolutely filthy too! You should see some of the texts I get—"

"Right, heard enough about Quinn. *Next*," Frankie cut in before she could really get going. Louise took her attention away from her own reflection just long enough to roll her eyes.

"You can be such a prude. How does James put up with it?"

"Trust me, James has nothing to complain about whatsoever," Frankie shot back, but not before flinching defensively. While it was true that their sex life was just fine, thank you very much, she knew that he would probably be more than up for a little more of the sexting and dirty talk Louise was always on about before she'd had the presence of mind to stop her. Frankie just didn't think she could do it without laughing hysterically. It was something she had always attributed to being Scottish; her people just weren't wired that way.

"And speaking of James," Louise drawled, wagging a finger entwined in her long dark hair, "you can tell him from me that just because he gets called away last minute to work on some fancy European merger, that in no way absolves him of the obligatory birthday gift. The invite was extended and accepted; a gift is therefore customary, whether he shows up to the event or not."

"Yes, yes – I'll be sure to tell him the first chance I get. How dare he mess with the gift ratio? Never mind that it's a huge honour for him professionally to have been chosen to go. I mean, just how selfish can one person be?" Frankie was struggling to keep a straight face, especially after that final comment. But she could hold back no longer, bursting into laughter once she caught site of Louise's pursed lips, crossed arms and the impatient tapping of her foot.

She managed to compose herself and turned the conversation back to Louise, a device she often employed to avoid just such a situation.

"Now, you were saying something about a third gentleman?" Frankie had half-turned away as she asked so that Louise would not catch her checking her mobile, just to be sure she hadn't missed a text or email from James. She mostly didn't want her to see the worried look on her face. It was unlike James to go for more than a few hours without some form of contact: a text, a short but sweet email, a Facebook poke or some cheeky Wall comment. She had known he'd been extremely nervous yesterday before leaving for his trip. It was the firm's oldest and most important client, and he couldn't wrap his head around the fact that they'd chosen him to broker such an important deal. He had only just qualified as a barrister a few months earlier.

"Oooooh, I've saved the best for last: are you ready for this? It's Alex Tompkins!! I am *so* getting diamonds…" Louise squealed, jolting Frankie out of her concern for her fiancé long enough to allow what she had said to fully sink in.

"Wait," Frankie held up a hand cutting her off again, this time in disbelief. "Do you mean Alex Tompkins, as in Tompkins Toffees? Um… couldn't that be considered a conflict of interest?"

"A what? How'd you mean?" Frankie rolled her eyes. Again.

"Are you fucking kidding me? Is Tompkins not a direct competitor to Chadwick's Chocolate? Or is comparing toffee and chocolate the same as apples to oranges and there is really no comparison, therefore no conflict?"

Frankie had known that Louise was never one for paying attention to such things but even for her, this was thick. Head-up-her-arse thick. How could she not think that there was something wrong with dating someone who happened to be a major competitor to her family's business?

"I don't know what you're on about, but Daddy actually approves of this one," she replied in a curt tone. "He was over the moon when I told him I was planning to invite Alex. Even offered to hand-deliver the invitation! We've known each other for ages, you know – since middle school – so really it was only a matter of time. And of him getting clear of that horrid girlfriend of his. Astrid, I think her name was. Assface, more like—" *Apparently she's gotten her head stuck so far up there the oxygen has been cut off to her brain*, Frankie thought.

"Right…back up a minute. Your father offered to deliver an invitation to his only daughter's birthday party to a bloke he pretty much knows will end up shagging her senseless that night right under his nose? Isn't there something a little bit eww about that whole scenario?"

Louise ignored the point Frankie was trying to make

entirely, choosing instead to fixate on the only thing that mattered to her.

"Ooooh, do you really think we'll end up shagging? So far it hasn't gotten any further than a quick drunken snog and some over the shirt—" She began to jump up and down, clapping her hands in excitement like a child at her first visit with Father Christmas.

"*Louise*! How many times must I beg… no details! I've got far too vivid an imagination, one that enjoys working against me at that."

"Okay fine – ruiner – but I still don't get what you mean," Louise pouted. "Shouldn't I be happy that Daddy finally approves of someone?"

Frankie sighed again. It was not an uncommon sound.

"I'm just saying it seems a little odd that a father would so willingly get involved with his daughter's love life, especially after showing such an aversion to it for so long, " Frankie explained carefully, trying to avoid sounding too judgmental. "That it's gross should go without saying. Makes me wonder what he's really up to."

"Why does everything have to be some huge conspiracy with you?" Louise scoffed. "Why can't it be as simple as Daddy just wanting what's best for me?"

Frankie shook her head. Another familiar habit.

"So naïve you are. Fathers don't want what's best for their daughters, not really. They want what's most comfortable for them, especially when it comes to men. Have you never noticed? My father has only ever been good with boyfriends who haven't posed too much of a threat, not all Rebel Without a Cause. The ones that are safe, non-threatening, kind of vanilla – you know? Like James."

"How flattering," Louise deadpanned. "I'm sure that James would love to hear that you think of him as vanilla. But it wasn't always that way, was it?' No sooner was the comment out of her mouth than Louise clapped both hands over it, eyes widening as Frankie shot her a deadly glare.

Although their relationship was built on a solid foundation of good-natured ribbing and general cattiness, there were lines that each of them knew not to cross. Most of the time.

"God, Frannie, I'm sorry. Went too far there, didn't I?" Louise was genuinely contrite.

"S'all right. That's all in the past now; there's no reason to dwell on it. Besides, James and I are in a much better place these days." Frankie tried to brush it off. It was Louise's party, and she wasn't about to ruin it. *Desperate times call for desperate measures*, she thought as she tried to come up with a quick way to break the uncomfortable silence that had befallen them.

Louise gave a little shriek and began to giggle as she dodged, rather deftly, the pink ruffled pillow that Frankie tossed at her head.

"No, no…I deserved that," she conceded once she'd finished laughing. Frankie smiled. And just like that, the awkward moment was gone.

"All I'm saying is that my dad just wants someone who can look after his crazy daughter, and who won't break her little heart. James is, in his mind, his ideal," said Frankie as she took Louise's place in front of the mirror, circling back to her original train of thought. "But your father is a power-hungry balls-to-the-wall CEO-type from a wealthy, world-famous family. He's going to want someone for you that he's comfortable with, someone more like him. No offence."

"None taken," Louise said thoughtfully as she toyed with the pillow Frankie had thrown. "You know, for a paranoid lunatic, sometimes you make a lot of sense. They are a lot alike. Alex is an arrogant ass, which is kind of what makes him so hot. Oh shit, wait– Daddy is not hot…"

"Ummmmm right. I think Freud might have a few

7

things to say about that." And it was Frankie doing the pillow-dodging – a red faux fur one this time – but fortunately for her Louise had horrible aim. The two began to giggle uncontrollably again as it bounced off the opposite wall, nowhere near its intended target.

"If I had to guess," Frankie said finally, returning much to Louise's delight to the initial question, "then I'd have to say all three of your boys are going to slip and land in puddles of their own drool once they get through the front door. You are crazy hot in that dress."

Her compliment, for once, was completely sincere. The gown's shimmering crimson velvet only served to showcase how physically perfect Louise was, clinging to the curves she had in all the places where they should be. She'd kept her makeup quite spare, save for her trademark glossy red lips. Her dark hair was swept up and piled loosely atop her head with just a few stray tendrils left loose to wisp strategically against her collarbone, her shoulder and the base of her neck, all of which were lightly tanned but not garishly so.

With Louise nothing was left to chance; strategy was everything. In this, as with so many other things, she and Frankie were polar opposites. It really was a wonder they got along so well.

Frankie had never really had much by way of strategy; with her, there was no agenda. When it came to her appearance she had always taken more of a wash and wear, take it or leave it approach. But in that moment, as she looked at her reflection standing side by side in the mirror with Louise, she was shocked to discover that for once in their many years of friendship Frankie felt like her equal. Physically, anyway. Most of the time that sort of thing never bothered her, but there were certain instants – like wearing a beautiful beaded velvet gown, for example – that Frankie wanted to be remembered for being something more than a bitchy smart-mouth ginger.

After a final primp they were ready to make their way over to the main house, to where the party was being held in the ballroom. Frankie knew that she should be more accustomed to her friend's lifestyle, but it was such a long way from the narrow two up-two down row house in the centre of Brighton she'd spent most of her own teenaged years in that she didn't think she was capable of it. Whenever she saw Chadwick Manor all dressed up for an event, its ancient Tudor beams lit softly from a rainbow of ground lights, she had the overwhelming urge to pinch herself to make sure she wasn't dreaming.

She often felt like she had been cast in a supporting role with the film that was Louise. And there was more melodrama to be found there than a full-scale Merchant-Ivory period production. Tonight, she was certain, would be no exception.

Guests were starting to arrive but Louise had insisted that they needed to make a grand entrance so they remained hidden, dressed in full party attire, peeking through the curtains to check out what everyone else was wearing.

"Lou," Frankie whispered, without really knowing why she felt the need to whisper seeing as it was just the two of them. It may have had something to do with the bottle of Veuve champagne that Louise had uncorked for them to indulge in as they waited.

"Oh look, there's that cow Marianne! What is she like wearing a dress that tight? She looks like a velvet-covered stuffed sausage," Louise cackled before realizing Frankie had spoken. "What was it you were saying?"

"I just wanted to ask you something, actually." This was definitely the champagne talking because Frankie, despite having always been curious, would never have had the guts to mention it otherwise. Louise continued peering out the window, only half paying attention.

"So…your dad. Is he, like…would he be the richest bloke in England?" To Frankie's surprise, Louise didn't even blink.

She considered the question carefully, almost thoughtfully, before answering.

"Nooo, definitely not the richest," she replied finally. "There's the Royal Family, obviously, so that's like three or four right there. And then there's the bloke with the beard from Virgin, and the woman who wrote the Harry Potter books. I think Daddy may be somewhere in between those two? Don't pay much attention, really... Ooh no – did you see how wide Sarah Jane's ass is in that dress? Some women were not built for bustles, that's for sure!"

Frankie could only shake her head. Partly out of disbelief, but more because she was annoyed with herself. Both for having the poor manners to ask such a thing, as well as for thinking that Louise would have given any real thought to such a thing.

It was at once her best and most baffling quality rolled up into one: the utter cluelessness as to just how important her family's empire was, not just to her personally, but to the country if not the entire world. The Chadwick family had been the major driving force behind chocolate becoming such a staple in the United Kingdom. It was Louise's great-great grandfather, if Frankie recalled her history correctly, that had made the leap from a lucrative Brighton shipping business into confectionary goods after picking up a failing chocolate factory at a bargain price. *Hell*, Frankie thought, *I'd wager I know more about her family tree than she does.* However, she did have something of an advantage there. She'd had to study those kinds of forgotten facts in school as part of her confectionary diploma.

And then again, I could just be a right jealous bitch and completely overanalysing the situation, as I am so prone to doing. When it came down to it, Frankie loved Louise: tantrums and dramatics and all. She couldn't give a fig about how much money her family had. She knew her friend well enough to know first-hand that money does not necessarily buy happiness. It just made some things in life a lot easier.

It was going on quarter past eight by the time Louise

and Frankie took the path toward the main house. In the dimming light of early evening Frankie could see the vast gardens stretch behind it, the winding paths between the hedgerows and flowerbeds glowing faintly with the light from wrought iron lantern posts, before almost appearing to drop over the edge where the horizon met the sea. She knew from countless games of drunken hide and seek that there was a rock wall that separated the garden from the edge of a cliff by several metres, but from this distance it just continued on into oblivion. They passed beneath the elegantly carved arches of the heavy oak doors into a large entryway that led to the ballroom. Frankie always thought every party was a spectacle at Chadwick's, but the event coordinators had certainly outdone themselves with this one.

The path leading to the ballroom was marked with a red carpet that wound its way from the edge of the circular drive, up the granite stairs and through the doors down to the ballroom, bordered with heavy velvet ropes and garlands of fragrant roses still on the vine. Silver urns sat around the edge of the room and overflowed with wild red roses and pink calla lilies – Louise's favourite flower combination – as the chubby fingers of small plaster cherubs drew back the silk chiffon draperies that cascaded down the walls and the floor-to-ceiling lead paned windows that were adorned with yet more flowers. A string quartet played strains of what sounded like Mozart from a platform mounted in the far corner. Rich red and pink damask-printed silk covered long tables that lined the walls opposite the door. One was piled high with gifts wrapped in brightly-coloured paper, while another appeared to be straining from the weight of the silver platters filled with food. Its centrepiece was a large seven-tiered damask print cake sumptuously decorated with red and pink buttercream and adorned with roses and lilies that had taken Frankie the better part of a week to finish. But the colours complemented her dress perfectly.

Strategically, of course.

Party guests decked out in full Victorian garb were milling about, gingerly balancing plates and glasses as they chatted and flirted. All conversation ceased once Louise and

Frankie stepped into the ornate stone and marble entrance. The band struck up a lively rendition of "Happy Birthday" as the guests joined in, clapping and singing along. Louise smiled graciously as she made her way slowly to the centre of the room whilst Frankie - ever the dutiful friend who knew her place - demurely fell into step a pace or two behind. This was not her moment.

Louise stopped in front of her father, who stood waiting for the song to end, and kissed him lightly on the cheek as the applause died down.

"Thank you Daddy," she said coyly, handling like a pro the wireless microphone her party planner had handed her. "And thank you, all of you, for being here and for humouring me by dressing up on such short notice. You all look so fantastic. But never mind that... don't let me keep you from your drinking!" The crowd laughed on cue as the band went back to playing and guests continued with their conversations.

"Happy birthday, darling," Frankie heard Louise's father mumble, giving her arm a squeeze as he moved off to speak with some of the more mature guests. Work colleagues he had invited, as tradition dictated, to come and pay tribute to the golden child. He murmured a quick greeting and compliment about the cake when he passed Frankie's way, punctuating it with a wink and a gentle squeeze of her shoulder.

For such an uptight businessman, she thought, there were moments where he bordered on nice...warm even.

"Incoming," Louise whispered, elbowing Frankie sharply. She looked up to see a rather nervous-looking man in a blue frock coat moving in fast. His eyes were locked on Louise in a hazy blend of panic, lust and liquor. He gulped down his last bit of champagne before closing the distance.

"H-h-happy birthday, Louise. You look bloody...ahh, that is to say, umm...positively radiant this evening," he stammered out, blushing madly.

Frankie suspected that he had practiced his opening line for almost as long as it had taken her to make Louise's cake. As faltering as it was, it was rather endearing nonetheless. Frankie's heart went out to him in that moment; she knew that Louise could so easily crush him like an insect. And he was Scottish, one of her people, making her feel all the worse. You poor bastard.

"Oooh, Dr. Jared, aren't you a sweetheart!" His blush deepened as he managed to stutter something nearly incoherent in reply.

"Oh, umm ah, Louise," he added, "you know that I'm not really a doctor. I just have a PhD in bio-chemistry…" Perhaps there was more fight in him than Frankie thought. Until…*uh oh.*

Louise oozed forward – oozed being the only term to describe such a move – so that she could lean into him, offering full view of her cleavage. She traced her index finger lightly across his cheekbone to the corner of his mouth down to his chin, which Frankie thought she saw tremble slightly.

Dr. Jared – or rather, just Jared – dared not take a breath.

"I know, silly," she giggled flirtatiously. Frankie was frequently astounded at the dizzying speed with which Louise could go from sex kitten to ingenue. "I just like calling you Doctor, Jared. Perhaps we could play sometime?"

"Play what, exactly," he squeaked, barely capable of a response. Louise leaned in further still, pressing her chest right up against his. It was a move Frankie recognised instantly.

"Doctor," she whispered. There it was. *The Kill,* as Frankie had often called it.

Louise patted Jared's jacket lapel dismissively and began to giggle as she turned away, leaving the poor man sweating and shaken. Frankie was certain he would be whipping a handkerchief out of his pocket to mop his brow once their backs were turned. Not that she could blame him.

"One down," Louise muttered as she sashayed away in triumph, with Frankie close behind, downing her own glass of champagne and grabbing another for each of them from a passing waiter's tray.

"You know, Lou, it really isn't nice to play with your food. I thought that poor fucker was going to have an aneurysm or something." But Frankie had to cut her lecture short.

"Two to go." Louise wasn't paying attention to her in the slightest, her sights too firmly set on her next victims.

Two young men were standing in a corner of the room, laughing, oblivious to what was headed their way. One of them sported a black top hat and coattails while the other was fully kitted out in English riding gear, complete with impeccably shined riding boots to the knee. Frankie pegged him as the American. But it was Top Hat who was first to notice.

"Louise," he crowed, arms opening wide. She allowed him a greeting kiss, one on each cheek. He took her hand and turned her slowly, pirouette-style, to get the full view.

"You could kill in that dress, my dear. You are perfection." He kissed her hand before releasing her. She giggled. What the fuck, Frankie thought in disbelief. Was she blushing?

"Why thank you, Alex. You aren't looking too shabby yourself," she replied shyly.

Could it be that Lou might just have met her match in this one?

Not to be outdone, Riding Boots grabbed her round her waist and spun her round so that he could plant a kiss squarely on her lips. Thank Heaven for him that he was ridiculously good looking, albeit in that irritatingly clean-cut American way, or that move could have easily earned him a swift punch to his finely-chiselled jaw. Frankie knew that

Louise didn't like it much when the prey manhandled the merchandise without permission.

"Happy birthday, baby," he breathed into her ear, making Louise visibly shiver as he kissed her again before noticing that she wasn't alone. "Who's your little friend?"

"This is Frankie MacSweeney, my bestest friend in the whole wide world who happens to be moving back to open a chocolate shop. She'll be staying with me, whether she likes it or not."

Frankie tried not to roll her eyes as she moved forward to shake his outstretched hand, not enjoying the way his eyes swept over her frame hungrily. Louise introduced Riding Boots as Quinn and Top Hat as Alex, although she had already managed to guess their identities by process of elimination and instinct.

The group chatted as the other guests came and went, stopping in to give Louise their birthday wishes. She was getting slightly distracted by the ever-mounting pile of loot that was accumulating on the gift table, and becoming a bit of a brat. Frankie decided it would be safe to leave her in Quinn and Alex's hands while she went out for some air on the terrace. It appeared that Dr. Jared had the same idea.

He was leaning forward with his elbows resting on the granite wall that separated the terrace from the gardens, staring off toward the sea in the distance as if pondering some great mystery of the universe, completely oblivious to everything around him.

"All right, Dr. Jared?" Of course, Frankie thought too late, I couldn't just mind my own business and leave him to it. He jumped as he turned round, startled.

"Oh, hello there. Just enjoying the evening. My apologies - I didn't have the chance to introduce myself earlier: Jared Skylar. You must be Frankie."

Away from Louise, Frankie couldn't help but notice that this version of Dr. Jared seemed much more friendly and confident, perhaps even a little bit charming. Bizarre, considering the quivering mess he'd been reduced to not but an hour earlier.

"I am indeed. How did you guess?"

"Louise speaks of you often –that and I recognised the red hair. She seems almost jealous, the way she goes on about it."

"Really?" Frankie didn't bother to hide her surprise, thinking he must have been mistaken. Louise had neither need nor reason to feel jealous of anyone. For anything. Ever.

"Oh yes – she adores your hair. And she's always going on about how clever you are. I sometimes get the feeling she wished she were a bit more like you."

"Well…um. That's news to me," Frankie finally managed after taking a few moments to process. "To be honest, that doesn't sound like the Louise I know at all. But then, you're obviously quite fond of her, so maybe you just see her a bit differently."

And with that, all of his awkward nervousness from earlier suddenly returned as Jared began to blush madly.

"It's true. I am, quite fond," he sighed. "But sadly I'm not even in the running. When other people are around, I just get so nervous and start babbling on like an idiot. She must think me just another lovesick fool. And can I blame her? That's exactly what it must look like."

Frankie patted his arm sympathetically.

"If it helps, it's not anything she isn't already used to. I've seen worse, believe me. And you have obviously had other, far better conversations with her than the one I just witnessed. Those mustn't have been so bad, eh?"

He gave her a sad half-smile, appreciating that she was trying to make him feel better about something they both knew was kind of a lost cause.

"I guess not, no. Thanks."

"Don't mention it."

They stood together in comfortable silence for a few moments, watching the sky above the sea turn from dark pink to a deep, rich purple as night took hold.

"I'm really not a doctor, you know. Louise just likes calling me that. I'm not sure why I let her," Jared said finally, almost as though he were talking to himself.

"Because you humour her, as we all do. So what do you do then?"

"I'm an industrial biochemist, actually. I've been hired in to evaluate the existing product formulas at Chadwick's and find where improvements could be made. It's all supposed to be very hush-hush, of course, what with everything that's going on with the company right now. But then, I'm sure you know all about that."

"How's that?" Frankie was genuinely puzzled.

"Oh," Jared replied, embarrassed again, "I just assumed because you were so close to Louise and the family that you would automatically know."

It seems that I'm not the only one giving Lou too much credit, Frankie thought, in thinking that she actually paid attention to the intricate machinations of the company that made her way of life possible.

"To tell the truth, I really don't know that much about it. I do know there's been talk of some sort of merger but with who or what's at stake, I haven't a clue. Lou rarely talks business with me. And it's not really any business of mine either."

"Not yet. But aren't you the one opening up the chocolate shop?"

Shit, Frankie cursed to herself. Had Louise told absolutely everyone about that? Good thing it was a plan that Frankie was in the process of actively following through with.

"Well, yes, but I would just be purchasing my chocolate from Chadwick's. What goes on in their boardroom really has nought to do with me. And it's not like I could really do anything about it anyway."

"Ah, but that's where you're wrong," Jared corrected her, a serious tone creeping into his voice that Frankie recognised instantly. It told her she might want to get comfortable because she was in for a bit of a lecture.

"What goes on in that boardroom directly affects you as a purchaser. That's where they make all the crucial decisions, from sourcing raw materials to labour costs to formulation changes. Basically, anything that could dramatically alter - for better or for worse - the quality of the chocolate they produce and by extension any product made by anyone who uses it. When you factor in that the trend over the past thirty years has been toward extreme cost-cutting with the sole goal of maximising profits, with everyone looking to do things on the cheap regardless of what it might do to the integrity of their product or their brand, what you're left with is an entire market filled with inferior product."

Frankie would typically have zoned out as soon as the term 'cost-cutting' was dropped: that was how little interest she had when it came to corporate affairs. But something in the way Jared was speaking kept her listening, almost hanging on his every word. His passion was infectious. It was like he made her care, at least in that moment, nearly as much as he did. A good thing too, seeing as she was on the brink of her own business. Like it or not, she was going to have to learn to start caring more about the things she'd always found mundane: the business side of having her own business.

"And there is absolutely something you can do about it,' Jared clearly wasn't finished, "you could find a supplier whose ideology might be more in line with your own. And there are a few out there, if you're willing to look hard enough. For example, I've heard about this one company, in Switzerland, I think… I've been trying to learn more and compare it to my own research for Chadwick but finding any information on this place is proving to be pretty damn difficult. Anyway, apparently the owner is trying to bring things back to the way they were before the only thing people cared about was money. He's focusing on things like quality and craftsmanship, on happier workers. On bringing a sense of pride back to it all."

"Oh," was all Frankie could think of to say in response. Somewhere in the back of her mind Switzerland seemed like it should be ringing some bells of familiarity, but the three or four glasses of champagne she'd already downed had seriously hampered her ability to focus on why.

Jared smiled, almost sheepish, as if by way of apology.

"Sorry for the rant. But it's something I feel rather strongly about. However, this is neither the time nor the place."

"Hey, I'm no stranger to the rant," she was quick to reassure him. "I'm also good friends with the tangent, so I can completely appreciate where you're coming from."

He smiled in response, not the sheepish grin from before but something closer to that of friends sharing a mutual understanding.

"So, tell me about your shop, then. Louise mentioned you were looking to open up quite soon…in the Lanes, is that right?"

Frankie brightened, as she always did when the conversation turned to her favourite topic.

"Hope to, yes – but space in the Lanes is not as easy to find as I'd hoped. Plus there's still that pesky bank loan business to deal with. But I've got that appointment set for later this week, so once that's sorted I can really get stuck in.

After I know what I'm working with."

"Well, yes – I suppose that would be important, wouldn't it?" Jared replied, "I've never opened a business myself. I'd imagine there's an awful lot to think about."

Frankie nodded in agreement.

"Oh, there is. I've even got lists for my lists now! But lucky for me I've been dreaming this shop up since I was a wee girl, so once I get going it should all come together. Unless, of course, I change my mind at the last minute, which I am very prone to doing. That's when things will really fall to shit, and I'll be well and truly fucked." Frankie shrugged in a matter-of-fact way before beginning to chuckle in spite of herself.

She didn't know Jared well enough to be nearly so candid, but it was the booze talking. He looked slightly taken aback. Frankie wasn't sure if it was her brutal honesty or the casual profanity that laced her statement. He seemed incapable of a reply at first, unsure of whether to laugh or offer condolences, and stood blinking at her in silence until Frankie reassured him that she was joking. He was visibly relieved, any awkwardness between them evaporating as he asked what the name of her shop would be.

"Oh, but that's the best part," Frankie clapped her hands together in a gesture that would have been more characteristic of Louise. "It's going to be called MacSweet. Like my name, but with Sweet instead. Isn't that absolutely adorable? It's like I was born to do something like this, isn't it, with a name like that…"

Jared laughed and nodded, although Frankie thought that she could detect a slight nervousness that still lingered beneath the surface. She decided it would be a good time to swap the champagne for some water. Paranoia and drunkenness were never a good combination.

Frankie realised that they had been on the terrace for quite some time. Exactly how long, she couldn't tell, but it had been enough for Louise and Alex to come round looking for them. The two of them did look quite cosy together walking arm-in-arm, Frankie thought. But she also noticed that Alex's eyes were not glazed over with lust in the way that Louise's were. It was possible that she was just confusing lust with drunk; the two so often went hand-in-hand with that girl. Her hair was a bit of a tattered mess, her mascara smudged across one cheek, and she was tiptoeing barefoot, weaving slightly with her Louboutin peep-toes dangling from one hand. And yet, she still managed to look better than most women did on their best days. Bitch, Frankie whispered to herself in admiration.

She was about to suggest that they hit the ladies for a bit of a clean-up when out of the corner of her eye she caught some movement in the garden.

"Wait -- who's that?"

All eyes turned to in the direction Frankie was looking. Although difficult to tell at such a distance, she thought she had seen a man – quite tall – dressed in what appeared to be a light grey top hat and frock coat. It stood out against the dark sky as the moonlight shone without obstruction. To Frankie, it was as though he'd stepped into the spotlight, centre stage. She watched, unable to breathe, as he stood facing the terrace from the very bottom of the garden where it met the wall near the cliff. And Frankie could almost feel that, had it not been so dark, they would have been locking eyes in that very moment. The thought of it sent an unexpected thrill through her.

The moon ducked behind the clouds, plunging the garden into utter blackness. By the time it came back, there was no sign of the stranger anywhere.

"Probably just another party guest out for a wander… maybe even a shag," Alex quipped dryly. Frankie cringed as Louise leered at him.

"Mmmmm. A shag sounds nice right about now, doncha think," she slurred lustily. Frankie thought she had been aiming for sexy, but had consumed far too much champagne to pull that off with much success. Alex looked more amused than anything else; Jared was equal parts horrified and devastated. It was the perfect time for that visit to the powder room.

"C'mon, Lou. Let's get you cleaned up a bit first, eh?" Frankie glanced in apology at both men and hurried Louise off to the nearest washroom.

"I don't think Alex fancies me," she wailed, her voice ricocheting off the wall tiles.

Frankie had Louise propped up against the vanity's counter in an attempt to keep her from swaying side to side, trying to wipe some stray eye makeup away with some damp tissue but her head kept lolling around like a rag doll.

"He won't even give me a proper birthday kiss," she whimpered. Frankie sighed.

"Well, maybe that has more to do with you being stinking drunk – and I do mean stinking, because you fucking reek – and he's just being a proper gentleman," she offered hopefully. Louise seemed pleased with that answer.

"You think so?"

"Stranger things have happened."

"He's so beautiful, though, I just want to—" Frankie cut her off before she could give any more detail. Louise had a long history of sharing her bizarre and graphic sexual fantasies, and she knew enough to stop her when the hand gestures started.

"Yes, Lou, he is - quite beautiful. But then again. so is Dr. Jared. In his own way." And Frankie was being honest.

While Alex could be considered universally attractive with his light brown hair that fell perfectly in place, crystal blue eyes and finely chiselled features, Jared was more an acquired taste that one could easily become accustomed to.

Dark reddish-brown hair and lively brown eyes behind tortoiseshell glasses, angular bone structure, and a smile that bordered on naughty when he wasn't busy flipping out over how beautiful Louise was.

"Well of course, Dr. Jared is nerd hot, but he can't compare to Alex or Quinn. Oooh…where is Quinn? I bet he'd shag me." So it was to be one of those nights, then, protecting Louise's virtue. What little was left of it, anyway. Frankie sighed again, this time in resignation.

"Let's get back to the boys, shall we?" She helped Louise off her perch on the counter and out of the bathroom. To her surprise, Dr. Jared was waiting just outside the door.

"Is she okay?" He looked genuinely concerned. Louise launched herself at him.

"Frankie thinks you're hot," she sang out loudly, wrapping her arms around his neck. Jared struggled to stay standing in spite of the sudden onslaught, quietly turning a deep shade of purple as Frankie felt her own face grow hotter. She managed to stammer something of a dismissal, laughing it off, then together they took the drunken Louise back outside for the fresh air of the terrace. Alex was waiting with a large bottle of mineral water.

"I can take care of her from here," Alex said, catching Louise as she threw herself at him. He had seen the doubtful look on Frankie's face, and was quick to assure her he had no ill intent.

"Don't worry, Frankie. She'll be safe with me, even from herself. I won't let anything happen to her. Promise."

From Frankie's perspective he seemed fairly benign, almost trustworthy, as he sat on one of the wrought iron benches with Louise's head in his lap. Every now and again she would lunge for his trouser zipper with her teeth, and each time Alex would gently redirect her face back to the water bottle. Jared and Frankie watched as Louise mewed in frustration, but after a few more thwarted attempts finally gave up.

Satisfied that her friend was in good company, Frankie pushed her way back into the party to look for the stranger she had decided to dub Grey Top Hat Man. She was convinced that he had not been at the party before she had spotted him in the garden. Someone that tall would be hard to miss. She weaved her way in and around the party revellers, some of whom were dancing, all of them flirting outrageously with anyone who'd pay attention. The air of desperation seemed so thick Frankie could almost cut it with a cake knife. There were moments she could feel herself being watched, that prickly feeling at the base of her neck, but when she turned she could not tell who it was doing the watching. At one point she thought she'd glimpsed the tails of a grey coat rounding the corner at the end of the hall. She followed, heart pounding. But there was no sign of him anywhere.

God, Frankie, get a grip, she muttered aloud to herself, aware she was close to spiralling out of control. *Why should I give such a fuck who this bloke is?*

She went back out to the terrace finally, almost walking straight past the bench where Alex was sitting in her preoccupation with the stranger. He had a completely passed-out Louise cradled in his lap like an infant as he gently stroked her hair. Jared stood to one side, pretending to be looking out to toward the grounds, but Frankie knew better. She knew he was there to ensure that Alex was being true to his word.

She also knew his heart must be breaking. Frankie quietly went over to stand beside him.

"She seems to be doing okay," Jared reported as he continued to stare into the garden.

"Well, yes, but that's only because she's passed out. I'll have to figure out how to get her to her bed after everyone leaves."

"I could give you a hand with that, but I don't think I'm the one she'd want helping," he replied miserably.

"I'm sorry, Jared. Louise is my best friend, but most of the time she has truly awful taste in men. You seem like a really decent bloke and unfortunately that's just not what she's looking for right now." Frankie was a firm believer that sometimes it was better to just tell it like it is. And from what she'd seen, Louise could do worse than Alex. She certainly had done in the past.

Jared seemed to agree.

"Alex seems pretty decent himself. A lesser man would have hurried her away into the garden and had their way with her." *Speaking of the garden…*

"So, any sign of our elusive top-hatted friend?" Frankie was trying to be nonchalant about it, but it sounded desperate even to her. And yet, she was powerless to stop herself.

"Not a soul, top hat or not," Jared frowned. "Why? Someone you know?"

"No, don't think so. Just curious." It wasn't something she could explain. It wasn't something that should even be affecting her at all in any way, but there it was.

"Maybe it's your fiancé coming to surprise you."

Frankie had mentioned in their earlier conversation that James was supposed to have been her date but had been called away on business at the last minute. The idea that he had come to surprise her made Frankie laugh out loud.

"James isn't that tall, for a start, and he wouldn't be caught dead in a top hat. It would flatten his hair. And considering I haven't heard so much as a peep from him since he left, I'm going to guess that he's far too caught up with this business deal to even be thinking about me."

She didn't mean it as a bad thing. James was a lot of

things, but spontaneous he was not. He's solid, sometimes forgetful but often practical. Like a favourite pair of trainers. They weren't terribly glamorous, but you loved them nonetheless.

"So do you think it's someone else you know, then?" Frankie tried not to frown at his persistence. Without much success.

"I've got no idea who it could be. Why do you ask?"

"Well, it's just that you seem rather...interested...in finding this person. A person that you don't think you know."

Guess I'm not quite as subtle as I thought, she thought in dismay. Which again begged the question – why did she care? Jared had just called her out on it, and she had no idea how to respond.

The entire situation left Frankie with only one option. Lie.

"I'm just naturally curious," she said again. "And if it's someone here crashing the party, like maybe a tabloid reporter looking for front page fodder, I'm sure that security and Mr. Chadwick would want to know about it." As answers went she thought it sounded fairly convincing, if a bit of dirty pool by throwing Jared's boss into it. But she wasn't sure she had him convinced as he looked at her for a minute or two longer than he should have. *When in doubt, change the subject.*

"Holy shit! Is that what time it is?" Although it was early by their past partying standards, Frankie couldn't believe it was only just passed midnight. Time seemed to have flown by. "Does that offer to help put Lou to bed still stand?"

Jared and Alex both helped Frankie carry the unconscious Louise out to the carriage house. Thank Christ she didn't wake up, Frankie couldn't help but think; she surely would have started shouting something about a threesome. But the trip wasn't without its perils.

En route, Quinn had emerged with a lazy smirk from somewhere amid the dwindling party guests, his ascot looking slightly askew. He asked if he could lend a hand after seeing the other men struggling with Louise's dead weight, but Frankie promptly assured him that they had the situation well in hand. While she was sure that he must've been a lovely bloke and all, there was something about him that just screamed 'date rapist' to her. Of course, that could just have been her natural mistrust of Americans talking.

The three of them deposited Louise safely in her bed, very much alone. Frankie returned to the main house and what was left of the party with Jared and Alex close behind to let Louise's father know that the birthday girl was officially out of commission and it was time to wrap things up. Fortunately, things appeared to be winding down of their own accord, with everyone either too tired or drunk to bother looking for Louise to say a proper goodbye.

She returned to the carriage house to get ready for bed herself. After locking the doors and making a final check to ensure that her best friend wasn't choking on her own vomit, she realised how completely exhausted she was. It was tiring business trying to protect Louise from herself, she remembered thinking as she drifted off.

Frankie had just settled into sleep when she was awakened by a noise somewhere outside her closed bedroom door. She bolted upright in bed, ears straining and nerve endings tingling. Another sound, that time the echo of footfalls on the slate tile that covered Louise's kitchen downstairs. But she was certain that she had locked everything up tight – she was just too paranoid not to. Maybe the latch hadn't worked?

Alarmed and bordering on terrified, Frankie reached for the closest thing she could find that might work as a weapon – which in Louise's house was a curling iron – and tiptoed downstairs to confront the intruder.

But there was nothing.

Only silence, save for the soft billowing of the silk sheers covering one of the French doors to the path to the main house, indicating that it was open. Frankie raced outside to find herself alone on the terrace of the main house in silence once again. The night sky had fallen to inky black darkness, with only a few slices of moonlight to light her way.

She turned to head back to the carriage house when, without warning, Grey Top Hat stepped out of the shadows.

"Who are you?" Frankie was finding it hard to breathe and was almost certain he could hear her heart pounding in her chest.

Without a word, the stranger took her into his arms and began to dance with her around the terrace even though there was no music at all. Frankie thought it was a waltz but couldn't be certain, having never waltzed before in her life. She tried to look up at him, to catch a glimpse of his face, but her attempts were in vain. The stranger seemed impossibly, unnaturally tall, his top hat a pale grey in the moonlight that somehow left the rest of his features obscured. It was so dark that the only thing that was clear was his profile, which held the promise of exceptionally fine bone structure. And the way he made Frankie feel. How he held her in his arms, how they moved together so seamlessly as they danced; for reasons she could not explain or even understand she felt safe in this faceless stranger's arms.

Safe. And happy.

Round and round the terrace they went, and soon he was spinning Frankie faster and faster. She wanted to cry out for him to stop, that she was going to be sick from the spinning, but she found that she was enjoying it far more than she maybe should have. She didn't want it to stop. In fact, she wanted more.

"Kiss me," she whispered, doing her best to parrot

Louise's sexiest *come hither* tone.

The stranger seemed only too happy to oblige and as he leaned in to meet her lips, a single beam of moonlight took that exact moment to slice across his face, illuminating it completely.

It was Dr. Jared.

Frankie's eyes flew open. She was in her bed once more, this time fully awake. At least she thought she was. The only sound was that of her own heart hammering in her chest.

What's wrong with me, she thought. She was happy with James, wasn't she? She most certainly didn't need to be dreaming about other men. Shaking her head to clear it of the lust and guilt she felt, Frankie got up to get some water from the kitchen.

Downstairs she noticed that one of the French doors was open. She felt a creeping sense of déjà vu begin to crawl beneath her skin. The silk curtains were blowing, the same way they had done in her dream. Cautiously she made her way toward them. And although it was the very last thing she wanted to do, Frankie reached for a curtain and yanked it open to look outside.

It was there that any resemblance to her dream ended. The night was so bright and clear that Frankie could see clearly all the way past the main house to the garden, and to the lone figure that wandered there. But this figure was not wearing a grey top hat, but rather a flowing gown. A nightgown that even from a distance looked suspiciously like the one she had slipped over Louise's still-unconscious head earlier that evening.

It was then that she remembered Louise's penchant for going walkabout in her sleep after having had too much to drink. And sure enough, it was her that Frankie could see at the back of the garden out past the terrace.

She sighed, berating herself for not locking the

bedroom door from the outside somehow, and slipped on some old Keds that that lay on a rug by the door before heading out after her friend. Louise was standing motionless in the middle of the large expanse of lawn that lay between the house and the wall, her back to Frankie, facing out toward the sea.

At least this time I won't have to chase her, Frankie muttered to herself in relief.

"Lou," she called gently. She had heard that it was a bad idea to wake a sleepwalker up, but she was tired and needed to get Louise back inside. There was a chill in the air that wasn't there earlier, with a mist moving up from the water below. It made the garden look uncharacteristically creepy.

"Louise," Frankie called again louder, more urgently this time. She was almost directly behind her when Louise spun around, so fast and unexpectedly that it startled her.

"Jesus!" Frankie shrieked in alarm.

Louise then collapsed in a dead faint at her feet. Frankie leaped forward in an attempt to catch her, but it all happened too quickly.

"Louise? Lou? Lou! Can you hear me?"

Frankie gently reached to check Louise's pulse at her throat: it was fast but mercifully there. Her initial panic began to subside. Louise was breathing in short shallow breaths, as if she'd been running all night and her lungs were struggling to catch up. Frankie sat, pulling Louise as far into her lap as she could and as she began rubbing her arms to try to keep the girl warm.

After a few minutes that felt more like a lifetime, Louise's eyes fluttered. She seemed to be struggling to regain consciousness.

"Where am I," she whispered, wiping at her mouth as if it were dry.

Louise tried to sit up and looked around, obviously confused. It was then that Frankie noticed for the first time that her mouth and cheek were smeared with some dark substance, something that she couldn't quite identify in the darkness.

"You went walkabout again in the garden. But Lou…what in the hell have you got all over yourself?"

Frankie could see once she'd moved that Louise was holding something in her hand. Louise looked down at it, frowning. In her hand she clutched a chocolate bar. Given where they were, Frankie thought that it wasn't so unexpected. But then she got a closer look at the packaging.

It wasn't a Chadwick's bar that Louise was holding onto so tightly; it was a Fitz Cocoa Cream, a bar that had been out of production for well over a hundred years.

TWO

September 10th

James checked his Blackberry again. No email from Frankie, no texts. He knew that she was with her best friend, who could very well be taking up all of her time and then some, but he also knew that it wasn't like his fiancée to go so long without so much as a quick 'love you' text. *Maybe she didn't get my email,* he thought. His host had mentioned that phone and Internet connections in the Alps were sketchy at best. But ever since he'd been picked up by the hired car from Zurich airport the previous afternoon and then driven up a narrow winding road to a house that appeared not only to be sitting on top of a mountain but built into the side of it, James had tried unsuccessfully to shake a growing feeling of unease.

Perhaps it was because this was the first big assignment with his law firm, also the first time he'd been allowed to fly solo, so he was eager to show them he was up to the challenge. Or maybe because he had been expecting more of a Swiss ski chalet like the travel adverts always described and not the sprawling behemoth of concrete, steel and glass that greeted him. Very cold and industrial the house looked, though its interior was almost like it came from a different space entirely: lots of dark wood and tapestries and a labyrinth of hallways branching out from the centre block. He felt as if he could get lost rather easily; one wrong turn and he'd never be seen again, which would be enough to throw anyone off their game.

Or perhaps it was the creepy butler, Guillaume, who had greeted him with hair as white as the snow that capped the mountains and skin that looked like bleached out parchment. Since there had been nothing but the listings of past properties and acquisitions in the file, James wasn't sure what to expect of the firm's most venerable client, the Comte Alfonse Defleur. He had naturally assumed that the small whisper of a man was he. As it turned out, he couldn't have been more wrong. The real Defleur was the polar opposite: tall and broad in that lean muscle sort of way that James had always wished he was, and just a few years older than he was himself.

It left him feeling both foolish and lazy, wondering what he'd been wasting his time on while this man was out conquering the corporate world, racking up accomplishment after accomplishment while apparently having enough time for regular visits at the gym.

James was soon surprised to learn that his host was not the uptight conservative businessman he had grown accustomed to dealing with in London, but much more of a 'Jack the Lad'. Not long after their initial meeting, they were getting on like a house on fire. *Perhaps even the beginnings of an epic bro-mance*, he thought in embarrassment. That is, until James and his nerves got in the way and he tripped over his laptop bag, sending both him and its contents sprawling across the dark-paneled library where the two men had been chatting. Defleur was on his feet in a flash, helping him retrieve the contents.

James shuddered in humiliation at the memory. He recalled the way Defleur had looked at a photo of Frankie he had picked up, one that James had taken just that past summer on a rollercoaster at Brighton Pier. Her red hair was flying in all directions, like a fiery halo, her cheeks slightly pink from the cold seaspray. She was laughing, but then again Frankie was always laughing. Usually at him.

It was his favourite picture of her, and it appeared that Defleur enjoyed it as well. Maybe a little too much for his comfort.

"Who's this?" James remembered him asking, his voice so low that he wasn't sure that he was speaking at all.

"Oh, that's Frankie. My *fiancée*," James had replied, trying to casually snatch the photograph from Defleur's hand. His unyielding hand; James had to really work at getting it back from him. It was only when his host seemed to realise the peculiarity of his behaviour that Defleur seemed to check himself, muttering something about how James was a very lucky man as he reluctantly let go of the photograph.

The event had marked a bit of a turning point in the evening. It was not long after that when Defleur had excused himself, citing some urgent business that he needed to attend to, but not before showing James to his suite of rooms that occupied one of the wings of the house.

James pulled himself out of his reverie, reminding himself that it was a brand new day. A whole new opportunity to make a good impression and hopefully get them back on track to that easy camaraderie they had shared earlier. *But in order to do that,* James thought, *I have to get my lazy arse downstairs. And stop feeling so damned jumpy.*

Someone had brought a loaded breakfast tray into his

bedroom while James had been sleeping, which only seemed to further add to his overall nervousness given that he was fairly certain that he'd locked the door before going to bed. He was a Londoner, and to not lock a door wasn't even an option. But he wasn't so disturbed by the food's appearance as to keep him from devouring everything he'd been given: soft, buttery croissants with fresh fruit and yoghurt served with a steaming carafe of freshly brewed coffee. He had realised that, between all his various travel connections yesterday, he had forgotten to eat. And the coffee, the smell of the coffee alone was out of this world. It made his eyes roll back into his head in pleasure. He wasn't sure if it was the altitude messing with his senses, but it was almost as though he were eating for the very first time in his life. He had never had food like it.

His moment of joy was cut short, though, when he realised that he had forgotten to adjust his watch when he'd landed and could not remember if Switzerland was an hour ahead or behind. A rookie mistake, to be sure, and one that could cost him dearly. If he had more time, he would surely have spent a few minutes quietly banging his head against the wall at his own ineptitude.

Am I early or late, he thought frantically as he threw on his clothes, quickly brushed his teeth and ran some water over his face and hair before hustling down the nearest set of stairs.

By the time he reached the bottom step, he saw to his own mounting horror that he had no idea where he was or which direction to take. He had been so tired and out of sorts the previous evening when Defleur had led him through the hallways that he could not recall how to get back to the library. The stark white walls and mahogany doors, even the Turkish-style floor runners, that all looked exactly the same did not help the situation in the least. James stood and listened intently for anything that might set him in the right direction. He could not detect any sound from anywhere. Nor could he see anyone down the seemingly endless labyrinth of hallways.

James shivered despite the woolly jumper he wore beneath his suit jacket. And that it was still technically summer. As he stood still attempting to recover his bearings, he could feel his head begin to spin. Rather quickly, that spinning gave way to nausea. It was making him feel even more disoriented than before.

He thought he heard a noise behind him in one of the passages that branched out from the base of the stair, the sound of a door that was just being opened. It was a slightly metallic jiggle of a doorknob turning, the subtle creak of hinges unaccustomed to use whining in protest. James's heart jumped into his throat and began to thump wildly as he whirled round, scanning the multitude of identical doors lining the walls. Further down the hall the light appeared to grow dimmer, as if the shadow of someone or something were physically blocking it. In his panic he couldn't be sure if it was a trick of the mind. He thought he could faintly detect a dark shape beyond one of the doorframes, a shape that he wasn't about to go investigate.

Enough, James, get a grip for Chrissake, he cursed his overly active imagination. *If Frankie were here, she'd give you a good slap back to your senses.*

After being frozen in place for what felt to be ages, James managed to calm himself enough to convince his legs to carry him down the hall as fast as they could. In the opposite direction of whatever it was he thought he had seen. Behind him he fancied that he heard a soft giggle - a distinctly *feminine* giggle - and the sound of a door coming to. He wasn't about to turn around to confirm it.

If only Frankie were here to slap me.

He rounded a corner, that last sound inspiring him to move even faster, where he suddenly found himself face to face with the library doors he'd been looking for. He stood outside them, panting to catch his breath as much from the quick sprint as the terror that had spurred it, trying to determine his next move. He wasn't familiar with the protocol in this situation: was he supposed to knock or wait till someone came to fetch him? *But how would anyone know I'm here if I don't knock or announce my presence in some way? A subtle clearing of the throat, perhaps?*

He didn't have long to weigh his options when the double doors suddenly flung open. Defleur was standing there.

James thought that his mind was playing tricks on him once again because, for a split second, Defleur looked utterly terrifying. His stature was much larger than what he'd recalled from their initial meeting the night before; his eyes were narrowed, shiny and preternaturally shrewd, like a shark sensing its prey. *Or maybe,* James thought dismally, *I've just been watching far too many shark documentaries lately on the telly.*

In an instant it was gone, as quickly as it had appeared, and Defleur was back to his confident and completely non-predatory self. *Gone because, of course, it was never even there to begin with,* James reasoned as he willed his heart to slow down to a more normal pace. He wondered again if there were such a thing as too much fresh air.

Defleur, ever the gracious host, asked how James had slept and if his rooms were to his liking. He was dressed casually, dark jeans and a grey knit jumper with a white tee peeking out from underneath, making James feel foolish in his Topman suit. He quickly removed his jacket, thankful for both his jumper and that he hadn't had the time to wrestle into a tie, as Defleur sank into one of the library's many leather chairs and motioned for James to take the one opposite.

"So how was breakfast? I wasn't sure what you would like, so I just had the chef prepare a little of everything."

James assured him that it was fantastic, and that he wasn't accustomed to waking up to food in his room. This made Defleur laugh out, a boisterous belly laugh that bounced off the high ceilings before being swallowed up by one of the many shelves of books lining the walls. It did nothing to calm James's nerves.

"I gather, then, that that lovely fiancée of yours does not serve you breakfast in bed? I'm sorry if it startled you. I realised that I'd forgotten to give you the tour so I had it sent up to make sure you didn't starve trying to find the kitchen. This place can be a little… difficult…to navigate at first."

Defleur was up again and moving restlessly about the room. James thought he could sense an air of the predator he thought he'd seen earlier, only this time it was more like the prowl of a caged tiger. A distraction seemed in order.

"So your house… It's not at all what I was expecting," James commented before hastily adding "in a good way, of course."

"Thank you. I actually designed and built it myself. The ancestral home is just south of Geneva, and that would be much more in line with what you would expect with a family such as mine. But I am not… anything like them, really. Not at all."

Defleur had stopped pacing to stare out the window, deep in thought.

"So you're a bit of a black sheep, then. I can relate."

James was trying to appear cool, but falling a tad short of the mark. In reality, he the only thing he knew about being a black sheep was what he'd learned from dating Frankie. James had always done his best to follow in his successful big brother's footsteps, which was exactly what he was expected to do. Becoming a barrister instead of a property developer was the closest thing to rebelling James had gotten when it came to his family.

Defleur appeared startled, as if he were just remembering that James was there.

"I suppose you could say that," he replied with a weak smile, which was soon followed with more silence.

James, unnerved with the abrupt change in his host's demeanour, asked for the time so that he could set his watch to rights and proceeded to prattle on about the work he had planned that day, like making charts and drafting out contracts in triplicate. Defleur seemed to have become lost in a world of his own as he turned back to continue staring out the window.

Without warning, he spun around, so fast it made James almost jump out of his chair.

"What would you be doing today if you weren't stuck here working with me," Defleur barked at him. His eyes had grown cold and hard again, similar to what James had thought he'd seen earlier.

"Well uh…I guess I would be in Brighton with Frankie. Her best friend is throwing a major party this weekend at her estate down there," he replied after swallowing hard, trying to collect himself.

"Estate, you say?" Defleur's eyebrows raised in faint interest. "Does she come from a wealthy family, then? I had family once in that part of England. I wonder if it's someone I might know?"

James managed to catch himself before he insulted his host by laughing laugh out loud. *Anyone he may know?*

"It would be unlikely that you wouldn't know them, actually," he chuckled. "It's the Chadwicks."

He wasn't prepared for what happened next. One minute Defleur was daydreaming out the library window, the next he was towering over James in his chair shaking with what seemed to be fury.

"Did you say *Chadwick?*"

James began to inch further back into his chair, wishing desperately that it would swallow him whole, as he tried to imagine what is what that he'd said or done to make Defleur so angry.

"Yes, as in Chadwick's Chocolate," he replied slowly, his voice shaking. "I just meant of course you would know them, because everybody does. But you especially, given the line of business you're in."

James knew he was babbling, something he had always been prone to when his nerves got the better of him. His babbling nearly gave way to a hysterical giggle before he managed to stop himself from adding something flip like they practically invented chocolate. *Because that,* he thought, *would be just about the wrongest thing I could say right now.* He was certain that Defleur was getting ready to tear him a new one as he slammed his hand on a nearby desk before swiftly moving across to the other side of the room.

"Oh yes, of course *everyone* knows them," Defleur hissed, finger jabbing into James's direction. "But what is it that you know? *Nothing*. Chadwick lied and cheated to get what he had. That bastard stole everything he ever knew from…"

If James had thought Defleur was scary before, nothing could have prepared him for how terrifying he was in that moment. His hands were shaking as though he was about to break something, his eyes flashing black with rage. But then, just as quickly, all of Defleur's anger was suddenly gone. As if he had just caught himself behaving badly and needed to put his suave billionaire mask back on.

And just when James believed that things couldn't possibly have become any more bizarre, Defleur smiled. He just stood there and *smiled* at him as if nothing had happened at all.

"I… I do apologize for my outburst," he said quietly as James struggled to keep himself from running out of the room. "It's just…that… I happen to feel very passionately about my business, and my business *is* chocolate. I – well, my family and I – have worked very, *very* hard for everything. For what you see here and in your files upstairs. I am – how would you say – easily irritated when people speak to things that they don't fully understand. Of course none of this is your fault—" He motioned for James to wait when he began to stammer an apology of his own.

"This is the history you've been given," Defleur continued, although James really had no idea what he meant by that. So far as he knew, history was history: it was the same for everyone. "It's been spoonfed to you. There would be no way you could know any differently. It's hardly common knowledge, and time has all but erased its memory. But some of us," he tapped the side of his head in a knowing gesture "have a longer memory than most."

Defleur appeared to have calmed down by the time he finished speaking, returning to the ornate leather chair behind the oak desk that dominated the room. James held his breath and hovered at the edge of his seat, waiting to see if he would explain further. He was rewarded with a long silence before realising that this was not something that Defleur cared to share, at least not any time soon. Not with him.

Still shell-shocked by the on and off anger switch that the Comte seemed to possess, James began his own apology.

"I'm so sorry, Mr—I mean, Comte—Defleur. It was never my intention to offend—" Halfway through, Defleur was waving his hand again, declaring that there was no need for any more apologies.

"If anything, James, I should still be apologising to you. That little… episode…was most unforgivable. Shameful, really. Believe me when I say that I will most definitely make it up to you." Defleur tapped his chin thoughtfully before speaking again.

"How does a little ski trip sound?"

James knew in his logical mind that he should have politely declined his host's offer, it being his first day and that he should really be working, not going skiing with someone as mentally unstable as Defleur appeared to be. Yet he was powerless to say no.

So yeah, maybe he did go a little American Psycho there for a minute, James reasoned with himself, *but he's just really into his work is all.* That kind of passion he had seen before, in his own life, through Frankie. Knowing full well that she would hurt him for even daring to think it, Defleur had reminded him a little of her just then. They shared the same sort of fire whenever they talked about chocolate. It was something James only wished he had. There was nothing he felt anywhere nearly so passionate for, save for maybe women or football. Even then, it seemed to pale in comparison to whatever it was that Defleur and Frankie felt.

James knew that the similarities between the two was likely the only reason he hadn't shat himself and cut out immediately regardless of the consequences. Because if he could handle a little Scottish firecracker like Frankie, he should be capable enough to hold his own here.

In her own way, Frankie was just as terrifying.

Defleur led the way out of the library down yet another passageway, this one appearing to head in the opposite direction from James's room. After a series of turns, he opened another dark wooden door that looked exactly like all of the other doors that they had been past. The sound of it reminded James of that morning, of what he had thought he'd heard outside his room. His stomach rolled uneasily at the memory.

He followed Defleur into what appeared to be a games room. A giant snooker table sat dead centre flanked by ultra-modern looking black leather couches. One wall supported a giant projection screen television, along with a cabinet housing the sort of elaborate sound system that James could only fantasise about and every single gaming console ever made. With games. The wall opposite was devoted to sports equipment. Skis and poles, goggles, scuba gear, rackets of varying shapes and sizes: everything that anyone could possibly need to go skiing or swimming, play tennis, or for any other leisure activity a guest might feel like engaging in during their visit to Defleur's remote mountain compound.

James could barely keep his jaw from hanging open. It was the bachelor pad to end all bachelor pads unlike anything he'd ever seen. His efforts to mask the admiration written so clearly on his face were in vain, earning a chuckle from Defleur as he closed the door.

"And here your butler told me that the *library* was your favourite room in the house," he muttered.

"Believe it or not, he's right," Defleur laughed out loud. "It is. I'm surprised the old man even noticed at all."

He was already across the room sorting out ski equipment for the pair, pulling out jackets and gloves and poles from a large closet that lay hidden just beyond the wall of sporting goods. James was beginning to wonder if maybe Defleur had a little resort business on the side.

"I take it you're a bit of a sporting buff, then?" James asked as a way of distracting himself from his own surprise. Even Louise – who did her fair share of entertaining – had nowhere near this kind of set-up at her father's estate.

"I actually don't come down here as often as you might think," he replied, tossing James a set of outerwear that happened to fit him like a glove. "I keep it around more for the benefit of my guests than myself."

As James was zipping himself into the ski jacket, he realised that something wasn't quite right.

"Wait a minute," he blurted, more to himself than anything else. "Isn't it a little early for skiing?"

Defleur was already making his way down another corridor that James could only guess led to somewhere outside. He wasn't sure if he had heard him.

"Not for us," Defleur called back over his shoulder. "Come on."

James struggled into the rest of his gear and hurried after him, trying without success to remember the last time he'd been skiing.

Defleur was well ahead of him, striding his way through a meadow that stretched beyond the door. Once outside, James was surprised to see that what he'd originally thought of as a solid rock face that the house was cut into was in fact part of more than one mountain. Two that he could see at least, perhaps more. He could see that the lake that lay directly beneath his rooms at the far section of the house was more of a river that threaded along a meadow that led into a small valley and another clearing.

James could hear what sounded like machinery humming away in the distance, a sound so completely at odds with the picture-perfect mountain landscape. It wasn't until he entered the valley and looked up that he could see where it was coming from. And what he saw had stopped him dead in his tracks. *A snow-making machine?*

He blinked, shaking his head to ensure he wasn't hallucinating. It seemed so impossible, like something that would only exist on a film set or one of those luxury resorts for the insanely wealthy he'd seen on travel programmes. Not on someone's private property. And yet there it was, churning out enough snow to keep a modest run going. It even had its own lift. James was officially speechless.

"I guess there really is such a thing as *too much money*," he mumbled as he forced his legs to move again.

"What can I say?" Defleur shouted back as if he had hear him, something that considering the distance James wouldn't have thought possible. "I love to ski. Come on!"

Defleur was in high spirits once more, more like the person James had met the previous evening, as he flipped his goggles down and patted the lift seat next to him.

James was quick to learn once he finally finished getting all his gear in order that skiing was very much like riding a bike: you never really forget how, but you'll still fall on your ass a few times. After a couple of runs, however, he finally started getting the hang of it.

And a couple more runs after that, he noticed that he was actually having fun.   For the first time since arriving in Switzerland, he was beginning to relax.

They had been skiing for a couple of hours in a comfortable silence, with James enjoying the feeling of the wind in his hair and the crisp mountain air in his lungs, when Defleur abruptly turned to him after he had reached the bottom of the run. James thought he had seen him typing on his mobile as he slowed to a stop and wondered vaguely how he was able to get reception. The last time he had checked, there were no bars to indicate service at all.

"I'm so sorry, James," he said quickly as he tucked his mobile beneath his ski jacket, "but I've been called away. To Geneva. A family emergency."

Must be serious, James thought as he watched Defleur pull off his gloves and step out of his skis as if he couldn't get away fast enough. James wasn't sure how to respond, then realised too late that his uncertainty must have been showing plainly in his face.

"Please, stay and finish your business here – I insist. I would hate to keep you from your lovely fiancée a minute longer than what's necessary. Guillaume will make sure that you have everything you need, and I shouldn't be more than a day or so. But in the meantime…" There he paused, looking as if he were about to say something more before deciding against it.

"Well… just enjoy yourself, James," was all he said after a long pause. "My home is your home."

Defleur had begun to walk away as he spoke but then he stopped, turning look back at James one final time.

"But please…just be careful not to wander about too much. These mountains all look the same if you aren't accustomed to them. And if you think the house would be much safer for exploring, you're mistaken."

His tone was serious, his eyes hard as stone. James watched in fascination as his expression changed again, like the flip of a light switch, into something far more jovial. Almost teasing.

"I just mean that the place can feel like a bit of a maze, and I wouldn't want you to get lost. Never to be seen or heard from again. Hah!"

His laugh was more of a bark that echoed back from the stone surrounding him, making James feel as though the whole valley were laughing at his expense. Far too confused by the entire morning's events, he didn't feel much like joining in. Defleur gave him a small, oddly formal salute as he said goodbye, reminding him once more to be careful. And with that, he turned his back and continued toward the house.

Apparently, there was to be no further discussion on the matter.

James wasted no time getting out of his gear and all but ran to catch up with his host, but the Comte was in far better physical condition. He resolved in that moment to cut back on his smoking. He saw Defleur disappear into the house but by the time he made it inside himself, there was no sign of him. He had simply vanished as if into thin air. So James did the only thing he could think to do – he made his way back to his rooms and got started with his work, just as he'd been told to.

He wasn't sure what to make of it all. He had no idea what could have made Defleur bolt so quickly. He had thought he'd seen him checking his phone so perhaps he had received some sort of message, but James was fairly certain it was not a family emergency. He didn't know why, it was just something he felt.

Everything is so surreal here, he thought, listening to the house and its silence close in around him. It was the isolation and the eerie quietness of it that unnerved him most; it was so different from the buzz and hustle he was used to in London. James couldn't imagine what life must be like for Defleur, up here in the mountains all alone with that creepster of a butler. But seeing that his host had just up and left, with no indication of when he might be back, it would appear that James was about to find out for himself.

Flipping open his laptop, James checked his email again. Still nothing from Frankie. His mobile gave him the same blank story.

He sighed and opened up a new email message, this time to his brother in Australia. He figured that he would just continue with his work and in his spare time keep emailing people until he got a response from someone. Until then, he got the distinct impression that he was in for some very long and very boring days ahead.

THREE

September 16th

Frankie was beginning to worry about Louise.

She had been behaving rather strangely ever since her party, even for her. Over the years she become accustomed to Louise's many special idiosyncrasies, but this time it was different. Something even Frankie herself had not seen before. And when it came to Louise and bizarre behaviour, she had thought that she'd pretty much seen it all. Perhaps it was something as simple as a birthday, the dismal prospect of yet another year passing with no real plan for the future to speak of, that had set her off. *But this is Lou*, thought Frankie. That girl wasn't in need of a plan. She was set for life.

And yet there she would sit, alone in her room, munching away on those bars of chocolate as if there were no tomorrow.

That the Fitz Cocoa Cream bars had appeared out of nowhere was in itself quite odd. If Frankie hadn't known better she would have thought that, considering Louise's father did own the most famous chocolate company in the world, finding chocolate at random throughout the property was to be expected. Her dad was constantly bringing work home when they were younger: prototypes of products not yet available in the shops for his daughter and her willing friends to sample and enjoy. And more importantly, to provide that all-important feedback, the essential cornerstone of any successful brand. But because Frankie had known something about chocolate history, she was well aware that the Fitz brand had been discontinued long ago, not long after the Chadwick family had purchased the struggling business in the late 1800's.

Although she was by no means an expert, she had written her final research paper on the history of English chocolate for school. She had found the whole story rather fascinating:

Fitz & Company had begun making chocolate in the late 1700s, at first in the back of a small bakery shop right there in Brighton. By the early nineteenth century they had devised a way of using the new industrial technology which led to the mass production of chocolate. The company had stayed a family company that was handed down in succession and quickly grew to become the largest confectioner in Britain, giving England the first ever chocolate bar. It was around then that the Cocoa Cream was created. However, what goes up must come down.

In the late 1870s the Fitz in charge at the time was killed in what history had vaguely labelled as a machinery accident at the factory. Not long after, his two sons who had taken over the business and were woefully lacking in experience found themselves incapable to cope. They had ended up selling the company that had carried their family name for the last century to Archibald Chadwick, a newcomer to the chocolate trade but no stranger to the world of big business. However, the formula for the famous Fitz Cocoa Cream bar had died with Thomas Fitz and, after several failed attempts to recreate it, Chadwick's decided to discontinue the bar all together in 1895. It went down in the history books as the nation's first favourite teatime treat. Frankie had seen a picture of it, had even downloaded one for her presentation. That presentation had earned her the best mark of her entire school career, and was something she wasn't likely to forget.

But how one of the wrappers from those long extinct bars had come to be sitting here in front of her in Louise's kitchen some hundred years later was a bit of a mystery.

Frowning, Frankie picked up the wayward piece of paper, just one of the many discarded wrappers that Louise had left scattered throughout the house in her wake. The colours on the label were faded, its typeface rounded and old-fashioned. If she wasn't already convinced that such a thing were impossible, Frankie might have actually believed that this bar had come from the days when Queen Victoria reigned. However, the silly romantic in her – and deep down, one did exist, contrary to popular belief – really wanted to believe that she was sitting here with this original bastion of British confectionery. But it was too much of a stretch. The pragmatic and practical side that had always won out in such situations understood that this was nothing more than a very clever marketing tactic, one that Frankie caught herself buying into completely.

Perhaps this was one of the formulas from Chadwick's that Jared had been talking about. It was entirely possible that he had somehow managed to recreate the original Cocoa Cream formula using modern methods not available to chocolate makers from that time period. From there, it wasn't too difficult to believe that the marketing team had taken and ran with that as the concept, devising a whole campaign right down to the painstaking creation of the packaging to original standards.

The whole retro thing is terribly chic these days, Frankie sighed inwardly as she tossed the wrapper aside.

She didn't have time to dwell on it. She would just have to remember to ask Louise later where those chocolate bars came from. And how she seemed to have a neverending supply. Because Frankie had much bigger things to worry about than the expanding state of her friend's backside: her appointment with the banking manager was today.

She had dragged Louise out yesterday, convincing her to put down the chocolate long enough to go location scouting with her, when they stumbled upon the sort of space that Frankie had only ever fantasised about for her shop. It was a rare corner unit in Brighton's most famous shopping and tourist district featuring quaint half-timbering and shuttered, leaded windows. It had also apparently operated as a café in a previous life complete with a fully functioning – and legal – kitchen area set up already in the back. And it was available for let.

A quick visit to the estate agent representing the property told her that the money her grandmother had left her would last about six months in this space. As it happened starting a business in the right location, specifically such a high profile spot as she had chosen, just wasn't feasible with so little money. Or so the agent kept telling her. Fortunately, Louise had come out of her chocolate-induced haze just long enough to take control of the situation and do what she does best. That poor young man didn't have a chance as she unleashed the full force of her charms on him. Expanding backside or not, she was still smoking hot by anyone's standard.

The agent agreed to hold the property until Frankie had spoken with the bank, promising her first offer rights. And again, luck appeared to be on her side: her bank appointment had already been set up for the following morning. Frankie decided not to mention that her original plan was to use her inheritance for the bulk of the costs and maybe get a five thousand pound business line of credit. She knew she would need to add an extra zero to that number if she wanted this place.

And want it she did, so desperately she could almost taste it.

Nervously, Frankie donned one of her grandmother's classic Chanel suits, another part of the bequest that had been left to her. This one was a cream tweed with navy detailing, and she took a moment to swoon over its exquisite tailoring. *It's too bad Nan couldn't have left her sense of style to go along with it*, she thought with a pang of sadness, rifling through Louise's oversized walk-in closet for some suitable shoes. And just when she'd become convinced she would be lost inside for all eternity, impaled on a Jimmy Choo stiletto, she emerged with some barely-worn nude Valentino pumps that looked responsible and practical, yet sexy nonetheless.

Valentino. She could picture her Nan's subtle nod of approval as clearly as if she were standing there in front of her. *With shoes like those my dear*, she could hear her say, *how could anything possibly go wrong?* Frankie felt her eyes mist dangerously. She missed her so much.

Facing the mirror and resolutely refusing to let any of those tears fall, she attempted to twist her stubborn straight hair into something resembling a chic chignon. Since Frankie hadn't a clue what she was doing when it came to those things, she was forced to call for reinforcements. Louise had managed to tear herself away from her latest pile of Cocoa Creams for the second time as many days, long enough to wipe her hands haphazardly against her yoga stretch pants and pin Frankie's hair up better than any professional ever could in less than five minutes. Frankie found the chocolate stains in the corners of her mouth more than a little disturbing and tried to avoid looking at her face while Louise reworked her makeup.

"There. All done."

Frankie stepped back from the mirror and examined the sophisticated stranger that stared back at her. This stranger's hair was not hanging off her head in some sad ponytail, but pulled back in a way that was elegant but not too stiff. Her makeup was far less slap and dash, and much more polished and understated. The suit and shoes ended up as mere set dressing in comparison. *Whatever Lou's done to me*, she thought, *it's genius*.

"Imagine you're a loan manager -- would you give me obscene amounts of money after meeting with me today?" Frankie asked with a twirl that ended abruptly with an awkward half-curtsy and the near-miss of a twisted ankle.

"In a heartbeat, as long as you don't do that. Ever." Louise replied without hesitation. She paused before adding somewhat acidly, "you know, you don't *have* to go through with this silly bank thing. They'll *drown* you in interest charges and penalties."

Frankie stopped admiring herself, and turned back to face her friend.

"We've been through this already, Lou," Frankie sighed. "Our friendship is far too important to me to risk fucking it up over money."

One thing that had been repeatedly drilled into her head during her business classes was how it was generally considered a bad idea to borrow money or go into business with friends and family. While there were exceptions, most of the time people ended up bringing along their personal history, issues and emotions which usually led to poor decision-making and trivial infighting. Ultimately it would lead to the destruction of not only the business venture, but the relationship. And for Frankie, she didn't think it was worth the risk. Louise also knew her well enough to realise it was useless to argue, that once made up her mind was nearly impossible to change. Not unlike Louise herself.

She let out a sigh of resignation, and nodded.

"You better get going. Don't want to be late, do you?"

She tossed Frankie the spare keys to her Mercedes and left the room without another word. As she left, Frankie thought she could hear the sound of another Cocoa Cream wrapper being torn open. She imagined she could hear the sound of it hitting the carpeted floor of her bedroom as the door shut behind her.

With another sigh, Frankie headed to the garage to figure out which Mercedes the keys in her hand belonged to, hoping to hell she could remember how to drive.

Stepping into Lloyd's bank branch in North Street had always felt a bit like stepping back in time. Frankie supposed that the same could be said for many other buildings in Brighton, but this one had always been her favourite. Built sometime during the nineteenth century, the glass on the teller windows shone like mirrors in ornately gilded frames, and the tiny offices that lined the walls on either side were dark wood-paneled cubicles with frosted glass for privacy.

She walked up to the heavy oak desk that held court in the middle of the room, following the directions of a sign indicating that was where visitors were to check in.

Frankie cleared her throat, practically gasping for air through her nervousness. The elderly, bespectacled lady manning the desk glanced up at her through wire-framed glasses perched at the end of her nose.

"May I help you?" With those four little words, Frankie felt as though she were transported back to school and had been sent to the headmaster's office for bad behaviour.

"Uh yes, actually," she managed to sputter, before steadying herself with a deep breath. *There's nothing to be afraid of.* "I have an appointment with Mr. Bradley at one. My name is Frankie—I mean, Frances. Frances MacSweeney."

The woman frowned, suspicious. Frankie guessed that she didn't look quite enough like whatever she thought a "Frances" should for her liking.

"Ah yes, here you are," she said more to herself as she appeared to scroll through the computer screen. "If you could take a seat in that first office, over there on the right. Mr. Bradley will be with you shortly."

She nodded her head toward the opposing wall of offices. Frankie scooted off to do as she was told. A receptionist who was seated behind a small desk inside looked up from her computer and smiled politely. The door to the office behind her was closed.

The air in the cubicle was dense with the smell of old wood, similar to what one might expect if sitting among the pews of a church. Frankie took that as a good omen, deciding a prayer or two in her head whilst she waited wouldn't hurt. It was cooler than usual for this time of year, hence the tweed, yet despite the gentle whir of the giant fans suspended above from the vaulted ceiling she still felt as though she were sweating like a common whore in said church.

Apparently I have the ability to go from pious to prostitute in the blink of an eye, she thought in wry amusement. *Who knew?*

"Ms MacSweeney?" *Oh crap.*

Frankie discreetly mopped her forehead and stood up with what she hoped was her best 'you want to give me shitloads of money, don't you?' smile. Out of the corner of her eye she thought she saw his assistant freeze at the sound of his voice. That was never a good sign.

"Oh hello. Mr. Bradley, is it?" The man who shook her outstretched hand was typical of what one might picture a loan manager to be. Short, slightly overweight, balding. But he seemed pleasant enough as he closed the door behind her and bustled past her to take a seat behind his own desk, shuffling papers as he went.

"So you are looking to open up a…chocolate shop, is that right? And it's to be called 'MacSweet'." He smiled at her in polite encouragement, tenting his palms under his chin as Frankie launched into the spiel she had been practising for what had felt like forever.

She told him about her main product line: traditional English chocolates and sweets with a twist to drag them into the 21st century. She described her accomplishments and background, making sure to remember to include some of the awards she had won. Finally, she outlined her marketing plan: she was planning to partner with some of the other independently-owned shops in The Lanes to cross-promote each other's businesses. Some of her ideas included regular contests that would entice new customers; for her existing clientele, she had already designed a loyalty scheme to be built around the number of purchases they would make.

Bradley seemed to nod in the appropriate places and appear interested enough, but Frankie was certain that he must sit through the very same conversation countless times on any given day. Although the types of business may vary and the ideas might radically differ from one another, there was one central point at which they would all invariably arrive.

"And what do you have by way of collateral?"

"I have thirty thousand pounds, with another seven hundred in personal savings."

This was where Bradley's polite interest was replaced by some no-nonsense number crunching. He frowned at the papers before him; Frankie guessed that they must have been her financial statements. Not really her biggest strength, if she were to be honest.

"The location that you're interested in, the one that's for let now is in The Lanes, is it not? That's considered prime commercial property – the rents there can be quite high. Not to mention that competition for a space like that is usually incredibly fierce, even in this economic climate. People have found themselves caught up in massive bidding wars, only to end up in way over their head."

He looked at her over the top of his glasses; it was the second time that had happened to Frankie that day. And the second time that she was made to feel like a child, only not a naughty one. More like a child who was about to be told no.

The phone's intercom buzzed loudly, breaking the tension in the room. The unexpectedness of it made Frankie nearly jump out of her seat; even Bradley looked affected. Red-faced and blustering, he pressed the reply button and barked that he wasn't to be disturbed. Frankie heard his assistant say how very sorry she was but that something had come up that required his immediate attention, and he was needed outside. Muttering his apologies as he left the office, he told Frankie that he would be back and then they would pick things up where they had left off.

I'd hate to be that poor assistant, Frankie thought. Although her timing could not have been better. It was going to take everything she had inside of her not to cry in front of Bradley when he would inevitably break the news that the bank would not be able to take such a huge financial risk on her little venture in such a volatile economic climate. She was almost thankful for that extra bit of time to prepare herself.

Frankie could see his shadow through the frosted glass window. After Bradley had stormed out, he didn't get very far, and appeared to be speaking with some force to the poor woman who was only doing her job. But his demeanour seemed to change rather dramatically as a third and much taller silhouette came into view. Bradley went from practically shaking with rage to cowering in fear, if Frankie was reading his body language correctly. As she continued to watch this silent drama unfold, she felt her own heart skip a beat. But it wasn't from fear.

This shadow seemed somehow familiar to her. If she didn't know better, she would swear it looked exactly like the mysterious Grey Top Hat man from Louise's party. Without the top hat.

Frankie was ashamed to admit to herself that she had not forgotten about him. She had also been unable to keep from dreaming about him, either. Dreams of dancing, along with other far less innocuous things, were a nightly occurrence since that first night she'd seen him across the garden. *Dreaming didn't qualify as cheating, did it*, she would often find herself wondering. If held to the theory that dreams were just snippets of unconscious desires trying to bring awareness in the conscious self, she realised that didn't really make it sound that much better.

But at least the stranger had not morphed into Jared the way he had done in that first dream. *Surely that would be worse*, she thought, *to have such dreams about a person you know versus a figure you spotted at a distance but have never even met?* Although in her dreams Frankie had never caught sight of Grey Top Hat's face, she felt as if she knew him. That she has *always* known him. But that day in the bank would mark the first time she had thought of him in the cold light of day.

Interesting, she mused, *that just when I'm about to lose one dream I would replace it with the thoughts of another.*

She shook her head as if to right herself, telling herself that she was just being a romantic asshole, and this was serious business.

Frankie continued to watch, mesmerised, as the tall shadow appeared to be saying something of obvious importance, if one could go by the fervent nodding of Bradley's head. The figure leaned over the desk for a brief moment, then shook Bradley's hand. She wasn't certain, but it appeared as though Bradley made a little bow as he left. The taller shadow faded slowly from sight until she was left with the shorter, rounder one of Bradley, who was on his way into the cubicle to continue with the meeting. *Or to stomp all over my dreams*, Frankie thought miserably.

The sound of the door opening dashed the momentary thrill she'd gotten from her imagined glimpse of an even more imaginary lover. And reality walked in.

"Terribly sorry for that interruption, Ms. MacSweeney. Now, where were we?"

Bradley had gone from red to decidedly ashen in the face, mopping his moisture-tinged brow with an old-fashioned-looking handkerchief. Frankie noticed that it had letters embroidered on it: H.R.F.

"Ah, yes," he clapped his hands together as he was about to sit down at his desk. "I was about to say that we can approve you for a line of credit of two hundred fifty thousand pounds to start with, with a review of that amount in about one year's time."

Well I guess I could always take Lou up on her offer, Frankie thought until the words that Bradley had actually spoken, not the ones she was expecting to hear, had sunk in. *Wait, what the fuck?*

"P-p-pardon me?" She managed to whisper. "Did you say…umm. Wait. Did you just say that you are going to give me *two hundred and fifty thousand pounds*?"

Frankie felt warm and cold all at once, her nerve endings tingling like pins and needles. She feared that she might have been going into shock. Bradley looked flustered, his face flushing deep crimson once more before he began to bluster again.

This man is like his own weather station, Frankie almost laughed out loud her own ridiculousness. And at the entire situation. She wasn't quite sure if it was real or something she'd dreamed up.

"Well, uh, you see…umm…your particular business is somewhat historic in nature, bringing back the sort of handmade tradition that the nation had left behind during the Industrial Revolution. And because of that, you qualify for a…a special type of loan scheme. Now, I'm going to need you to sign a few forms, then I can take you out front and we can get everything set up for you."

Why does it sound like he's pulling this out of his ass? Frankie couldn't help herself from thinking. It just seemed to good to be true. Loans based on historical value? Did that mean that there was going to be a sudden surge in traditional tannery, which involved the soaking of hides in lime, then a fragrant water and dogshit blend? Would that qualify as bringing back handmade tradition? *Or are some traditions just more marketable and... ahem...more palatable than others?* Is it based on a sliding scale?

So many questions chased each other through Frankie's mind as she followed Bradley from his office and into the main banking hall.

Ridiculously she felt as though all eyes were on her, that she was about to be greeted by great fanfare and much applause as she followed Bradley through the bank. Of course, no one else could have possibly known what had just transpired in that tiny cubicle. No one else could have suspected that Frankie had just, so far as she was concerned, won the fucking lottery. Her mind wandered back to that tall and familiar-looking shadow, wondering if her sudden reversal of fortune had anything to do with his rather timely appearance. Because, before that, she was almost certain the situation was on track to a very different and far less pleasant outcome. There was no time to consider the theory further, however, as more papers were thrust into Frankie's face that were in need of a signature.

She was practically vibrating with excitement as she took possession of a new debit card bearing not only her own name but the official name of her new business, MacSweet. It had just gone from nothing more than a pipe dream to something of a reality. But the celebratory drinks would have to wait.

It was time to call Louise and go back to that estate

agent. She had herself some prime retail space in The Lanes to secure.

FOUR

September 17th

Seven days had passed since Defleur had left on his so-called 'urgent business', leaving James with the distinct impression that his client had no plan for returning anytime soon. He was also beginning to believe that being left with so much time on his hands was not doing much good for his mental health. It was making him think too much. And the more time he had to think, the more James was convinced that he would never be seen or heard from again.

The noticeable lack of contact from Frankie was just the beginning. Louise's party or not, it was not at all like her to go for such a long time without so much as a 'how r u' text. James tried to reason that perhaps she was being polite, knowing that this was the first big opportunity James had been given and she didn't want to distract him from his work or risk making him look unprofessional by receiving messages from his girlfriend when he should have been working.

But then James realised that, regardless of how true his theory may or may not have been, it was just completely unlike her to think that way. It was part of what had initially attracted him to her: her unwavering ability to be blunt to the point of rudeness. She wasn't trying to deliberately set people off. It just always sort of happened that way.

To him, Frankie had always been this tall, fearless redhead who said and did whatever she wanted, whenever she wanted to. People either accepted it or avoided her. Either way, she really couldn't give a toss. For him, having spent much of his life in the shadow of his older brother and his endless string of achievements, it was an awfully appealing quality. He had always secretly hoped that some of her brazenness would rub off on him by proxy.

His next clue was the email he had sent to his brother. Not the first one where he confessed having doubts about the job before he had even gotten to Switzerland, admitting that he knew the only reason he had been asked was because he was the great Matthew Harris's kid brother. Matt had responded quite quickly to that one, especially given the time difference between London and Sydney and the myriad of building projects he had on the go, to basically tell James to put on his big boy trousers and man up. That this was an opportunity that could make or break his future career with the firm and he would do well not to panic like a little girl and get on with it.

No, it was the *second* email James had sent that, thus far, had gone without so much as an acknowledgement. *Maybe he's just busy*, James had reasoned once again, and hasn't had the chance to reply. Or maybe the tone of it was such that Matt had decided it didn't really warrant a response. That email had gone something like this:

Hi Matt – me again, if you get this email PLEASE just fucking respond. Even if it's just to say yeah got it. Been emailing everyone I can think of from Frankie to work even our parents and got nothing back. Not a peep. Is that not odd? Frankie I kind of expect it.

It's Lou's birthday weekend bender. Chances are she's too hung over to type. But work? Mum and Dad?? What the hell does Mum have to do all day..she's retired for fuck's sake!!

I know I sent that email before and you said I was just freaking myself out but there's more to it. Something else is going on here. Just look at the facts. First one being the bloke I came here to work for just up and leaving. Said he'd only be gone a couple days. That was four days ago. So I'm begging you, just send a reply even if it's just one word like Tosser *so that I will know my emails are getting out and I'm not going completely mad.*

James had sent the email three days earlier after finishing all the work he was able to without Defleur present. Financial statements and forecastings were done, contracts had been drawn up and cross-referenced, the offer paperwork was complete and ready to go. All he was waiting on was an authorising signature.

Guillaume had told him the fax machine was broken so he wouldn't be able to send anything through to him, but James didn't trust the creepy manservant as far as he could throw him. And he discovered, albeit a little late, that couriers in the Alps were non-existent regardless of how much money you happened to be dealing with. Perhaps the danger pay involved, what with the threat of avalanches, outweighed any chance of profitability. None of that changed the situation: James was stuck there until he could either get his documents out to be signed somehow or Defleur finally deigned to return.

He wondered which would come first, while knowing that the first one wasn't really an option.

He was well aware of how daft it would sound to the casual observer: him complaining about being 'stuck' in the Alps at a billion dollar mountain retreat. His colleagues, not to mention his brother, would be positively purple with envy. The whole place felt very much like what you might see in American beer adverts on television. But James had his reasons for feeling uneasy. And if ever there were a time when something was too good to be true, then this would definitely be it.

The layout of the house wasn't helping. To James, it felt very much like a hedge maze made out of concrete and glass. He literally didn't know if he were coming or going most of the time since all of the hallways and doors looked the same. He spent most of his time in his room simply because he didn't know how to get anywhere else. He had managed somehow to get back to the library a couple of times, but was never able to find that room with the sports equipment since the day he'd gone skiing with Defleur.

Shame, James thought, *I'd give my left nut to watch a game of footie on that fucking huge TV*.

He had no clue where the kitchen was, yet somehow food just magically appeared in his room, usually right before he woke up or while he was in the washroom. Never once did he see who was bringing it. Whenever he did make his way downstairs, the butler would always offer to fetch him something. But he was too scared shitless to eat it.

The butler. For James, Guillaume was like something out of some late night film entitled *The Butler Did It Then Ate My Liver with Some Shallots and A Lovely Merlot*. He gave off a serious serial killer-esque vibe. But then, James was mindful to the fact that it could have been the feeling of isolation combined with the man's unnaturally pale skin and ice blue eyes that were so light and clear they practically glittered like diamonds that made him feel that way. But still, James would frequently catch him watching him whenever he thought that he wasn't paying attention, which was more than a little discomforting. Face to face, Guillaume was all formal hospitality and deference, but once his back was turned those icy eyes would narrow and James could feel him monitoring his every movement. As if he were studying him. Maybe it was his butler training but to James it felt like whenever he left his room, Guillaume would be lurking there. Watching and waiting.

It was enough for James to make sure his door was locked up tight every night.

But it wasn't just the creepy butler. There were moments when James got the impression that he wasn't the only guest of the Comte. Even though he continued to try to convince himself that what had happened in the hallway outside his room that first morning was a figment of his imagination, he just couldn't shake the feeling.

James stood up from his desk and stretched before moving over to the windows. He didn't want to venture far from his room lest he run into his new friend Guillaume, but it looked like such a beautiful day out that he was reluctant to spend it trapped indoors. He glanced at the heavy double mahogany doors that he had gotten into the habit of keeping locked regardless of the time of day.

"There's got to be another way," he muttered to himself, not feeling quite brave enough to enter into that endless cold white hallway, butler or no butler.

He started toward the window and drew open the curtains even further. That was when he noticed that what he'd believed to be floor-to-ceiling windowpanes were actually a set of French doors that led to a small steel terrace bound by panes of glass and steel railings. James tried the door and was almost shocked to discover that they opened immediately, flooding his room with crisp fresh air. He had expected them to be locked; not just locked, but bolted in such a way that he would require a special key to open them.

He began to giggle aloud at his own foolishness. *Why would they be locked?* It wasn't as if there were any way to access the doors from the ground. The wing where his room was located was directly above the river that led into the valley with the mountain that held the ski run.

James stepped onto the balcony, taking extra care not to look down through the steel grates beneath his feet. He didn't need feel the need to remind himself how far he was above the water. He took a deep breath. After a week of breathing in the stale recycled air of the fortress he was staying in, its freshness had an almost narcotic effect. He felt dizzy, euphoric, then slightly panicky. To his relief, there was a small bistro table and chair tucked away on the other side of the doorway. He could feel himself begin to sway and quickly made himself sit before he could fall.

He let his head tip back so his face could bask in full view of the sunshine. Closing his eyes, he soaked in the moment of fresh air and freedom.

James wasn't sure how long he had been outside before he had begun to get that distinct and ever-increasing impression of being watched. It was the same prickly sensation you might get on the surface of your skin just before you look up to find someone staring you down. But that would be impossible since the only things he could see around him were mountains, snow-capped and silent. At least, that was what he continued to tell himself. However, the feeling remained.

After about an hour, James could stand it no longer.

He stood up from his chair and began to examine his surroundings more closely. He could see no one hiding in the deep craggy rock that lay directly across from his terrace, nor was there any indication that anyone was concealed in the peaceful silence of the valley below. Even the river seemed to flow without sound. As James slowly scanned the other blocks that made up the house, he saw a small movement in one of the windows at the opposite end.

It was a fair distance away so he couldn't be sure; for all he knew it could very well have been a trick of the sunlight on the glass. Upon further inspection, he was positive that he could see the outline of a very long, very shapely female leg, clad in what appeared to be a sheer white stocking and matching lacy suspender belt. And then it was gone.

James stood, blinking slowly, not really sure of anything anymore.

It wasn't like he had been flipping through *Playboy* or *Maxim* or any other lad's magazine, so there was no reason for that sort of image to pop into mind. Except, of course, that he was a bloke. But still, there was no context. He couldn't remember the last time he'd even seen lingerie like that, either in print or real life. Frankie was never into that sort of thing. Even the thought of it was enough to make him laugh out loud. The sound of the shrill bark bouncing back at him from the rock face made him jump.

He hurried back in to the relative safety of his room, firmly closing the balcony doors and making sure they were locked before leaning with his back against them to catch his breath. He'd been standing like that for an indeterminate amount of time when a soft knock at the door gave him another start. It was Guillaume, asking him if he had any preferences for dinner and if he would be taking it in his room or the formal dining room downstairs.

He decided that, for a change, his mental wellbeing might do well with a little company so he said that he would dine downstairs. Guillaume's silence seemed to indicate that he was as surprised by the answer as James was himself.

The meal was a simple one – some meat in a cream sauce served over some potatoes and green beans. Guillaume sat across from him at the massive oak table, eyeing him with what felt like suspicion. *But of course,* he thought, *I could be completely misreading the situation.* Perhaps the old butler was merely curious as to what had prompted James to eat dinner outside of his room. Or maybe that was just the look on his face.

James decided to test his newfound theory and mustered up the courage normally found after a few pints and reserved for pulling girls.

"So Guillaume," he asked, trying to sound as casual as he could as he all but yelled to the other end of the room, "is there anyone else staying here at the moment?"

He almost enjoyed watching the butler's pasty complexion pale even further. The old man was at a loss for words. James gave himself a mental pat on the back.

"*Non,* monsieur Harris," Guillaume finally replied calmly. "Why would you ask?"

"Oh, no reason," James was surprised by how much he was enjoying this. "I just thought I heard someone in the hallway near my room. And today I thought I saw someone in the window of one of the other wings."

"Is that so?" He thought he had heard a slight crack in the old man's voice. "I was cleaning windows earlier. Perhaps it was me you saw."

James found it difficult to contain his laughter, so he let slip a chuckle before he replied.

"Well, mate, unless you're in the habit of cleaning house in ladies underwear, then I highly doubt it was you."

He took great satisfaction in watching as the butler pale once more before his cheeks flushed to a deep, dark crimson.

Guillaume muttered something about going to the kitchen to see to dessert, and stalked out of the room muttering under his breath in French. James regretted not being better at the language in school; he would have loved to know what was said. His satisfaction was short-lived as the full implications of the butler's reaction dawned on him: he was definitely hiding something.

The best-case scenario was that he knew something that James didn't. He didn't want to think about possible worst cases, which ranged from simple lies to something far more sinister at play. James shuddered, suddenly aware of the emptiness of the room and the way the silence seemed to echo against the bare white walls. James had found that he had lost what was left of his appetite and wasn't in the mood to stick around for dessert.

He hurried back to his room without so much as a glance to see which direction Guillaume had gone or even if he was on his way back. As he approached the hall where his room was, having found it that time round with minimal difficulty, he thought he heard footsteps padding softly on the runner carpet behind him. He whirled, expecting to see the butler sneaking to that nightly post James had imagined him taking up each night, but there was no one in sight. Only the bare expanse of white walls punctuated with the dark wood of the doors. The ceiling's recessed pot lighting didn't cast much glow, leaving in its wake lots of shadow and an infinite number of hiding places. Not to mention the opportunity for one's imagination to run away with him.

Quickening his pace, James made it to the bedroom door. Gasping, his head snapped up as he thought he heard another sound, something more than a footstep, although he couldn't quite determine what it was exactly. Again, he was met with empty silence. He shook his head.

"Get a grip, mate," he muttered to himself.

Safely inside his room, with the door securely locked behind him, was the only place in the house where James felt like he could almost relax. But relaxation was something that refused to come easily that particular evening. He found himself pacing the floor restlessly, checking his laptop for emails he instinctively knew would not be there. His Blackberry had died a few days earlier and, as was typical for him, he had forgotten both his wall charger and the cable to connect to his computer. Not that it mattered, since he had not gotten any service bars since his arrival. He had noticed in the past few days of not having his mobile, though, how desperately attached he was to it. It was like losing a limb.

His laptop continued to refuse to make a connection with the Internet, so James was finally forced to entertain himself the old-fashioned way: by picking up a book to read. It had been so long since he'd actually read anything that wasn't on a screen, he couldn't recall the last time. He found himself incapable of concentrating on the words, given his jumpiness at every little sound the house made around him. He became frustrated and decided to make it an early night.

As he made his way to the bathroom, a familiar sound from just outside the bedroom door stopped him in his tracks. It was a sound he was positive he had heard before. A giggle... that *female* giggle.

James froze before bolting toward the sound in a rare fit of courage, wrenching open the door. Nothing. Not a sound, save for his own heart pounding in his ears. Not a soul to be seen.

He closed the door and cursed its lack of deadbolt. Not a rational thought, but one to be expected under the circumstances. It would have lent an extra layer of safety and security. Enough to completely put his mind at ease? Not likely. After a few minutes of straining to hear through the heavy wood of the door, he went on about his business with both ears alert for any more hallway sounds. He tried reading once more to try to take his mind off things, and realised how much time he had on his hands once television had been taken out of the equation. Too bad he was too keyed up to focus on, let alone enjoy, whatever it was he was reading. He finally gave up, turning the light out and turning over on his side to face the door.

He slipped reluctantly into a dreamless sleep for a few hours before waking at around three o'clock in the morning for no apparent reason. No reason, that was, until he happened to glance toward the bottom of his bed.

At the foot of its four-poster frame stood two of the most beautiful women James had ever set eyes on, Frankie included. This was the kind of beauty you didn't see every day; it only seemed to exist in Hollywood films. One was ice blonde, her eyes so light they appeared almost translucent in what little moonlight that streamed into the room through the curtains. The other woman was much darker; her skin was the colour of coffee, with long wavy dark hair that flowed over her shoulders. They were wearing matching lingerie in different colours: midnight blue for the blonde, ivory white for the brunette.

James squeezed his eyes shut and gave his head a

shake, convinced that he must have been dreaming or that the rich meat dish he'd had at dinner wasn't agreeing with him.

But they were still there when his eyes opened again.

He contemplated giving himself a good slap in the face but was lucid enough to recognise that, were he not dreaming, a move like that would most certainly get their attention. That was something that James wasn't sure would be a good or bad thing. Thus far, neither one seemed aware that he had woken up and seen them or if they did, they didn't care. They were too busy arguing with each other.

"He told us we couldn't," said the darker one.

"But it's been so long since we have had something so young, so full of life," the blonde purred. "Look how peacefully he sleeps. He would think it was nothing but a wonderful dream."

"We were told no." The dark-haired one was firm on this. "We only came to look."

"You're no fun. Where's your sense of adventure?" The blonde had moved closer to the head of the bed, forcing James to keep his eyes closed and pretend to sleep. He concentrated on keeping his breath even, something that became increasingly difficult when he felt the mattress sink beside him.

"This is not a game. He will be ours soon enough. Just be patient," the brunette replied.

James could feel the pressure on the mattress shift as if she were pulling the other woman back. Away from him. He heard the blonde let out a growl of frustration despite allowing herself to be pulled from the bed.

And then there was nothing. Only silence.

He waited for what seemed like an eternity before daring to open his eyes again. He was half-expecting them to be practically on top of him, that the silence was only a ruse. Taking a deep breath, he opened his eyes, exhaling sharply as he forced himself to sit up quickly. With any luck, he thought maybe he could knock one or both of them unconscious – perhaps even himself in the process – if they were hovering as close as he was afraid they might be. But the women were gone.

James scanned the room to be sure, even going so far as to switch on his lamp and get out of bed, hands shaking as he looked behind the closet doors and in the bathroom. But there was no sign of them at all. They had somehow slipped out of the room as swiftly and as silently as they'd managed to get in. He sat back down on the bed without turning out the light, trying to slow his breathing to a normal pace and will his heart to stop trying to beat a path from his chest.

There would be no sleep for him the rest of the night, of that much he was sure.

As for who these women were, how they had managed to get into his room through a locked door then out just as quickly without so much as a sound, or what they could possibly have meant by 'he will be ours soon enough', James was at a loss. Was it only a dream, perhaps inspired by that leg he had thought he'd seen earlier in the day? And should he be terrified by it or was it all right to be a little turned on? *I mean, it was a little hot until the cannibal talk*, he thought.

The only thing James knew for certain was that he was stuck in the Swiss Alps with a sociopathic servant and two gorgeous females who may or may not wish to make a meal out of him. *Young and succulent*: how else was he supposed to take that? If it was his subconscious that had come up with that little scenario, he feared he would need to see a shrink when he finally got back to London. *If I make it back at all.*

"All right, just stop," James told himself out loud. The sound of his own voice breaking the dead quiet of the dark bedroom made him jump. He tried again to tell himself that it was only a dream; the change in altitude was messing with his mind and heightening his already existing paranoia. But each time, he believed himself less and less because he *knew* that it wasn't a dream. He knew there was something going on that was beyond his comprehension.

Part of him felt that it may all be in vain, all of his self-reassurances. There was a very good chance that neither Frankie or his brother would ever see his emails, much less have a chance to respond. But there was a small part that remained inside him that had hope.

Hope that maybe someone might respond to his email.

Hope that there could be a perfectly rational explanation as to why two women were arguing over him in his bedroom in their underwear.

Hope that he would make it out of this place in one piece with his sanity intact.

FIVE

September 19th

Hi James - it's me, Frankie.

If the name sounds vaguely familiar to you, it should: I'm your fucking fiancée. The one you've left behind to rot as you party it up in Switzerland with your new fancypants client. At least that's what I've come to believe since I haven't heard so much as a peep from you since you left on your little trip. You know – the one you should have been back from ages ago? I mean it's fucking Thursday already! No emails, no voicemail, no texts…nothing. I've tried texting – no response. I can't even count how many times I've called your mobile just to get the same message repeated over and over that the customer I am trying to reach is out of range. WTF? I thought our plan was good for all of Europe? I was about to toss my mobile across the room it made me so angry.

I can only assume that you're just incredibly busy or that they haven't invented wireless technology in the Alps or that this deal is taking a hell of a lot longer than you thought it would. However none of that helps me in the least when I have such massively huge news to tell you. MacSweet is a go. Signed the lease today.

Now if that's not enough to get you to write back I don't know what is. So I guess I'll just wait to hear from you whenever you decide you've got the time then eh? Let's just hope that for your sake it's not too long.

78

You know how I feel about waiting.

xoxo Frankie

It took Frankie every ounce of self-control she could muster not to slam the laptop shut after clicking send on the latest email to her wayward fiancé. She could have kept on and on with the typing, there was so much to say, but she figured she would just save herself the time and hand cramping. She had gotten the impression that he wasn't terribly concerned with checking his personal email, and even though she had copied his work address on the one she just sent, she'd be surprised if it garnered a reply.

That had always been one of her pet peeves about James: his complete lack of ability to focus on more than one thing at any given time. But it was something she had often chalked up to her own impossibly high standards when it came to men. James really was a decent bloke, the first one who hadn't run screaming after witnessing her rollercoaster-style mood swings, so she figured she owed it both to him and herself to overlook a few things every now and again. However, a willingness to overlook something and forgetting about it entirely were two very different things, so as her way of coping she had a mental file she used as a way of channelling her irritation, disappointment or abject rage whenever James did something that would normally put her over the edge.

More often than not, it was what he *didn't* do. That happened to be the bigger of the issues.

Frankie's file was nearly bursting at the seams with the number of times James had forgotten they were having dinner and stayed at the pub with his mates without bothering to turn his mobile ringer on. Or plans they had

79

made to head down to Brighton to spend a weekend with Louise and whatever flavour of the month she had on the go, when Frankie was left waiting at the train station for him. He'd lost his mobile to so many pub toilets in London's East End she had lost count. And then there was the time that he had not only forgotten her birthday, but the surprise party he was supposed to have been co-hosting with Louise. That was the final straw for Frankie; maybe she didn't much care for celebrating her birthday in the same grand manner her best friend enjoyed, but she felt that if her boyfriend couldn't care enough to remember it then that was a bit of a red flag. She was going to end it with him.

As it turned out, his excuse was a valid one: he had become so caught up in choosing an engagement ring for her that he completely forgot about everything else. He had proposed the same night Frankie had planned on breaking up with him. She had been so flabbergasted by the situation, the very public display in the middle of her favourite restaurant near Brighton's famous pier, that she said yes almost involuntarily.

And it was because he had been so attentive and conscientious since they had become engaged, firmly positioning himself as the man who would never break her heart, that made this sudden and complete absence of contact troubling. Frankie was concerned that it meant that James might be slipping back into old habits. That he'd discovered that he wasn't able to make the effort to change as he'd promised, and had just been on his best behaviour until he couldn't hide it any longer.

Ohh hello, good old trust issues, Frankie thought.

She had been wondering how long it would take before that particular beast reared its ugly head. However tempting it was to dwell and wallow, she had neither the time nor the energy to think about James and why he suddenly decided to disappear. Or about Louise and her new best friends, those chocolate bars that had appeared from God knows where and in apparent unending supply. Frankie rarely saw her anymore without a half-eaten bar in her hand or an empty wrapper she was about to toss.

No, she needed to keep her eye on the prize: that perfect little piece of corner property in the Lanes that had just so happened to come onto the market at exactly the time that she needed it to. Although Frankie was never really one who believed in Divine Providence, she had to admit that this whole situation was falling rather smoothly into place. But of course, as always, her sensible Scottish upbringing and a healthy dose of paranoia made her question when it would all go pear-shaped and what exactly was going to go wrong. As her mother always told her, better to be prepared for the worst than to hope for the best.

That way you'll never be disappointed when things don't work out, dear. Frankie's mother was a charmer.

"Right," Frankie said out loud, taking a deep breath. "That's about enough of that."

She knew herself well enough to know that when she started thinking about those little pearls of wisdom her mother had passed onto her in childhood, it was time to pop a pill or busy herself doing something else. And it just so happened that she'd forgotten her pills at Louise's.

She took another look around the empty space she had just signed a five-year lease on, something in itself that would have normally caused her to hyperventilate. But, although it was the most important step Frankie had taken in her life thus far, she felt a strange sense of calm. She didn't even question how quickly the transaction had gone through, accepting Mr. Bradley's vague and bizarrely sweat-laden explanation that it was down to a very motivated landlord. The shop was gorgeous enough on its own, with its beams and gables and leaded glass. The works. She had wasted no time once the keys were in hand, deciding to get straight into prepping for the painting she was planning on doing just as soon as she could get started. She knew that she could have just as easily hired someone in to do it for her, but she wanted to give it a go herself first. Frankie had always been someone who preferred to do things on her own, but when it came to something this important she knew that she wouldn't be satisfied leaving her vision in someone else's hands.

"Guess I really am a bit of a control freak," she mused out loud.

The sound of her voice echoing back at her reminded her that she needed to get moving. October wasn't that far away, and there was lots of work to be done if she was going to be open in time.

Frankie took stock of her internal checklist, noting some of the things she'd already been able to get in such a small amount of time. She'd found a gorgeous set of gilded glass cabinets in one of the many antique shops in the neighbourhood; the walls already had lots of built-in shelving, a feature she was so fond of if only because it meant she wouldn't need much else for display. Louise had spotted an antique gilded cash register in that same shop on their way out, so she bought that as well. Both items were being professionally cleaned and would be delivered later in the week. She had already contacted a graphic designer – the boyfriend of someone she had gone to culinary school with – who was working on signage and promotional items for her with the mid-October opening date.

It's amazing how much you can get done when you don't have to worry about how you're going to pay for it all, she thought again for the umpteenth time.

But her list wasn't even closed to being complete. There were still so many things yet to do: source out suppliers for packaging and other sundry items, fine-tune a few of her recipes and of course, make all of the product. *Which is why*, Frankie told herself firmly, *I need to pull my head out of my ass and get to work.* Otherwise, opening day would come along and she would have nothing on the shelves to sell. And that would be a disaster.

The sound of her mobile brought her back into the present. She looked down to see who was calling, fully expecting it would be Louise or possibly even James finally deigning to respond to one of her many messages, but it was a number she didn't recognise. And she wasn't in the habit of picking up calls from numbers she was unfamiliar with, a behaviour trait she supposed she would need to adjust rather quickly once the shop was up and running.

"Because you can't very well ignore people when they call the shop," she said out loud as she hit the answer button.

"Hello?"

"Oh hello there, am I speaking with Frances?" chirped a male voice at the other end. Obviously someone she didn't know, what with the use of her birth name.

"Yes, but it's Frankie, actually. I don't really go by Frances," she responded warily. Probably someone trying to sell her something.

"Oh, my apologies. I was going by the letting application I have in front of me."

Oh shit, Frankie moaned to herself. What with all of the chaos the past week had brought, she had completely forgotten about the application that her and James had submitted to an estate agency for a flat a few weeks earlier.

"I'm just ringing to tell you," the estate agent was saying, "that we do have a flat available at the end of this month. It's a lovely two bedroom in a converted Victorian row house, with a view of the sea from the master bedroom. I was trying to contact James Harris as it says here that he would be the principle on the lease but I haven't had any luck getting through…"

That makes two of us, mate, she thought ruefully before realizing that the agent had asked her a question.

"I'm sorry – what was that?"

"Would you like to book a viewing to see the flat?" came the question again. And a very good question it was.

"Actually, it isn't really a good time for me to think about a move like that. But I appreciate the thought and please do keep us in mind for the future," she replied without hesitation, effectively cutting what may have been left of the conversation short.

Now why would I have gone and said that, Frankie wondered.

Granted, she was angry with James at the moment. But, as she toyed with the small diamond on the ring finger of her left hand, she found herself thinking that there was maybe more to it. Admittedly, she was a little freaked out by all this newfound responsibility she'd been given, never mind the huge amount of money that had come along with it. Living with Louise, despite whatever was happening with her and those chocolates, had given her more stability than she'd had in quite some time. Since she had last lived in Brighton, in fact.

Truth be told, she was somewhat relieved that James hadn't been around that week as she was rushing around, taking care of things for the shop. Otherwise she would have felt an obligation to take care of him, to make sure that he felt welcome and included. Brighton wasn't his home; he was an Essex boy, born and raised. The only reason he was moving there was for her. And although they'd spoken about it at length and he had always insisted that he was happy to relocate with her, deep down Frankie wasn't entirely convinced. Even this recent absence almost seemed like a test of sorts. For her or James, Frankie wasn't sure.

The only thing she felt for certain, as she sat alone in her empty shop thinking too much, was anger.

She hated not knowing what was going on. For the first time since they had become engaged, Frankie was beginning to wonder if there would be a future for her and James after all. But she had stop wallowing and get back to what she was supposed to be doing in the first place: painting.

How did that old saying go? Be careful what you wish for; you might get it. Frankie was busy mixing yet more primer for the walls, wondering for the tenth time that day if she'd made a mistake in electing to do all the painting and design for the shop on her own. There were so many other things she could be doing with that time.

But no, she thought, *this is exactly where I'm supposed to be right now.*

She had scored high marks in the conceptual design

classes she'd taken at culinary school. Maybe those had more to do with creating interesting-looking treats than anything else, but then she had earned a perfect score for a project where she had designed the layout and colour scheme for a storefront. She was just going to have to trust that actually meant something. But she was confident she'd be able to execute the floorplan she'd had floating round her mind for so long she figured she'd be able to do it in her sleep.

The colours she had chosen were simple. Pink was second only to purple when it came to Frankie's list of favourites, and would go far better with chocolate brown trim of the baseboards and mouldings making it the more logical choice. In the end, it was a soft blush pink that perfectly punctuated with the rich chocolate brown border and darkly stained hardwood flooring. Since she knew next to nothing about refinishing wood she'd had to swallow her pride and hire someone in to do it, but even the perfectionist in her had to admit that the bloke had done a hell of a job. He was quick to come in and get things done, even left some extra dropcloths to protect the floors from the painting she was still insisting on doing herself, despite his offer to do it for her for a pittance. There was really no question over his quality or price; he had come highly recommended to her by Louise's father.

And from Louise herself, but for a completely unrelated reason.

"Ooh, oh yes...I remember him," Louise had recalled rather lasciviously in between bites of her Cocoa Cream. Apparently she was so far gone on the stuff that she'd taken to eating whilst they were on the phone.

"He was quite a goer in the sack, that's for sure. He'll polish your floors but good, if you know what I mean." Unfortunately Frankie had known exactly what she meant as the unwelcome image leapt into her mind.

"Yes, *thanks* SO much, Lou," she had replied before ending the call as quickly as she could with a shudder.

She wasn't sure which was the worst of it: the idea of Louise cavorting with the floor man, or the sound of the incessant open-mouthed chewing sound that had echoed directly into Frankie's ear as Louise inhaled her chocolate bars one after the other at the other end of the line.

She sighed at the memory, and then shook her head in an attempt to rid her mind of it entirely. Frankie was accustomed to thoughts drifting away from her – it was something she'd lived with all her life – but these days she couldn't help but notice it had become more difficult to control than ever. She knew it was means of escapism. In this case, it was her mind's way of escaping the enormity of the situation.

Her very own shop, at last. If only it were that simple.

Lately her mind had gotten into the bad habit of meandering back to that tall shadow she'd seen through the frosted glass at the bank, and then from there inevitably to the stranger from Louise's party. Dreaming about him wasn't enough anymore. While part of her realised that this constant fantasizing about a stranger she'd barely caught sight of in the dead of night weeks ago wasn't exactly healthy, it clearly was enough to create quite an impression and a symptom of a much deeper issue. But it was an issue she wasn't prepared to tackle head-on at the moment, so it would just have to continue to fester.

Frankie frowned. She was losing daylight quite quickly, and the primer wasn't going to apply itself. The walls of the shop had been painted a very odd shade of terracotta, dark and flat, so it was proving more stubborn to cover than she'd anticipated. It was going to take another coat or two of primer not to bleed through and mess with her perfect light pink.

"Third times the charm," she muttered out loud through gritted teeth as she heaved the bucket back into what would become the main shopfloor.

She had already decided to make one wall a design feature, painted entirely in that delicious deep chocolate selected solely because it made her mouth water just looking at it. It would most likely serve as a backdrop to the antique cash register. *At least that will save me some primer*, she thought as she reached the middle of the room with the bucket. She just needed to decide which wall that was going to be. Since Louise had declined to come meet her – she must have wanted to be alone with her Cocoa Creams – so she was going to have to make that particular choice on her own. Something she supposed she would have to get used to.

The Lanes were usually a hive of bustle and activity but not at half seven on a Tuesday evening, Frankie noted as she stood inside, peeping through a small tear in the papered glass at the streets in front of her shop. There were a handful of people milling about on the cobblestones outside a pub, perhaps sneaking a fag before going back to their pints, but overall it was fairly desolate. She guessed that summer's high season was winding down, offering a bit of respite until the Christmas rush took hold, which would likely change everything.

As she stood quietly inside, she felt her breath catch again at the idea that all of this was *hers*, just as it had done since the first time she'd unlocked the lead-paned door and opened it to hear the charming bell peal overhead. *And charming was the perfect word for it*, she thought.

The interior layout of the shop was fairly unassuming. The front room had an angled ceiling supported by exposed beams, and built-in dark wooden shelving that ran along the two walls parallel to the front door. To the left of the entrance was an enormous leaded glass window that overlooked the street, with flower boxes on the outside and a generous banquette inside that Frankie had already decided would be perfect for the elaborate displays she was planning. Its tiny pot lights didn't give off so much heat as to melt the chocolate, and were just bright enough to attract the attention of the passersby who would be her potential customers. Directly opposite the front door, a small corridor led from the main shop into a small kitchen and office area in back, anchored by an expanse of wall that she had just decided in that moment to paint in the dark chocolate shade. She walked over and confirmed that it would give her the best vantage point to keep an eye on everything.

And as she stood there, she could suddenly see it all laid out before her: the shop finished and glorious and teeming with eager customers. The shelves had become home to a selection of boxed chocolates, wrapped with brightly coloured paper and being pondered over by well-intentioned husbands and boyfriends who had stopped in on their way home. Frankie imagined herself behind the antique register, chatting and laughing as she rang purchases through. Customers stood patiently waiting for service, peering into the enormous glass cabinets beside the register that housed the individual truffles, chocolate bark, and other bonbons that sat waiting to be personally selected and packaged. Uh-oh, it looks like that silver platter Frankie had planned on using as a taster tray on the dark cherry table in the middle of the shop is in need of a refill again: it's looking pretty empty.

And that would be another fine example of why I haven't been able to get any bloody work done, Frankie sighed again. Too much fucking day-dreaming.

She reluctantly pulled herself free from her fantasy and pushed up her shirtsleeves to start making it a reality when she remembered that she'd left her roller and painters tray in the kitchen sink. As she rinsed them until the water ran clean, she heard the brass bell above the door ring out. It echoed loudly in the empty space. The unexpectedness of it froze her in place.

Oh shit. Had she somehow forgotten to lock the door behind her?

She could hear the sound of hard-soled shoes walking across her newly refinished wooden floors. Heart pounding, she called out something that sounded that sounded like 'be right there' and tried to dust herself off enough to at least look presentable.

It was probably some local resident or perhaps a fellow shopkeeper who saw the lights she had just switched on and had gotten curious, she decided as she tried to calm herself down. She quickly grabbed her tray with the rollers so that the person would get the hint that she was very busy and wouldn't have much time to chat, before reminding herself that she needed to be polite. This could be a potential customer, and she would have to be nice. She checked that her mobile was still tucked into her back pocket as a precaution, no doubt getting dust all over her bottom in the process.

Great. Way to make a first impression, she rolled her eyes at herself before she ventured out, taking a final deep breath and plastering a smile on her face with as much sincerity as she could muster.

Her unexpected caller was standing waiting just inside

the door. Frankie could feel her heart begin to pound again as she took in the stranger's height. He was so tall that he towered in front of the door, and may have even had to duck down to gain entrance. Then she noticed his beautiful trench coat. Dove grey, and so meticulously tailored that it could only have come bespoke from Savile Row. He stepped forward to greet her, and she felt a lump form in her throat.

"Ms. MacSweeney?" His voice melted over her like honey. *No, not honey, exactly*; it was smoother than that. More like a fine Belgian milk chocolate at perfect temper. But his voice was nothing compared to the face. It was indescribably perfect, so perfect that Frankie was beginning to feel lightheaded just looking at him. It was a symphony of cheekbones, full lips, and long eyelashes. The features that men so often take for granted, and most women would kill to have.

Her throat had suddenly become very dry as she tried to swallow, heart still thudding away like a hammer in her ribcage.

"Umm y-yes. And who are you?" Not the most polite way to start a conversation, but it came out less as a demand and more a mystified whisper. She was amazed that she'd had the ability to speak at all.

The stranger smiled warmly, his eyes crinkling attractively in the corners, and Frankie was relieved that she hadn't offended him. Something she seemed to do with so many people.

"I apologize for the intrusion, but I was just passing by and noticed that the light was on. And since I was already planning to drop by tomorrow to introduce myself anyway, I thought that maybe I would try my luck tonight. My name is Henry Roberts." He extended his hand.

Frankie was barely able to concentrate on the words as they left his beautifully shaped lips. She'd heard him speak, but his voice seemed to slide right over her. She watched, mesmerised, as a lock of hair the colour of lemon buttercream slipped onto his forehead.

"Frankie MacSweeney," she replied as she managed to pull herself together and moved forward, fighting not to sweep that lock of hair back as she did, to shake his hand. It was strong but smooth, and it made her knees weak.

"You must be with the bank?" She reasoned before mentally giving herself a smack. Given that he'd known her name and just finished telling her he was planning to come in to introduce himself, wouldn't that be the only reason he'd know who she was? *Nice one.*

He chuckled, almost nervously she thought, although again she wasn't really paying attention. She was far too occupied trying to hold herself together. *Christ, what's wrong with me*, she thought. *I don't usually go to pieces over an attractive man.* But rarely had she encountered a man such as this. *Okay, scratch that. Try never.*

"Yes, you could say that," he replied. "I've been appointed as your mentor under the loan scheme Mr. Bradley had set you up with. I'm surprised he didn't mention it to you."

It was entirely possible that he had mentioned it, but she had been on such a high over getting the loan in the first place that she had stopped listening after hearing the amount. *At this rate, I'm going to make the best businesswoman ever.*

"I'm not sure if he did, but I guess he thought I could use all the help I can get," Frankie joked lamely.

"I don't think you're giving yourself enough credit," he

said softly as he looked intently into her eyes. His were a soft blue-grey, almost the same colour as the sea after a storm. The kind of eyes a girl could get lost in, she noted, making them just as dangerous.

Frankie was suddenly very aware that he still had hold of her hand. He seemed to notice at the same time she did, and he pulled it away quickly as he continued.

"It looks to me like you have the makings of a very profitable business here." He had begun to walk around the room looking around him with interest. Inspecting the space on the bank's behalf, Frankie assumed.

"The wall colour not to your liking, I gather?" He nodded at the bucket of primer that Frankie had almost forgotten was laying at her feet. She laughed, giving it a nudge with her foot.

"Yeah, it was less than appealing. Kind of a cross between puke and baby shit," she replied off-handedly before realizing what it was that she had said. Then she froze, wide-eyed.

It had come out of her mouth before she could stop it, even think about it. *Bugger, bugger, bugger,* she thought desperately, *why do I have to be so...me sometimes?* She felt herself begin to blush a dull shade of burgundy before risking a peek just to see how appalled he was by it. By her.

To Frankie's relief although Henry's eyes had widened to the size of milk saucers, he began to laugh. Not an uncomfortable titter, but a genuine, shoulder-shaking chortle.

"That was a...ahhh... remarkably *vivid* description."

He wiped at his eyes, still smiling at her. There was no sign of disgust or even disapproval. She felt her knees

93

weaken again slightly and her mind go blank, unable to draw up some witty remark that would save her from herself. For once, this time not mercifully, words failed her.

"Would you like some help?" he asked.

She looked up at him, startled. He was serious.

"Um, I'm not sure priming walls would be quite what the bank had in mind when they appointed you as a mentor." But Henry appeared undeterred, giving her a smirk that made Frankie's stomach flip as he removed his overcoat.

Mother of God, that's a well-fitted Thomas Pink shirt he's wearing.

"Well now, we just won't tell them then, will we," he replied as he began rolling up his French cuffs.

Frankie wondered how it was humanly possible to make a white button down shirt tucked into plain grey trousers look so pornographic. And why he was affecting her in such a way.

She came to the logical conclusion that she was in need of a good shag. *Of course, that must be it.* James had just been gone too long without contact – no flirty texts, no naughty emails, nothing – and his absence had left her with the hormone levels of a horny teenager. And then, to make matters worse, there he was bending over in front of her to pick up the roller. All Frankie could do was silently repeat *must... not...squeeze... his ass* over and over until she was sane again.

It was turning into one fucking long night. At the rate things were going, she realised, the only thing that would be accomplished that evening was the female equivalent of blue balls.

But somehow, through a combination of deep breathing and sheer force of will, she pulled herself out of the frenzy of lust she had worked herself into and grabbed a paintbrush. She had a job to do, after all.

And, she reminded herself, *I'll be fucked if I let some bank-appointed mentor-type come in and distract me with his perfect V of a back and the masterful way he's gripping his roller.*

Although that may not have been the best choice of words.

Or maybe they're exactly *the right words right about now.*

Oh fuck, just STOP.

Just don't look at him.

Pay no attention to the blond godlike creature painting next to you. Make some small talk if you must, but for Christ sake DO NOT *look at him again.*

On and on went the running commentary in Frankie's mind until Henry broke the silence.

"So, what sort of colour were you planning to paint over this shade of baby shit?"

Just respond, don't laugh – don't even look at him. Frankie could tell that he was smiling without even having to glance in his direction. She could hear it in his voice.

"A pale pink. Something light but at the same time has a little bit of warmth to it. If that makes any sense at all," she managed to reply in a neutral tone.

"Perfect sense. And what about trim? Will you be leaving it white?"

"Nope...that's going to be chocolate brown—"

"Of course," Henry and Frankie finished in unison.

She finally gave in and risked a glance over at Henry, and together they burst into laughter. To her surprise, she found that being in his presence was getting easier. More comfortable. The tidal wave of pure lust she'd experienced earlier was quickly subsiding. However, it was being replaced with a flood of some other emotion that though Frankie couldn't precisely pinpoint what it was, she knew it could prove far more dangerous.

Best not to think about that now, she thought. Best just to ignore it until it went away.

"So are you from Brighton then?" Frankie had never been very good at small talk. Henry seemed to pause before responding, as if considering his words carefully.

"My family is, yes. But I've lived here and there. All over, really. I've only just come back recently. I suppose to become more acquainted with my roots."

Henry smiled to himself, as if the thought pleased him a great deal. *Oh crap,* Frankie scolded herself. She had forgotten that she wasn't supposed to be looking at him. And she definitely couldn't handle it when he smiled. She was doing well, but not that well.

"What about you? I can tell from your accent that you're not from around here..."

Frankie giggled for what felt like the thousandth time that evening. And she had never been the sort of girl one would refer to as a giggler. It was a trait she loathed, actually.

"And here I thought I'd managed to rid myself of the

telltale Scottish brogue, I haven't lived there for so long. Since I was a wee girl. You'd think it would be gone by now."

"Ahh, but that's where you're wrong. Some things never go away." Henry had stopped painting to turn and face her, his eyes thoughtful but serious as he continued with his train of thought. "Perhaps they might fade a little, but there are some things that are so inherent to who you are as a person that they will never go away. Not entirely."

Frankie had stopped painting as well, mirroring his movement. They stood looking at one another in silence for what felt to her like an eternity, letting the words hang between them, before Henry spoke first.

"Well now, that was a little too deep for polite conversation, wasn't it?" He laughed uneasily. Frankie began to laugh as well. Or rather, giggle.

"Hmmm, now that you mention it, maybe just a little," Frankie was relieved she was able to at last serve up some of her infamous caustic charm, that although Henry made her giggle he hadn't rendered her completely useless.

He made a face in response, then moved as though he was planning to toss the excess paint in the roller tray in her direction.

"No!" She cried out theatrically, faking her best look of horror, "think of the hardwood floors!" They laughed together again, harder this time.

Laughter was quickly becoming something of a theme for the evening. It seemed to come so easily and often. The conversation continued with much more ease as they painted. Or, more accurately, Frankie talked while Henry listened with great interest.

She told him about her childhood in the Scottish highlands, how they'd first moved to Southend-On-Sea for a few years before heading on to Brighton, a place that she had always considered home above any of the other places she'd lived. Especially London.

"I wonder why that is," he mused out loud.

They had finished with the priming, three coats in total to get rid of that horrid brown shade completely, and had begun cleaning off the rollers and tray in the kitchen's sink. *For a drop-dead gorgeous bank-appointed mentor with excellent taste in clothes,* Frankie mused, *this bloke isn't afraid of a little hard work.*

"I'm not sure. It's not something I can really explain in words, you know?" She stopped washing and turned to face him, frowning as she struggled to find the right words to express how she felt about the city. Of course, Frankie wasn't one to let that stop her.

"Brighton just feels like home for some reason. It always felt... I don't know, wrong in London. Like I was pretending to be something I'm not. But as soon as I got back here, there was this huge sigh of relief. Almost like, 'phew... at last'."

"I can relate to that," Henry nodded in agreement, leaving Frankie relieved that she was at least making sense and not prattling on like a twat. "I've lived all over Europe and travelled most the world, but as soon as I arrived here - to Brighton – it was as if a weight I wasn't aware I was carrying had been lifted from my shoulders. A sigh of relief would be an excellent way to describe it."

Henry smiled again. The most beautiful, genuine smile, Frankie couldn't help but notice. It made her feel as though they were the only two people left in the world. Until she remembered that they weren't.

"Shit! What time is it?" She had taken her phone out of her pocket for safekeeping once they'd started painting, but promptly forgot all about it. To say that Henry was a distraction would have been an understatement. She grabbed it from the countertop. 3:30am, it read, as well as a few missed calls from Louise. They had been painting and talking and laughing for the past eight hours, but it had felt like no time at all.

"I didn't realise it was so late." Henry had glanced over Frankie's shoulder and hurried to rinse the sink free of primer residue. He washed and dried his hands hastily as she put the bucket and tray with the rollers in the storage closet, then they made their way out to front of the shop.

"May I walk you to your car?" *Such a gentleman. Fuck.*

"It's just parked down the street. I'm sure I'll be fine. There's no one about." *Honestly, you should be more concerned with your own safety, all alone here with me in the dark.*

"I gather that came out as more of a question, but it's not really up for debate." His voice was firm, sending a shiver down Frankie's spine as he was shrugged into his coat and looked at her expectantly. "I insist on seeing you safely to your vehicle."

"Oh fine, if you're insisting," she tried to reply jokingly, even rolling her eyes. Giggling again like a schoolgirl, she followed him out the door.

"Where is your coat?" There was genuine alarm in his tone.

Frankie shrugged as she was locking up.

"Must have forgotten it. Too pre-occupied. Besides, it's really not that cold," she replied as she attempted to nonchalantly rub at her arms, clad only in a thin long-sleeved t-shirt, for warmth.

Henry gave her a stern look of disapproval before removing his trench and draping it over her shoulders, moving so quickly that it left no room for her to argue. On Frankie's reed-thin frame, the trench looked more like a cape. She sighed a little, and figured that she must have been really tired and thinking way too much about the shop because Henry's coat smelled like chocolate. Earthy and sweet, maybe a little bit smoky. And utterly intoxicating.

"Thank you," she said softly.

"My pleasure," he replied just as softly, his hands resting on her shoulders just a half-second longer than they may have needed to.

They walked to the car in silence.

"Thank you again for all of your help tonight. And it was lovely to meet you a day early," she said as they stopped in front of her borrowed Mercedes.

"Again, it was my pleasure, Ms. MacSweeney. I'm glad that I noticed that your light was on." *Oh, my light's on, all right. No.*

"Call me Frankie. That Ms. business just sounds so odd to me."

He laughed. Frankie was hoping that it was because she was incredibly witty. And not being completely ridiculous.

"And you must, in turn, call me Henry. I was thinking: will the primer be dry by tomorrow? Because I'd really like to come back and finish what we've started here tonight. If that would be all right with you, of course."

He was looking at Frankie with such earnest, as if his next breath hinged upon her answer. *As if it would be possible for me to say anything but yes.*

"Of course," she said finally, and he seemed to relax. "I was hoping to be back in for around ten, but don't quote me on that. It's pretty late." *Who am I kidding?* Like she would be able to get to sleep after tonight, regardless of how shattered she was.

"Shall we say around noon, then? Would that be fair?"

"Sounds good. I'll see you then." Rather reluctantly, Frankie removed Henry's beautiful coat from her shoulders and stole one last look at him. He was smiling at her again. *Why must he do that?*

"Thank you, kind sir, for the use of your coat," she tried to sound light and teasing, but his smile had taken some of the wind out of her.

"And as I said before, it's my pleasure. Good night, Frankie."

She felt a thrill course through her veins as he said her name, although it was strange because it sounded so formal. She even thought she had detected a hint of a bow in his posture. But then, the potent combination of lust and lack of sleep could have just made her delusional.

"Good night Henry," she replied as she swiftly got into her car, sitting with her hands on the steering wheel for a few moments as she tried to steady her nerves enough for the drive home. She was acutely aware that Henry was watching from the opposite curb, ever the gentleman, determined to see her off safely. She glanced through the window in his direction; he gave her a little wave and a nod. Frankie managed a weak smile in return as she started the engine.

Pulling away from the curb, she was surprised to discover that driving in the opposite direction of where Henry was far from easy. It was as if the further away she got, the more anxious she started to feel. By the time she'd made it back to Louise's house, she was in need of a warm bath and cup of tea to calm herself. She kept telling herself that it was just the cold chill, the seaside air that can seep into your bones and freeze you from the inside out. But again, she wasn't fooling anyone, let alone herself. Whatever this was that she was feeling was ridiculous. Not to mention dangerous, for at least two reasons.

First, she happened to be very happily engaged. Well, she was until a few days ago, at least. And second, Henry had been sent by the bank to help Frankie with *her business*. The same bank that had just given her a rather large sum of money to open the business she'd been dreaming of since forever. To throw all of that away, or even to risk it over some silly horny crush, would be utter madness. One thing she knew all too well: you just don't shit where you eat. Frankie inhaled deeply to steady herself. She just needed to take a minute to remember where all of this angst and apprehension was coming from. She was diving headfirst into new and alien territory; it would be perfectly natural, almost expected for things to feel off-kilter. Her fiancé has evidently disappeared from the face of the earth. Louise was acting like a complete freak. And to top it all off, she'd been handed a fortune by the bank who also happened to throw in the most beautiful man she had ever seen in her life to serve as her mentor.

Maybe it's a trap. Did they do that just to fuck with me? Does the money come with some sort of morality clause? It was that final thought that told her it was clearly time for sleep. When the conspiracy theories started, that was often the only remedy. And by the time Frankie would wake up in the morning, everything would have gone back to as normal as it could be. Of course, no amount of sleep would make Henry any less beautiful. In fact, she was almost positive that seeing him in the late morning sunlight was going to cause some considerable pain.

No, this wouldn't be an easy night. *But come tomorrow*, Frankie told herself determinedly as her head hit the pillow, *everything will be just fine*.

SIX

September 20th

As Frankie drifted off, she tried to force herself to dream about the shop instead of about Henry. And it worked. Sort of. She did dream that she was in the shop. She just wasn't alone. She should have known that there would be no way her subconscious would give in to such an unreasonable demand, especially once it had given her grey top-hatted stranger not only a face, but a name. It was a temptation far too great to resist.

In Frankie's dream, she was in the back of the shop just as she had been earlier that evening. She heard the same clang from the bell above the door. When she walked out to see who it was, there stood Henry -- but not as he had looked before. Her mind had dressed him up in her phantom lover's grey frock coat and hat, but he was still very much the Henry she had met earlier. She wasn't surprised to see him there, because it made perfect sense in the way that most things do when dreaming.

Without a word, dream Henry began to remove his frock coat. He was wearing that lovely Thomas Pink shirt underneath, but he had quickly begun to unbutton that as well as he made his way toward Frankie slowly. Frankie tried to speak but he put a finger gently over her lips to stop her. He kissed her then, with much more passion and urgency than he'd had in any of her other dreams, pulling the thin shirt she was wearing up and over her head as he walked her backwards toward the kitchen area.

His skin felt warm and soft, and smelled faintly like the chocolate she thought she had smelled on Henry's trench earlier. It tasted of chocolate as well, she was quick to discover as she moved her lips from his to kiss the smooth skin of his throat and shoulder. He pulled her mouth back to his hungrily; that time, it tasted like melted caramel. Frankie could feel the cold stainless steel of the kitchen island pressing into the small of her back as he continued to push forward, his lips not leaving hers for a moment. He scooped her into his arms and up onto the island, his hands working nimbly to shed what remained of their clothes. She shivered in anticipation.

But then, just as things were starting to get good, the scene abruptly changed. She was still lying on the kitchen island, but it was no longer Henry who was standing there all sculpted and shirtless beside her. It was the stranger in the grey top hat, his face in shadow as it always was in her dreams. Without a word, he began to drizzle dark liquid over her naked body. It felt warm and vaguely like treacle, and Frankie was more than a little alarmed to see that in the dim light streaming in from the windows it looked a lot like blood. The faceless man began to lick the sticky substance off her body, slowly and deliberately, as if he wasn't willing to risk missing a single drop of it.

She was caught in a state somewhere between terror and ecstasy.

He moved to kiss her again, looking like a wild animal

with the way the dark substance stained his lips. Convinced it was blood, Frankie started to scream and twist out of his grasp, but he was faster. His mouth pressed firmly over hers and she tasted something all too familiar. It was spicy with a hint of sweetness: dark chocolate. Frankie was at first relieved to discover it hadn't been blood then found herself overwhelmed with lust, throwing herself almost frantically into the kiss. He broke free long enough to look down at her.

"The chocolate is the life," whispered the stranger who had previously been Henry.

Frankie bolted upright in her bed, very alone, covered in a thin sheet of perspiration. This dream had felt far more real, more than any of the others had, which was saying quite a lot considering how vivid those ones had seemed. Once her pulse finally slowed, Frankie reasoned that it was yet another opportunity her subconscious had taken to taunt her, this time merging her fantasy man in the grey top hat with the scorching hot reality that was Henry Roberts in a new and special way to torture her. She groaned out loud in frustration when she grabbed her mobile from the nightstand to check for any missed calls or texts from James and found nothing. *Where the fuck is he?*

Was he really so busy with work, or was there something seriously wrong? And which sort of wrong was it: the 'he's had an accident' kind or 'he's found a less crazy, more voluptuous Swiss Miss to distract him' kind?

Frankie noted the change in her temper as it gave way to something far more contemplative. Typically, any thoughts of James cheating would leave Frankie feeling like she'd been punched in the stomach. It was enough to knock the wind right out of her. But not this time. Maybe it was because she had been so caught up in the shop that it held all of her attention, so much so that she hadn't had the time for her usual overreactions. But then, a little voice inside whispered insistently, was she not having some remarkably vivid dreams about a man who doesn't even really exist and has the face of a man who is so far out of her league it's almost laughable?

So then, she thought, *what does that say about me?* It says *I'm an ungrateful and unrealistic fickle bitch,* that's what.

Instead of behaving like the kind of fiancée that James deserved, Frankie felt like a self-absorbed brat who'd been too busy dreaming about seducing some random man when really she should be worried sick about her own. She wasn't being a very good girlfriend. Then again, that was something she had never been very good at it. But, since the engagement especially, she was almost proud of how well she had been doing.

Much better than before she had started dating James, of that she was certain.

* * *

Frankie had met James at the restaurant where she had been working before her most recent bout of unemployment. She was the executive pastry chef at London's hottest eatery; incredibly arrogant and quite certain that she was untouchable. So certain, in fact, that she had succumbed to a rather bad habit she'd had of sleeping with her managers on a semi-regular basis. That time, it was the head chef who also happened to be part owner of the establishment. That would be where she had learned, the hard way, that all-important lesson about not shitting where you eat.

The two of them had just gotten into a massive row: she had caught him taking the credit for a chocolate and blood orange soufflé she had created as a special request for a famous footballer and his posh wife. Considering that it was the only thing she had eaten to completion that evening, her overjoyed husband wanted to thank the chef personally. Of course, Frankie realised after the fact, it was way too tempting for him not to accept all the glory for himself.

She was in the alley at the back of the restaurant next to the staff entrance, furiously puffing on a menthol cigarette and shaking with rage, when James sauntered out. From the corner of her eye, she could see him giving her the once-over as he leaned casually against the wall a few feet away. It was early March, cold enough that she'd had to wear a winter coat over her chef whites.

"Err, excuse me love? Can I trouble you for a light?" Frankie couldn't hide the rolling of her eyes. *Here we go*, she thought as she fished a lighter from her pocket and handed it over without so much as a glance his way.

"Cheers," was all he said in return, though she'd thought she could detect a note of disappointment in her less than exuberant response. From what she could tell, he was a decent enough looking bloke. Green eyes, dark hair, smartly dressed in dark-rinse jeans with a slim-cut jacket and tie. The tie was off-centre, almost adorably so. Frankie couldn't tell if it was on purpose in that ironic hipster way or if he'd just had no clue how to tie a tie correctly. What intrigued her most about him, though, were the slightly worn black Converse trainers he was wearing. It was an ever-so-subtle two-finger salute to the smart casual dress code enforced by so many of the restaurants in the city, hers included.

She could see that he was taking slow hauls off his cigarette, as if he were trying to buy himself more time to think up another way to start a conversation.

"These strict no smoking rules are a blatant affront to our civil liberties, don't you think? I mean, I feel positively persecuted, having to take my 'filthy habit' outside as if I were some common criminal. D'you know what I mean?"

Ahh, Frankie thought, *he was going to try his luck with the intellectual rebel routine in the hope that she would be impressed with his large vocabulary and "damn the Man" mentality.* Too bad for him that Frankie had heard that particular tune before. Her father had been a rather vocal critic about the government's increasing invasiveness into the lives of its overtaxed and underserviced citizens. But she wasn't sure this young man would care to hear that he reminded Frankie of her father.

She turned to face him.

"I agree. Perhaps we should walk back inside, smoking our faces off, as a great big 'fuck you' to society and its rules at large," Frankie replied straight-faced, looking him squarely in the eye.

Right, that should do it. Frankie fought the urge to gloat, confident that she had scared him off successfully.

At first, he did seem slightly taken aback. But then, all of a sudden and much to her surprise, he began to chuckle.

"Of course: you're Scottish. That makes so much sense."

For some reason, the comment made her laugh out loud. Perhaps because it wasn't at all what she was expecting. But she knew she had to hold her ground and not allow herself to get distracted by a little unexpected charm.

"Now, what the fuck is that supposed to mean? Was it the red hair or casual use of the F word that gave it away?"

"Both, I guess. But let's not forget the accent. That sort of clinched it for me." And then he winked, the cheeky bugger.

Sarcastic and charming with a hint of cockiness was a deadly combination. One that worked, for her, every time.

"I'm James," he said, holding out his hand. Exactly two minutes later, he asked for Frankie's mobile number, which she had handed over without a second thought.

She then went back inside the restaurant and promptly told the manager she'd been shagging exactly where he could stuff his chef whites, knowing that there would be no way he could sack her. They were in the height of both the opera and theatre seasons. It would be another three weeks before she would finally receive her pink slip.

It took James all of a week, during their first real date, to confess that he had been in her restaurant that night on a date that hadn't been going very well. It went from bad to worse after he'd met Frankie in the alley. Well, for that other girl, at least.

For James and Frankie, it was only the beginning.

* * *

Unsure of exactly when she had drifted back to sleep while she was remembering the night she'd met her fiancé, Frankie was awakened by the shrill ring of her mobile phone laying beneath the pillow.

She glanced at the caller ID, hoping once again that it would be James calling at last to say he was fine and there was nothing wrong, but in her heart she knew it wouldn't be. And she wasn't wrong. It was only the technician reminding her that they would be coming into the shop later that afternoon to install her phone and computer lines. The phone call was a courtesy in more ways than one: it reminded her that she needed to actually pick up a computer and telephone, as well as all of the other basic supplies she'd need for the office. She had been so focused on how the shop was going to look that she had completely overlooked one of the most important parts of running a business – all that boring backend stuff that makes you *function.*

She yawned sleepily and sat up to stretch, checking the time quickly. It was 10:04am.

Frankie had not forgotten that she had agreed to meet Henry at noon. She hopped out of bed and all but skipped to the bathroom to begin getting ready, taking extra time and care on her appearance than she would have normally done. Her outfit had been chosen after some careful planning. It needed to be casual with a slight hint at sex appeal, but not in an obvious way as though she was trying too hard. In the end she settled on dark grey skinny jeans with a light turquoise v-neck jumper.

The mirror seemed to approve of her choice.

She had dug Louise's large-barrelled curling iron from underneath the tangled mess of hairstyling instruments that littered the bottom of the bathroom vanity, and managed to curl her fickle hair into something that resembled soft waves. Pleased and encouraged by the outcome, she decided to continue. She flicked a bit of mascara onto her top lashes, winging them out in the corner for a wide-eyed effect. It was a little trick that Louise had taught her years earlier, but Frankie had never fully appreciated its usefulness until that morning. She dusted some light peach-coloured blush over her cheekbones to brighten her pale skin, which had started to betray signs of her sleepless nights. A bit of lip gloss swiped over her lips was about as far as she was willing to go as far as lipstick was concerned. *After all,* Frankie reasoned, *Henry had stumbled in last night to be greeted with the zero makeup and old pair of jeans version of her -- primer dust on the ass and all.* It was a miracle the man hadn't run screaming. She decided, going forward, that she couldn't risk meeting her neighbours or future customers in the same lacklustre state. It just wouldn't be professional, and that meant it was potentially bad for business. It sounded convincing enough, even to herself.

As she was about to race downstairs, she paused briefly at Louise's bedroom door. It was closed and she detected no sound from within. She wondered if she maybe should knock, invite her to go in to town with her, if only just to get her out of the house and away from those chocolate bars.

No, Frankie's nastier inside voice sneered back. *Even at her worst she's ten times more gorgeous than you*, it taunted. *Don't you want Henry all to yourself?* Well, she did, didn't she? She took a deep breath.

"Lou? You awake?" Frankie knocked gently, pressing her ear against the door.

She thought she heard a muffled groan, as if Louise were rolling over in her bed then covering her head with a blanket. It was a move she was quite familiar with.

"I'm going back to the shop now. You should come down later. You know, if you're feeling up to it."

No response. Frankie sighed in resignation, and reminded Louise that she had her mobile with her and that she was more than welcome to ring any time. She worried as she left the house and got into the Mercedes that should things continue the way they had been, she would need to deal with Louise sooner rather than later. Yet another one of her friend's messes she would have to clean up.

It took everything Frankie had to keep within the speed limits on her drive into Brighton. The Lanes were definitely busier during the day, especially for a mid-week morning, which meant that parking was a bit of a nightmare. She had to walk a few more blocks than usual, and worried that she was going to be a little late. As she neared the shop she could feel her pulse speed up, and it wasn't from the pace she was walking alone.

Frankie strained her eyes, trying not to look obvious as she tried to see if Henry was there as he said he would be but the sun was proving far too bright, making it difficult for her to see anything at all. She cursed herself for forgetting her sunglasses in her haste to leave the house to get there. To get to him. Once she was about a block away from the shop the sun disappeared behind a bank of clouds, casting a sudden shadow over the cobbled streets. Once her eyes had adjusted to the change, she glanced once more in the direction of the shop but could not see past the press of people in front of her. Then she passed a pack of twenty-something girls heading in the opposite direction and overheard whispering and giggling.

"Blimey, he's gorgeous," one of them had exclaimed.

She knew that could only mean one thing. She was about five stores away when she looked up again. And there he was.

Henry was leaning casually against the shop's front door, not looking at anything in particular but simply enjoying the morning sunshine like everyone else. It appeared as if he were deep in thought. Something pleasant, if the smile on his face were any indication.

Rather unexpectedly, he turned in Frankie's direction in time to catch her watching him. His smile broke into a wider grin. She couldn't help but smile in return even through her embarrassment.

"Good morning, Frankie," he said as she reached the

door, extending his hand again for her to shake. It seemed so formal, but then maybe that was how things were done in certain business circles. *I guess I have a lot to learn,* Frankie thought. *But the first lesson, and perhaps most pressing of all, would be how to control the fire in my pants every time this beautiful man is anywhere near me.*

"Umm, good morning," she returned somewhat awkwardly, taking his hand after subtly sliding her own across the top her thigh to rid it of any excess moisture. Again, she imagined that he held it for longer than what could be considered customary.

Henry waited as Frankie began to unlock the door. She prayed silently that her hands would not shake and the keys wouldn't drop.

"No alarm system?"

"Not yet, no. There's nothing really here to steal. But that's next on my to-do list. And I have the phone company coming today to check the phone and Internet wiring."

"That's a good idea – a list," he said thoughtfully. She hated to burst his bubble.

"Actually, that's more of a metaphor," she admitted somewhat sheepishly. "For this part, I have no list. I guess I'll go make one now."

Henry laughed and shook his head.

"You're very entertaining, Frankie."

"Umm…right. Thanks, I guess?" She wasn't sure what he meant by that. Her reply seemed to make him laugh even louder.

"I meant it as a compliment. I honestly cannot

114

remember the last time I laughed this much," he said sincerely as he stood smiling at her.

They stayed that way for a few moments. Frankie could have stood like that forever, if she were being completely honest and at the very real risk of making herself sick. She was not what one would commonly refer to as the romantic type.

"So what are we doing today, Boss?" Henry rubbed his hands together, appearing rather eager to get started and awaiting her direction.

"Well, I was hoping to finish with the painting. But wouldn't you be considered The Boss in this situation, Mr. Mentor from The Bank?"

Henry chuckled, ignoring the dig as he strode into the back room to retrieve the paint brushes. She followed him to grab the paint that she had stowed beneath the sink, taking care to keep her eyes firmly on the floor. On anything but his flawless frame.

"It's your shop, so that would definitely make you the boss," he replied airily, armed with brushes, paint rollers and a tray as he passed by her on the way back to the shop floor.

Frankie must have given him a dirty look, which he responded to with a wink. She felt her heart stutter. *What is it about men who wink?* This was bad. Very bad indeed.

They painted together in companionable silence, much the same as they had done the night before. To the casual observer, at least, Frankie was certain it would appear that way. But what was going on inside her was anything but companionable or casual. She'd had to force herself to concentrate on painting to avoid looking at him because that could quickly give way to dropping her brush and jumping him. And she was definitely trying to avoid picturing herself rolling around on the floor, naked and covered in paint with him.

What is wrong with me?

Even when she was supposed to have been a horny teenager, Frankie could not remember behaving like this. She'd always felt that she had a normal, healthy interest in sex. It was nothing quite on par with Louise's bedhopping ways, but she wasn't completely frigid either. Never had she experienced this level of obsession, for anyone or anything. It was so irrational and overwhelming, and getting to the point where she didn't even really feel like herself anymore. And, more disturbingly, it was all directed at the one person that it really shouldn't be. Not her fiancé, but this gorgeous stranger whose only crime was to have been assigned to help her build a viable business. If the poor bastard knew what sort of things she were doing with him inside her head, Frankie was positive that he would be so horrified that he'd never set foot inside her shop again.

She took a deep breath and, despite her mind screaming in protest, decided to sneak a glance at him anyway. Henry was busy painting the wall opposite her, utterly oblivious to the thoughts that had been continuously running through her dirty, dirty mind. Frankie knew that she wouldn't be wrong: seeing him in the sunlight did hurt.

Henry seemed to have developed something of a knack for catching her looking at him.

"Am I doing this right? Does it look okay? I'm not terribly familiar with painting walls," he asked with genuine concern. She couldn't help but laugh. As if he could do anything less than perfectly.

"Well I'll admit, I'm no expert, but from the look of it it's almost as though you've been doing this all your life."

And it was the truth. As Frankie had struggled not only to keep her lurid thoughts under control but her brush strokes even, Henry seemed to have been having no trouble at all. His walls were so well painted, it was as if they had been professionally sprayed. Frankie's were somewhat spotty by comparison, but nothing that couldn't be fixed. Provided that she could keep her mind on the job at hand, of course.

"If you don't mind my asking," Henry began with some hesitation. "Why did you decide to do the painting yourself? Surely you could have worked it into your budget somehow."

"I'm sure I could have. But I would much rather do this sort of thing myself," she answered without thinking about it, "and not just because I'm a control freak. I want to do all of it – all the work, even the painting – because I'm just so… happy that it's mine to do. It may sound stupid, but I've been waiting for this for so long, I don't want to miss a single minute of it."

Henry had stopped painting and turned, standing motionless as he looked at Frankie. Much like he had done the day before. This time, however, Frankie thought she detected a slightly different look in his eyes. It was one she recognised immediately, because it was precisely the way she feared she would look whenever he caught her ogling him.

Lust. Pure and unadulterated.

And as much as parts of her – the lower parts, in particular – were reluctant to, Frankie knew that she had to act quickly to diffuse this situation lest it become very bad indeed.

"Whew," she forced out a giggle. "I guess it was my turn to get a little deep this time. Sorry about that."

She was expecting him to laugh along with her. He didn't.

"Don't apologize," he replied somewhat hoarsely, almost as if he were forcing himself to speak and not cross the room to kiss her. *Or maybe that's just wishful thinking on my part.* "You're obviously very passionate about what you do," he continued, "which is important when you're starting your own business."

He smiled at her again, the moment gone. Frankie was saddened and relieved.

"So you never did explain," she said a few moments later, "apart from demonstrating your superior painting skills, what else is involved with this mentoring program?"

She knew it was a bit cheeky of her to speak to him that way, but she needed to ensure for her own sake that the earlier moment was well and truly gone. Henry burst into laughter, as she'd suspected he would. Wasn't she, after all, very entertaining? Not unlike a performing monkey.

"Well," he began, " I suppose that it can be whatever you want it to be. It's very much a self-directed program. I'm here to help with whatever it is that you feel you may need."

Somehow, Frankie didn't think the bank would agree on certain things she felt she might need from Henry. She must have frowned without realising because he was quick to continue.

"I understand how vague that must sound, but until you get all of the groundwork done I get the impression that you won't be able to concentrate on the business aspect," he said in a rush. "So then isn't it better for me to help get this out of the way so you'll be able to give me your full and undivided attention when it comes to the more important things?" Frankie opened her mouth in rebuttal, but Henry hadn't finished. "Not that store design and curb appeal aren't equally important."

She was impressed. He had known her for less than twenty-four hours and already he'd been able to pick up on so much of what made her tick. It was more than some people would get after months. James included.

He must be the best mentor the bank has ever had, she thought.

"After BT comes to wire the place for me, I'll be able to bring my laptop in. That has my business plan and everything on it. If you want to take a look," she offered, feeling somewhat lame in her attempt.

He nodded, agreeing that it would be a good place to start. She was pleased that she hadn't come across as a complete idiot.

"So Henry," Frankie asked after another stretch of silent work as he was checking his walls and she was touching up her own, "what do you do when you're not out mentoring people like me?"

"Oh you know - a little of this, a little of that."

He chuckled when he saw the frustration flicker across her face, and seemed to struggle to give her a real response.

"I'm not sure if I can explain it, really. I work with different kinds of confectionary businesses, both large and small, to help them restructure and streamline their workforces to be productive in a more ethical way. In a way that would preserve not just the integrity of the product, but of the company itself. I guess you could say I'm a bit of a consultant."

Frankie was reminded of Jared's rant about the ills of modern globalization on the terrace at Louise's party, and recognised the opportunity to say something that would make her sound more clever and worldly.

"That must be quite the task, when the global trend is to favour aggressive cost-cutting and outsourcing of cheap labour in order to maximise profits," she parroted almost verbatim before being hit with a pang of guilt. It wasn't like her to take credit for someone else's ideas. *Why do I want to impress Henry so badly*, she wondered, to have him regard her as something more than 'entertaining'? Like it would make any difference either way. *I'm engaged and he's quite out of my league. End of story.*

"Yes, quite. That's spot on," he replied, seeming pleased with her observation. It did nothing to assuage Frankie's feelings of shame.

"It can be quite difficult, especially when you're dealing with a bunch of stuffed shirts in the boardrooms who have no clue as to how much the work their factory staff does actually *matters*. They fail to realise that, without that commitment to quality, their product is nothing. Yet they are always first to take the glory of other's hard work and claim it for themselves, while constantly cutting back on basics for everyone else."

He reminded Frankie of Jared then, of the way he had been talking about Chadwick's. She could tell it was something that Henry, like Jared, felt quite deeply about.

They were interrupted by the wiring technician

knocking at the front window, and decided that they'd done enough painting for one day. Together went to rinse out their brushes and tray leaving the serviceman to do his work.

"What time should I come back tomorrow?" Henry asked as he scrubbed at his brushes. Frankie's heart skipped a beat at the thought of seeing him three days in a row.

"I'm having an early night, so I'll be here for nine."

"No plans for this evening then?" Her heart went from a skip to a deafening pound she was positive Henry could hear where he was standing.

"Nope," she managed to squeak. "Just going home to watch some telly and go to bed early."

She knew that she should mention something about her fiancé, how he was out of town. Anything to indicate that he even existed at all. But Frankie just couldn't bring herself to do it.

"You've worked hard today. You've earned a good night's sleep."

Henry had finished with his own brushes, and Frankie stepped up to take her turn at the sink. Without warning he took the brushes out of her hand, their fingers brushing as he did. *Pound-pound-pound-thud* went the beat of Frankie's heart.

"Let me," he said softly. "My hands are already dirty. You should go check on the wiring. Make sure he's not messing up our walls?"

He had the brushes under the tap and was shooing her out of the kitchen before she could protest. In an uncharacteristic show of obedience, she did as she was told. *Was this going to be the new trend*, she wondered: *doing as I'm told?*

The thought made her laugh out loud, although she wasn't sure it was from the humour of it.

Walking back into the retail space of the shop sent Frankie's heart racing again, this time in a very different way than it had before. It was beginning to look exactly as she had always imagined it would. The dark chocolate trim looked good enough to eat set against the soft pink walls, and together the two colours leant the space a inviting glow. She was pleased to note that the technician was taking great care not to destroy their hard work as he checked the connection wires and made some updates. Fortunately, he hadn't had to do any drilling, he had told her: only staple some wire leading from the shop to the office so that they could run on the same network. After a quick test of the phone points, he was gone.

Henry emerged from the kitchen, wiping his hands on some paper towel and leaned to pick up his jumper from the floor. It was dark blue, almost the same colour as his eyes. *Oh, just stop already. Who the hell cares if his jumper matches his eyes?*

"Well, thank you once again, Frankie, for a very lovely and productive day," he said as he held out his hand. She took it, not willing to miss any opportunity she had to touch him.

"And thank you again for all of your help," she replied. "I promise I will bring in my business plan tomorrow."

This time, it was a full minute before he let go of her hand. Frankie counted the seconds off in her head.

"I look forward to it. See you in the morning, Frankie."

For a split second, she thought he was going to kiss her hand, but he released it instead. Seventy-four seconds later.

"Have a good night, Henry." She forced a light tone into her voice as he followed her outside, locking the door while he waited beside her.

"And you," he replied, pausing before adding. "Shall I walk you to your car?"

She wanted desperately to say yes, but there was still plenty of light and people around so there was really no need to take him out of his way. Regardless of how badly she wanted to.

"No, no, it's fine. I'm just parked over there." He smiled, almost sadly Frankie thought. As if he were hoping she had said yes. *And there I go, projecting again.*

"Well then, I know how independent you are, so far be it for me to infringe upon that. Good night, again, Frankie. Sleep well." And with a nod, he was walking away and around the corner.

The emptiness that Frankie had felt the previous evening consumed her, slamming into her with a blow to the chest that nearly knocked her to the ground. Reluctantly, she walked toward the car, forcing herself to turn in the direction of home rather than to follow wherever it was that Henry might be going. She realised that if she were to allow herself, she would happily follow him anywhere without hesitation. And that thought alone should have been enough to scare the crap out of her. If it were anyone else Frankie was feeling this way toward, she would be looking for any excuse to cut them out of her life completely. But not this time. Not with Henry.

As she drove back to Louise's house, which had become her house, Frankie knew that she really had no reason to feel empty or sad. That she would be seeing Henry again soon enough. Much sooner than the next morning, in fact. Because, after last night's dream, she recognised a certain pattern was emerging.

Her mystery lover and Henry had become permanently and intrinsically linked in her subconscious, regardless of how ridiculous concept it was. And it was useless to even try to force herself to dream of anything else. Despite her best efforts, she would dream only of him. And the more she thought about it, the more she became aware of another important fact.

That she could not wait to get to sleep that night.

Ah, we men and women are like ropes
drawn tight with strain that pull us different ways.
Then tears come, and like the rain on the ropes, they brace us up,
until perhaps the strain become too great,
and we break.

- Bram Stoker, *Dracula*

SEVEN

September 20th

Frankie pulled into the estate's sweeping driveway looking forward to nothing more than a long hot bubble bath, some mindless television, and a deep and dream-filled sleep. She was surprised to see another vehicle, a beaten up Fiat Spider convertible from the 80's parked in front of the carriage house, and knew that her evening might not go off exactly as planned.

Dr. Jared was there, pacing nervously outside the front door of the carriage house.

"Louise hasn't answered any of my calls or texts," he blurted out anxiously. "I'm afraid I must have done something to offend her, so I've come to make amends. But she's not here. Has she said anything to you?"

Frankie looked at him with pity. He looked positively crestfallen. *And there goes my relaxing evening,* she thought before becoming dismayed with her own selfishness. After all, it had to happen some time and she supposed that it was as good a time as any to deal with the issue at hand. After the fantastic day she had just enjoyed in Henry's company, it would be hard to put a damper on her mood. Perhaps the timing couldn't be better.

"She's here, Jared," Frankie sighed as she opened up the front door, "it's just…well, she doesn't really come out of her room much these days. Except for supplies, I suppose."

Jared followed her inside, clearly confused. He had no idea what she was on about. Frankie grabbed one of the several Cocoa Cream wrappers that littered the kitchen island. It was as if it had been left there on purpose to illustrate her point.

"It's not you. *This* is the only thing Lou seems to make time for lately."

She held up the wrapper to show him. Jared took it from her hand slowly, as if not really quite believing what he was seeing.

"Where on earth did you get this," he breathed, his eyes widening.

"I was kind of hoping you would tell me," Frankie replied with no small amount of concern.

Over the past couple of weeks, she had been able to comfort herself with the assumption that Louise had gotten her endless supply of mystery bars from Jared. But judging from the way he was examining the wrapper now, he was just as clueless as she was to where they had come from.

"So, let me see if I have this right. You're telling me that you've never seen this before." A chill ran down Frankie's spine as she considered other, less innocent options.

Jared looked up, startled, as if he'd forgotten she was there; he had been absorbed in examining the candy wrapper.

"No, never. I mean, it's the sort of thing you dream about but you never think would actually happen," Jared began babbling excitedly. "Do you even know what this is? This is like the Holy Grail of candy bar-making."

Frankie couldn't help but roll her eyes. Despite his doctorate degree, apparently Jared had been as taken in as she was by the clever marketing.

"Of course I know *what* it is: it's a Fitz Cocoa Cream. But it's obviously not a *real* one. It's just the imitation wrapper that makes it look real." *That's all it was. Wasn't it?*

Jared was shaking his head in disagreement.

"Ahh yes, but how can you be so sure it's not real? Look at the ink; commercial wrappers now use laser printing for their wrappers. Do you feel that edging around the lettering? That's an indent made by a machine press. That method of printing hasn't been used for at least eighty years."

Frankie felt her mouth go slightly dry.

"Maybe they're just going that extra mile in the name of authenticity?" It sounded plausible, at least to her.

"But who? Who would do that?" Jared asked simply. "And why go to such lengths and expense merely for the sake of looking authentic? For what purpose? Where did you think they were coming from?"

"I... I'm not sure," Frankie replied, her voice faltering. "I thought it was you. Well, Chadwick's, I guess...but that it was you who had given her the bars. Maybe it was one of those formulas you told me you'd been working on."

Frankie sat down on one of the kitchen stools, her legs starting to feel weak. She had been on such a high after spending the day with Henry, and wasn't prepared for what was becoming a far bigger issue than she had originally taken it for. Jared leaned over the island, his expression earnest, clasping her hands in his. There was nothing untoward in the gesture; she knew that it was down purely out of concern. For her, for the whole situation at hand, but most of all, for Louise.

"Now Frankie, I know this is a lot to take in, and believe me – I'm not trying to scare you. It's probably just an elaborate prank. But I want you to think very carefully. When did you first see Louise with this candy? And where?"

Well, that's easy enough to answer, she thought.

"The night of her party. Lou has a habit of sleepwalking when she's been drinking. I heard some noise outside and figured she was at it again. When I found her at the bottom of the garden, she had a bar in her hand. And has continued to have one ever since." Jared had begun pacing restlessly in front of her, deep in thought.

"So you're telling me that she has somehow been able to get more of them?"

"Oh yes, loads more. But I have no idea how. Like I said, I thought it was something you'd been working on and you gave her some to try. But she's gotten a little…crazy with it."

"What do you mean, crazy?" He stopped pacing.

"Well, I really wasn't joking when I said that she doesn't come out of her room much these days. Ever since she's gotten hold of that chocolate, I've barely seen her. And I live with her. When she does come out, she's just finished a bar and is cracking into another. It's like that's the only thing that matters." As Frankie spoke, the guilt set in with a vengeance. How could she have let this go on for so long, she berated herself. *What kind of raging bitch lets this happen to her best friend?*

Jared seemed alarmed, but she could tell he was trying to play it cool for her sake. She didn't have the heart to tell him he was a horrible actor.

"Where does she keep these bars now? I'd like to take one back to the lab for analysis."

"I have no idea where she hides them. What, you don't think it might be tainted or something, do you?" Frankie wasn't about to try to play cool.

"Her behaviour, as you've described it, sounds to me like some form of mania. And since she's not the manic type by nature, it may be more of a… a chemical dependency. Would you say she's otherwise healthy? No dramatic weight loss or anything?"

Frankie felt numb as Jared continued to fire questions at her. It was obvious he thought that someone had been poisoning Louise right underneath her nose with some tainted hundred year-old chocolate, while she had done nothing but flirt with a man from the bank. *Some friend I am.*

"No, no weight loss. Quite the contrary, actually," Frankie heard the raging bitch inside her, the one that was apparently content to kick Louise while she was already down, reply absently. "All of that chocolate is starting to show."

Jared didn't seem fazed by her outrageous cattiness. In fact, he looked almost relieved.

"Okay, well, that does sound like a normal physiological reaction. I would like to examine her myself, though, just to be sure."

"I thought you said you weren't a real doctor."

"Well no, I'm not, but I have taken several first aid courses. And I'm familiar with the signs of substance abuse. Is she upstairs?"

"She is," Frankie replied warily, suddenly protective. "But maybe you should let me go up first. I think we'd stand a better chance of getting her out of her room that way."

She rose from the kitchen stool, motioning for Jared to stay put. She knew that Louise would never come out if there were a man present. She may have been acting like a complete lunatic lately, but one thing that could be counted on with Lou is that vanity always wins out in the end. She climbed the stairs to her closed bedroom door.

"Lou?" Frankie knocked softly, hesitant at first. No response. She knew that the time for soft and hesitant had come and gone.

"Louise!" She banged louder and did not stop until the door finally opened.

She was her best friend, and they had been through a lot together. Frankie had seen Louise at her very worst: passed out in a public toilet in Blackpool, knee-deep in a pile of her own puke after an all-night bender in London, crawling out from beneath not one but three boys covered in God knows what after crashing a Trinity College party in Dublin. But Louise looked like a supermodel then in comparison to what stood before Frankie now. If she hadn't have known for sure that it was Louise, she scarcely would have recognised her at all.

She was witnessing first-hand the effect two weeks of

consuming nothing but chocolate bars can have on one's appearance.

Louise's skin was slick with grease, littered with angry red spots and the occasional smudge of chocolate. Her hair appeared to have not been washed in days, and it looked as though she hadn't slept in that long either. Dark rings rimmed her eyes – or maybe it was chocolate, Frankie couldn't tell. She was dressed in a faded t-shirt that clung to the newly formed rolls on her normally well-toned midriff and an old pair of yoga pants that were tighter than they should have been in most places. Frankie recognised them instantly: it was Louise's 'period party' uniform.

Louise looked at her with an expression that was equal parts misery and resignation. And only a moment passed before Frankie noticed the smell.

"Jesus," she whispered, covering her nose. "Open a window or something, please."

Louise shrugged and moved mechanically to the window to do as she'd been told. Something she would never normally do.

On her way back to the bed, where a large indentation indicated the spot she rarely moved from, she reached for yet another Cocoa Cream from a pile on her bedside table. Her bed appeared to be floating in a sea of more torn wrappers. Before Louise could sit down and become trapped in that world again, Frankie knew that she had to do something to snap her out of it.

"Jared's downstairs to see you."

It was as if the sun had come out from behind the clouds. A glimmer of the old Louise shone through this filthy stranger's eyes. A hand went to her hair, completely subconsciously, in true Lou fashion. She was more herself in that small moment than Frankie had seen over the past fortnight.

"Do you think he'd wait while I grab a quick shower? I'd hate for him to see me looking like this."

So she's aware of how poorly she looks, Frankie mused, *but powerless to do anything about it?* Again, that just didn't make any sense. That had always been Louise's sole purpose in life: to look good at all times. It was a very rare occasion when she did not succeed.

"I'm sure he won't mind," Frankie replied softly, turning to hide her smile. Not that she was being smug: she was more just relieved that it had been so easy. She had been prepared for more of a struggle to get Louise out of her room, knowing full well how stubborn she could be. She tried to swallow another twinge of guilt for not addressing the problem earlier, for not knowing how far her friend had gone over the edge.

Frankie waited until she heard the water in the ensuite shower turn on before going back downstairs, satisfied that her friend would keep to her word. But she remembered to grab something for Jared before she did, something he had mentioned he needed.

Jared looked up anxiously when he heard footsteps on the stair, and did not bother to conceal his disappointment when he saw that it was only Frankie.

"She's just in the shower. She'll be down in a tick," she breezed as she handed him the Cocoa Cream she had swiped from Louise's upstairs stash.

"Here you go."

For the first time that day, Jared looked pleased.

"Fantastic. Thanks for that." He began turning the chocolate bar over and over in his hands, gazing at it in unabashed wonder, before stowing it away in his laptop satchel.

"I'll take a look at it as soon as I get back to the lab tonight."

"Let me know if you find anything."

"Of course – yours will be the first call I make. The only call, really, since Louise isn't answering her phone."

"Well, she's in the shower getting ready to come downstairs, which is more than I've seen her do in over a week, so that's something," Frankie offered by way of consoling him. *After all, if anyone should be feeling guilty, it's me.*

They sat in silence until they heard another set of footsteps on the stairs.

"Hi... Jared," Louise half-whispered, almost shyly.

Frankie had never known her to be shy or quiet about anything before. She also made a mental note to commend Jared on the stand-up job he was doing of masking his shock as he got up to greet her. The look of horror at how she had changed so much in so little time was clear when he caught Frankie's eye in passing. He went to hug Louise hello, but she flinched out of his reach.

The sting of rejection wasn't quite as easy for him to hide.

"Louise," he began before faltering, lost as to how to continue. "Umm, sooo... How have you been?"

Louise looked uncomfortable as her eyes shifted nervously from the floor to the counter to the kitchen cabinets, then back again. As if she would rather be looking anywhere else than at them.

"Okay," she answered in a whisper.

Frankie knew it was a lie, and they'd known each other long enough that she that Louise knew it too. Because anyone could tell by looking at her that the girl was anything but fine. Although she was clean, at least, she looked like a completely different person.

Her makeup, once so carefully and artfully applied, was now slapped on in a vain effort to cover up some of the spots and sallowness. Her jeans and t-shirt, although stain-free, were far too tight, not in a sexy or fashionable way but in the way that is seen far more often than it should be. In young girls, racked with insecurity, trying desperately to look cool and sophisticated as they stuffed themselves into clothing two sizes too small. That is what Louise looked like then, and as Frankie made the connection, she knew that something had to be done at once.

"Louise," she began, her voice gentle but firm. From the corner of her eye, Frankie saw Jared tense up, ready to leap to Louise's defence if necessary.

"You know how much I love you," she continued, speaking faster to get it all out before anyone decided to try to stop her. "And so it is from a place of love that I say this to you now: you look a right bloody mess. What the *hell* is going on here? Because whatever this is," she made a waving gesture over Louise's outfit, "it's definitely not you."

Frankie was afraid that poor Jared was going to pass out on the floor. He had no way of knowing the history the girls shared and that for her, this was almost kind. But she

135

wasn't about to let his reaction make her back down. She couldn't. Her friend's wellbeing was too important. And so there she stood in front of Louise, arms folded, waiting for an answer.

Louise continued to stand, awkwardly silent, not looking at anyone or anything in particular. But Frankie sensed that she had been heard through that chocolate-induced stupor. The muscles in Louise's face had begun to twitch, particularly around the mouth and eyes.

Frankie decided to press a little harder.

"Lou," she said softly, taking a step toward her. Jared reached out as if to stop her, out of the instinct to protect Louise, but again Frankie ignored him and forged ahead. This…whatever it was that was happening, needed to be stopped.

"I'm not trying to be the asshole here for once. We just want you back. We miss you." And it seemed that was enough to crack it.

Louise crumbled, both figuratively and literally, before Frankie's eyes. Fortunately, she was prepared and quick enough to catch her before she hit the ground. Déjà vu set in. *Wasn't this how it all began, that night in the garden just a few short weeks ago?*

"I don't know what's happening to me," Louise sobbed, rocking back and forth as Frankie held her in her arms.

Jared was standing over them, with all of the panic and despair and fear and love written on his face at once. He held himself back in spite of what he was feeling, as though he understood that Frankie needed to take care of this part. She appreciated knowing that he was there for them both, and hoped that Louise could pull her head out of her ass and see what kind of man he really was. Had it been Alex or Quinn, Frankie felt certain that they would have been out the door as soon as they'd spotted her coming down the stairs.

She held Louise as she sobbed it out on the floor in the kitchen, waiting for the right moment to start asking her where this had all started and how it had gotten this far. When the rocking back and forth subsided, the crying slowing to the occasional sniffle, Jared stepped in.

"Louise." He had knelt down to her level and was speaking in a low, soothing voice as he stroked Louise's hair softly. This time, she did not flinch from him.

"I want you to think back, now. Can you remember what it was you were doing, or even where you were when you first got the candy?"

Louise blinked rapidly and began taking deep breaths, trying to calm herself down. Jared gently wiped away the remaining tears from her cheek with his thumb, but left his hand resting there. Again, Louise did not shy away. No, Frankie quickly noticed that this time, it was a very different look that she was giving him. She moved to get up, and he quickly jumped to his feet to help her. He then offered his hand to Frankie for which she was grateful; one of her legs had become numb from the angle it was sitting at.

He swiftly went back to tending to Louise, who sat perched rather unsteadily on one of the kitchen stools. Frankie watched, trying desperately to pound some of the feeling back into her upper thigh. Jared was holding Louise's hands, urging her to speak.

"I... I can't really be sure," she stuttered.

Her face was red and puffy, eyes swollen but no longer

leaking tears. She puckered her lips in concentration.

"I can remember being there in the garden with everyone at my party then going to bed and all of a sudden, they were there. And they've just...been here ever since." She had a far-away look in her eyes, as if she had gone back to that moment in an effort to remember. Or more worryingly, feeling the irresistible pull of the bars.

Frankie had already decided that the chocolate had to have been drugged. It was the only way she could explain Louise's completely uncharacteristic behaviour.

"When I found you in the garden, you were sleepwalking. You had a bar in your hand then. Was someone out there with you that night? Did they give you the chocolate?" Frankie was firing questions at her, her own thoughts going back to that night as well. And to the stranger with the top hat, before inevitably skipping forward to Henry. She shook herself out of it. *This isn't about you right now.*

"No, there was no one in the garden. Just me."

"Well, how did you even find the chocolate then? Did you just pick it up off the ground? Was it on something, in something? How did you end up with that one, then all the rest?"

It was clear that Louise was trying as best she could to remember, and getting ever more frustrated with her mind the more it refused to cooperate. Her exasperation must have become infectious; both Jared and Frankie were becoming agitated as well. Jared began to pace the kitchen floor, taking over the rapid-fire line of questioning in effort to help jog Louise's memory, while Frankie went for the one thing that always helped in a crisis.

"Anyone fancy a cup of tea?"

She had crossed over to the other side of the kitchen island to rummage through the tea cabinet by the range. She chose an Earl Grey from Louise's vast collection, this one for its packaging: it made her smile. And anything that could do that at a time like this had to be worth a taste, Frankie reasoned. The tin was designed to look like the wooden trunk she imagined it must have been imported in, distressed and weathered, weary from its many travels overseas by ship. Like a pirate's treasure chest.

As she put it down on the granite countertop and turned to put water in the kettle, she heard a small gasp behind her. Spinning round, spilling water on the tile as she did, she found Louise with the tea tin. She was turning it over and over in her hands as if entranced by it.

"It was in a chest," Louise whispered. "The chocolate was in a chest in the garden."

Frankie nearly dropped the kettle in her excitement.

"Where is the chest now, Louise?" Jared could also barely contain himself.

"It's in the same spot where I first found it. It was too heavy to move so I… I just brought in as much chocolate as I could carry. And I've been going back for more whenever I run out."

A ripple of shame ran through Frankie once more, for what felt like the millionth time that day. Had she spent more time with her, or even paid attention at all, she would have noticed all of this much sooner.

"Show me where it is." Jared was holding his hand out to Louise. Not about to be left behind, Frankie followed. Tea would have to wait.

It was not yet nightfall so the three of them had more than enough light to see where they were going. Together, they traipsed through to the back of the garden to a spot not far from where Frankie had found Louise that night.

A few yards away, almost hidden by the dense shrubbery that dotted the back garden, sat a marble bench that faced out over the sea. Years ago, Frankie recalled Louise's father and countless housekeepers warning the girls not to come out this far, that it was too dangerous, which only made them want to do just that. Just a few yards beyond the bench was the edge of the cliff that towered over the rocks below, hemmed in by the low rock wall that rimmed the back end and sides of the estate. It was set low so as to leave the magnificent view unobstructed, but wide enough to prevent tripping and falling. Frankie found it fitting that she would remember such a detail on that particular evening.

Tucked beneath the opposite side of the bench closest to the crook formed by the joint in the rock walls, sat an old wooden crate. It was similar to what you might see in museum vignettes or black and white pirate films: weather-beaten, bound with rope that had been chewed through in spots by rats or the ravages of time. Its lid was almost half open, resting at an angle yet managing to both conceal and protect the contents within. They stopped once they had gotten within a couple feet of it, and stood in silence.

"How did you even know where to look for this? I mean…what did you… It's impossible."

It was as if Jared had taken the words out of Frankie's mouth. How Louise had managed to find the chest all the way back there, much less get it open in her unconscious state, was anyone's guess.

Louise shrugged silently in response. She had no

answer to offer.

Jared moved forward cautiously to further examine the chest. It had some faded lettering on the side, too difficult to make out at the distance they were standing. Frankie edged closer, feeling silly. It's just an old wooden box, she thought, nothing to be afraid of.

Fitz & Company, it read, *established 1780*. Frankie could feel her heart begin to pound. Whether it was from fear or excitement, she wasn't entirely sure. She knew one thing for certain: this was no elaborate marketing scheme. Whatever this was, it was real.

Jared opened the chest with what she could only imagine must have been the same blend of emotion. Inside, amidst layers of dusty brown craft paper, lay more bars of Cocoa Creams. About half of the crate had bars that were still packaged and waiting to be eaten, but among them were empty wrappers and half eaten bars. The chocolate had begun to bloom, a fine greyish film resulting from unstable cocoa butter crystals as if objecting to being left in less than ideal conditions.

That was part of what Frankie enjoyed most about working with chocolate: its notoriously fickle nature often reminded her of herself.

Louise has been busy, she thought grimly. *And hungry.* Frankie noticed that she had been keeping her distance after they had made the discovery, keeping herself well behind the shrubbery. In her friend's eyes, she saw a hint of the mania they'd witnessed earlier, and she could sense by the set of Louise's jaw that she must have been locked in some epic internal struggle to restrain herself.

Frankie looked over worriedly at Jared, who was picking up the crate as if it were the Grail itself. She could hear him muttering about the remarkable condition the bars were in.

"I'll need to take these back to the lab as well. I hope she won't put up too much of a fight about it," he said to Frankie in a low voice, casting a worried glance at Louise.

Louise had begun to chew on her fingernails restlessly. She made no move to stop Jared, however, as he carried the chest back toward the house where his car was parked. Frankie put an arm around her, guiding her gently along behind him. She could feel her shoulders shaking, then her entire body grow tense when she saw Jared open the trunk of his old car.

"It's okay, Lou. Everything's going to be all right."

But even as she spoke, Frankie wasn't at all sure that it would be. While yes, she was happy that Louise was out of her room and relatively unharmed, that Jared was taking the bulk of the bars with him to examine, it still did not explain how or why they had come to be on the property in the first place. Or if it would be the last they would be seeing of them.

By the time they had gotten back inside, Louise's demeanour had abruptly changed.

For all the calm she'd displayed earlier, they should really have been expecting the massive fight she put up. Louise began to scream and cry uncontrollably as Frankie and Jared removed the last of the Cocoa Creams from her room. Frankie could see that Jared wanted to give in; he couldn't bear to see Louise in pain and know he was the cause of it. But she also knew that they had to see it through if Louise was going to move past this and get back to herself, so they needed to be strong when she couldn't be. It was in every sense an intervention and at that moment it may as well have been crack cocaine or crystal meth instead of chocolate because, for Louise, it made no difference. The effects were basically the same.

After what felt like hours, Louise finally seemed to understand that no amount of begging, crying, cursing or threats were going to make Frankie and Jared give the chocolate back to her. She fell into a deep sleep, curled in fetal position on her bed, with the occasional whimper and mumbled profanity. Jared had left with the chocolate bars, almost as anxious to get to the lab to test them as he was to not have to watch his beloved Louise suffer.

Frankie stood up from the armchair beside the bed where she had been waiting out Louise's tantrum and was about to close the door, confident her friend was out for the night, when something her friend mumbled made her blood run cold.

She turned, certain that she mustn't have heard her correctly, when Louise said it again louder as she tossed about fitfully in her king-sized bed.

"The chocolate is the life," she muttered to Frankie's mounting horror, and repeated the phrase once more so there was no mistaking it. "The chocolate is the life."

EIGHT

September 21ˢᵗ

Frankie would have loved to have been able to say that she'd had a restful sleep, that she had woken up refreshed and ready for another day. But that would have been a complete lie.

Dealing with Louise and the violent symptoms of withdrawal she seemed to be experiencing after they had removed her chocolate was emotionally draining, but nothing in comparison to the effect the five little words she uttered as Frankie had left her bedroom.

The chocolate is the life.

Those words, innocent as they seemed, had kept Frankie awake for most of the night until exhaustion finally claimed her in the wee hours of the morning. The rational part of her tried to explain it away as something they must have heard or said themselves before, maybe even joked about. She could definitely see them doing that considering the nature of Louise's family's business. And the girls have been known to get quite dramatic with their silliness, so that fit nicely into the theory as well. *Maybe my subconscious decided to drag it into my dreams now just because I'm staying here,* Frankie thought. The connection Louise would have had to the phrase was obvious: she had literally been living off the stuff for almost two weeks.

But the fact that it had been brought up twice in completely unrelated circumstances over the past forty-eight hours was odd, though it could easily have been nothing more than a coincidence.

Except that Frankie didn't believe in coincidence. She never had.

She believed that everything – absolutely everything – happened for a reason. As to how that philosophy would apply to the events of the past few days, she had no clue. Yet she could not shake the feeling that the answer was clear as day, somehow right in front of her while remaining stubbornly out of reach all the same. And if she didn't have MacSweet to open in a few weeks, she might be able to put some more time and energy into puzzling it out. But neither were a luxury she had at the moment.

She had already racked up some large bills over the past few days that would need paying back and, though the bank had been quite generous with their payment terms, she couldn't push her luck by taking personal time just a week after acquiring the property. *Besides, they might take Henry away. And fuck knows that would never do.*

At least it was a comfort to know that Louise wasn't entirely alone, she was reminded as she rounded the staircase headed to the kitchen. There was Jared, fast asleep on the sofa in the lounge. Frankie tiptoed around him, trying to make her morning tea as quietly as she could.

It wasn't enough for him to just call the night before, as he had promised. He had insisted on coming back to the house after finishing with the first series of tests on those

Cocoa Creams he'd taken. After he'd arrived, he announced that he was taking a personal day, and possibly again the day after; he was undecided. His reasoning was sound: in one way he was relieved that he hadn't found anything immediately wrong with the chocolate, but he was still concerned about Louise's mental state. And, since he knew how busy Frankie was with the shop, he wanted to be here to keep an eye on her as much for himself as to take the load off her shoulders. Whatever his reasons, Frankie was grateful. Maybe it would help with the remorse she'd been feeling.

"So, since I couldn't find anything, I've decided to call in some outside help on this," Jared had told her. "I'm sending a couple of bars to my old mentor at Cambridge. He specialises in organic compounds and their various mutations, so if anyone can determine if there's anything out of the ordinary about this chocolate, it will be him."

Frankie had nodded as he spoke, but by her own admission, whenever she heard words like compounds and mutations she had the tendency to zone out.

As she sped around her room getting dressed, she reflected on the situation with a smile. She got the impression that, even after this mystery was solved, Jared was here to stay. That made her happy, unlike the predicament she found herself in at the moment which was trying to decide which colour jumper would be best at detracting attention from the giant bags beneath her eyes. After some trial and error, it turned out to be teal green. She hadn't the energy to curl her hair again, but at least had had enough presence of mind to not soak her head while in the shower, thereby managing to salvage some of her previous day's handiwork.

Was it really only yesterday that I spent over an hour dolling myself up for Henry? It had seemed like so much longer than

146

that. Like a whole lifetime ago.

Frankie quickly checked the mirror. She had told Henry that she would be at the shop for nine, but of course she'd woken up late so was rushing round like a madwoman. She was going to have to break the speed limit along with a few other traffic laws in order to make it on time. At the last minute she whisked on some more of that blush from yesterday and dabbed on some clear gloss, and sighed as her reflection in the mirror glared back at her with disapproval. It was the best she could do. At least she wasn't going to offend anyone with her appearance. But then again, she wouldn't be inspiring any love songs either.

She drove to the shop once again as if her life depended on it, desperate to make it there before Henry. Frankie was glad she was able to park much closer than before because the shopping day was only just beginning, and that meant she would only be about five minutes late.

Henry was waiting for her. *Of course he was.* Always respectful, never late, a man whose word was his bond: that was the impression she'd got from him. And he looked perfect as well. She had not had the benefit of seeing him in her dreams the previous night for the first time in days and, as pathetic as it was, Frankie was once more struck dumb by how beautiful he truly was. They were finished with the painting, and as such he was dressed for business. He was wearing a light blue button down shirt, Thomas Pink again by the look of it, and a flawlessly fitted pair of grey pin-striped trousers. She couldn't help but notice, as he stood leaning casually against the wall by her front door, how nicely they curved around his behind. Again, perfection.

"Good morning." He looked up with a smile as he saw her hurrying toward him down the sidewalk. Frankie hoped that he hadn't seen her openly ogling his posterior only moments before.

"Good morning, Henry," she replied, trying for a casual tone as she brushed past him to unlock the door. She felt a small shiver of pleasure run through her as her shoulder met his chest, albeit briefly. Stop, she had to remind herself. *Just...stop.*

"Frankie? Are you all right?" His eyes had narrowed, his voice sounded concerned. She had been trying not to yawn as she put her keys away and wasn't aware he had been watching her. *He's worried about me? How sweet.*

"Yeah, just a little tired, that's all. There's some...stuff going on at home. Didn't quite end up being the relaxing evening I was hoping for," she replied, too mentally exhausted to try to edit.

She busied herself with putting her laptop bag on the counter in the kitchen area, silently thanking whatever deity had helped her remember that she'd promised to bring it, and didn't notice how close he had gotten to her until his hand was on her shoulder.

"Is it anything you feel like talking about?" Henry asked softly. He let his hand continue to linger on his shoulder; Frankie felt it would be rude of her to remove it.

She managed to smile up at him, not that the smiling in itself was so difficult. It was more the managing not to giggle and stutter like a schoolgirl while doing it that she had trouble with.

"I'll be fine, but thank you, Henry. For your concern."

He continued to look in her eyes intently, as if to confirm that she was indeed telling him the truth. His hand stayed put right where he'd left it. After a long minute, he smiled.

"Well, I'm here if you need someone. To talk to." Henry's tone was so completely sincere, Frankie was afraid she would break down into tears.

I think I might love him. Wait… what?

Then suddenly, it was all business again. His hand was gone from her shoulder, and the moment had passed as though it never existed. It made her head spin.

"I see you brought your laptop," he said. "Let's take a look at that business plan then, shall we?"

They stood together, hovering over the computer screen, since there was nothing to sit on as they waited for the documents to load. Frankie decided that the next purchase needed to be actual furniture, which Henry agreed might be an excellent idea. When he gently but purposefully brushed by her to take control of the laptop, her being the drooling idiot she had become around him Frankie allowed it with no questions asked. She realised that it was kind of nice to be around someone so take-charge, so authoritative for a change. James had the tendency to be so laid back, especially lately, so they usually ended up doing whatever it was she wanted to do. There was no real challenge or mystery there. Henry on the other hand was nothing but mystery, wrapped up in so much more.

And… *oh yes, that's right, also completely off limits.*

"This looks good, you seem to have a pretty solid business plan in place. I like the idea you have of partnering with other businesses in the area to build each other up. Neighbour helping neighbour seems to be a bit of a lost concept these days," Henry was nodding in approval as he read. "But what I don't see is your product offerings clearly defined or outlined. And that is, for lack of a better term, your bread and butter. So let's start there. What type of chocolate do you plan to sell here?"

Henry had turned toward Frankie expectantly. All she could do was stare at him blankly in response. She knew the concept well enough: traditional chocolates with a twist had become something of a mantra of hers. She had always just come up with all of her ideas and flavour combinations on the fly. *But have I gone so far as to break that concept down item by item?* She had to say that she had not. She had been so caught up in the other aspects of the shop that it would seem she had overlooked the most important thing of all: the chocolate itself.

Panicking and weary from the weight of last night's events, she could feel her eyes begin to well up with tears she fought desperately to hold back. *There's no room for crying in business*, the horrid voice inside her taunted, *stop embarrassing yourself.*

"No, no...Frankie, please. There's no need to cry," Henry had become alarmed, reaching an arm around to pull her closer to him. "We'll figure it out, together. The ideas are there, I'm sure of it."

She let him hold her and stroke her back in comfort, totally aware of how many lines it was crossing both professionally and personally but not caring one bit. As she rested her head against his chest, Frankie revelled in how wonderful he smelled. She thought again that it must have been her own wild imagination, but he really did smell like dark chocolate. She could hear the echo of her own heartbeat thudding in her ears, gradually slowing down as she relaxed into his arms. It was beating so loudly she could detect nothing else.

It felt like forever, and yet it felt like no time at all.

Henry pulled away from Frankie abruptly, perhaps recognising himself that things may have gone too far. She knew that she imagined the disappointment that ghosted over his face before he began to pace in front of her, thoughtfully tapping his chin.

"Hmm, let's see. Is there anything, any sort of confection that Brighton in particular is known for? Customers love those little touches, something that ties them in with the local history," he was saying, thinking out loud as he walked the length of the kitchen and back.

"Well," Frankie began as she eased herself up to sit on the counter beside the laptop. "Years ago my friend's housekeeper would make these little vanilla cookies called Brighton Buttons that Lou and I would eat by the bucketload after school. They're these little sandwiches held together by an orange flavoured jam. I could maybe do a play on that; something in a white chocolate to keep it traditional, or even try it with a dark chocolate. That could be a nice combination."

"Yes! I remember those myself, actually. That's good… very good." Henry's eyes had lit up encouragingly. "Keep going – what else do you think might work?"

And then it was as if Henry had unlocked something inside her other than lust. The floodgates had opened, and ideas for flavours, fillings and shapes were coming from Frankie faster than Henry could type them into the computer. There was no time for him to continue to pace; his fingers were too busy flying across the keyboard.

Sweet lavender white chocolate buttons.

Dark chocolate laced in Scottish whiskey, filled with

sea salt caramel.

Ginger-chili ganache covered in milk chocolate.

Delicate, yet ever-so-classic, English violet and rose creams.

Pink champagne, heather cream and cognac truffles.

Dark chocolate hand-dipped almond pralines.

Tartly flavoured lemon mint creams in white chocolate.

Cherry cordials, soaked in brandy, enrobed in a dark chocolate shell.

English butter toffees infused with raspberry and blueberry.

Frankie's mind had begun to race ahead with thoughts of the upcoming holidays: chocolate-covered caramel apples, candied orange slices and sugarplums, images of happy children hopped up on sugar racing through the shop. She didn't see that Henry had stopped typing and sat quietly watching her as she continued to list off her ideas. She had drifted into her own version of Candyland, where she was Queen. When she did notice, it was back down to reality. Sadly, she realised that her reality could not include Henry as her Prince Consort.

"What?" she asked him, suddenly embarrassed that she'd caught him looking at her so intensely. "What is it?"

"Nothing," he said after a few moments, with a shake of his head. "Please, do continue."

It was something Frankie had seen him do more than once. And once again the moment passed by and disappeared without a second thought, leaving her with the same sense of sadness as before.

They continued to brainstorm together, with Frankie talking and gesturing wildly as Henry typed furiously, until they noticed that it was getting dark outside. Once again she had forgotten a watch in her haste to get there, so Henry checked the time at the bottom of the screen. She was alarmed when he announced that it was past six in the evening. They had been so busy talking, brainstorming and laughing that they hadn't even bothered to stop and eat all day. Her stomach growled loudly, arriving at the same realisation.

"We should get you something to eat." Henry had obviously heard its protest as well. Frankie flushed with embarrassment, almost missing the context of what he was asking. "Would you care to join me for dinner?"

And there it was, out in the open.

Frankie glanced at him through lowered lashes, not intending to be as coy as she was sure she must have looked. She was trying to assess the situation and buy herself some much-needed time to consider her response. To weigh her options and the possible consequences carefully. There was no way to misread the intent: it was written on his face. On the surface, it appeared to just be an invitation to a business dinner. But upon further scrutiny, Frankie could see from the look in his eyes that it was more than that. He wanted more of her company. He wasn't ready to let go of her just yet. And his casual invite to dinner confirmed it.

"Okay," she said simply, as much to herself as in answer to him.

It was just business, after all; men in suits in any given hotel bar or restaurant do the same thing almost every night. Wasn't the business dinner a time-honoured tradition? *Who am I to fuck with tradition?* The more Frankie continued to lie to herself about all the ways that it was purely business, the bolder she became.

"Where should we go?" she asked. Henry seemed pleasantly surprised, not only by the response but her assertiveness.

"I'm not sure. I'm not really familiar with the area anymore, but I keep passing by a place not far from here that looks promising. The House, I think it's called?" And then reality came hurtling in like a comet, as swiftly and brutally as if it meant to destroy everything in its path.

Frankie knew the restaurant he was suggesting. She knew it very well.

It was where James had proposed to her but a few months ago. James: the fiancé she had never, ever mentioned to Henry. Not even once. The horror and shame of it must have written itself on her face, because Henry was quick to react.

"Frankie! Are you all right?" He had her by the shoulders with both hands, holding on as though she might faint on him then and there. "You look like you're going to be sick." *Oh, if only it were that simple.*

"No, no. I'm fine, Henry. Thanks. It's just... I'm not... that is to say,"—*oh, just spit it out already*—"I'm not entirely sure that dinner with you is such a good idea after all."

Frankie could see his confusion over her sudden change of heart, certain that this time she had not imagined the hurt expression on his face. She was compelled to explain.

"I'm engaged, Henry," she blurted out.

She wasn't quite sure how she was expecting him to react. After a pause, he smiled. A smile that did nothing to ease the sickening knot twisting of her insides.

"Frankie," he began softly. "I'm asking you to dinner as a friend, a business colleague, so that we can continue to discuss your product line. I think we've made some real progress here today, and would be sad to see it end now when it feels like we've only just gotten started. Surely your fiancé wouldn't begrudge you that, would he?"

The way he put it, so simply and so succinctly, made Frankie feel foolish for having any romantic notions about it at all. Of course that would be the reason. Of course he could never be interested in her in a romantic way. *As if you would ever be good enough for a man like that.* When he had put it that way, whatever she had thought was there before seemed laughable.

"Of course," she laughed finally. "I mean, of course he wouldn't."

To her relief, Henry laughed too. Seeming pleased with her answer, and that she no longer looked like she was about to throw up all over his fine Italian shoes, Henry saved the document he had been working on and closed the lid to the laptop.

Theatrically, he offered her his arm as he stood up.

"Shall we, Mademoiselle?"

Frankie giggled and took it without a second thought, happy that the earlier awkwardness had been laid to rest. This was business, nothing more. She knew her place now, and Henry knew his.

"We shall," she replied just as theatrically.

This isn't flirting, she told herself. They were just kidding around, in much the same way other work colleagues would be doing elsewhere at any moment in time.

After Frankie had completed her rounds of turning off lights and checking that doors and windows were latched, pausing to stroke the antique glass casings that had been delivered earlier that day during the brainstorming marathon, they locked up the shop and began walking to the restaurant together. It was quiet on the streets for such a nice evening.

Frankie excused herself quickly to call and check in on Louise.

"I'm *fine*, Frankie." She could practically hear the eye roll over the wireless connection. It made her smile; it was an indication Louise was coming back to her old, bitchy self.

"And hello to you too. I'm fine as well – thanks so much for your concern."

"I was getting to that. You on your way home, then?"

"Um… no, not quite yet actually. Got some things to do still," she lied quickly. Louise would ask a million questions that Frankie wasn't about to try to answer with Henry in such close range.

"All right, don't work too hard eh? Jared wants to go see a movie, this new sci-fi flick that's just come out. So we may not be here when you get in. I'll ask Mavis to leave some food out for you."

Frankie almost dropped the phone. Louise hated science fiction with a passion that bordered on murderous, and scarcely ever thought about anyone but herself. For her to go see that kind of movie, as well as think to ask her housekeeper to leave Frankie some dinner in the same conversation, was mind-blowing. Dr. Jared was turning out to be a very good influence.

"No need – I'm running to grab something now." It technically wasn't a lie. More of a half-truth. *Better than that really*, she thought. It was more like three-quarters or four-fifths truth.

"Then I guess I'll see you when you get home or we do. Whichever happens first."

"See you later, Lou. And I really am pleased to hear you're feeling better," Frankie added with sincerity. She paused for a moment, unsure if she'd spoken out of turn.

"Thanks. So am I." Another pause. "I mean it, Frankie. Thank you, for everything you did for me last night. Well, both you and Jared, I guess. It was pretty scary there for a minute."

Frankie could hear Louise's voice begin to waver and decided to cut it short before they both ended up in tears.

"No worries Lou. It's what I'm here for, ain't it?" She laughed and agreed.

After telling her that she needed to get back to work - another three-quarter lie - she returned to where Henry was politely waiting for her round the corner.

"Everything all right?" His eyebrows were slightly raised, out of curiosity or concern, she wasn't sure.

"Yes, fine. Let's go. I'm absolutely starving now."

Frankie's stomach was quite upset that she had gone so long without giving it food, and made persistent gurgling sounds which made her hold herself round the middle in an effort to quell the racket. She was thankful that the two of them were no longer in the silence of the empty shop. The noise was loud enough that she was sure it would have echoed.

The restaurant was less than a five minute walk away, and soon they were inside waiting for a table. The host showed them to a quiet corner in front of the bay window, an intimate table for two. It was obvious, particularly in the way he winked at her knowingly, that the host thought it was a date. In truth, Frankie was feeling much the same way. The hunger sounds weren't the only reason she kept clutching at her stomach – she was trying to keep it from doing backflips and cartwheels as well.

Henry moved past him to pull out Frankie's chair. Admittedly, that didn't help the whole date situation in the slightest. She reminded herself that he was a gentleman, and that's simply what gentlemen did.

"Thank you," she smiled up at him, struggling to keep her voice even.

"A pleasure," he replied as he slid smoothly into the seat opposite hers. Frankie could have sworn she saw the host's knees buckle ever so slightly at the fluidity of the movement. If she hadn't been the person being seated, hers may have buckled a bit too. *But this was business, remember? Just business.*

Not one to waste any time, Henry asked that the waitress be summoned straight away. Frankie was staggered when she seemed to appear almost immediately. It had never ceased to amaze her how quick people were to jump at the request of the exceptionally good-looking and extremely wealthy. Many dinners with Louise had proven the theory. She was fairly certain that had she been on her own and made the same request, it would have taken quite a few minutes longer.

She ordered their renowned fillet steak, a decision that made her stomach growl one last time in approval, and was surprised when Henry declined to order anything at all. Instead, she noticed that he had turned to the side and discreetly drew a flask from his inside jacket pocket.

Her heart sank. *He's a drunk.*

She knew that he had been too good to be true. Part of her was almost relieved to find out that he wasn't so perfect after all. The flask seemed to make him a little more…human.

"It's not whiskey, of that I can assure you," Henry said quickly. He must have seen the look on her face, Frankie supposed, and felt the need to explain himself. "I'm on this special detox program, and my naturopath has me drinking this concoction."

He wrinkled his nose as he uncapped it and took a couple of quick sips. Again, Frankie caught that familiar, unmistakeable scent of dark chocolate. It was there, and then it was gone again. She shook her head. *Wow, I am seriously losing it.*

"Do you mind if I ask you something?" Henry said suddenly just as Frankie went diving into the bread basket. "Your name is Frances, but you go by Frankie. Most nicknames for Frances would be Fran or Frannie, so I'm curious: why Frankie?"

Frankie had begun to nod in understanding before he'd even finished his train of thought. It was a question she'd answered often, starting in nursery school.

"My grandmother's name was Frances, and I am

definitely not her. I mean, I wish I was even half the woman she was, but I'm just not. I'm also not really a Fran or Frannie. You can probably thank my dad for it, actually. He's obsessed with Frank Sinatra. " Henry smiled.

"Tell me about her. Your grandmother," he urged. Frankie tilted her head, chewing on her Italian breadstick as she tried to find the words that would do her formidable grandmother justice.

"Hmmm. For a start, though she was barely five feet tall, she struck terror in the hearts of almost everyone around her. She had this commanding way about her, like when she walked into a room she was impossible to ignore. That could've been the flaming red hair, I suppose." Henry was still smiling, encouraging her to continue.

"But although she was terrifying, she had the biggest heart of anyone I've ever known. She just had very strong opinions, and wasn't shy in the least about sharing them."

Henry started to laugh.

"Sounds to me like you're more like your grandmother than you give yourself credit for," he chuckled. Frankie bristled at first, then laughed in agreement, recognizing that it was meant as a compliment.

"I guess you're right. My mother named me after her as a way to try to heal the relationship there, but it sort of backfired. As soon as I was old enough to talk, Nan and I ganged up on her. She would always complain that we were way too much alike…" Frankie smiled ruefully, struck by how much she missed her.

The waitress came by with the food, lifting the mood as she did.

"So, back to what I was saying earlier at the shop," Henry began, leaning earnestly over the table to talk as Frankie tried to eat as daintily as possible. Really, she was so hungry that all she wanted to do was shovel the steak into her mouth one forkful after another, but was impressed that she was able to hold herself back remarkably well.

"I think you've come up with a brilliant product line to get yourself up and running. But, have you given much thought to your suppliers? Because where you get your raw materials from is just as important as what you choose to make with it." *At least that's an easy question to answer.*

"I was planning on going with Chadwick's. I have a good relationship already with the family. Well, personally, anyway—" She had barely gotten the words out before she stopped abruptly.

As for what happened next, she wasn't sure.

Perhaps it was something in Henry's detox mixture that had made his face suddenly turn purple, then red before fading to a pale greyish-white in what appeared to be anger. His eyes darkened and she saw his hand clench into a fist and come down in one swift motion, narrowly missing the table. With the force of it, it may have been enough to split the wood.

"Why would you choose to go with Chadwick's?" Henry managed to whisper through gritted teeth. *Right. Maybe it's not the detox, then, after all.*

"Well for one thing," Frankie began warily, completely perplexed at where all of his anger could be coming from. "I've known the family since I was a teenager; the daughter is my best friend. Right now, in fact, I am staying as a guest at their estate."

She watched his face carefully to see if any of this was calming him down. Finding his expression unreadable, she continued.

"The company also employs the majority of people living in the area and happens to make some of the finest quality chocolate in England. Didn't you just mention something to me earlier about how it's better to keep things local?"

Henry remained silent. *What is the problem?* Then, as quick as the flick of a switch, all of his anger was gone. Henry's face returned to its usual, handsome self. *A good thing too*, thought Frankie, *because inexplicable rage is not a good look for him.*

His expression became serene. Frankie found that it unnerved her as much as his earlier response had done.

"You do make a valid point, I suppose," he said coolly as he began to absentmindedly play with his dessertspoon. "But I would urge you to do your research first, into Chadwick's or anyone that you plan to do business with, really. To be sure that they are indeed everything that they make themselves out to be."

He smiled slightly, but it did not extend beyond his perfectly formed lips. A bitter smile. Frankie shifted uncomfortably and was struck by the strange sense of having been there before, in having almost the same exact conversation. It was not dissimilar to the one she'd had with Jared on the terrace the night of Louise's birthday. Making it the second time in as many days that Henry had reminded her of Jared.

What was it I was saying about coincidence?

"And why wouldn't they be, everything they appear to

be, that is?" Frankie knew it was a bit of a risk to push, considering what she'd witnessed earlier. But it was out before she'd had the chance to even think about it, as with so many of the things she would say.

Henry smiled again, a little tightly this time, and leaned forward over the table as if he were going to tell her a secret. She backed up in her chair without really knowing why.

"Nothing is *ever* what it appears to be."

His eyes were not as hard nor as hollow as his words were in that moment. As strange as it seemed given his earlier display, and indeed equally as strange as the whole conversation had been, they were quite the opposite. He looked almost sad.

The two sat in silence when the waitress came along to ask if anyone would like some wine, perhaps some tea and dessert. It was enough to break the uncomfortable tension that had set in. *Thank Christ for that waitress.* Frankie realised that she was very much in need of a strong cup of tea.

Once she had left, Henry swiftly changed the subject to something about the restaurant's charming decor as if nothing had happened between them. Neither of them went back to the topic of Chadwick's. In fact, it seemed that they were talking about anything else but that on purpose. Frankie enjoyed the fact that, when he wasn't being cryptic or cagey, Henry was remarkably easy to talk to. She had always felt completely at ease with him; well, when she was trying to keep herself from jumping him. And considering that she felt the need to censor herself around most people, it said quite a lot.

"So, tell me about your fiancé. What's his name?" Henry asked unexpectedly, casually leaning back in his chair. As he took another haul off his flask. The look in his eyes was anything but casual. It was hard, like ice.

"His name is James. He's an estate agent. Well, a barrister now, actually. We've been together about eight months," Frankie replied, unable to drum up much enthusiasm.

Why didn't I want to talk about James? Should a girl not be excited to talk about these things?

"How lovely," he answered, in a tone that seemed to indicate that he really didn't think it was that lovely at all, before pressing on.

"I must say, I really had no idea that you were engaged. You aren't wearing a ring. That's usually one's first clue."

Frankie's gaze flew to the third finger on her left hand, and saw that he was right. She had removed her ring before she started painting for safekeeping. The night she first met Henry. With a sharp intake of breath she remembered that, what with all the excitement and chaos that happened at home, she had simply forgotten to put it back on.

Again, what does that say about me? She didn't realise that Henry was still speaking, apparently not yet finished with his line of questioning.

"How is it that I have yet to meet him? I have been with you all day for the past few days. Surely he should have stopped by to see how you were doing?"

"He's away on business right now. And he still lives in London." *And I haven't heard from him in about two weeks, so that's why you haven't met him yet,* she decided not to add.

"I see. He must be very proud of you. Was that him you were on the phone with earlier?" Henry was quite persistent. At least on certain subjects.

"No," Frankie half-whispered, her voice surprising her by almost catching in her throat, "I haven't actually spoken to him since before he left."

She couldn't look up from the table. She knew that if she did, he would see the tears forming in her eyes and get the wrong idea. Because they weren't tears of sadness or panic, as one might think they should be given the situation. They were tears of regret. Of remorse.

Frankie regretted that she wasn't more concerned about her fiancé and his sudden departure without word as the days went by. She felt remorse over how much she had been enjoying the time she spent with Henry. And, based on Henry's questions and the uncanny ability he possessed in reading her mind, she knew he would see that. Since that was a risk she wasn't willing to take, she continued to stare fixedly at the table.

"I'm sorry," Henry said after a long pause. "I let my curiosity get the better of me and I've obviously upset you. Forgive me."

When Frankie trusted herself to look up again, his eyes had definitely softened. She took that opportunity to change the subject. Or rather, turn it back round to him.

"So what about you, then? Are you married, engaged?"

Of course she had already checked his ring finger, so she knew that if he was married there would be no way he would admit it. He was too clever for that lame of a trap. But to Frankie's surprise, his smile disappeared. It was replaced by a look she could only describe as sadness, bordering on despair.

"No, things like love and marriage have never been in the cards for me, it would seem. But really, I have no one to blame but myself," he seemed to pause before Frankie urged him to continue.

"I was always too busy with my work to bother with that sort of thing. If anything, you might say that I'm married to my job. Much in the same way that a priest would be married to God." He looked so vulnerable with his eyes lowered and shoulders slumped as he went on.

"My father died when I was young, and there was really no one to take over for him when it came to running the family business. My brothers couldn't cope, and I myself was little more than a teenager caught up in my own world. Part of me will always blame myself for not caring more when Father was alive to learn... Perhaps I could have done something. Helped my brothers, so that they wouldn't have had to sell. Since then, I have devoted every moment I've had to building something my father would have been proud of. To make up for failing him, I guess."

Frankie's heart lurched, and wordlessly she reached across the table. Not necessarily to touch him, but more as a gesture of comfort. She let her hands rest on the tabletop.

Henry looked up after a few seconds, smiling sadly.

"I know you've mentioned that you have a rather...tense relationship with your mother but Frankie, if I could offer you a little unsolicited advice on the subject: don't let that get in the way. Because before you have the opportunity to make amends, it might be too late."

Quite unexpectedly, he reached across the table, hesitating just before his hand touched hers as if he were rethinking what he was about to do. Impulsively, Frankie moved her hands forward as well, this time in encouragement.

"To answer your earlier question, my life can be… complicated. Hectic at times, and more than a little surreal. It would take a very special woman to keep up with it. I guess you might say that I haven't met anyone who has fit that tall an order." He cut himself off abruptly, as if he'd said more than he'd intended to.

She wasn't aware that she was holding her breath until he spoke again.

"Frankie," he sighed, almost as though he wasn't aware of saying her name. His fingers brushed over the back of her hand. It ran through her like an electric shock.

"What is it?" Frankie held her breath again, wondering what he was about to say this time. He closed his eyes, and exhaled as if in defeat.

Once again, the waitress with her excellent sense of timing returned to save the day with the bill. They were both surprised to hear that it was almost midnight; the restaurant was getting ready to close. The hours had literally flown by, as Frankie had discovered they so often did whenever she was with Henry.

He insisted on settling the bill himself though he hadn't eaten, saying it was a tax write-off since they had been talking about business. Mostly.

"It's late,' he said as the waitress returned with his change. "I'll see you to your car."

Again, this wasn't so much a question as a statement of intent. And since Frankie wasn't remotely interested in saying good-bye to him just yet, she nodded and allowed him to pull out her chair while she stood up.

They walked together in silence. It was neither uncomfortable nor awkward; they were enjoying the quiet of the evening together.

"Frankie," Henry said abruptly. She wondered vaguely if her heart would ever stop stuttering whenever he said her name. "I know I probably shouldn't say this since we've only just met and I'm helping you with your business, but here it goes. I think your fiancé is a fool."

Well, that was certainly unexpected.

Frankie stopped in the middle of the empty sidewalk. The streetlights were dim compared to the brightness of the full moon that shone down and reflected off the water, illuminating the harbour.

"Okay. And…what's that supposed to mean exactly?" She wasn't quite sure how to take his comment. Was he implying that she too was a fool, as in guilt by association? Aware that they were standing dangerously close, she took a step back, folding her arms across her chest.

Henry had stopped as well, his hand reaching out as if he meant to touch her shoulder. It stopped in mid-air before dropping to his side, its mission aborted. He took a deep breath.

"What I mean is, that if I were lucky enough to have you—I mean, someone like you in my life, there would be no way I would let a day go by without talking to you at least twice."

"Why twice?" Frankie was confused, and she thought that it could have been the exhaustion but she had no clue what he was saying. She needed him to spell it out for her.

And she felt that it was high time for Henry to squirm. But of course, he didn't.

"Well, once would be first thing in the morning, so I would get a proper start to my day." There he paused, head turned slightly to the side and chin lowered, looking at her through lowered lashes.

"And?" Frankie swallowed hard, waiting, not daring to breathe.

"And then the second time just before bed, so that you would be the last thing on my mind as I went to sleep." Henry stood motionless, looking at her, as if waiting for a response.

He would be waiting a long time, because for once Frankie was at a loss for words.

Whatever he meant by what he had said, it was out and it couldn't be taken back. She wasn't sure if she should just laugh it off and ignore it or respond. It seemed so heartfelt. But she wasn't sure what to do, just as she was not really sure of anything at all. Of James, of Chadwick's, of Henry... or even of herself. Everything was changing, she felt as though she was running to catch up.

"I'm sorry," he said as the silence stretched between them. "Not that I didn't mean it, but that I've made you uncomfortable and for that I apologise. I spoke out of turn."

Frankie couldn't help but laugh. It was a knee-jerk reaction to any situation she didn't know how to handle.

"That's okay. It's not like you offended me or anything," she said, a little too quickly. She managed to pass her laugh off as relief at his apology.

They began to walk again, and found themselves next to the car sooner than Frankie would have liked. She found herself sad once again knowing that it was time to leave him, but at least this time there was a plausible explanation for it. They had covered so much ground tonight, professionally and personally, that she didn't want to stop there. She didn't want to stop, ever, if she were being honest. But she knew that it had to.

"Well, this is me. Thank you for dinner. It was lovely."

She was fishing her keys out from the bottom of her handbag when she felt his eyes on her. She looked up to find him twisting his hands nervously in front of him, as if lost without the dessertspoon to play with.

"Frankie," he sighed her name quietly, much as he'd done at the restaurant.

She felt her heart lurch forward, which pushed her a half-step closer to him without her being aware of what the gesture might implied. He also took a step, closing the polite friendly gap between them. They were standing so close they were almost touching. Dangerous territory.

"Again, I know that I have no business saying any of this. But it needs to be said. It doesn't seem like your fiancé is worthy of you."

Henry's eyes burned into her. Frankie felt like she could have entire conversations with those eyes alone.

"What do you mean?" *Why must he be so confusing?* Or, Frankie thought in answer to her own question, *is it more that I'm just allowing myself to be confused because I want to be?*

"You deserve to be with someone who worships you every minute," he whispered, lowering his face to hers and

170

brushing his lips against her left temple.

Frankie shivered, not realising that he wasn't finished. Not remotely.

"All day," he continued softly, this time allowing his lips to drift across her forehead and rest lightly against her right earlobe.

"Every day."

His lips remained at her ear, and when he spoke again she could feel his breath feather lightly over her neck. It was too much for her to bear. Nature took over. Her face turned toward his as her mind screamed that she shouldn't, that they mustn't. But it was too late for that.

The first thing that Frankie became aware of was how soft Henry's lips were as they pressed into her own. Soft, but firm. Almost demanding. There was no hesitation; he knew exactly what he was doing.

Their lips melted into each other as if they had been doing this all along. In that moment, kissing Henry felt like exactly the right thing to do. It was like coming back to Brighton, like opening up a shop; it felt as though it was what she was meant to be doing. It felt like she was home. And then, just as quickly, it changed.

Frankie felt a scorching heat spread rapidly from where their lips first met to every nerve ending in her body. There was a tingling sensation, quickly followed by a deep ache that was concentrated in the pit of her abdomen. A white-hot tide of desire washed over her, causing her knees to fail her. Henry had a firm hold of her around the waist; she let out a whimper as his hands dipped lower, catching her by the bottom and turning her so her back was supported by the nearby wall of a closed shop. She wrapped her legs around his waist out of instinct, a move that elicited a low growl in his throat that made Frankie's pulse throb.

She knew in her rational mind that all of this was very wrong indeed. That she should not be kissing and grinding herself into this man who was little more than a stranger like her life depended on it, let alone be enjoying it as much as she was. Yet she was powerless to stop. And because it felt so natural, as natural as breathing, she didn't want it to stop. Ever.

When she felt Henry's strong fingers gripping her hips in a way that was almost painful, making her cry out in pleasure, she knew that it had to. If only because they were so close to escalating into something far worse.

"I'm so sorry," Henry gasped abruptly once Frankie broke free from the kiss and managed to wriggle away from him, panting. He paused long enough to catch his breath before continuing.

"Not for kissing you because, dear God, that was amazing. But for the situation we find ourselves in. You are not mine to kiss. And that...that just complicates everything."

There was something in the way he said those final few words that stood out to Frankie, as if they held a hidden meaning of which she wasn't aware. But she was in no condition to figure out why or what that meaning might be.

Henry was leaning over her with his arms on either side, his hands pressed against the wall. With a deep breath he stepped back, sliding his hands from the wall to her shoulders and down her arms in one languid movement, stopping only when he held both her hands in his.

"I'm sorry too," Frankie said softly once she trusted

herself to speak. *After all, there were two sets of lips involved here.* "We don't have to tell the bank about this, right?"

Henry blinked at her slowly before erupting into a roar of laughter.

When in doubt, Frankie would deploy yet another of her famous defence mechanisms: humour. This time, it worked as it often did. As perceptive as Henry was, Frankie was relieved that he hadn't seen through the ruse and noticed that she was barely able to keep herself from trembling. But she felt confident that being able to laugh about it was a good sign. A sign that this momentary lapse in judgment would not cast an ugly shadow over what had been a comfortable working relationship.

"I had better get going. Have to get up early and do some research tomorrow. On suppliers," she added, if only to let him know that she had not forgotten his advice from earlier that evening. Regardless of how strangely she might have thought his advice had been delivered, not to mention the other myriad twists and turns their evening had taken.

Henry smiled warmly, the most beautiful smile Frankie had ever seen. She could have stood basking in it forever before he abruptly smacked himself on the forehead, putting an end to the almost trance-like state she'd fallen into.

"I cannot believe I forgot to tell you. I have to go out of town for a few days."

Frankie could feel her heart sinking down to her toes. It was coupled with the growing suspicion that it was the beginning of an exit strategy. Once again, Henry was deftly able to interpret the look on her face. He tilted her chin up gently to face him.

"I won't be gone long, Frankie. Only perhaps a day or

two. You won't be rid of me that easily, I'm afraid," he offered her a lopsided smile that made her stomach flutter.

Damn, he really can read me like a fucking book. Cover to cover.

"But there's a situation that needs taking care of. But should you need anything, and I do mean *anything* at all, just call."

Henry produced a flat silver case from inside his jacket and handed her a small business card. It was plain white but made with exceptionally fine quality. *Henry Roberts, Consultant, H.R.F. Holdings Inc.* was embossed on its front in black elegantly scripted lettering, along with a phone number. Nothing frivolous or flash; the simplicity of it exuded sophistication and refinement. It was all of the qualities Henry possessed himself. *Except for when he had just been kissing you like a beast...no, don't go there.*

He kissed both of Frankie's hands and lingered a few seconds longer before letting them go. He opened her car door and waited as she got herself situated. She prayed that he wouldn't see her hands shaking as she gripped the steering wheel.

"Good night, Frankie. We *will* see each other again very soon, I promise you that much," he said solemnly, as if swearing an oath, dropping a quick parting kiss on the top of her head as he began closing her door.

Frankie struggled hard to swallow the sob that seemed to be building in her throat as she fought the urge to throw the car door open, wrap her arms around him and start kissing him again.

"Good night, Henry," was all she managed to get out.

She knew in her heart that he would be coming back, that she would see definitely see him again. They had unfinished business between them, both literally and figuratively. But the emptiness tugged at her as it always did whenever she drove away from him, gnawing at her with every passing mile. Tonight it was worse than ever. It threatened to swallow her whole.

It was entirely irrational, she knew. As was the uncontrollable shaking that she was no longer capable of holding back once left in the privacy of the car. Never had she felt such an all-consuming emptiness or this rollercoaster ride of emotion. For James or anyone else for that matter. Only Henry. And it was for precisely that reason, among a whole host of others that had cropped up over the past few days, that she knew she would have a lot of hard thinking to do and some not-so-pleasant decisions to make in the days ahead. But before she could do any of that, she needed to find James. Now more than ever, she needed to sit him down and really talk to him, heart to heart. Something that under even the best of circumstances was often easier said than done.

Where the hell could he be?

NINE

September 22nd

James woke up to yet another morning of Swiss mountain sunshine spilling across the king-sized bed of the room he'd begun to think of as home inside the Defleur mansion. Home was a far better way to think of it rather than the prison it had become.

He'd allowed himself to become somewhat resigned to the idea that he would likely never leave that massive house, let alone get out of Switzerland and back to England. Since then a strange sort of peace washed over him.

It had been almost two weeks since his host had departed without warning, and James was very nearly certain that he wouldn't be seeing him again. He discovered that he had forgotten to bring both the charger and the electrical cord for his laptop; with its battery quickly dying, a bit of the hope he'd held onto that he would hear back from one of the many emails he'd sent along with it. As for the remarkably realistic hallucination of those two lingerie-clad beauties that had visited him in the night almost a week earlier, nothing had happened since. He had convinced himself that it really was too much fresh air and the high altitude messing with his mind.

And that morning, he was resolved to do something about it.

Of course, it was something stupid, he realised as he went over his plan again in his mind. He had decided that the only way to overcome the elements was to fully immerse himself in them. That meant he was going back out to ski, alone. But before he could do that, he needed figure out how he was going to get back to that room with the equipment he'd need, without having to enlist the help of creepy butler Guillaume. He had thought that would be the trickiest part of his plan and to date he'd been right; he was on day three of exploring the labyrinthine-like compound without any sign of the Comte's glorious mancave. After downing the fresh coffee and hot buttered croissants that appeared each morning on his bedside table despite the room's locked door, he set off.

He felt as though he were doing something naughty, although the last thing that Defleur had said before leaving was that he should enjoy himself. James didn't think that meant sitting in his room cowering like a puppy in a thunderstorm. He crept downstairs, trying as much to remember the direction they had taken that day as to not squeal like a little girl at every sound he heard. He knew it was a completely irrational fear. *I mean, it's not like I'm really being held prisoner here or anything – it's just I have no idea how much longer I have to stay with no way to contact the outside world. Oh wait…*

His biggest obstacle was that all the doors seemed to look identical, as did the walls and floors of the infinite number of hallways he encountered, making it near-impossible for him to get his bearings. Cursing himself for not having paid more attention, he snuck down a corridor he couldn't remember trying, testing each door as he got closer to where he thought he should be. Some were locked. Others opened to rooms that were nothing but empty space with bare concrete walls. Very odd.

What terrified him most, though, was the thought of opening the door on one or both of those women from that night. Well, it both terrified and thrilled him in equal measure. They were, without doubt, the sexiest women he had ever seen. Somehow he had sense enough to be afraid of them at the same time.

When he opened the second-last door of the hallway, he was neither thrilled nor terrified. He was just bewildered.

It looked like some kind of drug lab. Or, having never seen such a thing himself, what James would imagine one to look like. There were test tubes and Bunsen burners, if memories of A-level chemistry served correctly, bubbling away with what could only have been something illegal. The worktops were stacked high with half-opened crates, with more crates in a small storage area further back inside the room. The odour hit him as he took a step inside, so heavy and dense it nearly brought him to his knees.

It was pungent and sweet and achingly familiar; a scent he couldn't seem to place. It seeped into his clothes and hair to such a point that he feared he might never be rid of it. It was at once maddening and intoxicating. He could feel his head begin to swim as he backed out of the room. It was an unexpected discovery, one that led to more questions than answers. Was Defleur a businessman, a scientist, a drug dealer or someone who was just mucking about with a bit of all three? He dismissed the last possibility outright. From his experience, Defleur was too intense for mucking about with anything.

As he stood in the front of the door he'd just closed, struggling to make sense of what he had just seen, he heard the faint click of another door closing not far away from him. The sound was enough to bring him back to his mission. There was no time to wonder about an out-of-place lab or what it may have to do with any of the infinite number of strange things that went on here. James had one more door left to find and open.

The last door of that particular hallway held his prize, and he found himself once again standing in the room dreams were made of. But before he could allow himself to get too distracted by the big screen television and high-end gaming consoles, to the point where he'd never get anything else done, he quickly grabbed some of the ski gear and launched into Phase Two of his plan to naturalise himself in his environment. *After all, it's not like I'm going anywhere anytime soon...*

James made his way outside, and was pleased to discover that the sun was high in the sky, telling him that it was just before noon. He had little concept of time these days, but he was relieved that he hadn't wasted another entire day in finding the room. The air around him was completely still, unmoving, with a hint of foreboding to it. It wasn't making him feel any better. *No better, no worse – at least it's a draw*, he thought.

He rounded the corner and noticed that the ski run had been laid with fresh powder. It hadn't occurred to him that it may not have been, but that could have been a very real possibility. It was far too warm for snow this time of year and, without Defleur around, there was no one to use the run. Once he started to really think about it, he was shocked there was any snow there at all.

As he drew even closer to the slope, he could see what

appeared to be recent tracks. A chill ran through him. If Defleur wasn't around, then who was using it?

Somehow he couldn't quite picture Guillaume up there, goggles covering his watery blue eyes, poles flailing as he flew down the slope. The thought made him laugh out loud. He jumped at the unnatural-sounding bark that echoed back at him from the surrounding mountains.

The ski lift was waiting at the bottom of the run, as if it had known he was be coming. James was half-expecting its motor to be running, and almost fainted in relief to discover it wasn't. He was just as relieved that the mechanics of the lift were simple enough for someone as non-mechanically inclined as him to start, which was something else he hadn't considered. James felt a small sense of satisfaction, something he had not been familiar with that entire trip. Almost able to relax, he settled into the lift seat and slowly made his way up the mountain, taking note of the view that had eluded him when he'd been there before with Defleur. It was truly spectacular. And very, very isolated.

From the vantage point offered by the lift, James could see that the remote mountain chateau of concrete and glass offered the ultimate in solitude. There was nothing around it apart from more mountains and trees interspersed with green velvet carpeting that he took to be other valleys. The air was so pure, not at all like what he was accustomed to in London. Not like anywhere in England, in fact. It was intoxicating, and made James feel like he'd been drinking something more sophisticated than his usual lager. Something more refined, like an old fine wine. It lent more weight to his theory that the air was a major factor in the way he had been feeling.

As he reached the top of the run and readied himself for the first descent, he detected a hint of movement at the bottom of the hill. Looking closer, he felt his breath catch in his throat.

It was the two women he had seen in his room.

Although it was a fair distance to the bottom, the white blonde hair of the one and the creamy cocoa complexion of the other were unmistakeable. James could see the skintight lines of their skiing outfits even from that height. Once again, they were dressed to match: the blonde in blue and the brunette in white. The latter lifted her hand in greeting.

James froze, unsure of what to do.

When he had last seen them, half-asleep in the darkness of his bedroom, he was certain that they had been out to make a meal of him in some way. Yet there in the brightness of the early afternoon sunshine, they seemed more like two fellow houseguests out enjoying a bit of early-season skiing. Totally harmless. It was making James feel more than a little foolish for his earlier hysterics.

He waved back in something akin to relief, feeling all of his tension and anxiety slip away as he pushed off from the top of the run. He hoped that he would glide down the hill with elegance and grace; the women were watching his every move with what appeared to be great interest. He silently prayed that he wouldn't cock it up and wipe out in typical James-like fashion. It would appear that, for once, luck was on his side.

James landed at the bottom, upright on his skis, somehow managing to come to a smooth stop not far from where they were standing. If he had thought that they were the most beautiful things he had seen while he was imagining them in his room, he was unprepared for what he was in for as they stood before him now. There were no words to describe them. Particularly the darker-skinned brunette. Her eyes were sea-green.

And the way she was looking at him from underneath her dark lashes was making him weak in the knees.

"Hello ladies," he said as suavely as he could. Inappropriate feelings toward the houseguests of the man who was employing him ran through James without warning. He was trying desperately to think of Frankie, but found it wasn't doing much to subdue his urges.

"Hello," the brunette responded. Speech had to mean she was real, James reasoned with himself; this was not just a figment of his mountain air-addled brain. The blonde remained silent but he saw her watching him in a way that made him feel very uncomfortable. If he were to hazard a guess and had a way with words, he would have said it was 'lascivious'.

Frankie would know, of course. But then she'd fucking kill me.

"Do you mind if we join you?" The brunette asked, so politely that it brought his attention back from where he had lost it.

"Of course... I mean, of course not. Join me. More the merrier and all that" James babbled nervously, wishing it were just the two of them. The blonde was making him uneasy.

The brunette introduced herself as Shaye, and her blonde friend as Marta. James, relaxing all the more now that he was certain that these women were real, jumped at the opportunity to find out more as they climbed the hill, tightly wedged into the ski lift.

"So, do you two live here?" he asked point blank. He saw no sense in tiptoeing around the issue.

Shaye giggled, while Marta snorted without much

humour.

"Something like that," Marta replied coldly.

It struck James as odd that Defleur would leave a key detail like that out. He knew that, because he was there for work, his employer didn't really owe any such explanation. However, considering the way he had explained so many other things, James wondered why it wouldn't have come out in passing. Something along the lines of *oh by the way I share my home with two incredibly gorgeous women* would have sufficed. And had Defleur not specifically told him there was no one else there apart from the creepy butler, that he lived alone? Or had James just imagined it?

He felt the line between imagination and reality growing thinner by the day, stretched to the point where one had become the other.

"Marta is Alfonse's cousin," Shaye was explaining, the use of his host's first name throwing him off even more. "I'm just... a friend who stays now and then."

Her last comment made Marta laugh out loud. James wondered just how close a friend she was, and with whom.

"Oh." He wasn't sure how else to respond. "I wasn't aware there was anyone else here."

"*He* doesn't let us out to mingle much with the guests," Marta sniffed as the lift came to the top of the ski run.

It could have been James imagining things again, but he thought Shaye smiled as if by way of apology for Marta. It was sweet, but entirely unnecessary. From what James understood about women, when you came across one who looked like that, you'd expect there to be a little attitude. It was part of the package.

What he didn't understand was his extreme anxiety whenever Marta so much as glanced in his direction. Or how he'd become so completely smitten with Shaye.

They skied together for what seemed like hours, until the sun started to fade behind the mountains. But because Defleur had thought to string some lighting along both the ski run and the path that led back to the house, they were able to stay out till it was full dark. It was more fun than James had had in the entire time he was there. More than he'd had in his whole life, if he was being truthful, and that included the past few months he'd spent with Frankie.

Shaye was turning out to be a lovely girl: sweet, beautiful beyond reason, and really good fun. Marta? Not as much.

"I'm bored," she whined as they hit the bottom of the hill.

Shaye and James were having too good a time tossing the fake snow at one another to pay attention. Marta began to pout, her behaviour quickly eroding as they continued to ignore her.

"Let's do something fun," she wailed at last, tugging on Shaye's arm like a two year old threatening a tantrum.

Annoyed, Shaye stopped trying to stuff snow down the front of James's ski jacket and turned toward Marta.

"What did you have in mind?"

Marta bit her lip and pretended to hmm and hah, but James got the distinct impression that she knew *exactly* what it was she wanted to do.

"How does some nice hot cocoa sound?" There was a

twinkle in her eye that let butterflies loose inside James's ribcage.

His thoughts flashed back to that strange room he had found, the one with all those flasks and test tubes. He tried to reassure himself that she meant the traditional kind of hot chocolate with marshmallows, that time-honoured ritual commonly engaged in after any outdoor wintertime activity. *Again, harmless*, he thought as he followed them back to the house. Its huge panes of glass were lit from within, and it beckoned to them invitingly. He'd never seen the house from outside at night before; it was breathtaking. But there was also a sense of something ominous, something that lay just below the surface, out of reach of his understanding. He shivered.

James sighed and shook his head. He was letting his imagination get the better of him again. There was nothing to be concerned about. No danger was coming his way. It was the slight chill of the night air that was making his hair stand on end. Nothing more. However not more than three hours later, when James found himself bound by both hands and feet to the green felt top of the snooker table, Shaye and Marta on either side of him in various stages of undress taking it in turns to lick warm chocolate off his bared chest, he felt the need to re-evaluate his previous opinion.

Especially because he had no recollection of how he had gotten there.

There were flashes of steaming mugs of hot cocoa that had appeared as if from nowhere. Laughter and more flirting. He could vaguely recall that the chocolate had been thick and dark, with a hint of spice and much more bitterness than he was accustomed to. And definitely no marshmallows. Maybe that was how the Swiss did it, he remembered thinking. Right before Shaye had plunked herself squarely in his lap and began to run her hands down his chest, nibbling on his neck in a way that made his eyes roll back into his head. The last image he saw with any detail was Marta, unzipping her coat and unbuttoning the shirt beneath it as she moved toward them.

The male part of his brain realised that, for most men, this wouldn't qualify as the worst way to pass an evening. Yet for all its eroticism, he was terrified beyond all reason. Not least of all because of what Frankie would do to him if she were to find out. More because he could have sworn that the look in Marta and Shaye's eyes was at times more animal than human. As if he were nothing more than prey to them.

At least they had made good on their promise of hot cocoa.

Everything had happened so quickly he was clueless as to the when, where or how of it. One minute they had been laughing and messing around outside in the fake snow at the bottom of the ski run, and the next they were suddenly in the recreation room. Recreating, so to speak.

There were moments over those strange hours when James's conscience surfaced and asked how he could have become engaged in all of this, although engorged may have been the better word for it, without so much as a second thought for his beloved Frankie. But then the thought would be gone again, lost somewhere between a nibble here and a scratch of fingernails up his thigh there. Although James knew he would have to face up to his own guilt soon enough, it wasn't enough to keep him from gorging himself over the next several hours on Shaye and Marta and their magical cocoa. It felt more like a compulsion, as though he couldn't help himself though he knew how wrong it was.

They spent some time in his room, a few hours in

theirs. Their room was set up like something he had only been privy to while watching porn in university with his flatmates. These things just didn't happen in real life, he kept trying to tell himself as Shaye blindfolded him with a silk scarf and he felt a leather paddle bite deliciously into his backside. But in the end, he found himself back in the room where it had all began, strapped to the snooker table. A return to the scene of the crime, so to speak.

James was able to reassure himself that he was a victim, that there was something in the cocoa to blame for this. There must have been, because not only did he feel completely powerless to resist the temptation once he began to drinking it, but he had also regained the stamina and libido of an eighteen year old virgin who was just getting to use his equipment for the very first time. Time ceased to exist. The only thing that mattered was the chocolate and the women licking it off of him.

Guilt be damned, he never wanted that feeling to end.

James was lying on the now-destroyed snooker table, his body languid from a mix of ecstasy and near exhaustion. But they weren't finished with him. Shaye seemed to have a thing for blindfolds, and though he would have enjoyed seeing the action unfold he found that he rather liked not knowing whose hands were whose as they roamed over his naked flesh. That way, he could imagine it was only Shaye. Or better yet, Frankie and Shaye together. The thought made him shiver, but it wasn't out of fear.

That changed when he heard the door to the room burst open, struck by a force so strong that he was sure it had been knocked off its hinges. Through his haze, James struggled to free himself, willing his eyes to focus once Shaye snatched off his blindfold and hurried to untie him.

Defleur was standing in the doorway. Enraged. He began to stride forward as Shaye was pulling James from the table.

"Run," Shaye whispered, her beautiful face pale and drawn tight with fear. She had half-dragged him to the door his host had just come through and pointed in the direction of where his rooms, before closing the door quickly in his face.

Echoing in the hallway behind him, James could hear Marta and the Comte screaming at each other in a mix of languages ranging from English to French to something that sounded vaguely Eastern European in origin. From what little he could gather, Defleur seemed more angry about the use of the cocoa than what had been done to his snooker table. He wasn't exactly steady on his feet as he half ran, half limped his way through the halls, the boxer shorts around his ankles threatening to topple him. He paused to pull them up and his mind went back to Shaye and her look of terror as she pushed him out of the room to safety.

In that moment, he knew that he loved her.

As James continued to run in what seemed to be a hall that had no end, he thought he had heard Defleur bellow his name and something about being right, but he couldn't be certain. He was far more focused on not wetting himself to care.

Reaching the safety of his room, he closed and locked the door before realizing how pointless it was. It wasn't like a locked door had ever barred anyone from entry before, whether it be a creepy butler bearing coffee and croissants or two gorgeous women in their skivvies. At any moment, James knew that Defleur could come storming in and end it all. His career, his bright future at the firm, his life as he knew it. Everything. And in spite of it, he had no regrets.

Meeting Shaye had been the best thing to ever have happened to him, and not just for the many wonderful ways she could use her tongue. He had felt their connection out on the ski hill even before all the crazy chocolate-licking sex games had even started. For the first time in weeks, he had felt like he could make it out of there if he had Shaye by his side.

With her, it felt like anything was possible.

Of course he loved Frankie still. Part of him always would, and it tore him up to have to end things with her like this. *I'm not good enough for her,* he thought as he rummaged frantically through his desk, *never have been.* She deserved so much more than James could give her and, what with all her big plans for her shop and how excited she was to be moving back to Brighton, all he wanted was for her to be happy. It was all he'd ever wanted.

Opening the lid of his laptop, James prayed silently that there would be enough juice in it for one final email. Not that this email would be any different from the others he had sent that went unanswered, but it was something he needed to do. Like an electronic version of his last will and testament.

But who to send it to? Certainly Frankie was the most deserving, but would some cryptic goodbye email from a fiancé she may never see again really help the situation? James didn't think so.

As he hit the send button, he could hear footsteps approaching from down the hall. Expensive Italian shoes striding over the carpet runner with purpose. Or possibly wrath.

The door handle began to turn. James had known that it was locked as much as he knew that a locked door meant nothing in that place. *Or maybe my hand was too slippery from all that chocolate*, he thought with a sinking feeling, watching helplessly as the door swung open.

He closed his eyes and stood up.

To: Matthew Harris
<mharris@harrisdevelopment.com.au>

Subject: well this is it

Dear brother,

This may be one of the last emails I write and I don't even know if you'll even receive it. I know now that I will not be leaving this place anytime soon. And as much as I'd like to say that I'll write Frankie her own email, I'm not sure I have that kind of time.

In my defence I didn't intend for it to end like this. Really I didn't. I just came here to do my job. But you know what they say about intentions. I have no regrets... how can I when what I've gotten is worth so much more than work experience? It's been life-changing. I'm left questioning everything I've ever held to be true. The only thing I know for sure now is that nothing is what it seems.

If you speak to Frankie please tell her that I love her and I'm so sorry, but it's better this way. She'll be better off without me and though I can't say the same, this is the way it has to be.

The chocolate is the life, Matt. See you on the other side - J

TEN

September 25th

Frankie's dearly-departed Nan had a saying: *if you go round digging in the dirt, best be prepared for the shit you'll stir up with it.* She missed her terribly.

She also knew for a fact that were she around to see how her granddaughter had been carrying on, she would not hesitate to give her a good swift kick in the arse. And she knew that she would deserve it.

Frankie had never really considered herself a romantic person. Ever. In fact, she was usually the first person to scoff at the notion. The whole topic made her uncomfortable. She had quickly dismissed many past suitors for overtures of the publicly romantic nature. Even James had not been spared from the cynical character of her heart.

The first and only time he had brought her flowers, Frankie all but laughed him out of the room. When he had proposed to her in the restaurant that night, the very same place she had so recently spent hours enjoying the company of another man, James had learned that it was in his best interest to keep it simple. There was no hiding of the ring in a glass of champagne, no violinists appearing tableside to pluck out strains of Vivaldi's *La Primavera*, no getting down on bended knee in front of Queen and country to ask for her hand. No.

He had kept it simple and practical with a short speech about how they had only been dating a few months but were so good for one another, why prolong the inevitable? Looking back, she could see that it had served as an effective metaphor for their relationship.

James and Frankie have never been that sweaty palms and heart-pounding excitement sort of pairing. She'd always thought that was more of a Hollywood movie myth and, if it did indeed exist, surely the spark would fizzle out almost as quickly as it had ignited. Those feelings could never last. Were she in need of supporting evidence, she need look no further than Louise and her constantly revolving affections. Until recently, it would seem.

Glancing over to her engagement ring sitting on the vanity in its velvet-lined box, its modest diamond winking at her in mocking, she wondered if maybe all this time she had been wrong.

Louise's bedroom door was shut by the time she had returned home from dinner with Henry. Frankie had wanted so badly to talk to her, to tell her all of the things that she couldn't while her friend had been caught up in her chocolate-induced mania. But as she was about to knock, she heard a low yet undeniably intimate giggle on the other side, one she was all too familiar with. It was closely followed by nervous male laughter. Frankie knew that rather than hesitate, she needed to go straight to her own room and put on her headphones immediately with the volume cranked as high as it would go on the iPod, or she would quickly regret it.

It was comforting, at least, to see that Louise was getting back to her old self.

Frankie hoped that Jared could handle it, getting everything he's ever wanted and probably a whole lot more all in one night. She also hoped that he would be different, that Louise wouldn't just chew him up and spit him out as she had done with the countless others that had been in and out of her bed before him. The fact that she had gone willingly to a science fiction movie with him meant that the odds were heavily in his favour.

It made her smile. Jared was a good man. Like James. *And Henry.*

The emptiness tightened in her chest, and was accompanied by another not entirely unfamiliar emotion. One that threatened to choke the joy right out of her. Guilt.

With the way that Henry had been making her feel in those past few days, Frankie wasn't convinced that she was the same cynic she once was when it came to matters of the heart. Funny how quickly some things could change. For example, she was almost positive she would not laugh Henry off the premises were he to show up in her shop with a bouquet of roses. Even if they were red. She was fairly certain that if it were Henry getting down on one knee to declare his undying love and beg her to marry him, she wouldn't mind in the least. She'd be lying if she said she hadn't thought about it, maybe more than once. Perhaps even daydreaming the whole scenario in painstaking detail right down to his impeccably fitted, if inexplicably wet and clinging, Thomas Pink shirt. It wasn't something she was proud of, but it was true nonetheless.

But where the guilt had snuck in uninvited was on a minor technicality, hinged on something Henry had said and been wrong about. It was Frankie who wasn't worthy of James at the moment, and not the other way round. And the nasty little voice in her head wasn't about to let her forget it.

Frankie gave her head a shake and stretched.

If she was hoping to get anything done, she couldn't continue to dwell on these things. She was having a difficult enough time as it was dragging herself out of bed each day that Henry was gone. There was still far too much work to do. The shop wasn't going to stock itself, and hadn't she made a promise to do some research on alternate suppliers?

Frankie was barely motivated enough to take a quick shower and throw her still-wet hair into a ponytail. No need for anything beyond that; Henry wasn't around. Part of her despised the fact that she had suddenly become *that girl*, so she tried to make up for it by telling herself it was more a matter of practical choice. She was going to pick up some bar stools she'd spied earlier that week in the window of one of the antique shops just round the corner where she had gone in and immediately put a deposit down. She knew they would look fabulous somewhere on the shop floor, and hadn't Henry said furniture would be an excellent place to start?

Of course, despite her best efforts to the contrary, her thoughts would always come back to him. Like a moth to a flame.

She sighed in frustration and threw on some jeans she'd found lying on the floor and a lightweight grey v-neck jumper, then made her way downstairs. Louise's door was closed, with no sign of the happy couple anywhere on the lower floor. Frankie hadn't seen them in a couple of days, not since before that night she'd had Henry for dinner.

I mean, dinner with Henry, she corrected herself.

She decided she would ring Louise later and persuade her to come into town. After all, she had not seen the shop since it had been painted and the fixtures installed. And Jared would have to go back to work sometime, much as he may not want to, so it would give Louise something to do apart from obsess over those Cocoa Creams. And it would give Frankie the chance to talk to her alone, best mate-to-best mate style. Mobile in one hand, Frankie rattled off a quick text - *ring me later nerdfucker* - in case she got too caught up in her research and poured herself some coffee to go with the other.

She ran into Mavis on her way out to the car, and managed to snag some freshly baked banana muffins the housekeeper had made and was bringing down from the main house. Although she didn't hover as much as she had when the girls were younger, Frankie could tell that she had sensed something off with Louise and was as relieved as she was that her former charge was on her way to being well clear of it. Growing up, Mavis was more like a substitute mother than mere hired help for both Louise and Frankie; the main distinction was that Louise's mother had passed away when she was four and her own was very much alive.

The simple act of baking muffins was also her subtle stamp of approval for Jared, whose car had remained parked in plain sight in the drive, just as it has been for the past few nights. *That makes two of us,* Frankie thought with a grin.

As she made the drive into town, thinking about how happy she was that Louise seemed to be finally maturing as a human being, Frankie's thoughts inescapably turned back to Henry and that night. She wondered again what had made him react with such violence when she mentioned Chadwick's. It made no sense. How could *anyone* hate the country's most beloved chocolate-maker so much?

Frankie was quick to acknowledge that there may have been some bias on her part, given her personal relationship with Louise. However, she barely knew anything about her best friend's father and had never given him much thought until the night of Henry's outburst. For all she knew, maybe he was a complete bastard to work for and had rubbed everyone in the industry the wrong way. He didn't strike her as particularly evil but, again, she hadn't really paid much attention. Intimidating, yes, but to run a corporation of that size the way he had done for the past thirty-odd years, she supposed that he would have to be a bit of an asshole. It could well be considered a prerequisite.

It could also have been something as simple as Henry having had some kind of run-in with Chadwick's, like a business deal gone sour or some such, and he was harbouring a bit of a grudge. As hard as it was for Frankie to believe that Henry could hate anyone, the look on his face and his anger had been terrifying. He was as likely to be as much of an asshole as Louise's father when it came to the business side of things. Maybe he was only being nice to her because he was her mentor.

But then there were other reasons, the ones that she had discovered at dinner. Frankie felt her face turn crimson and her stomach tie itself into knots at the memory.

It was after she had unlocked the front door and dragged her new antique bar stools inside she remembered once more the similar tangent that Jared had gone on at Louise's party. It hadn't been directly related to the company itself; it was more a general diatribe about corporate responsibility than the unadulterated fury Henry had reserved exclusively for Chadwick's. But the similarities struck her as more than simple coincidence. Frankie decided then that she would include Chadwick's in her research. It couldn't hurt to be more informed, to not pass judgments based solely on personal perceptions or the opinions of others. She'd never been inclined to do so before, so why start now? She owed it to the future of her business to develop a well-rounded picture of all of the supply options available. It was the responsible thing to do. *Wasn't it?*

With that in mind, she opened her laptop and typed 'Chadwick's' into Google. The first entries were typical – the main corporate website, details of current share prices and stock options, various national and international retailers advertising the Chadwick's products that were available in their own shops.

Buried somewhere in the middle of the third page of search results, though, Frankie found something interesting. A website entitled *www.savechadwicks.co.uk*. Curiosity mounting, she clicked on the link.

Frankie was greeted by a mocked-up version of the Sex Pistols' *God Save the Queen* promotional poster from 1977, with the iconic image of the monarch overtop a Union flag backdrop with bands of text strategically placed as if to simultaneously blindfold and gag the subject saying 'God Save Chadwick's' instead. However, rather than an image of the Queen, it was the Chadwick's logo with its patented sunshine yellow lettering that stood in her place.

She was both impressed by the image's cleverness and intrigued as to what she might find inside. After clicking on the image to enter the site, the old-fashioned typewriter text inside wasted no time in delivering its message:

Save Chadwick's!

There's a plot afoot to merge our beloved
National Treasure, Chadwick's, with Tompkin's
Toffees and another unnamed American confectioner
with the sole purpose of creating a global candy

monopoly.

As with all mergers, there are the immediate
risks of job loss, quality concerns, and damage to the
nation's economy as a whole.And to what end?
Nothing more than greed.

Please have a look round this site to get the full
picture of what's really going on at Chadwick's.

And don't forget to sign our petition which will be
sent to the only remaining family member on the
Board of Directors:

Archibald Chadwick III, CEO of Chadwick's PLC

Let him know that England will not sit idly buy
while he sells out a piece of our nation's proud and
delicious history!

Riveted, Frankie continued reading.

She quickly discovered a number of things about
Chadwick's. Some things she had known already, but there
were others there that she was fairly sure Daddy Chadwick
wouldn't want anyone finding out about. For starters, she
knew that the company's local factory provided a large
number of jobs for the Brighton-Hove area: roughly seventy-
four percent of the working population, the site noted. But
what she wasn't as aware of was that the chocolate it
produced in the local factory was shipped worldwide. There
was only one other Chadwick's manufacturing facility, and
that was in the United States and had been built to supply
exclusively to that market.

That's a fuckload of chocolate, Frankie thought. On a larger
scale, it meant a lot of money in both revenue and taxes for
England's coffers.

According to the information the website had gathered together, which included what appeared to be internal company memorandums and shareholder bulletins, should the merger go through all manufacturing would be outsourced to a production facility in some as-yet-unnamed country. Probably, if the way most corporate entities worked were any indication, it would be a country with little by way of quality control protocols or pesky labour laws. And this was just one of a whole laundry list of Chadwick's planned 'cost-savings measures' exposed by this website.

The more Frankie read, the more it was beginning to sound like a license for printing money.

Not that she had any real clue about large corporations and their politics. But this site seemed to indicate that this was a hostile merger with a twist. Instead of the board or legal departments on either side holding up the process, it seemed like it was the shareholders themselves that were most resistant, citing the same concerns over quality and job cuts. Possibly because a large number of those shareholders also happened to be long-time employees who had been given stock options as part of their compensation packages, which was another thing Frankie hadn't known. Thus far, they had been able to ignore the vast amounts of money being flung at them, but who could say how long that would last. Apparently it was the board, led by Daddy Chadwick himself, who was attempting to force the merger through by any means necessary.

Frankie found it amusing that the site had christened her friend's father with the same nickname she had used for him for years.

Browsing through the different page links, Frankie found more surprising news in a section aptly named *Scandal!* It detailed a number of alleged lawsuits that had been brought against Daddy Chadwick for sexual harassment, all of which were quickly and quietly settled out of court for undisclosed sums of money. It even had some grainy images of rather official looking legal affidavits taken from a number of London call girls who had allegedly spent several evenings entertaining Chadwick and his friends on the company tab, but it wasn't clear if any formal action had been pursued to that end. Their only purpose, it seemed, was to support the defendant and damage his character.

It was that last piece of information that she had found particularly disheartening, on a more personal level, as she thought of her poor friend. Louise worshipped her father as much as he adored her; they were all each other had by way of family. Frankie was sure that Louise was blissfully unaware of her father's other life. If she had known, Frankie was certain she would have heard something about it. If this kind of news were to ever get out, regardless if turned out to be nothing but lies, it would destroy her.

Frankie sighed heavily. Could this have been what Henry meant when he said nothing is ever what it seems? Thinking of him made her smile even as she could feel her stomach twisting into those painful and familiar knots.

Another thought occurred to her, just what she needed to get her mind off the unsavoury goings-on behind the scenes that she'd just uncovered about her best friend's family business. She would do a search on Henry's company. Just to get the facts, of course.

A responsible business owner would have done such a thing straight away, Frankie realised in embarrassment. Instead, what had she done? Spent the bulk of her time having chocolate-coated dreams about him before snogging him senseless in an alleyway not far from the shop. Not to mention, she was frequently fantasising about doing it again.

Her hands were shaking as she dug his business card out of her handbag. She couldn't decide if she was more excited or terrified to find out more about her mysterious Henry. It occurred to her that he had never really divulged any real information about who he was. Although they had spent several hours a day together, he had somehow always engineered it that he was doing more listening than talking. Frankie was able to admit that it was near the top of the list of many things that she selfishly enjoyed about her time with him. It wasn't often she'd had the chance to talk so openly without interruption. She supposed it was one of the hazards of having both a boyfriend and a best friend who loved to chatter on incessantly and, more often than not, about themselves.

She typed the name *HRF Holdings* into the search engine, not without some trepidation. As she watched the little globe turning in the top right corner of the screen, her heart rate sped up as if to keep time. *A watched globe never stops spinning.* When it finally finished and produced its search results, Frankie was astonished at what it had come up with. Or rather, what it *hadn't* come up with.

One would have thought that a multi-national corporation, one that permitted Henry to travel so extensively and dress so impeccably, would yield at least a few hits in Google. If not a few thousand. And yet, there was nothing to be found. At least, nothing to do with him.

Apparently HRF also stood for Hypoxic Respiratory Failure, a medical condition that affects newborns, occurring when the cells in the body cannot receive enough oxygen. It sounded terrifying, but not anything remotely like a confectionary conglomerate. There was one mention of a corporation of the same name located in the West Midlands that, although in the wrong location entirely, may have held some promise until Frankie clicked onto its web link. They sold farming equipment, not chocolate bars. Another dead end.

She huffed in frustration, which soon gave way to a quiet panic as she realised something. She really didn't know anything about Henry or his company at all. In fact, she had made a number of assumptions about him without having been given a lick of proof that he was who and what he said he was. Really, for all she knew, he could have been some high level corporate spy masquerading as a mentor appointed by the bank.

Wouldn't the bank have sent me some sort of letter, so as to avoid this very situation? Yet, she had received nothing, just simply accepted Henry's word on blind faith. Well, maybe it wasn't altogether blind.

Would I have been so willing to accept Henry so easily if he had a face like a smacked ass? Probably not. Although Louise and Frankie had many differences, they were also very much alike in just as many ways. Shallowness was one of them.

As she was quickly spiralling from panic into something closer to total paranoia, Frankie could here someone knocking at the shop door. How long they had been there, she'd had no clue. She jumped up from the laptop, racing to the door with the hope that it would be Henry, back from whatever mysterious place he had gone to explain everything and wrap his arms around her so she would no longer feel so empty inside. She was so elated at the prospect that she forgot to berate herself for such a lame thought as she wrenched open the door.

It was only Louise.

Frankie stepped aside rather dejectedly, and in swept her friend in characteristic fashion. She looked lovelier than

Frankie had seen her look in weeks, almost back to her pre-Cocoa Cream-crazed self.

"What's up there, sourpuss? You don't look too thrilled to see me. Do you fear my wrath for that nerdfucker comment?" She was eying Frankie up and down in suspicion, before getting distracted by the shop. "Place looks fab, by the way. You must be well pleased."

And that was all it took. Those few words, and Frankie couldn't stop herself. She did what she'd always done in times of crisis, the very thing she had done since they were teenagers and would probably continue to do well into their sixties. In one breath, she told Louise everything.

It came spilling out almost faster than she could form the words. Everything that she had been dying to say for weeks, from the night she had caught that first glimpse of the grey top hatted stranger in the garden to meeting Henry, then on to describe the dreams where they had become merged into one and the same in both her conscious and subconscious mind, before finishing with the kiss that she hadn't been able to stop thinking about from the other evening. She decided to leave out that morning's exercise in cyber-stalking and the subsequent freak-out that had ensued. She was too embarrassed to admit it had gone that far.

When Frankie was finished, breathless and in desperate need of a strong cup of tea, she found that she'd achieved what she had previously dismissed as impossible. Louise, who always had an answer for everything, was gobsmacked. Stunned into complete silence.

When she finally found her voice again, however, she burst into peals of laughter.

"Well hell, I never thought I'd see the day," she choked out as she wiped a tear from her eye. "I'm so proud of you,

Franniekins."

Frankie glowered in response, not really sure what she meant.

"Lou, this is serious. I've started actively fantasising about another man. I just *cheated* on my fiancé—" Louise cut her short with a dismissive wave of her hand.

"It was just a kiss, Frankie. Not the end of the world. Although I suspect it's been tearing you up inside. Hasn't it?" Frankie nodded as Louise continued, sipping thoughtfully on her iced Frappucino.

"You've always been so chronically monogamous…it's quite tragic, really. Such a waste of a cute little ass."

"Messing around indiscriminately might work for you," Frankie replied quietly, "but it's just not me."

"Right, because shagging your boss is a much more noble path to take?" Louise raised a perfectly manicured eyebrow. Frankie grumbled in response but could think of nothing to offer in rebuttal. Louise became silent once more, this time more contemplative. She moved to perch atop one of the new stools Frankie had decided to set up in front of one of the glass display cabinets.

"What - no caustic retort? No sign of the F word? Blimey, Frankie, this is serious," she breathed. "What has this bloke done to you?"

"I don't know!" Frankie wailed in frustration. It felt good, despite that the force of it had nearly knocked Louise off her seat.

She proceeded to reveal all of the parts that she had previously left out, the ones that made her look like what she felt was a pathetic cross between lovestruck teenie-bopper and manic-depressive cyber-stalker. She tried to put into words the depth of the emptiness she felt whenever she was away from him, the utter elation she felt when they were together, the unreasonable terror that hit when she realised that he may not be everything he was claiming to be. To Frankie's surprise, Louise listened without interruption. Or poking fun.

She felt like their relationship had evolved a little in that moment.

"I think I know what's going on here," Louise began after Frankie had finished, then bit her lip as if weighing her next words. "But you aren't going to like it."

Frankie waited for her to finish, vibrating in anticipation.

"You're in love with him," Louise stated simply. "And that scares the crap out of you, so now you're going to try to convince yourself of all the reasons why you shouldn't be in the hope that it will all just go away."

What the… ?

"No," Frankie began to shake her head furiously as she began to babble her objections.

"No, just… no. That's ridiculous. I mean, I just met him… well, days ago really. How could I lo—? You're wrong, Lou. *I love James.* You know, the man I'm going to *marry*?"

"There you go again," Louise replied as she calmly swirled the melting ice round her cup, barely giving Frankie a second glance, 'convincing yourself that just because you've agreed to marry James, that must mean you love him. And that because you've only just met Henry, you can't possibly love him."

Frankie was silent for a moment.

"But I do love James," she said finally, almost miserably. "Really, I do. And I can't love Henry. I don't know anything about him. I just...I just...I can't. I *can't*."

"That's right, Frankie. You just keep repeating that until you think it's true. And maybe someday I'll believe you. But I wouldn't hold my breath or anything."

Louise was beginning to sound annoyed. Frankie was looking for something to throw. She was out of arguments, Louise had had a rebuttal for everything. So unlike her, and so unlike Frankie to not be capable of arguing her way out of something. She was usually so certain about her every conviction. But not this time, not with this. This time, all she could do was sputter 'No' and 'I can't' over and over with the occasional 'it's not possible' thrown in for good measure.

Louise had lost interest in poking holes in her bubble and sat looking at her steadily, waiting for reality to kick in. And the more Frankie tried to deny what she was feeling and declare it preposterous, the clearer it became.

Louise was right. Frankie did love Henry.

She loved him more than she had ever believed she could love anyone. She didn't even think it was possible. And that was exactly what it was: an impossible love. She sank to the floor. In retrospect she may have been aiming for one of the bar stools but her bottom didn't quite make it.

Louise was up and beside her in a flash, fearing that she'd just sent her best friend catatonic.

The Chocolate Is The Life

"Jesus, Frannie! Get a grip – it's only love, for fuck's sake. Nothing to go to pieces over." She was tugging Frankie to her feet and helping her onto the stool.

"Now, don't go getting all broody over James. He's tougher than he looks, and he'll understand. Deep down, he's probably seen it coming anyway."

Frankie looked at her sharply.

"What do you mean?" *Was I honestly the last person to know that I don't really love James? Am I really that thick?* She hoped that she wasn't.

"It's so obvious, Fran," Louise replied, softly stroking her hair. "You only stayed with James because you thought it was what you *should* do. You needed to prove to your mother that you could be part of a real grown-up relationship and stay with a man for more than a few weeks. But as lovely as James is, he's just not that man."

Frankie sat back, looking at her friend with admiration. When Louise decided to get profound, something that didn't happen very often, she didn't mess around.

"And just when did we switch places, exactly?" Frankie asked, making them both break into laughter. Louise gave her a quick squeeze of reassurance before taking a seat herself.

"Christ, I have no idea. But if that's what it feels like to be you all the time, then I don't want any part of it. It's exhausting being so... enlightened," she replied playfully as she commandeered Frankie's laptop and noticed what she had been Googling.

"Amateur," she muttered under her breath as she typed in a new url.

"What are you doing?" Frankie had no idea that Louise was a closet cyberstalker. Not like she didn't have more than enough time on her hands, so it was entirely plausible. Frankie just found it surprising; she'd had no idea that her friend could be so ambitious.

"You have to do a little more than just bash a name into Google. If you hope to get real results, you have to identify your search parameters," she muttered half to herself as she began to type furiously.

"Who the hell are you right now?" Frankie was utterly bewildered. *Did I pass out and hit my head on the floor on the way down? Stumble into some sort of alternate reality where Louise is a genius computer hacker?*

Louise shot her a dirty look as though she knew exactly what she was thinking before pointing at the screen in triumph.

"Hah, I knew it! A company that predates the Web or keeps an otherwise low profile is harder to locate, so it needs more than a simple search to find it." Mystified by the words coming out of her friend's mouth, Frankie peered past her to the website blinking on computer screen.

Louise had managed to access some registry database that provided basic company information for corporate entities of a global nature. It indicated that HRF Holdings Inc. had been registered as a corporation in 1896, and that its status was active. Although she toyed with other combinations of search terms, it was the only tangible result Louise could come up with. Even she thought it was somewhat odd to find so little.

As Frankie's mind began to race with yet more questions, she thought of something else Louise could try.

"Try 'Henry Roberts'," she suggested quietly.

Louise muttered something that sounded suspiciously like 'ooh so he does have a name' as her fingers clicked over the keyboard.

"Hmmphh," she soon snorted in disgust. "Unless he's a dead English architect, an ex-footballer, or any number of short fat bald blokes, I'm not getting anywhere with that either." Frankie wasn't surprised.

If they couldn't get anywhere apart from vague references to his company's origins, she was almost positive they wouldn't find anything on Henry himself. In all of her various interactions with him over the past few days, it was only now that she was starting to think about it when she recalled that he had been very careful to divulge only the most basic information about himself as he actively encouraged her to spill out her entire life story. At first, she had thought he was just a very private person, perhaps even a little on the shy side. And she didn't mind because she loved looking at him, and could do freely as she spoke. Far too often those moments could be spoiled when a beautiful man did too much talking.

But with her newfound paranoia, Frankie was becoming convinced it was because he had something to hide.

The two women sat together in silence in front of the laptop, pondering their next move.

"Oh!" Frankie jumped up in her seat as she remembered something. Digging into her back jeans pocket, with Louise watching her as if she had lost it completely, Frankie pulled out Henry's business card in triumph. She must have stuffed it into her pocket before Louise had arrived.

"Try the F. Maybe that means something?" she offered, suddenly not so sure about her epiphany.

Louise typed in the extra letter, and together they waited impatiently for the search results.

"Hmmm," Louise sighed thoughtfully, "are we sure he's not a stonemason from America?" The first few entries were for a Robert F. Henry from a tile company in Alabama.

"What? Tiles can be sexy too…" she replied in mock defense as Frankie eyed her derisively, taking back control of the keyboard.

Together they continued to scroll through, but again nothing was coming up that in any way resembled Frankie's Henry F. Roberts. They were about to give up and go look at shoes on asus.com when Frankie spied something at the bottom of the third page of search results.

It was an online encyclopedia entry. For Fitz & Company.

A sliver of fear shot down Frankie's spine. *Could this be just another coincidence in what was becoming a long line of coincidences?* She felt her throat go dry as she clicked the link that would take her to the webpage:

'Fitz & Company began as a small bakery and pastry shop owned by Thomas Robert Fitz of Hove before his trade turned toward chocolate in 1780. In 1805, he developed a way to grind cocoa beans using the technology of steam, which then led to the first mass production of chocolate in the United Kingdom. Fitz quickly patented the process and incorporated the business as Fitz & Company. By 1850, Fitz & Co had become the largest commercial chocolate producer in Britain with a diverse range of product that included the country's first chocolate bar, the Cocoa Cream. It remained a family-run business, with Thomas Fitz II officially taking charge in 1858.

In 1878, Fitz was killed in what was officially deemed an accident at the factory while working, although the particulars of exactly what happened were sketchy at best. The prevailing theory is that the grinder press had overheated and when he moved to fix it, his hand slipped and was severed when the press released without warning. His radial artery would have been cut, a key detail that was further supported by official police reports indicating Fitz had bled out onto the factory floor. He was found the next morning by two of his three sons who had worked alongside him at the factory, Thomas III and George. Little more than teenagers, they suddenly found themselves in charge of a company that employed fifty to sixty people. Their lack of business experience made them vulnerable to a takeover in 1880 orchestrated by Archibald Chadwick, the son of a prominent shipping magnate whose own chocolate business in nearby Brighton had been floundering. It has been suggested over the years that Chadwick had somehow been involved in the accident, but no conclusive evidence has ever surfaced to prove such a claim.

After the sale of the company, Thomas Fitz III went on to become a pastor in the nearby village of Worthing. He married and had two daughters, Isabel and Jane. George Fitz stayed on as a foreman at the factory, which had become the centre of operations for Chadwick's. Fitz's youngest son, Henry, disappeared the day after his father was found dead. He was sixteen at the time, and some officials took the timing of his disappearance as an admission of involvement with the accident, but again there was nothing to support the allegation.'

Frankie couldn't bring herself to read any further; it was a story she was already well familiar with. That, and she felt physically ill. She wasn't sure if it was the details of how Thomas Fitz had died, the implication that Louise's great-great-whatever grandfather may have been responsible, or Google's helpful yellow bolding of the search terms they had entered.

But one thing was clear: what the letters H.R.F could stand for.

"What'd you find?" Louise was trying to peer over Frankie's shoulder.

"Another dead end," she replied as she quickly closed the browser and closed the laptop screen, "and bugger, we forgot to plug in the cord so the battery's gone."

Frankie wasn't prepared to deal with what this new information might mean, let alone share it with Louise. Especially since it could very well end up meaning nothing at all. Chances were that it was nothing more than another series of rather closely related circumstances her overly active imagination was busy piecing together into something significant. She was also not prepared to tell her friend any of what she'd just discovered about her ancestor, or her father earlier.

What Frankie needed was time to turn it over in her mind a little more. And in absence of any other options, she did what she had always done best in those situations. She turned the spotlight back on Louise.

"So… you and The Doctor, eh?" Frankie nudged Louise in the ribcage with her elbow, giving her best oafish wink. To her amazement, Louise blushed and looked at the floor.

"Shut it," she whispered quietly, her tone becoming wistful as she continued. "I can't myself. Jared's wonderful."

"Sorry, not trying to take the mick. I'm actually really happy for you. I happen to think he's a fantastic bloke." Louise brightened instantly at her friend's approval.

"I know, right? He's so funny, and totally brilliant. And I feel like he really... I don't know. He just gets me, you know?"

Oh yes. I know, thought Frankie. She imagined that it was much the same way that Henry made her feel when she was with him. But she only nodded in reply, then noticed Louise giving her a sideways glance.

"It's okay to fall in love with someone else, Frannie. Because at the end of the day, if you try ignoring it and marry James anyway because you think you should or you have to prove something or any of that other bullshit that goes along with it, you'll just end up miserable and divorced in the end. It's just not worth it."

Amazing. Love has apparently made Louise remarkably astute. And though the newfound worries about who that other person Frankie may have fallen in love with sliced at her insides like a hot knife, she was determined to push all that aside for the moment. There was work to be done.

Frankie stood up and announced, in another abrupt change of subject, that they needed to do some shopping for supplies. That was enough to do the trick: Louise quickly forgot what they were talking about, jumping off her stool in excitement. Shopping always brought out the best in her. Frankie only wished it could be as easy.

In spite of herself, though, she managed to salvage what remained of the day into something productive. It wasn't to say that Henry and HRF Holdings and the tragic story of Thomas Fitz had not been on her mind the entire time, simmering on the back burner. *Although threatening to boil over would be a far more fitting analogy*, she mused as she drove the borrowed Mercedes back to Louise's house, following closely behind her friend's bright red Bentley. Even as she had oohed and ahhed in all the appropriate places over the various appliances and other pieces they had found for the shop, she was more convinced than ever that her earlier irrational paranoia was spot-on. But instead of your garden variety corporate espionage committed by a potential business rival, she got the feeling that this was something far more deep-rooted and sinister.

To Frankie, this reeked of vengeance.

It was an illogical leap, with nothing more to support it than weak circumstantial evidence, a couple of erotic dreams, and a whole lot of happenstance. But her subconscious had connected the man in the grey top hat to Henry a long time ago, and only now was she beginning to understand why.

ELEVEN

September 25th

As they pulled into Louise's drive, Frankie felt her stomach take another flip as she noticed a new car parked there, next to Jared's old Fiat. A Toyota Prius. The presence of an unfamiliar vehicle was something she had begun to view as a bit of a bad omen.

"Must be one of Jared's mates," Louise remarked with a shrug, nodding at the car as they made their way up the walkway to the house.

Frankie was surprised to hear that she was so nonchalant about it. The Louise she knew had always been oddly guarded when it came to strangers coming to her home unannounced.

"Hello ladies," Jared rose and greeted Louise with a kiss. She smiled up at him with such unabashed adoration Frankie feared she was going to throw up or stab her own eyes out in jealousy. Since neither was going to help her current situation, she turned her attention instead to the other seat at the kitchen counter, which was occupied by Jared's guest.

215

If those pictures of Einstein that you see in science journals could come to life, only minus the bushy moustache and with slightly crazier-looking eyes, it would come close to the gentleman who rose and stepped forward to be introduced.

"This is Dr. Johann Von Hoffstatler. He's the director of biochemistry at Cambridge, and he made a special trip down to discuss those chocolate samples I'd sent him in person."

Jared made the introductions around, blushing with pride when he came to Louise. The doctor was quite effusive in greeting her, kissing her soundly on both cheeks and sniffing surreptitiously at her hair. When it came time for Frankie's turn, he kissed both of her hands slowly and, to her surprise and revulsion, inhaled deeply as he did. It was all she could do not to yank herself away from him.

"Dr. V has a highly-tuned sense of smell," Jared offered by way of explanation, "almost extra-sensory, at times, it would seem."

Frankie noticed that the doctor was studying her carefully, as if to lend further proof to Jared's claim.

"You are deeply conflicted," he announced suddenly in an accent she could not place. Austrian or Dutch perhaps, especially with a name like Von Hoffstatler. Maybe even Afrikaans?

"You're so accustomed to knowing exactly what you want and what you need to do to get it. But something has happened – quite recently, I'd say – that has turned it all topsy turvy. Or no. No, it's not just something. Perhaps I should say, *someone*."

What the hell... What kind of doctor is this?

216

He turned his attention then to Louis, looking her up and down with approval.

"Your friends got to you just in time, I see. It would appear that it's almost worked its way out of your system. You must take care, though." Here his tone became solemn as he raised an index finger in warning, "for you could still succumb to it at any time."

At that point, Frankie had had more than enough of being polite. It had been rather a long day.

"Right, and just what the hell is that supposed to mean?" Her arms were crossed in front of her chest, her right foot tapping with impatience.

Louise looked a little shaken, more vulnerable than Frankie was accustomed to seeing her; Jared moved quickly to take her in his arms. It was clear he hadn't expected any of that. The doctor, however, did not seem fazed by the stir he was causing. If anything, he looked slightly amused.

"My apologies if I have alarmed you, my dear, for that was never the intention," he replied, giving Frankie a curt bow. "But what I mean is that your dear friend must be careful, lest she slip back under the spell."

"The spell. What spell?" Frankie was annoyed but at the same time intrigued, wondering where he could be going with this. Then it was the doctor's turn to look surprised.

"Are you not the young lady who works with the chocolate? I would have thought that you, of all people, would know."

"Well I do have a theory, but I'm not sure how much it really has to do with chocolate," she began haltingly, before deciding to take the plunge.

With a deep breath, Frankie began to tell them everything right from the beginning, just as she had done earlier that day with Louise. She even included a little of what she had discovered during her online research, holding nothing back save for the part about Louise's father and the prostitutes. She decided that was irrelevant to the situation, and better off saved for a more private conversation. If at all.

She described Henry and the physical similarities he bore, though fully admitting she could have been remembering it wrong and that it had been at a distance, to the man in the grey she had seen that night at Louise's party. Before she found Louise with the chocolate.

"I think I remember you saying you'd seen someone when we were on the terrace," Jared corroborated.

"I don't understand," Louise interjected. "What does this have to do with anything?"

Frankie realised that not everyone was following with her logic. Or maybe it was more that she wasn't explaining herself properly. More likely, though, it was some combination of the two.

"I think that maybe Henry isn't who he says he is," she began slowly, piecing all of the things that she had been mulling over in her mind from earlier that the day and putting them into words.

"In fact, I think he might be part of the Fitz family, and that he's come back to Brighton looking for revenge against Chadwick's for what his family lost. And it somehow involves planting those old chocolate bars onto Louise's property. And me..." Frankie trailed off as she was met with silence and empty stares.

She knew that it sounded a little ridiculous once she said it out loud. Or maybe a lot ridiculous. But it had all sounded completely feasible when it was just rolling around in her mind.

Which, Frankie mused, *could say a lot about the way my mind works.*

"Hmmm. That's verrry interesting," Von Hoffstatler said after a long moment of silence. He was quickly up and out of his seat, walking around the kitchen as he thoughtfully stroked his chin.

"But would anyone care to hear my theory?"

He indicated that they should take a seat, and they made their way to the lounge area. Frankie got the impression that this might take awhile.

Once everyone had settled in, Von Hoffstatler began to speak.

"How much do you know about chocolate?" His audience looked at him blankly at first, unsure of what he was looking for.

"Umm, it's made from the cacao bean?" Frankie offered flippantly.

"It comes in dark or milk… oh, and white but that isn't really proper chocolate. It just has cocoa butter in it." Louise added.

"It's widely considered a stimulant, but also has significant antioxidant properties," Jared contributed.

Von Hoffstatler seemed pleased with their responses as he circled the room, deep in thought, as if considering what he was going to say next.

"You are all correct," he said finally. "But how much do you know about its historical uses?"

That was where they hesitated. There were so many answers Frankie could have chosen from: the Aztecs used cacao beans as currency, the Mayans crushed the beans into a paste to make the first chocolate drink, the Spanish were believed to be the first to bring it to Europe where it was used medicinally. His question was too broad, too vague, perhaps even more than the first one. What sort of answers could he be looking for?

"The Mayans held the belief that chocolate was divine in origin and reserved it mainly for use in their sacred rituals. I don't think it's a coincidence that the scientific name for cocoa is *theobroma cacao*, or 'food of the gods'." Frankie was beginning to feel her frustration from earlier bubbling up inside.

"This is a lovely history lesson, doctor, but what does any of it have to do with what happened to Louise? I mean, that *is* why you came all the way down here, isn't it?" Frankie could appreciate dramatic tension as much as the next person, but she didn't see any value in wasting more time, be it his or theirs.

"Patience, my dear, I'm getting there," he replied. "Would you not prefer to get the full picture, rather than the abridged version?"

Point taken. Frankie shifted in her seat and glanced over at Jared. He met her gaze and shrugged his shoulders. *At least we're all in the dark here,* she thought.

"Now, where was I? Oh yes, Mayan rituals and chocolate's role in them. Jared, my young protégé, you were quite right when you said that cocoa is a stimulant and an anti-oxidant. The way the science journals read, you'd think that this was just discovered yesterday. But the Maya were aware of it long ago, over a thousand years in fact. And they were able to harness and redirect some of that power in a most remarkable way."

He glanced around the room to see if his audience was following. They were not.

"The Maya were an advanced civilization, to be sure. A clever and resourceful people. But one of their greatest achievements also happens to be one of their best kept secrets."

More blank stares.

"They discovered the mystical powers of chocolate."

With that, Frankie could hold herself back no longer. She snorted out loud. All eyes, previously fixed on Von Hoffstatler, turned in her direction.

"Seriously," she spat, exasperated. "Mystical powers of chocolate? I mean no disrespect, doctor, but really? What are the so-called *powers* that chocolate possesses?"

Von Hoffstatler looked at Frankie as though she were nothing more than a child, something she didn't much appreciate since she was smarting from the sting of her own failed theory. She was equally disturbed at the way Louise and Jared were hanging onto his every word as if it were gospel. It was clear to her if no one else that, regardless of how brilliant he may be, the professor was stark raving mad.

"Well, Ms. MacSweeney," he began, speaking as slowly as one would to a four year old, "cacao beans in their purest form are extremely high in theobromine, a substance similar in effect to caffeine. A stimulant, as Jared has already mentioned. But when you mix theobromine with a very specific and somewhat complex blend of spices, it transforms into something else entirely. It becomes what the Maya referred to as *Water of Life*."

Frankie felt the back of her neck begin to prickle with unease.

"What does this Mayan 'Water of Life' have to do with anything? I thought you were here to discuss the chocolate Jared sent you. He had tested it himself and found there was nothing special about it. Nothing mystical," Frankie was confused, and began babbling when she could feel the panic inside her beginning to build. "And that chocolate was from England, not South America."

As far as she could tell, this man – this doctor – just seemed to be talking in circles. Frankie's head was starting to spin as a result.

"Oh, but there is a connection, my dear. Make no mistake about that," the doctor responded, his tone turning hard and cold.

Crackers or not, he had her attention.

"The ritual, according to my findings, went something like this: a young man, usually a great warrior or someone of high importance to the tribe, was first blindfolded then tied down at the wrists and ankles to a stone platform. It was a symbol of trust and faith, an offering of himself in a way. His body would then be anointed with the Water of Life by the tribe's most beautiful priestesses, as the holy man recited an incantation imploring the gods of death to pass over their subject unharmed, that the Water of Life was the sacrifice in his place. The ritual would be complete when the subject drank whatever remained of the Water of Life as the priestesses wiped him clean, a gesture that signified the washing away of his ties to this mortal life in preparation for the one granted to him through the gift of The Water. It wasn't meant to be eternal life per se, but the process would allow the subject to age at a far slower rate, giving them the appearance of immortality. Like a god among men, but at a price."

"Isn't there always a price?" Frankie muttered half under her breath. Her head was no longer spinning and she could feel her earlier frustrations building again, along with a prickly sensation she couldn't identify.

Von Hoffstatler ignored her, as did everyone else.

"The subject would have to continue to consume the Water of Life in order to sustain its effects. He would not be able to eat regular food or…" There the doctor trailed off.

"Or what?" Louise breathed, completely captivated by the yarn he was spinning. Frankie shifted in her seat uncomfortably.

Von Hoffstatler shrugged and threw up his hands in response.

"I don't know. I can find no definitive answer to the *what would happen if* question. Some research seems to indicate that the person would begin to rot from the inside in a matter of days or weeks, their cells deteriorating at an accelerated rate, depending on how long they had been consuming the preparation. But then again, there are also suggestions that nothing would happen at all, that the subject could be successfully weaned from the Water without any consequence. Apart from the same fate that awaits us all, of course."

The room grew quiet as they considered what he had said.

"I'm sorry, Doctor. I'm just not seeing the connection here." Though Frankie was refusing to buy into whatever he was selling, that prickly sensation had refused to go away. It had spread from her neck, and was working its way down the length of her spine.

"There are stories throughout South America that there was one Western man, an Englishman actually, who was held in such high regard by a tribe in the Amazon that he was granted the ritual," the doctor replied, his eyes locking with Frankie's. She glowered at him with suspicion, but it did little to quell the sickening feeling growing inside of her.

"I believe you know who that might be, Ms. MacSweeney."

Frankie found it difficult to qualify what happened next. It seemed to go in stages, as if she were moving in slow motion.

First came the denial.

"No," she shook her head firmly as her mind spun through the implications of what the doctor was suggesting, "no. That's just...well, it's not possible."

"What do you mean?" Louise asked, still confused, before turning to face her friend. Frankie remained silent, her head continuing to shake in disbelief.

"I don't understand. How would Frankie know who it is," she asked as she turned back around to the doctor.

Jared stood quietly at her side, looking at Frankie as if waiting for confirmation.

"The doctor doesn't just think that Henry is *a* Fitz," Frankie finally said without emotion. "He thinks he is *the* Fitz—"

"The one and only Henry Robert Fitz, born to Thomas and Georgianna Fitz in 1862," the doctor interjected, "although I'm guessing you would be hard-pressed to recognise him as the scared sixteen year old boy who disappeared the day after his father's accident."

Louise gasped. Jared remained silent. Frankie continued to cling to her state of denial by trying to reason with the doctor.

"But… okay, wait," she stammered. "That would mean that he's been alive for over a hundred and forty years. Henry looks like he's barely over thirty. Never mind that it's not even physically possible for someone to live that long. The notion is just…well, it's absurd."

"You're right. It's not physically possible, no," the doctor corrected. "Metaphysically, on the other hand…." With that, Frankie felt anger kick in.

"Who are you?" she demanded. "What kind of respectable doctor would spout this kind of crap? This isn't science you're talking about, it's voodoo."

It was as though Louise and Jared were watching a tennis match with the way their eyes drifted back and forth between the doctor and Frankie. They were staring at one another in silent standoff.

Jared finally broke the silence.

"Actually, voodoo and science are really not so far apart from each other," he began softly, stepping toward Frankie as he spoke. "Both seek to better humanity as a whole and are equally as misunderstood. One system operates on blind faith, the other on proven hypothesis. Maybe this is the sort of situation that could benefit from a little of both."

Frankie waited impatiently to see where he might be going with this train of thought. She respected Jared, believed him to be an intelligent man of rational thought. Surely out of all of them, she felt that he would be capable of making sense out of something so nonsensical.

"Science has already offered us the proof that chocolate has a number of therapeutic properties. Like lowering high blood pressure, affecting the body's serotonin levels, and reducing the formation of free radicals that cause cellular damage. And that's just what *we know*. Over all my years of studying its chemical composition, I've read some studies which suggest that chocolate can prolong the life of lab rats by upwards of ten to fifteen years. That's not even to mention the effect it can have on intra-species attraction…"

Uh-oh, here comes the science talk. In her peripheral vision, Frankie could see Louise's eyes beginning to glaze.

"Yes," Von Hoffstatler picked up where Jared left off. "What you might refer to as charm, charisma or sex appeal, science calls pheromones. It's the chemical trigger designed to elicit a physical response among members of the same species. From the Maya texts I have managed to transcribe, many of them indicate that the beneficiary of the ritual is considered far more physically attractive, more charming and generally more appealing than their village counterparts. There are other markers as well, I've discovered. Most interesting is that it is said the individual has a distinctive…aroma about their person. It's spicy and earthy, not unlike—"

"Chocolate," Frankie finished for him weakly, sinking back down onto the chaise she had jumped up from when she felt her legs begin to give out from beneath her.

"I thought it was just my imagination..." she whispered in disbelief.

The doctor, on the contrary, seemed quite pleased with her revelation and was eager to learn more.

"So it's true? How splendid!" He clapped his hands together. "And what of his nature, or rather your response? Do you find yourself completely taken with him without really understanding why?"

Swallowing the lump that was forming in her throat, Frankie could only nod in reply as she thought about her unnatural lust for him. About her willingness to put complete trust in him without giving it a second thought. And her despondency at the notion of being away from him.

"Of the few documented reports of interactions with the man believed to be Henry Robert Fitz, all of them indicate that he is preternaturally charming. He would have had to be, to have been able to work his way up from a simple apprentice with no formal training at a patisserie in Bruges to owning a small chain of chocolate shops throughout mainland Europe in the course of a decade. Those shops in turn quickly developed into factories, and those factories have since become the basis of a massive chocolate empire far surpassing that of his father."

"But," Frankie sputtered. "It just...it *can't be* the same person. Perhaps it's a member of the Fitz family, a relative with a case of mistaken identity or personality disorder. It just doesn't make any sense. It's not possible... It can't be the same Henry."

But it certainly sounded like him. Frankie had progressed to the bargaining stage, attempting to use logic as a form of currency. Except that logic had no place in this situation, and it was beginning to feel as if she were fighting a losing battle.

Wordlessly, Von Hoffstatler walked back to the kitchen and pulled a sheaf of papers from his tattered valise. He rifled through them, muttering in a language that was not English, before finally producing a small square of paper yellowed with age. He handed it to Frankie.

"Is this the man you know as Henry Roberts?"

It was a faded photograph, done in those sepia tones that served as hallmark for early photography. It was a little blurry, its subject a young man barely more than a boy, but there was no way she could deny who it was. The intensity of the eyes, the angles in the face that she had so firmly committed to her memory, the hint of a smile she had come to rely on almost as much as breathing were unmistakeable. It was Henry.

Louise had come up behind her, too curious to sit still, and gasped.

"I think he was at my party," she said, her voice little more than a whisper. Frankie spun around to face her, almost knocking her down in the process.

"What? What do you mean? And why the hell is this the first I'm hearing of this?" *And why was I so full of jealous rage all of a sudden?* Louise could only shrug helplessly.

"I just remembered, seeing this photo. I think I ran into him when I was alone on the terrace, but I was so drunk I could barely speak. I can't even really recall what it was he'd said… I think he just wished me a happy birthday and said to give my father his regards. But he turned and disappeared before I could ask who he was. I mean, there were tons of people there from Daddy's company who all knew me and I have no idea who they were. I didn't really think anything of it at the time."

Her eyes widened.

"Oh my god," she grasped at her shoulder. "I – I *dreamt* about him! That night, in my dream, he was the one who told me where to find the Cocoa Creams."

Frankie recalled her own dream from that night, when he was the mysterious yet totally benign fantasy man in the grey top hat. She blushed as she recalled that he had morphed into Jared, of all people, a gem she wouldn't be sharing with Louise anytime *ever*. Besides, none of that mattered. That had all happened before the stranger had a name and a past and an apparent vendetta that seemed to include a permanent recurring role in her fantasies, starring as himself.

"Doctor," Frankie began cautiously, "these pheromones you were talking about. Are they powerful enough to make you... *dream*...constantly about that person?"

"Absolutely." The doctor responded without hesitation.

"Pheromones act on a very basic level, both behaviourally and physiologically," he explained. "They can tap into all of those subconscious desires or senses or intuition that you may not understand on a more conscious level. The Mayan texts refer to receivers of The Water as something beyond human; the ritual apparently elevates them to an almost god-like state of being. It's difficult to sort the facts from the legend and folklore but all accounts share a central, common theme. An unnatural allure, combined with the ability to use that as a tool to bend others to their will – whether they be male *or* female, and regardless of sexual orientation."

Frankie nodded, though it was the opposite of what she was hoping to hear.

"Would you say this power, this 'allure' as you call it, is almost similar to hypnotic suggestion?" Jared asked, tapping his finger against his bottom lip as he seemed to ponder a theory.

Von Hoffstatler tapped his nose at him as if he had just won a round of charades.

"Excellent analogy, my boy. Absolutely brilliant," he exclaimed. "But it can only suggest those things that the chocolate would itself."

"What do you mean?" Louise was struggling to follow, trying to grasp the many unbelievable revelations that were being bandied about on what was supposed to have been a quiet evening at home.

"Chocolate is capable of invoking a variety of feelings in human subjects, although each person has the potential to react differently," the doctor replied. "Desire, joy, obsession, mania, depression, longing… chocolate can both inspire and inhibit all of these basic human emotions. The Water of Life allows its recipient to tap into that emotional framework, both within themselves as well as in those around them, and manipulate those feelings to their advantage. It could be as a means of self-preservation, like a defense mechanism of sorts. Or it could be a circumstantial by-product of the ritual itself and not mean anything at all."

Frankie sat in silence looking at the floor, trying to sort

through everything Von Hoffstatler was saying, drawing parallels with the Henry she knew to this Henry Fitz immortal-like being and growing ever more despondent. It was becoming clear that she could no longer trust herself to know what was real and what wasn't. For all she knew, everything she was feeling for him could have been some ritual-related spell Henry had cast over her, some suggestion that he'd planted in her feeble little mind as a means to wield power over her in some plan that had yet to unfold.

Despair set in, unreasoning and relentless, not dissimilar to how she felt when she was away from Henry for any length of time. Perhaps she should have been more relieved to know that those feelings were not necessarily her own, that she was being manipulated by a man who was somehow beyond human and not necessarily experiencing a total personality transformation. But she could take no comfort in any of it. The emptiness had become more hollow and all encompassing than ever. It left her believing that what she'd been feeling, which had felt more natural and real than anything she had felt for anyone before including James, had been nothing more than an elaborate hoax. If so, what did that say about her?

There was only one thing she knew for certain: if she were to love Henry, it would be on her own terms. Not some hocus pocus that had been cast over her.

She managed to excuse herself, citing the busy days she had ahead of her. As she got ready for bed, she wondered how she would be able to sleep at all. But sleep was what she needed more than anything. Tomorrow she would have to start making stock for the shop or she would never be done in time for the grand opening that was a month away. Fortunately, making chocolate was the one thing she was able to do with her eyes shut, and possibly in her sleep as well. And, equally as fortunate, chocolate making also helped her to think. A good thing, considering that Frankie would need to do a lot of that over the next few days.

When she woke the next morning from a not entirely dreamless sleep, Frankie had no idea what her day would have in store. Given the events of the past few, she knew that she should be prepared for anything. Because it would seem that those simpler days of her knowing exactly what she would be doing at any given time were gone for good.

The way Frankie saw it was, if the man of her dreams could suddenly stumble into her shop out of nowhere and make her fall madly in love with him when he should have been dead for well over a hundred years, then anything could happen. *What's next, a unicorn? Is Santa Claus real as well? If so, perhaps we could come to some sort of arrangement. Exclusive distribution rights in chocolate stocking stuffers and the like.*

Frankie amazed even herself at times with the random thoughts that popped into her head without warning.

She crawled out of bed much later than usual and threw herself into the shower. No need for anything fancy; there had been no word from Henry about coming back, after all. Not that it mattered anymore, anyway. She put on whatever clothes she'd had strewn throughout the room that appeared vaguely clean and realised that she would need to do laundry at some point. She tied her hair back into a loose knot at the base of her neck and patted some clear lip balm onto bare lips. The weather was turning cool now that fall was fully in swing, and being this close to the ocean meant that the air was much harsher on delicate skin. Or so Louise was constantly telling her. And on the rare occasion, Frankie listened.

As she made her way downstairs, Louise strolled out of her bedroom wearing Jared's blue button down Oxford and gave her a sleepy wave.

"Come down to the shop later, yeah?" Frankie called back to her. There was no time for idle chit-chat. She needed to get going and start her prep work while she waited for the rest of her deliveries to arrive.

She was starting to panic, to believe that perhaps she had left it all a bit too late this time. But then she remembered some of the epic stunts of food craftery she had been able to pull off at the last minute when working the restaurant circuit, like that night she cranked out twenty individual chocolate soufflés inside of fifteen minutes with absolutely no notice whatsoever, and realised that she could totally do this. More than that: she could *rock* this. *Chocolate is kind of my thing,* she reassured herself.

Frankie drove into town quickly, but not as recklessly as she would have had she been late to meet up with Henry. She felt that familiar twinge of longing as she remembered some snippets of the dream she'd had, something about him feeding her roasted cocoa nibs in the cool darkness of the Amazonian rainforest. She couldn't recall all of it and its clarity was fuzzy, which kind of upset her. Whenever Frankie dreamt about Henry, she preferred it to be as clear and as memorable as possible. And then she realised how pathetic that sounded, which just depressed her all the more.

She had become painfully aware that the emptiness that she had always felt in Henry's absence was slowly, almost imperceptibly, subsiding as the days passed. In fact, she found herself looking for it that morning to confirm that it was even still there at all. It made her worry more when common sense indicated that really, it should have had the opposite effect. If Henry were to be gone for much longer, chances were good that she may not feel anything by the time he returned. Were he to decide to return at all. And were it simply an issue of the chocolate concoction's power, she knew that she should be pleased that it seemed to be wearing off. But the splinter of unease that drove itself straight through her heart down into the pit of her stomach said otherwise.

Did she not want to be let go of Henry's apparent spell, to be free to feel whatever it was that she felt for him without the unnatural interference suggested by the quack doctor the night before? That was soon replaced with a simpler but far bigger question: *What exactly should I feel?*

Frankie heard her mobile buzz somewhere inside her handbag with a new message alert. *Must be Lou,* she thought. She would have to wait. Frankie made her way to the shop after managing to find a prime parking spot. As she unlocked the door, she felt the mobile vibrate again, reminding her of the unread message.

"Keep your knickers on," Frankie muttered as she pushed the door open with her hip. She couldn't allow herself to get distracted today; there was far too much work to be done. She put down her bag and set to it.

Carefully, almost reverently, she laid her tools out onto the stainless steel worktable that dominated the kitchen area, and dug out what ingredients she had on hand. She adjusted heat settings on the tempering pots, got out the mortar and pestle to grind spices and wiped down the cool marble slab to work the chocolate into its final shape and texture. She quickly forgot about everything else.

Frankie pulled out the well-worn notebook she used for her recipes, its handwritten pages spattered with chocolate that looked more like stains of dried blood, and carefully thumbed through it, planning her day. Chocolate was precise, it had to be timed very carefully especially considering she was limited to what she had on hand. That first, vitally important delivery she had placed with Chadwick's would bring her the bulk of her supplies. And thankfully she did not have long to wait before it arrived; the delivery man was knocking on the door not long after she had arrived. Bar upon bar of glossy and gloriously rich dark chocolate, smooth milk chocolate that both instinct and experience told her would melt like butter, creamy white chocolate whose texture was not unlike that of soft velvet. Frankie sighed in pleasure and a twinge of relief.

This was where she belonged.

Not caught up in some frenzy of irrational lust or embroiled in some impossible romance. But here, where her heart and mind were safe with the delicious simplicity that she had only ever found in chocolate. The only thing that mattered was the chocolate at hand, and she was determined to give herself over to it freely.

Once she had the order unpacked was when the real work began, which Frankie threw herself into it with complete abandon. She had just finished the rose and violet cream fondants and was up to her elbows in the remaining sugar paste, which she was planning to use to wrap the liquor-soaked cherries she had begun preparing last week before hand-dipping the lot of them into a perfectly tempered pot of that gorgeous dark chocolate, when her mobile began to ring. Rather predictably, it was Louise.

"Shit – sorry I didn't get back to you. I've kind of been on a roll here," Frankie said by way of greeting. There was a short pause on the other end.

"What? What are you on about?" Louise sounded confused.

"Your text. Didn't you text me earlier?"

"Um no, wasn't me. I just got up to say goodbye to Jared and the Professor. They're going round the lab to examine the chocolate again and mentioned something about control samples, although I'm not sure there can be much more to tell us after last night's freakshow. Seriously, that Dr. Von Hoffstatler is one major whackj—"

Frankie was only half-listening as her heart had begun to hammer in her chest. Who was it who had texted, if not Louise? Was it James maybe, or possibly even... Henry?

Louise was prattling on, unaware of the silence st the other end, something about how she would be coming in later to do some taste-testing of her own. Frankie cut the conversation short, making up an excuse that the chocolate was about to burn. It was a risky lie that should have set off some warning bells, since Louise knew well enough to know that Frankie would never have picked up the phone if there were a danger of anything burning. But she seemed to buy it, and let her go without comment.

With shaking hands, Frankie clicked over on the icon that told her she had a new text message waiting. The number was unknown, but she knew exactly who it was.

My dearest Frankie,

There is so much I wish I could tell you, so many things you deserve to know. But it must wait until the time is right. I promise you, however, that it will be very soon.

Ever yours, Henry.

P.S. If you are still researching suppliers, might I suggest you look up Defleur of Switzerland?

Frankie smiled in spite of herself. *He texts just like he's writing a letter.* Of course, just as Frankie thought things between them couldn't possibly get any more cryptic or weird, it made complete sense that she would receive something like this. At least he was consistent. She supposed that for that, she should be grateful. But this was going to do nothing for her productivity.

What is it with men, regardless of age or era they happen to be from, that they can never just come out and say what they mean? They were so quick to accuse women of playing games when they themselves were just as guilty, she fretted. And why did she feel that post script was fraught with hidden meaning?

The name Defleur. Was there a reason it should sound so oddly familiar? She felt it must have meant something, something she already knew but had long forgotten due to recent, taller and blonder interests.   And then, for the second time that day, she felt like she'd been run through with an icepick. Although it wasn't unease that shot through her.

No, this time it was far worse than that.

She raced to where she had left her laptop folded shut, fingers fumbling over the keyboard as she hastily typed in her password. She managed to get it wrong twice. It felt like forever as the computer started to load its files, and another lifetime for the internet browser to come up.

She logged into her webmail account and waited again for what seemed an eternity until she was able to scroll down through her recent emails. Fortunately, that part didn't take as long. If you didn't count all of the spam that the filter didn't catch, Frankie generally didn't receive a lot of email. In fact, there was really only one person she communicated with in that medium. And it was his last email that she sat reading through before finding what it was she'd been looking for, but desperately hoped would not be there. No such luck.

There it was, staring her in the face.

Defleur is one of WBM's oldest and richest clients... His main interest is in the food industry, specifically confections – candy, chocolates, sweets and stuff.

There really is no such thing as coincidence.

She sank back into her new ergonomically designed desk chair, trying to catch her breath. She felt as though the wind had been knocked out of her. And in a way, it kind of had.

Was it not enough that Henry could be some sort of... immortal being, kept alive by a ritual she would never really understand? Or was Fate really so cruel as to allow him to ferret her fiancé off to some foreign land, in this case Switzerland, keeping him so busy and distracted that he would have no time for anything else so Henry could come here to seduce Frankie to somehow get to Chadwick's? Or has her mother been right all along, that the day has come where her vivid imagination has finally gone too far and she was about to experience a psychotic break from which she might never recover? *After all, am I not sitting here having a conversation with myself?*

For all Frankie knew, she could have been talking out loud. It wouldn't have been the first time. Taking a deep breath, she tried to reign in the parade of paranoid thoughts that threatened her sanity and made a solid effort to regroup. To try to look at the situation from a place of reason and logic, while knowing that neither applied.

From Louise and her obsession with the Cocoa Creams, to James disappearing off the face of the earth after going to work for this Defleur person, then to Henry and how strongly Frankie felt for him despite how wrong she knew it was and finally now to who or what he appeared to be. There was one common thread: Henry. He was the link that tied all of these seemingly unrelated threads together, motivated by… By what exactly? Resentment? Revenge?

None of it did anything to quell Frankie's desire for him. It would have been convenient for her to simply dismiss it as a side effect of the Water of Life ritual, as Von Hoffstatler had asserted. And for the time being, that was exactly what she planning to do. However, it appeared that there was yet more research ahead.

She had to wait for the batch of cherry cordials to set before she could start dipping them and she'd finished all the truffles she could make for the moment, she told herself, so surely she had earned a quick Internet break.

Obviously, at least to Frankie, Henry mentioned the Defleur name for a reason. Perhaps it was a clue. She typed it into Google. This time, she had far more luck than when she had tried to look up anything regarding Henry. Until she found out way more than she'd bargained for. In fact, there was so much that, being someone there considered herself an up and coming chocolatier and all round know-it-all, Frankie was embarrassed she hadn't recognised the name when James had first mentioned it to her. She attempted to comfort herself with the fact that she was aware of the plethora of Swiss and Belgian brands of chocolate that the company owned, and that the Defleur name was usually at the bottom in fine print and therefore very easy to miss.

A click on the company's main website told her what she had already begun to suspect: Defleur SA was the largest confectionary corporation in Europe, and was working rapidly toward world domination in the category.

How could something like this have escaped her

attention? *Oh right,* she answered herself, *because sometimes I have my head so far up my own self-important ass that I can't see anything beyond it.* Or, more recently, she had been more preoccupied by the attentions of a certain tall and incredibly charming distraction when she should have been working on her business.

She wondered how long it was going to take before she let that go.

Frankie had already felt like she was messing things up before she even got started. If her mother were there, she knew exactly what she would say and how it would come out. *"Typical,"* she would sniff indifferently, while inspecting her perfectly manicured nails. She was constantly berating Frankie for the state of her own hands. Her palms seemed to be permanently stained with cocoa powder regardless of how hard she scrubbed them, and there were often times when her nails looked like she was an avid gardener who thought that gloves were for sissies.

But your mother isn't here, Frankie reminded herself, *and fucking this up is* not *an option.*

Shaking herself free from the memories of her mother's near-constant disapproval before their teeth had the chance to sink in, she soldiered on through the Defleur company website. She clicked on the link in the navigation bar that said *News,* which seemed the most logical place to start. And judging from the headline that greeted her, Frankie was relieved that finally her instincts were dead on. It read:

Defleur SA makes historic first purchase across the Channel

For immediate release: The name Defleur has long been *synonymous with luxury chocolates and confections that have been*

240

enjoyed throughout mainland Europe for almost a century. Finally, the United Kingdom will get its first taste of what Defleur has to offer. The majority share purchase of Tompkins Toffees PLC was completed last week, thanks in large part to the diligence and perseverance of one Mr. James Harris, a broker agent with UK-based estate firm Wright, Blake and Massey Commercial PLC—

She couldn't read anymore. She didn't have to. Almost everything that Frankie needed to know was contained in that short opening paragraph. It only served to cement her earlier, if perhaps somewhat delusional, suspicion of a connection between Henry and the Defleur company. Perhaps not to the full-blown conspiracy she had initially imagined it to be, but it established a firm relationship nonetheless. *Why else would he have brought it to her attention in his message if not to serve as some kind of hint*, Frankie thought. *Especially after all his 'there's so much I want to tell you' crap.*

Answers? She'd found a few. Conjecture? Yes, that most certainly was the order of the day. And yet, as always, she was left with still more questions. Most of them beginning with *why*. Why James? Why her? Why now? *Why? Why? Why???* When it came to Henry, however, Frankie was quickly learning that it seemed like questions were the rule rather than the exception.

She sighed heavily. It was beginning to look like God enjoyed a cruel joke after all.

Frankie shut down her laptop and went back to her chocolate. She figured that since it was the only thing left that made any sense anymore, she might as well stick with it. As she began to dip the rose creams, however, her mind began to wander. There seemed to be no stopping it. This time, however, it took a detour from its usual destination. This time, it wandered to James.

With as little as she knew about Henry, Frankie realised that the same could be said about her fiancé as well. They had only just met and been dating for about a fortnight before she had moved into his flat, and from there it only took another few short months for him to pop The Question. There hadn't been a mention of an actual wedding or marriage since. That ring had been sitting idly on her finger for the past few months. Until recently, when she had taken it off in fear of damaging it while she worked on getting the shop in order. Or so she would continue to tell herself until she actually believed it.

She moved on absentmindedly to dip the cherry cordials as she racked her brain to recall the last conversation, those last moments she had spent with James. To her shame, she found that she could not. Her every thought had been entirely consumed by Henry. Despite repeated attempts to focus on memories of James, her mind was completely dominated with thoughts of Henry Roberts.

Or rather, Henry Fitz, as she supposed she should call him. Regardless of who he was or wasn't, Henry had eclipsed almost everything in her life.

Not good. Shaking her head once again to bring herself back to reality, she discovered that she had finished the cordials and a fair amount of chocolate remained. Another indication that she wasn't working in the right frame of mind; it was quite unlike Frankie to overestimate the amount of chocolate she needed for dipping. She decided that, rather than leave it to cool and reheat for another day, she would smooth what was left over the marble slab and follow with a liberal coating of some almonds she had toasted earlier to flavour a truffle filling. The makings of chocolate bark, ever the crowd-pleaser. *Christ only knows why,* she thought, having never much cared for it herself. In the grand scheme of everything else chocolate, she had always found it rather bland and boring, not unlike the bark of a tree after which it had been named.

Maybe that was what made it so unappealing, she thought.

Perhaps if she were to come up with something with a little more…substance to it, so to speak, then she wouldn't despise it so much. She searched round the kitchen for inspiration, a new name and some other ingredients she could add to enhance the texture, and quickly discovered both at once. As she reached for the bag of pistachios that had arrived conveniently shelled, her gaze happened to fall upon an empty crisp packet Louise had left behind from a previous visit. *Slob*, Frankie thought as she reached to throw it in the bin.

And then it hit her.

She reached for her palette knife and, working fast, began to carve and shape the rapidly cooling chocolate bark into little rounds that resembled potato crisps. Inspiration can truly come in almost any form, she thought triumphantly as she set them aside to dry and set. She would have to think up some clever way to package her little chocolate crisps later.

As for what little was left of the dark chocolate, she decided that it would make an excellent dip for that bit of peel she had candied earlier, taken from the fruit she'd used to flavour fondant for fruit creams. She left nothing to waste, a character trait that she had often attributed to her Scottish heritage. She felt the more delicate flavours of lemon and orange fondants were better suited to the milk and white chocolate she had used to cover them. But once caramelized in sugar, the fruit peels were bold enough to hold their own against the dark chocolate.

As an analogy for her current situation, it was not lost on her.

Henry was very much like the dark chocolate she was working with. Addictive, intoxicating, and impossibly rich; strong but ever so slightly bitter, and never failing to leave her wanting more regardless of whether or not it was any good for her. Time would reveal which of the flavours she would turn out to be, whether she were more fruit cream than peel. With a sigh, she suspected that despite all her posturing, that deep down she was more of a cream than she'd care to admit. She wished she were more like the peel, with its resilient caramel-encrusted shell, able to withstand most anything it came into contact with.

So absorbed was Frankie in the chocolate she had been creating, her senses overwhelmed by its aroma and smooth texture, that she hadn't heard the knocking at the door. Until it came again, sharper and more insistent, almost rattling the window in its pane.

I have to get an electronic doorbell, she thought as she emerged from the back room. She was startled to see that it was almost nightfall. The shop's interior was dark, and Frankie could not make out through the drawn shade who it was who had been knocking so repeatedly. But there was really only one person it could have been. She prepared herself to give Louise a tongue-lashing about minding her windows, but the words quickly became caught in her throat once she'd opened up the door.

She had to grasp the doorframe to keep from reeling in shock.

Her fiancé James was standing in front of her, looking slightly dishevelled as he often did in the only suit he owned, with Henry right behind him.

TWELVE

September 26th

"James?"

It was the only thing Frankie was capable of sputtering after taking a long moment to determine that he was actually there and not an elaborate hallucination. He shifted uncomfortably, refusing to look directly at Frankie, choosing instead to look anywhere but. At his shoes that were in desperate need of a good polish, at the cobbled stone of the street, then past her into the shop which had been faintly illuminated from the glow of the streetlamp outside the door that had just blinked into life.

"All right, Frankie," he said at last, his eyes finally resting on hers for a brief moment before continuing to roam.

"Shop looks good," he added, nodding past her as he hunched his shoulders to stuff his hands deeper into his pockets and examine his shoes.

Frankie continued to stare at him in disbelief as she felt her initial shock give way, replaced by an anger that began to burn. Slowly at first, but then soon spreading like a poisonous venom through her veins. From the corner of her eye she saw that Henry shot James a disdainful look, snorting in what sounded a bit like disgust.

"All right?" she finally managed to choke out. "*All right?* After weeks with no call, no email, *nothing,* and *that's* the best you can do? *'All right, Frankie'?*"

She was aware that her voice was rising dangerously, that very soon she would be at risk of causing an all-out public scene. But Frankie could not keep her rage held in any longer, so out it came.

"All of your blasé bullshit might have been charming once upon a time, James, but it's not going to save your ass now."

She noticed a couple that were walking arm in arm, likely on their way to dinner, had slowed down and were casting worried glances in their direction. Henry saw them as well.

"Well, I'm certain that the two of you have a lot to discuss," he said quickly, "so perhaps you should take this inside. I should be on my way—" Frankie raised a hand to cut him off abruptly; she was having none of it.

"Oh Henry, please. What's the rush? I'm sure there are plenty of things we can *all* find to discuss," she shot back as she grabbed each of them by an arm and yanked them inside, slamming the door closed behind them before either one could protest. *I might be fairly slight,* she seethed, *but do not underestimate the power and fury of a pissed off woman.*

The three of them stood in the silence of the darkened interior of the shop. Henry looked somewhere between bewildered and slightly awed; James just looked frightened. He had been on the receiving end of Frankie's temper many times before, so he knew a bit of what was coming.

"Why don't I wait back here while the two of you sort things out?" Henry suggested quietly, already moving in the direction of the lighted kitchen.

"Don't sample any of the merchandise, Henry," Frankie called after him, her voice dripping acid. "Oh wait. Guess we don't need to worry about that, now, do we?"

She saw Henry pause, almost turning back round to face her before he thought better of it. Although his face was obscured in shadow, she could have sworn that she saw him pale a little. She wasn't ashamed to admit that the thought of his discomfort pleased her.

"So," she turned back to James who was continuing to fidget in front of her. Frankie took a deep breath in an attempt to calm herself.

They had been there before, though nowhere near this extent, and she knew that if she were to let her temper get the better of her he would completely shut down as he had so many times before when they'd argued. It was something of a pattern of theirs. Frankie almost found it funny that she was remembering something so insignificant in that moment. Some things seemed so obvious in hindsight. *No*, she thought, *I must not scream and rant and throw things this time*. She knew that it would accomplish nothing. What Frankie needed were answers, answers to at least some of the myriad of questions that had been brewing over the past couple of days. And to the one big question that showed up today and was standing in her shop kitchen.

Acutely aware of Henry's presence as he waited his turn, she decided to put her best face forward. Not to impress him, mind, but because she had a few questions for him that would be in need answering as well.

247

"Now," she began again, slowly and less angrily as she forced herself to be pleasant through gritted teeth. "Would you care to explain why I haven't heard a peep out of you till today?"

The look James gave her made Frankie feel like a beleaguered parent reprimanding a badly behaved toddler who was convinced they had done nothing wrong. It was all she could do not to slap that sullen self-involved pout right off his face. *Calm down*, she reminded herself. *Just breathe and we can get through this without drawing blood. Maybe.*

After another awkward, drawn-out pause and yet more scowling, James spoke at last.

"It's not what you think," he said, refusing again to make eye contact, "and you won't even believe me if I tell you what really happened. I just went there to work, nothing more, and then... and then it all just went to shit from there—" He broke off as his knees appeared to give out fleetingly, and he started swaying a little before righting himself.

It happened so quickly that Frankie barely had time to react, let alone make a move to help him. It was only then that he was able to look her in the eye at last, and she could see why he'd avoided it for so long. She was close enough in the near-darkness of the shop to see that they were rimmed red from either complete exhaustion or tears. Or both.

She felt her resolve weaken as her hand reached out to comfort him out of habit. She quickly snatched it back.

"Why don't you talk me through it then, eh?" she gestured for him to take a seat on one of the stools at what would soon be the chocolate bar, suddenly wishing that they were sitting down at a real bar. Perhaps in a cozy pub somewhere with a pint and some shots.

A shot or five of something may not be a bad thing right about now, she thought to herself as she eased onto the stool next to him.

In the muted light that streamed in from the kitchen in the back, she waited in silence for James to collect himself. He was trembling weakly as he sat, holding his head in his hands, before he straightened up and began to tell Frankie what had happened in Switzerland.

He started at the very beginning, with his first impressions of the strange cubes of concrete, glass and steel that formed the Swiss mountain retreat of the eccentric European aristocrat he had been sent to work for. He went on to describe, in great detail, the creepy butler who had led him through the stark white maze of hallways with their identical mahogany doors and remembered how sharply it all seemed to contrast with the warmth of the library.

He was red-faced when he admitted to the initial man-crush he'd had on Defleur, but Frankie had to give him credit for manning up enough to tell the whole story regardless of what light it painted him in.

James continued, to the point where he was almost raving like a lunatic over how his mobile wouldn't receive reception regardless of where he was in the complex and how frustrating it was that all of the emails he was trying to send out – to Frankie, to his brother, even to his mum and dad – had gone unanswered. How he had become convinced that he was being held prisoner under the façade of his host's genteel hospitality, and that he was not alone in the house. He told her about the unnerving feeling he was not able to shake of being watched, and how he'd even begun having nightmares of strange women stealing into his locked room at night to hover over him. Well, perhaps nightmare wasn't the right word for it, judging from how awkward Frankie thought he looked in telling her. There was definitely more to those dreams than he was letting on.

Her suspicions were confirmed when he stopped abruptly just as he came to the part about meeting his fellow houseguests on the ski hill, his description of them sounding more like something you might read in a dirty men's magazine than real life. Frankie knew then what direction this story was going to take, and began to understand why he was having such a difficult time facing her.

"It's all right, James. Go on," she urged as gently as she could manage, reminding herself that she wasn't entirely innocent in this situation.

His head hung low, and she knew it was going to be bad.

She tried to prepare herself for it mentally: *don't scream, don't punch, don't kick, and just keep breathing.* And though he was kind enough to spare her the details, James admitted to being intimate with those women. Both of them. At once.

"I'm so sorry," he whispered, so quiet that she could scarcely hear it.

He raised his head to look at her again, his eyes heavy with shame. Frankie could not return his look. She was concentrating on keeping herself from shaking uncontrollably. With a strength of will Frankie wasn't even aware she possessed, she managed not to slap him. Or scream, or cry, or any other reaction she would normally have had under such circumstances. She simply sat there with him, waiting for his story to continue.

"I know that this is going to sound like such total shit,' James said after a long minute, "but there were times when it honestly felt like I was under some sort of spell or something."

It was almost unnerving how calm Frankie had become. She was fairly sure that it must have been freaking James out as well; he kept looking at her warily and flinching at every tiny shift she made in her seat. Admittedly, a small part of her enjoyed that.

After several minutes of uncomfortable silence, once James was reasonably sure that Frankie wasn't going to completely flip out and start choking him, he continued. She only became tense when he got to the part where Defleur had come home unexpectedly and caught him, quite literally, with his pants down. And it wasn't necessarily because of that detail, but something that had very nearly escaped her attention.

"Wait, what was that again?" Frankie could feel the tiny hairs on the back of her neck begin to bristle with anticipation. James was confused.

"What, the part where I was trying to email my brother? I'm sorry, it was just inst—"

"No, no, not that," she waved her hand impatiently. "What did Defleur say?"

"Oh, that I didn't deserve you? I mean, he *is* right, I really—"

But Frankie had stopped listening, her mind instead wandering back to that last night that she had seen Henry before he had shown up on her shop's doorstep with her missing fiancé in tow. To the night that Henry had kissed her; well, when they kissed each other until she could no longer breathe. Something he had said only moments before that.

It doesn't seem like your fiancé is worthy of you.

Frankie froze, but knew enough what question she needed to ask next. Although she had a sinking feeling that she already knew what the answer might be.

"But.. How would this Defleur bloke know anything about me?"

"I… I'm not sure what you mean?" James was looking at her like she had three heads, utterly amazed at how calmly she had been taking this. When he realised that she was waiting for him to elaborate, he continued.

"Well, I'd told him quite a lot about you when I first got there," he said. The hammering of her heart began to slow, hopeful. *Maybe there is such thing as coincidence after all.*

"But beyond that, you obviously know him. He's standing in your kitchen right now."

Frankie's stomach jumped at the same time her heart threatened to pound its way out of her chest.

"It's all right, Frankie," James was looking at her sympathetically. Or perhaps it was more empathy. "He already told me that he had been here. With you."

It was clear that James had taken her reaction to be guilt rather than for what it truly was. A combination of so many emotions, Frankie was powerless to pick just one. He reached over tentatively to take her hand.

"Maybe we've both done things we're not so proud of, eh?" he half-smiled, pleased that she had not flinched away from him. Frankie barely realised that he was touching her at all while he continued. "I'm just kind of relieved that you don't think I'm a total lunatic. That you believe me."

And he was right; she did believe him. Had Frankie not experienced all that had transpired in the past few days, there would have been no chance of that. It all seemed so fantastic, who in their right mind would believe any of it? But because she had gone through and discovered so much herself, it left her with no choice but to take him at his word.

The most curious of all, Frankie felt, was that she was actually more angry with Henry whom she barely knew than with James who had been her friend and lover for months. Not to say that she was thrilled at the prospect of being cheated on, and so repeatedly, but at least James was being honest with her about it. It was becoming apparent that Henry had done nothing but lie from the moment he tapped on Frankie's shop door and walked into her life. And there he stood in her kitchen, having come full circle, waiting for the chance to tell his side of this sordid tale.

How much of it will be true, she wondered. *And how will I even know the difference?*

Frankie was content to make him wait. She needed time to absorb what she had just been told, and at that moment she was far too pissed off for words. Well...civilized words, anyway. And it was James who sitting in front of her, anxiously awaiting his fate. Their fate. He had begun to drum his fingers on the top of the glass cabinet in front of him, a nervous habit he knew Frankie despised. One look from her was enough to silence him.

Guilt really was a powerful weapon.

"So what happens now?" He had grown tired of waiting.

The fear was written plainly on his face, for which Frankie couldn't really blame him. Their fights had always been explosive: epic screaming battles that seemed to wage on for hours and, if victory was based on the use of profanity and volume alone, historically James had always come out on the losing end. So, having him look at her as if she were a ticking time bomb was exactly the sort of the reaction Frankie would expect from him. What he failed to realise, as harsh as it sounded, was that his actions no longer mattered to her. As ridiculous as Frankie felt admitting it, Henry was the only thing that mattered. He had begun to matter as soon as he helped paint the walls of the room she was standing in, which was only other thing that meant anything to her.

It made all of Henry's betrayal and subterfuge that much more devastating.

Of course, she would never admit all of this to James. Although she was often known for being spiteful and vindictive, Frankie could never be that deliberately cruel. She had to figure out her next move.

"I'm guessing that the engagement is off and you'll be giving back my ring," James persisted when her silence continued. He glanced at her hand sadly, a look that was followed by a quick double-take. "Oy, speaking of ring, where is it anyway?"

It was enough to snap Frankie back into the moment as she realised that the ring was still sitting in its box in her room back at Louise's house. The same place it had sat since Henry had come along.

"I've been leaving it at home for safe-keeping. Didn't want it to get damaged, what with all the renovations," she lied smoothly, immediately backing it up with the sort of caustic remark she'd become famous for. "What's your hurry? Someone else you're planning on giving it to instead?"

Deflection was something that came so naturally to her, though she felt like a bitch saying it. *You can't fight who you are.* James flinched and then nodded in understanding, making Frankie feel that much worse.

"Yeah, I deserved that, I guess," he agreed, before adding with a small smirk. "But at least I know you won't be left out in the cold."

Apparently James had grown a pair when he was in captivity. Frankie was impressed, almost a little turned on by it. Almost.

"How do you mean?" she asked defensively, knowing full well what he was inferring. James smirked again.

"When I said before that Henry told me he was here, I mean he told me *everything*." He paused, letting the full implication of his words hang between them.

Frankie flashed back to that last night she'd had with Henry. *Could Henry have really told him everything, or was he just bluffing?*

"You never finished your story," she replied drily, deciding not to take his bait. "Why don't you tell me what Defleur – I mean, Henry – said after he caught you with those two women?"

It was almost a subject change, while still managing to remain very much on point. When in doubt, deflect. James got the message, having been down that road before with her on more than one occasion.

"Well, I'll admit it, I thought I was done for when he came in and found us like that," James raked a hand through his hair before continuing with his story. "But he'd completely calmed down by the time he got to my room. Actually apologized for not warning me beforehand about his 'permanent houseguests', he called them. Then he started asking some weird shit like what they had offered me to drink, what the taste of it was.

He only seemed angry because of the chocolate drink we'd been drinking almost the whole time we were... together. But he wasn't really mad at me; it was more Marta and Shaye. I tried to defend them. Well, Shaye mostly, because that Marta is one evil bitch. He pretty much confirmed that for me, and agreed that Shaye was as much a victim as I was. Not quite sure what he meant by that, though."

Frankie tried to swallow the jealousy she felt building up inside her over Henry's two houseguests. Not because of James and his indiscretions with them, but because they lived in such close quarters with Henry and had done for Christ only knows how many years. And then she realised that James was still talking.

"He apologized again for what he'd said about not

256

deserving you, that he just said because he was angry. But I had to agree with him, because he was right. I've always known it, that one day you would come to your senses and leave me for someone better. He said that there was more to it than that, that there was something of a confession he needed to make.

And then he told me that he had come here to Brighton on business, and he'd met you quite by accident as part of some local investment program he'd become involved with at one of the banks here. Thought that was weird, because why would he come to Brighton of all places to do it? But then I figured maybe it was just something all big business-types did.

He admitted that he'd become quite close to you, that he knew how wrong it was because he'd recognised you immediately from that photo I showed him. He then told me that he'd taken you to dinner, and that at first it was totally to talk shop. He told me about the kiss and how after that he had to leave because he didn't want to put you in any more of an awkward position than he had already, because you had made it clear to him that you were engaged. Thanks for that, by the way. I know most women would be like 'what fiancé?' if a bloke like that gave them the time of day—" Once again Frankie found herself tuning him out, drowning in her own thoughts rather than listening to what James was telling her.

How dare Henry turn this around on me? If what James was saying was true, and Henry was being more conscientious than cunning when he had left her that night, it was going to make it that much harder for her to lay into him the way she planned to once she'd finished with James. *Damn him*, she cursed under her breath.

She needed to wrap this up before she softened any

further.

"James," she began haltingly, surprised that her eyes were tearing up as the impact of what she was about to do hit her. Frankie wasn't sure what would be considered proper etiquette when ending an engagement, but tears seemed appropriate.

"You've been through a lot, that much is obvious. And thank you for being honest with me, even as you tried to spare my feelings. I just want you to know that whatever happened in Switzerland... well, I don't hate you for it. It wouldn't be fair for me to blast you for cheating when I could be painted with the same brush."

James was standing still, having braced himself for whatever was coming, with mouth gaping. He seemed relieved that he would get to leave without a broken nose or worse. Frankie had to stifle her laughter.

"F-F-Frankie," he stammered. "I – I don't know what to say. You're taking this ...umm, really rather well. Looks like having your own business has really brought out the best in you."

Frankie was surprised by James's observation, and supposed it was true to a point. A lot had happened to her, both professionally and personally, while he had been gone.

"So, uhh...do you think we could be friends?" James was asking her.

"Yeah of course, James. We're still friends," Frankie replied without hesitation. "And don't worry, I'll get you your ring back as soon as I can."

And in an even more surprising and evolved move, she stepped forward and put her arms around James. She saw his eyes widen at first, then squeeze tightly shut as she grew closer. His shoulders stiffened as she hugged him, as though he was thinking *oh shit, now I'm fucking dead* and trying to brace himself against the blow.

That time, Frankie couldn't contain her laughter.

"Don't worry," she choked out in a fit of giggles, "I'm not planning on hurting you."

She had stepped back, but her arms remained around his shoulders. She could feel them slowly relax and then start to shake as he laughed along with her. Together, they laughed until tears started rolling down their cheeks.

"God Frankie…" James sighed as she walked with him toward the front of the shop. "You really are amazing." He paused as she reached to open the door for him.

"Go easy on him, eh?" He jerked his head meaningfully in the direction of the kitchen. "He's really not such a bad bloke. And if *anyone* deserves you, in spite of everything and all, my money's definitely on him."

He had both of Frankie's hands in his, looking her straight in the eye with earnest for the first time that evening. It was quite touching, she thought, or at least it might have been had she not been so murderously angry at Henry. James and his impassioned plea on his behalf only served to further remind her of the depth of his betrayal. She didn't respond, only half-nodded in acknowledgement as she unlocked the door and patted James gently on the back as she said goodbye to her now-former fiancé.

Closing it behind him, she leaned against the door to catch her breath and collect herself. Breaking up with James, although she knew without question that it had been the right thing to do, had taken a lot out of Frankie emotionally. But she also knew it was a cakewalk compared to the conversation she was about to have with Henry.

Knees shaking, not so much from fear and nerves as it was from rage, she marched toward the kitchen.

Henry was standing in its doorway, the light illuminating him from behind like an angel who had been sent from heaven just for her. *Or some other crap you'd read in a romance novel,* she thought bitterly, *since that's what I've been reduced to.* As much as she was loathe to admit it, that was exactly how she had come to see him. As her angel. But recent revelations, from Dr. Von Hoffstatler and from James, had suggested that maybe Henry wasn't quite so angelic after all. Perhaps the complete opposite. In fact, she was starting to believe that he might have more in common with that less celestial, far more southernly address.

Guess I'm about to find out either way, she thought as she took a deep breath and stepped forward to face him.

THIRTEEN

September 26th

Frankie stood facing Henry. Neither one of them seemed capable of making the first move. Not him, still standing in the lighted doorway of the shop's kitchen. Not her, as she stood in the middle of the shop with her thoughts reeling, trying to figure out where to even begin with all of it.

There had to be a better starting point than her gut reaction response, which would mean a lot of shrieking and clawing.

Henry was first to break the deadlock.

"Frankie," he began in earnest as he moved toward her, hands reaching out imploringly. "I'm not sure where to start with this except to say that I am truly sorry. For everything. But if you would just give me an opportunity to explain, then perhaps w—"

"Oh I see, fine. You're sorry, are you?" she countered coldly, arms folded over her chest in an effort to keep herself from shaking as she continued. "And what is it that you're sorry for, exactly?"

Henry had never experienced this side of Frankie before. Up until then, there was no reason for him to have. It was enough to stop him cold.

"I'm not sure what you mean?" He was confused, not unlike James had been, which only made Frankie all the more angry since he was the only one of the three of them who could explain exactly what was going on.

"Well," she began, forcing her voice to remain even. "Let's see... where should I start? Are you saying that *you're sorry* for basically holding James hostage in Switzerland? Or is it that you're just sorry that you *left him alone with those*...women? I suppose that it's possible you might be sorry for pretending to be someone *you're not*. Or no, wait, I've got it! You're sorry for *lying to me about absolutely fucking everything*."

Frankie had lost any semblance of composure by that point, screeching with rage by the time she had finished what needed to be said. It was by no means pretty, and definitely not one of her finer moments. It had stunned Henry into a shocked silence, confounded as to what to do next.

He sank to the floor, where he sat holding his head in his hands, not unlike James had done earlier.

In the dim light Frankie thought that she could see his massive shoulders heaving. *Oh no*, she thought, heart lurching as she inched closer. He looked up as she drew near, and she was relieved to see that his face was not damp from tears. *At least I didn't make him cry. Though that might make me want him less...*

"If you would *please* let me *try to explain*," Henry whispered, looking up at Frankie in what she took to be weary defeat, "I promise, I'll tell you everything. No more secrets, no more lies. I'm done with that now."

He looked so vulnerable, completely at odds with his usual cocky demeanour. He motioned for her to sit down with him on the floor, but somehow she resisted. *Shocking that*, she thought. It seemed implausible that anyone would be able to resist him at all. Pride, especially when wounded, can be a stubborn and unmovable force.

"Frankie, please, won't you sit with me? Don't make me beg," he whispered hoarsely, probably having no idea how ridiculously sexy it sounded to her. And the prospect of having him beg made Frankie feel slightly light-headed.

No Frankie. Keep it together, she urged herself silently.

Henry continued when she didn't respond. When she was *unable* to respond.

"I have no problem doing that, begging, I mean. But I fear I may only have enough energy left to tell you what you deserve to know." His eyes had not moved from hers.

She felt her throat go dry, could hear herself swallow in what sounded like more of a gulp for air. But for the most part, she was amazed at how well she was doing. She could not allow herself to get distracted by something as mundane as how perfectly the fabric of his jacket stretched over the curve of his shoulders as he sat beneath her.

He sighed heavily then with such genuine anguish it was almost her undoing.

Frankie chewed on her lip in indecision. It would be so easy to give in, she knew that; to just sit down and forgive him for whatever it was that he was about to say. But she couldn't. She had always been the strong one, unwilling to be anyone's doormat or faithful puppy, so why should that change now just for him? *Regardless of how glorious his hair looks from this angle.*

When he saw that Frankie was refusing him, he slowly got to his feet. Wiping one hand over his eyes, he leaned wearily against the wall behind him looking completely drained. Still ridiculously handsome, even with the heavy bags that clung just below his dark blue eyes.

"I don't even know where to begin," he said simply, shaking his head and throwing his hands up in a gesture of defeat.

"Why don't you start with who you are?" Frankie suggested. "I mean, who you *really* are?"

Henry regarded her carefully, his face set in his now-familiar mask of composure. It gave her chills, and not the good kind, how quickly he seemed to switch back and forth from total rage or abject misery to behaving as if nothing had even happened at all. It made her wonder if there were anything about him that was real, or ever had been. The silence hung between them like a thick cloud, with neither one willing to budge any more than they'd already felt they had. It seemed that they were at an impasse.

And then something changed. Frankie saw his carefully crafted façade begin to crumble.

She watched fascinated, as the veneer of arrogant confidence Henry hid behind began to crack, and what lay beneath was at once beautiful and terrifying. Terrifying in that he looked so frightened and alone, with the painful transgressions of his life written on his face for the world to see. Beautiful, because it was finally real.

Frankie decided it was time to end the standoff.

"Telling me who you are would be as good a place to start as any," she urged, deliberately softening her tone to as gentle as it had been that evening. "Are you Henry Roberts, international confectionary consultant and dashing man-about-town? Or are you the Comte Alfonse Defleur, the eccentric aristocrat whose family has been in the business for centuries? Or… someone else entirely?"

She was trying to help, to make this easier on him, but the look on his face said that her encouragement was having the opposite effect. He was at odds with himself; Frankie could almost see the inner battle raging inside his head. When he spoke, his voice was laced with regret.

"I want to tell you everything, so badly… I really do," he said quietly. "But at the same time I'm absolutely terrified that you won't believe me, that you'll tell me to leave and that you never want to see me again. Or worse than that: you do believe me but you still want nothing more to do with me because of it. Either way, I lose you. And I'm not sure that's a risk I'm prepared to take." He finished with hands outstretched as if he were weighing his dilemma.

A hush had fallen between them as they waited for the other to decide their next move. Since it was clear that Henry was incapable of making the decision, it appeared to Frankie that she was going to have to do it for him.

"Well, Henry, or whatever the hell your name is," she said frostily. "I'm afraid that it's a risk you're going to *have to* take. Because if you don't tell me who you are and what exactly it is you are doing here right now, I promise, this will be the last you see of me."

Frankie prayed silently that she had not just made the biggest mistake of her life, that her massive gamble would not simply blow up in her face. She wondered what she would she do if he just shrugged and turned on his heel without so much as another word.

"Frankie, no. Please," he pleaded, "please, don't say that."

She had to hide her relief behind a mask of her own as she waited for him to continue, tapping her foot ever so slightly in the anxiety of the moment. He took a deep breath and exhaled slowly as if trying to figure out how he was going to say what he needed to.

"This is going to sound maddeningly cryptic, but I guess you could say that I am both of those men and neither of them, all at the same time..." Henry trailed off for a moment to gather his thoughts for the next sentence, but it was just a half second too long.

"All right, enough with the 'riddle me this' bullshit – just get on with it already!" The tension had become too much for Frankie to handle.

Henry waited patiently, eying her as one might a toddler in the middle of a tantrum. Frankie fully expected to be put in the corner in a time out, a thought that quickly lead to some vivid imagery of the last time Henry had her backed up against a wall. *God, woman, have you no shame?* In such an emotionally charged moment, how could she be so inappropriate as to start thinking dirty thoughts?

"I'm sorry," she grumbled without looking him in the eye, "I'll try not to interrupt you again."

Henry gave her a bemused half-smile before continuing.

"Well I'm glad to here it, because for a minute there, I thought I was going to have to put you over my knee," he replied huskily, complete with a suggestive wink. A wink. *How dare he?*

Frankie was convinced that she had turned three shades of magenta as she struggled to control the swell of longing that coursed through her veins. She managed to tell him to behave himself and continue with his story. He apologized, saying it was only an attempt to lighten the mood.

"And to hear you laugh again," he added with genuine contrition. "I must admit: I have very much missed that laugh." Again, Frankie felt her resolve slip a notch.

It would be so easy to just... no.

"I'm sorry, Henry, but this isn't something that you're just going to be able to charm your way out of." He nodded in understanding and picked up where he had left off.

"As I was saying, I am both the Count and the consultant. Although the Comte Alphonse Defleur is an almost total fabrication, an exaggeration of certain elements from my mother's Gallic history, it has nonetheless made for a convenient pseudonym when building that first tiny sweet shop into the empire it has become today. An aristocratic history has the uncanny ability to open a lot of doors and chequebooks in the right sort of company. And Henry is my given name, that much is true, but Roberts is not my family name. It is a part of it, in that Robert is my middle name. But my birth name is actually—"

"Fitz," Frankie finished for him. She wasn't too childish to admit that it gave her a great deal of satisfaction to watch his eyes nearly pop out of their sockets.

"But...what..." he stammered, struggling to form the words. Finally, all that would come out was "How did you know—?"

"When a series of strange events suddenly crop up in an otherwise boring life," Frankie replied calmly, allowing herself to thoroughly enjoy the moment, "like when your best friend starts obsessing over a cache of chocolate bars that haven't been in production for over a century, or the bank gives you more money than you ever thought possible, and when the world's most perfect man stumbles into your shop and you suddenly begin to find yourself changing in ways you never thought you could... You start to look around for answers. And sometimes two plus two equals four, but then you take another look and find it adds up to something quite incomprehensible but there it is, staring you in the face nonetheless."

How she had managed to get all of that out so succinctly, all of the things that she had been wanting to say out loud but was too afraid of messing it up, Frankie would never know. Henry was looking at her in what appeared to be silent amazement, and something she took to be admiration shining in his eyes.

"When were you born, Henry?" Frankie asked him pointedly.

"July 23rd," he replied with a smirk that bordered on playful.

"What year?" She rolled her eyes, suppressing the urge to either smile or slap him. With the mischievous gleam in his eyes, she should have expected that sort of response.

"What difference should that make? All you need to know is that I'm much older than I look." Henry was toying with her, and it was making her angry again. Even the way he was standing there so casually with his hands in his pockets was making Frankie furious beyond reason.

"I'm glad you think that this is all so entertaining, Henry. But if you won't keep to your word and tell me everything, you can get the fuck out," she spat at him with surprising venom, taking yet another risk by pointing the way to the door.

Before she knew it Henry was in front of her, both hands encircling the one that was directing him to leave. Gently, he touched it to his lips as his eyes begged for forgiveness.

"I swear to you, Frankie, I don't mean to make light of this situation we're in. I'm simply trying to enjoy these moments with you, since they might well be my last. But obviously I'm upsetting you more, so I promise: no more jokes, no more stalling. I'll just close my eyes and tell you everything. And we will have to see what happens next."

Frankie hesitated, the stubborn bitch inside her not wanting to give in. But of course, all it took was a single look into those pleading dark blue eyes that seemed to whisper 'Just give me another chance' and she should have known she was done for.

"Start talking, then."

Henry kissed her hand again in gratitude, turning it over and planting a light peck on her wrist that made her very nearly swoon from the intimacy of it, before reluctantly letting go. He crossed to the other side of the room, and sighed heavily.

Then, as promised, he closed his eyes and began to speak:

"I was born not far from here actually, at my family home, the youngest of three boys. It was clear from the start that I was not like the others. My brothers were short and dark like my father, built for honest labour and quite shy. Both were keen to learn the family business, which was chocolate, from an early age which pleased my father to no end.

Not so much, me. I took after my mother's side, both in looks and temperament. I was tall and fair like her, and just as social and outspoken, often getting into trouble for it. Most of the time, however, it served me rather well. My mother would say I could charm the birds from the trees with just a bat of my lashes, and she wasn't far wrong. My father tried everything he could to involve me in the business, to pique my interest in some way. But I was having none of it, always too busy charming the young ladies outside in front of the shop on the high street when I was supposed to be working behind the counter, or delegating duties at the factory to men twice my age who were happy to help simply because I'd listen to their stories.

It drove my father mad, to where he eventually gave up and we drifted apart as fathers and sons with so little in common so often tend to. It was my mother who had wanted me to go to the factory that night with my father, the night that he died. She wanted us to be able to connect on some level, not realizing it was like mixing oil and water.

We quarrelled, as we did most nights, but that night it was a blazing row. One of our worst, actually. He did not approve of my… ahem… relations with the various young ladies in town. I was, shall we say, rather cavalier when it came to my affections, and Father firmly believed that I was at an age where I should be thinking about my future. He thought I should have been looking to settle down with a lady from a respectable family and find some meaningful employment since I refused to become part of his little chocolate empire. Sixteen was a very different age then, not at all like it is these days. At sixteen, you were considered a man.

Of course, I was far too busy having fun, with no intention of falling into line the way he expected me to. And I was not shy about telling him, either. He claimed that my behaviour was a blight on our family's name, the very one that he'd spent most of his life building up, and as a result I was bad for business. He especially disapproved of one particular girl I was courting at the time, Archibald Chadwick's youngest daughter. Lucinda."

Frankie knew it was completely ridiculous, but that did nothing to stop the sudden surge of jealousy that had come over her as she listened to Henry talk about the many women he'd 'courted' all those years ago.

She wondered if courting was the polite Victorian term for shagging. Mercifully she didn't have much time to think about it as Henry seemed determined to make good on his promise to tell her everything.

"Father despised the Chadwick family. Brighton was a much smaller place then than it is now; no more than a village, really, where everyone knew everyone else. And there wasn't a soul around for miles who didn't know the name Chadwick, although not for their fine or upstanding reputation. Quite the opposite, actually. And young

Archibald was the worst of them all."

He paused then, his jaw suddenly tightening. Despite the darkness, Frankie could see his eyes narrow at the memory.

"Henry?" She didn't want him to get so lost in the past that he would end up stopping there. He shook his head slightly as he threw her an apologetic smile that almost knocked her on her behind.

"Sorry. Now, where was I? Oh yes, Archibald. They had started out as friends, my father and him. They had grown up together and where my father had to work for everything he'd ever had, young Archie Chadwick had it handed to him on a gold platter. By the time they had grown into men, things between them had changed dramatically. You see, Archie always seemed to want anything that my father had for himself. And for the most part, he always got what he wanted. Except for my mother." He smiled softly then.

"My mother was so unbelievably beautiful, with no shortage of suitors. And yet she chose my father, which was a constant surprise to him." Henry's eyes were distant, caught up in his memories. At least these memories were happy ones, Frankie noted by the way he was smiling softly.

"Why? Why would it surprise him, I mean," she asked, almost as wrapped up in his past as he was.

"My father was never what you would consider handsome, so he'd always thought himself very lucky. And his family, though successful in their own right, did not have the same desirable prospects that custom dictated at the time... Well, when compared to the mighty Chadwicks, that is. Fortunately though, my mother's parents had been working class immigrants from France, and had more respect for the company my father's family had built from the ground up.

My mother's father had owned a modest patisserie on the high street, and my father used to deliver their chocolate supplies. He always said that he ended up learning more about chocolate there than he'd ever learned while working at his own family factory. It was also where he met my mother. And when her father passed away suddenly, the shop was left to my mother as the only living heir. But in those days, as my mother had three young children at home and the idea of women owning property was a not common one, it meant that my father was running both the factory and her family's shop at the same time.

I'm assuming, since you have studied the history of chocolate in this country, that you're familiar with the Fitz & Company story?" Frankie nodded quickly.

Once Henry seemed satisfied that he wasn't boring her with the backstory, he continued.

"Something history may not have told you is that Archibald Chadwick decided to open up a very similar shop just down the street and had nerve enough to call in almost every day to harass our shophands; telling them how it was destined to fail so they should convince my father to sell it to him and avoid the embarrassment. He would even go round town saying that he had seen rat droppings on the counter, or witnessed the rodents scurrying about the displays after hours.

Thankfully, the only thing Chadwick succeeded in doing with that little scheme was further sully his own reputation. My father may not have been born a wealthy man, but he was honest and well-respected by everyone who knew him. And brilliant in his own way. He found the alchemy that went into chocolate-making fascinating, something I'm sure you can relate to yourself, so he went about learning everything he could the same way he did with anything – through trial and error. He started with the more traditional chocolate recipes used in the factory when he wasn't much more than a child, and found ways to expand on them. He wasn't afraid to experiment with flavour and texture. He wanted to improve on the famous Fitz Cocoa Cream."

He seemed to catch Frankie's flinch at the mention of the bar that had caused so much chaos in her life in recent weeks, and moved on.

"Enough with the history lesson," he said, "let me just skip ahead to that night, then." He paused, squeezing his eyes shut before finishing. "To the night I lost my father."

It made Frankie feel guilty despite knowing she had done nothing wrong.

"If it's too painful for you," she said gently, "you don't need to go into it. I wouldn't want to make you relive something like that. I'm not that cruel." Henry gave her a forlorn look.

"You aren't making me relive anything, Frankie," he replied, his voice hollow with so much sadness it nearly brought her to tears. "There has not been a single day in the last one hundred and thirty-five years that I haven't thought about that night."

He paused again. The silence stretched between them

like an elastic band, taut and ready to snap until he began his account of the night that had changed everything.

"I've already told you that we had fought," he began softly. "After that, I stormed off to see Lucinda, hellbent on adding fuel to the fire like the self-centred brat I was back then. And continue to be, so it would seem. I took her to my mother's shop because I had the key, it was private, and it served to further entrench my sense of rebellion. Bringing the enemy behind battlelines and into main headquarters would have been tantamount to treason for my father. Of course I was foolish enough to revel in it.

She liked to sample our biscuits and pastries, saying on more than one occasion that they were far superior to those on offer in her own family's shop. At the time I liked to think that she enjoyed being defiant just as much as I did, but after that night I started to wonder if there wasn't more to it than that."

"Wait, what does that mean?" Frankie interrupted him without thinking. "Do you think she was working for her father, that she was acting like some sort of… double agent or something?"

He grinned suddenly, in spite of himself.

"And *that* is one of the things that makes you so wonderful. You're either incredibly perceptive or unbelievably paranoid, I haven't worked out which one it is just yet," he exclaimed, before adding wistfully. "If only you were around back then to bash me over the head with something… I didn't see what was staring me straight in the face."

His tone seemed to hold a hint of hidden meaning,

something she couldn't quite grasp that lay just below the surface.

"Well, in your defense, you were a hormone-riddled teenager blatantly violating your father's wishes. To be honest, that's a pretty intoxicating combination." Frankie reasoned before pausing mid-ramble when she noticed him staring at her intensely.

"What?" She demanded, suddenly worried that she had a bit of chocolate on her cheek. She would have to install a mirror in the kitchen.

"I won't make the same mistake twice, you know. Not seeing what's right in front of me." Frankie felt her stomach flip over. She knew she would have to act quickly if she was going to keep this conversation on track. *Not to mention my panties intact.*

"What happened when you and Lucinda left the shop?" she somehow succeeded in choking out, feeling the need to cross her legs with the way he was looking at her. *Guess that connection is back in full force,* she thought as she felt her face grow hot.

Henry sighed, almost reluctantly, but continued.

"I was feeling guilty about the way I had left things with my father, so around midnight I escorted Lucinda home and made my way back over to the factory. It was not unusual for him to be there at such a late hour, especially after a row like the one we'd had. As I approached the door, I could see someone rushing out. I couldn't see who it was at first, I was too distracted in wondering how to make amends. But I knew from the frame it was too large to be Father and since I didn't feel like being questioned by one of his workmen, I hid behind a storage shed until he was gone. I'm not sure why I'd felt the need to hide since I had as much right as anyone, if not more, to be there. Again, perhaps it was the guilt. Anyway, that doesn't matter. What does matter is that as the figure came closer, the moon broke through some clouds and I could see them as plainly as if it were daylight.

It was Archibald Chadwick. But he didn't look like his normal self. His face was pale, and he was sweating profusely despite a chill in the air that had rolled in earlier that evening. He kept looking behind as if he were expecting someone, and every now and then would rake a hand through his hair. I watched as he hurried past the gate then broke into a flat-out run. I knew then that something was wrong." Henry paused, swallowing hard, then leaned against the wall again as if needing the support to get through what he was about to say next.

Frankie could barely keep herself from yelling at him to get on with it. *The man knew how to tell a story, that's for sure.* She couldn't remember the last time she had sat still for so long.

"I could smell blood as soon as I opened the door. The factory back then was not the massive building it is now; it was basically just a large room with an office. I could see my father's body lying on the floor in a pool of dark liquid but, knowing him, that could have just as easily been chocolate. But I somehow knew this time it wasn't. I ran toward him, praying that he had just slipped and bumped his head, but as I got closer I could see that his eyes were open and empty. Staring at nothing. Then I saw that… that his hand still on the table, where it wasn't attached to anything. And I believe that I was so overcome with horror and grief that I blacked out." He exhaled loudly, wiping a hand quickly over his eyes. They had grown damp as he spoke.

277

"I've never told anyone that before." He smiled at her without mirth. Frankie wasn't sure whether she should be flattered or guilt-ridden because she had been the one to force the issue.

"Is that a good or bad thing?" She couldn't bear not knowing.

That time, his smile was genuine. As was the short bark of laughter that followed.

"Good, I think," he said finally. "It feels as though a huge weight has been lifted from my shoulders. Perhaps religion makes a valid point after all: confession might indeed be good for the soul."

Silence fell again as Frankie waited for him to continue his story. She was trying to be patient and not prod him as she had done before. It was clear that this was taking a toll on him; she felt that the least she could do was give him as much time as he needed to take. Regardless of how desperate she was to hear what happened next. After what felt to her like an eternity, he began to speak again.

"When I came back to my senses, I was on the factory floor next to my father. I'm not sure if I'd slipped and fallen, but I was covered in his blood. My brother George was shaking me, slapping my face. I guess Mother had sent him and my other brother Tom to check on us since we had been gone so long. I remember George kept yelling at me 'What did you do?' and Tom just stood there beside my father's dead body, his face ashen, his mouth opening and closing but nothing was coming out. I think, looking back on it, that he had gone into shock. I believe that I may have done as well. I was trying to tell George to stop, that I'd had nothing to do with it, that I had seen Chadwick leaving as I arrived – but none of it would come out..."

"Because you were so traumatized by what you had seen." Frankie finished for him, when Henry trailed off and grew quiet.

He refused to look at her at first, just stood with his head angled down and the opposite direction. When he finally did look up, she could see that fresh tears had pooled in his eyes.

"No," he replied quietly. "It was because a part of me knew he was right. It was my fault. Had I *been there* with him at the factory, like I should have been, none of it would have happened." Then he sighed again, but this time it sounded more like a sob.

"Henry, no," Frankie began in an effort to console him. "You can't seriously blame yourself for that? You weren't much more than a child. There was *nothing* that you could have done. In fact, had you been there, who knows? You could have gotten hurt yourself."

Again she fought against the temptation to go to him, to put her arms around him, but remained firmly rooted in place.

"How can I not, blame myself? I can't help but think that if only I'd returned even ten minutes earlier, I could have done something."

Frankie realised then that it was useless to argue with him. He had believed that he was to blame for his father's death for well over the past century, and it was unlikely there was anything she could say or do to convince him otherwise in the span of a single evening.

"Well, perhaps it hasn't all been in vain," Henry said pensively after a lengthy silence. "If things had not happened they way they did, I would not be here with you today."

She could feel her face growing hot again as she tried not to smile. She knew that he was watching, waiting for a reaction. When she did not oblige, he gave up and carried on.

"By the time I'd managed to explain what I'd seen and that I had not even been there, my brothers had already decided I was guilty. At the very least for abandoning my rightful post. They told me to leave before the bobbies got there so they wouldn't be forced to turn me in. Because of my reputation, the police would not think twice about pinning it on me.

I went home to my mother, and told her everything. Holding her in my arms while she wept will haunt me to my grave. It was then that I realised what needed to be done. I had to get away – far away – so that the police could maybe have a chance to find the real perpetrator. I knew that by running it risked the appearance of guilt, but it was a risk I was prepared to take. My brothers were right; had I stayed, the police would have focused their investigation on me and the Chadwick money would have taken care of the rest. Flawed logic, I admit, but it was what I took to be the truth.

My mother understood what I was doing and why. She even agreed to help me do it. She put together a small bag with clothes and some food, and gave me some money out of the safe. Saying goodbye to her was one of the hardest things I've had to do. From there, I went south to the Chain Pier, where some large Scandinavian merchant ships were known to dock on their way to...well, anywhere. A few shillings were enough to secure safe passage in the cargo hold and a little bit of food."

This was where Frankie had to interrupt. Again.

"I'm sorry, Henry, but I have to ask. What was a shilling worth again?"

"Twelve pence," he replied with a smirk.

"Not sure what that's worth in today's sterling, but please forgive my 21st century ignorance. Continue."

Henry laughed, and had no choice but to join in though it was at her own silliness.

"Now, where was I? Ah yes, in the belly of a Swedish cargo ship on my way to parts unknown. I did not know the language back then so I couldn't even ask. It seemed like I was on that boat forever, but it was the first time I had ever been so far away from my family. I remember I would often dream that I could venture out on my own, free from the obligations I had to my family and its business. But there, on that boat, I don't think I have ever felt more empty or alone.

I spent my nights in the darkness of the hold wondering what I had done. Wondering what I should do next. Wondering if I would ever see my mother and brothers again. I think what surprised me most was how badly I wanted to see them again, how desperately I'd hoped I would just wake up at home in my bed to find that this had all been a horrible dream. That I would walk downstairs, and my father would be there in the dining room having breakfast with the rest of the family. But then I would wake up in the cold and the dark, utterly alone save for a few ship rats, and realise that it was my life now. And it had turned into a complete nightmare."

Frankie found herself nodding along with Henry as he

spoke. *In a bizarre sort of way*, she thought, *our stories are similar.* Not quite so extreme as being suspected of patricide and having to escape in the hold of a Swedish cargo vessel, but they both shared the same strained relationship with one of their parents and had to struggle to find their own ways in the world. To determine their own identities, ones that were quite separate and perhaps even at odds with what their respective families had expected of them.

"One morning I woke up," Henry was saying, "and after what must have been several weeks at sea I found the hold was buzzing with activity. From the limited Swedish I'd managed to pick up, I was able to decipher that land had been spotted in the distance and they were preparing to disembark. I stepped out on deck, eager to find out where we were, and was instantly struck by the blazing sun and an oppressive layer of heat. Ahead on the horizon I spotted an untamed mass of green, which I could only assume was the land of which they spoke.

Having only ever ventured as far away as London, I of course had never seen anything like it. It made me feel a bit like Robinson Crusoe. I soon learned that the Swedes had gotten thrown off course, that they had been trying to reach the West Indies in search of sugar and other spices but had ended up much farther south. Where we'd landed, I was able to determine by going back years later, would have been what is now known as the Amapa state of Brazil, ninety percent of which to this day is still dominated by the Amazon rainforest. It was, and still is, stunning. When we went out exploring, I was so completely caught up in how green and lush everything was, how every branch and leaf seemed drenched with a vitality that's not seen even in the most beautiful parts of England, that I wasn't aware I had fallen so far behind my Swedish shipmates."

Frankie was completely captivated by Henry's story, particularly the manner in which he was telling it. She had a fondness for detail and was glad that Henry did not disappoint. But he was becoming so lost in his own memories, she was afraid he'd never come back to the point at hand.

"What happened next," she urged him on breathlessly when he happened to pause for another second too long. Henry seemed amused at her eagerness and obliged.

"Well, I found myself alone in the Amazon jungle and it was growing darker as night approached. The very scene that had seemed so steeped in beauty suddenly grew menacing. I've never experienced a blackness anywhere like it. It was while I was stumbling around, panicking in the dark, trying to listen for voices or anything that might lead me back to the ship and my comrades that I fell into a ravine and was knocked unconscious. If it weren't for the tribesmen who found me and took me back to their village, I most surely would have succumbed to the elements. I guess you could say they saved me. Well, both saved and condemned me to this… whatever this is."

"Why would you say condemned?" Frankie blurted without thinking. Henry smiled sadly before answering.

"Perhaps condemned is too strong a word," he conceded, "but it's not natural, this existence. That's not to say that I haven't enjoyed myself over the years, but what joy I've had always seems to have come at the expense of others. Vengeance can be a demanding mistress."

Sometimes, very rarely, I hate being right. Frankie tried to keep herself from interrupting again, to let him finish his story as he'd promised. But it was proving to be much more difficult than she could have possibly imagined. She was bursting with questions.

Like when he began to tell her about the Maya tribespeople who had believed him to be the Golden One from one of their ancient prophesies, the one who comes to lead the tribe out of a period of strife and hardship, she was dying to ask if he was terribly frightened. And how did he know that they weren't cannibals planning to make a meal of him? And if they didn't speak English and he didn't speak whatever language it was they did, how was he able to tell?

Of course, if she were the patient type, she would have realised that all would have been revealed in due course. But Frankie was not known for her patience. At least she did not wait long for the answers to those questions she'd somehow forced herself not to ask. They had been able to communicate using drawings and gestures, Henry explained, and from there they began to understand each other. To develop something of a language of their own between them.

When he was describing the Water of Life ritual, Frankie was amazed that the crazy professor Jared had brought in was pretty much bang on in his interpretation of it. She reluctantly admitted to herself that she could no longer refer to him as Professor CrackerJacks. As for why he had been the one chosen to receive such an honour, and why the tribe had come to think of him as their Golden One, she learned that it was because Henry had found the reason so many of its members were becoming ill and dying.

The village's main water source, a stream which ran from a nearby river, had become contaminated by a large rubber production plant miles away that was dumping used machine oil and other toxic waste into the river. It was only by sheer luck that he himself had not been so affected; his nursemaids had used water that ran in a separate stream closest to his recovery tent which happened to be on the opposite side of the settlement. He had recognised the symptoms from something similar that had happened with a school that had been built too close to a factory just outside of Brighton. Another in a long list of casualties of the Second Industrial Revolution, he had called it.

Frankie wanted to ask him what Brighton was like back then, in a world where the Kyoto Protocol and forty-hour workweek did not yet exist. But she kept quiet. However, when he got to the part where he returned to Europe on Belgian cargo vessel whose crew had become lost searching for cacao beans a year or two later, she could hold herself back no longer.

"So wait…you just up and left at the first opportunity?" She burst in again, as was her nature. That, and her inability to keep her mouth shut. "I mean, how could you just leave them like that, the ones who had taken care of you for so long? Did you even bother to say goodbye?"

As soon as it was out, she realised that she was no longer referring to something that had happened well over a century earlier. She was talking about something much more recent, something that hit far closer to home.

And Henry knew it.

"I'm sorry, Frankie, for leaving things the way that I did. It was never my intention to have that happen."

Frankie was beginning to sense a pattern in Henry's behaviour that was not entirely unfamiliar, and she cursed herself for being so blind to not have seen it in the first place. A lot of things had never been his intention.

"To have what happen, exactly?" She bristled in response.

"To fall in love with you," Henry answered simply, his eyes holding steady on hers. She held her breath while he continued.

"I have fallen so utterly and completely for you, Frankie, that I... I just didn't know what to do. I didn't even see it coming. Of course, in retrospect, I wonder how I could have missed it."

She couldn't respond. The simple truth of his declaration was impossible to ignore. Of course, that wasn't enough to prevent her from trying.

"So, when did you realise all this then? Was it before or after you kidnapped my fiancé? Or maybe it was after you got my best friend hooked on some old chocolate for the express purpose of making her crazy?"

Frankie always felt she was at her best when backed into a corner. Always one to come out swinging, whether she should or not. Henry looked wounded at first, then bewildered. And then, he was angry.

"That would make the second time you've accused me of kidnapping your fiancé," he answered stonily after a long pause, "and I think this should be the first point to be resolved before we move any further. Let me be quite clear with you: *I did not kidnap anyone.* James came to work for me, and work he did. But make no mistake: anything else he may have done during his stay was entirely of his own free will."

His eyes had turned hard, a deep slate grey as he spoke, his mouth set into a firm line once he had finished. Frankie could clearly see that her accusation had upset him a great deal.

Was he serious? If he wants to get arsy, she thought, *two can play at that game.*

"Really," she responded, her tone equally as cold. "Well, by all means, Henry, enlighten me. What do you think happened with James, in your *seasoned* expertise, while you were here in England with me? For example, why could he not send or receive emails or call anyone while he was there?"

There was no mistaking his flinch at her exaggeration of the word 'seasoned'. It pleased Frankie, if for no other reason than it proved how well she was handling herself through this. She was calm, she was in control. She in no way resembled the screaming banshee she'd been known to become when she was this angry. But then again, she had never really found herself in a situation quite like this.

Henry seemed to be choosing his words carefully, taking the time to consider his response. And then he smiled. A supercilious smirk that nearly pushed Frankie over the edge.

"It's a fairly simple concept, Frankie," he responded caustically. "Wireless connections are notoriously unreliable in the Alps, so it's entirely possible that his phone and laptop were unable to maintain it. Or did James fail to mention that he did not remember to bring his mobile charger so its battery died, and that he neglected to correctly log in to our secure server *despite* the instructions I'd left in plain view on his desk, therefore he had been working offline on his laptop the entire time without noticing? Before the battery on that died too, of course."

Frankie felt her chin drop before she had time to catch it. Her reaction appeared to satisfy him, as his smirk morphed into a smug, borderline cheeky grin.

But she was not prepared to concede defeat quite yet.

"Fair enough," she replied serenely, not willing to let on how much he had shaken her. "And what of the two women you have living with you? Why did you not tell him about them? Or tell me, for that matter?"

It was her turn to look smug as she watched the grin slide off Henry's face. It may have taken some of the colour with it, too, if she weren't mistaken.

"It's not what you're thinking. I'm not with either of them. Shaye was... how can I put this without making it sound so much worse than it really was? She had come with me from South America, to become my wife."

Frankie opened her mouth to interject something she knew she would surely regret later, but Henry pressed on.

"Her father was the new chief of the tribe that had taken care of me, and I believe it was on my second or third trip maybe fifty years ago to purchase cocoa beans when he... offered her to me. It was out of gratitude for continuing to do business with them. To refuse him would have been professional suicide; I have never found an equal in the flavour or texture of those particular beans. And to be truthful, I had become somewhat lonely. But it was never anything but friendship. And she really is a decent young woman. Sadly, I cannot say the same when it comes to Marta."

He paused to see if Frankie had any further questions. When, to the surprise of them both she remained silent, he carried on.

"Marta is a very distant relation on my mother's side, a legitimate Defleur. She had come sniffing around when she'd learned that there was another Defleur in Switzerland. Like a leech, she latched on to me and has refused to let go ever since. She's more of an albatross around my neck, to be honest. When I realised that she wasn't going to go away, I decided to find a way to use her to my advantage."

Frankie frowned. *What the hell did* that *mean?*

"Marta has her certain…charms, I guess you could say," Henry explained quickly when he realised she wasn't following his train of logic. "She can be very persuasive, and most men are powerless to resist her. It can come in handy during negotiations. Though it almost makes me feel sorry for them." Frankie was hit with an uncomfortable realization.

"So what… are you speaking from experience here? Have you also fallen victim to these so-called 'charms'?" she asked with some hesitation, arms folded protectively across her chest, unsure if she really wanted to know the answer.

In a flash Henry was at her side again, his arm already outstretched ready to offer comfort before he appeared to think better of it. He let it drop before it touched her.

No, no – *no*," he insisted, "it isn't like that. With Marta or Shaye, I swear it."

He paused as if he were deliberating over what to say next, how best he could explain himself. From where Frankie stood the longer he was quiet, the worse it would be for him.

"Since I lost my father that night, and the way that I lost him, the only thing I've thought about has been revenge. I wasn't kidding when I said that vengeance is a demanding mistress. The only mistress, actually. To be honest, I've not had feelings for anyone until I met you. And those feelings are quite unlike anything I've ever felt before."

Henry hesitated again for a moment, then took a deep breath and grasped Frankie by the shoulders, turning her gently to face him.

"Frankie," he began softly. "I could keep going, and tell you about everything I did when I returned to Europe, but I feel I've given you quite enough to think about for one night. I've told you who and *what* I really am. And I'm sure you must understand why I would have kept that from you."

Henry paused, waiting for a response. Frankie wasn't really sure where to begin.

"You're right. This has been quite a lot to take in. But what I still don't understand is where Louise fits into all of this? Why would you hide chocolate on her property then tell her where to find them? Did you know that it would drive her insane? I get the revenge bit, but why not just go after the company, or straight for her father who runs it? Why her? She has nothing to do with any of it."

"Vengeance also rarely listens to reason," Henry answered after a long pause.

"When I returned to Brighton a few weeks ago, I happened to see Louise first. At a distance, in town, and it was purely by chance. But she was so like Lucinda, in both her looks and the way she acted, that it pushed me over the edge and I decided to launch my plot against Chadwick's earlier than planned. And from a different angle, I suppose..." That was when Frankie decided that she had heard enough.

"So basically, getting close to me was just another part of the plan. I was your angle," she finished for him, feeling her anger building again.

Henry's eyes widened, as if the implication of what he'd said suddenly dawned on him. His hands were on her shoulders, and there was no hesitation this time. Almost desperate.

"No, *no*. That's not it at all. Frankie, please, I realise how this—" He broke off as he noticed the look on her face. She had been looking at the hands that held her by the shoulders.

"I'll thank you to take your hands off me now, Henry," she said in a low voice that hovered between a whisper and a growl.

Henry's hands dropped. Frankie stepped away from him, toward the shop door.

"Right." She had to keep moving so he would not be able to see how badly she was shaking. "It's been a *really* long day, and I think I need to get some rest. You should go."

Henry seemed taken aback at her abrupt about-face, but hastened to grab the jacket he had tossed carelessly on the floor at some point during his story.

"Of course. I'd be happy to see you back—" Again, Frankie had to cut him off. With words she never thought she would ever say, and with no idea how she even managed to get them out.

"No, Henry. I've brought my own car. I can see myself home just fine." She could see that he was about to interrupt her again, no doubt to offer to call again tomorrow, but she could not allow it.

"Henry, look. I've just ended my engagement, and you said yourself that you've given me enough to think about for one day. But I'm afraid it's going to take a bit longer than that for me to process. So I would appreciate it...if you could give me the time and space to do that. Alone."

Frankie could feel her heart fracture into tiny pieces as she watched his beautiful face fall. After a minute that seemed to more like a lifetime, he nodded.

"Of course. Take as much time as you need. Just promise me when you're ready, you will let me know. I'll be waiting, however long it may take." He hesitated again, and then walked toward the door.

"Good night, Frankie. I wish you sweet dreams and much success until our paths cross again," Henry half-whispered into the darkness, before he unbolted the door and went to walk out of the shop for what may well have been the last time.

He paused once more, looking back at her as if hoping that she might reconsider.

"Good night, Henry," Frankie whispered.

He gave her one last look, one that was impossible to decipher between the lack of light and the turmoil of emotions that had been stirred up over the past few hours, and let the door close behind him. She walked over to lock it, and stood for a long moment, her cheek leaning against the roughness of the wood.

"Goodbye Henry," she whispered. And with that, Frankie did something that she had not done since she was a very small girl.

She slid to the floor and cried until she could no longer breathe.

FOURTEEN

October 12th

Frankie knew that things could not continue the way that they had been, that she was going to have to say something. And despite how much it might hurt the both of them, she would just have to live with the consequences. With a deep breath and fingers crossed, she launched in.

"Enough with the fairy lights, Lou. You can see the shop from the London Eye as it is."

Louise whirled around to glare at her.

"Frankie, this is your grand opening for God's sake. I'm just trying to create the right ambience."

It had been less than three weeks since Frankie had asked Henry to give her space to consider everything that he had told her. She was pleased with herself that she hadn't spent the time pining for him or wallowing in self-pity. At least not in any way that was immediately obvious to anyone. Instead she had managed to get quite a lot of real work done, and they were winding down to the final preparations.

But she knew she couldn't take all the credit. She'd had a little help.

Louise had stepped forward on a day not long after Frankie's last evening with Henry to announce that she was going to plan the shop's grand opening party… by herself. No army of party planners, no event management team to move this here and that there only to move it all back again. This time, she declared, she wanted to do it all on her own.

Frankie's initial response to the offer had been *I'm sorry, what?* She wasn't sure what to make of this brand new person Louise was becoming, and was left wondering what the hell had happened to her self-centred but ultimately well-meaning best friend. It was fast becoming a fairly consistent theme in her life; she found herself wondering what happened with a lot more than just Louise. But Frankie had made herself far too busy with last minute details that come with getting ready to open up shop to obsess about those other things. *But let's be real. It's really only the one thing.*

Henry had proven to be a man of his word. Frankie had neither seen nor heard from him since she had shown him the door just sixteen days earlier. Sixteen of the longest days she had ever experienced. In that time she had come to recognise that, although Henry had covered a lot of ground that final evening, there were still a number of questions for which there she'd gotten no answers. And worse, no means of getting answers. Until one day, about three days after Henry walked out of her shop's door, she had happened to check her email. Just in case he'd grown tired of waiting and decided to drop her a line himself.

* * *

Her heart had danced a little jig when she saw that

there were a number of unread messages waiting. She scanned quickly, looking for any sign of his name, only to find that most of them were the sort of insignificant patter that tends to build up unnoticed in one's inbox. There were a couple of bulletins from the Trust she had taken her small business course through reminding her that it was time to gear up for the holiday season, a time when most retail shops made the bulk of their profit. Then there was an email from her mum saying that she had marked the date for the grand opening in her calendar, and that her and Dad would be ever so pleased to attend. Frankie could feel her molars grind as she imagined the bored yet polite interest that would have been her tone as she typed it. She knew her far too well.

But when she noticed two emails that were time-stamped from a several days earlier, one titled 'well, I'm here' and the other 'hello…anybody there', she sat up and took notice. They were from James.

A quick scan told her that these were the emails he had written to her whilst he was in Switzerland.

The first one included a highly detailed description of the house, although perhaps compound was the more appropriate term for it. It described his first meeting with Defleur—no, Henry—how her picture had dropped to the floor, and how Henry had reacted to it. She guessed that would have been when Henry decided to make a small change in tactic when it came to his master plan, and drag her into it.

The second email had been a little more frantic in tone, recounting how he had felt like he was being watched and how Henry's mood could turn in an instant, something she herself had experienced on more than one occasion. He did not mention the women, for obvious reasons. And yet it made her feel a little better, a little more understanding of what James must have been going through when he was there. It in no way absolved him or Henry of the things that had happened, but it allowed her to see the sequence of events from another perspective.

And, perhaps most important of all, it proved that James had not lied to her.

He might have been a few things – technically inept, morally bereft, a philanderer in the end – but a good liar he was not. The same could not necessarily be said for Henry.

It was while she was reading through the emails James had written in Switzerland that Frankie suddenly remembered one of the many things she had forgotten to ask Henry as he was spilling all his secrets. It was quite important, potentially life-changing, and she was angry that she had let the opportunity slip by. But a half-second later, she realised that there was more than one way that she could find the answer. It involved a bit of legwork, and a lot of mental preparation for what she could potentially uncover. Not to mention, the possible ramifications the discovery could have both personally and professionally.

But Frankie had made up her mind. For better or worse, she was going to pay Mr. Bradley the bank manager another visit.

A few days after that, in the first week of October, she was on her way back to Lloyd's bank. She had left Louise at the shop to continue boxing and stocking the shelves with the product she had been purposefully banging out expressly for the opening. It was such an important task that under normal circumstances she would never have been able to entrust it to anyone else, but having this new version of

Louise there was almost as good as being there herself. Frankie did leave a few instructions for her. Perhaps it was more of a detailed planogram of what was to go where, one that may or may not have been colour-coded and drawn to scale., but that wasn't the point. The point was that she was finally delegating, a skill that she would need to cultivate if she had any hope of becoming a successful businessperson. And with that in mind, she passed through the beautifully carved doors of the bank as if she were on a mission.

It had a very different feeling to the first time she had been there. She was beside herself with nerves, having come with hat in hand and the desperate hope that they would give her some money. This time, however, she did not hesitate as she strode confidently passed the grim grey haired matron who held court at the imposing desk that dominated the main hall. She looked appalled at Frankie's apparent lack of respect for the protocol, which made her hold her head up that much higher.

"Excuse me, miss, but you'll need to check in with me if you have an appointment," she barked. Without so much as a misstep, Frankie continued on her way to Mr. Bradley's office.

"Oh don't mind me, I'm just popping in for a quick visit with my loan manager. I won't be but a moment," she called back over her shoulder.

The clerk stood stunned, blinking slowly, before beginning to huff and puff like an old steam engine. Frankie had to bite her lip to keep from laughing out loud as she breezed into Bradley's office, startling his assistant and her busy afternoon of Internet browsing.

"Oh hell—I mean, good afternoon," the girl

stammered, her words tumbling over each other. "How can I help you?"

"I'm here to see Mr. Bradley." It was quick and to the point.

"All right," she answered, turning back to her screen to scroll through the agenda. "Do you have an appointment?"

"No, not today," Frankie answered, quickly following that with "but I was here a few weeks ago arranging my small business loan. I just had a few more questions for him."

The assistant looked at her, frowning.

"Well, unfortunately, Mr. Bradley only sees people by appointment," she replied turning back to her screen to check for the next available time. "He has some time next Tuesday at 3:15pm. Would that work?"

Frankie knew she was going to have to slip into bitch mode, something she was reluctant to do since the assistant was nothing more than an innocent bystander in this situation. A casualty of war, so to speak.

"No, that won't work at all, I'm afraid. Apart from today I'm all booked up," Frankie said, leaning forward with both her hands on the desk to punctuate the urgency of the situation.

"Now, Janine," she continued, reading the name off of her lapel tag. "If you'd be so kind as to let Mr. Bradley know that Frances MacSweeney is here to ask him a few questions about the so-called mentoring program that he forgot to mention, I'd be more than happy to let you get on with updating your Facebook status."

Janine's cheeks reddened as she bolted from the desk, stammering something about seeing if he could spare a few moments. When she returned, she was as red-faced as her blustering manager was pale.

"Ms. MacSweeney," Bradley said quietly, not looking her in the eye. "Won't you please come inside?"

He held his office door open for her, closing it stiffly once Frankie had moved passed him to take a seat inside. He resumed his place behind the desk, hands folded in front of him in a gesture of authority.

"Ms. MacSweeney, I think I know what brings you here today," he began before Frankie interrupted him.

"Do you, Mr. Bradley? Do you really?" It may have come across as poor manners, but there were moments when she was incapable of keeping her mouth shut. If Bradley was rattled, he didn't let it show.

"Well, yes," he replied smoothly, "it's quite common amongst new business owners. They tend to burn right through their credit line, finding themselves with nothing left before they've even opened. No need to be embarrassed by it, we can simply readjust your credit terms."

Oh, could we now? But she couldn't allow her anger at his patronizing tone deter her.

"I'm so glad you brought that up," she began meekly, playing along to let him believe he'd had it right. "I wasn't sure how to. I'm just so relieved you mentioned it first."

Bradley nodded at her sagely, urging her to continue. Something she felt fairly sure he would soon regret.

"There is something I would like to ask you about the mentoring program." And that was when the sanctimonious nodding gave way to more visible discomfort. But Frankie wasn't even remotely finished.

"I was actually wondering what other businesses in Brighton have been a part of this mentorship scheme? I'd like to ask them a few questions, you know, maybe get some advice on how to get a richer experience from such a unique opportunity. I'm just not sure that I'm getting everything I could be out of it."

God, I can be such a brilliant liar when I really work for it. Frankie's tone was no longer meek; by the time she had finished speaking, it had become one of artificial innocence laced with a touch of menace for good measure. She watched, gloating silently, as Bradley hummed and hawed, spluttered and steamed, before conjuring up something of a response.

"It's quite a new program, Ms. MacSweeney," he said finally once his face had gone back to its usual colour, his tone more confident, "and I believe that yours is the only business at the moment that has qualified." Bradley seemed quite pleased with himself for being able to come up with something on the fly.

Frankie had to admit that, had she not known better, it might have sounded entirely plausible. She could see that her tactic of playing along wasn't going to work as well as she had hoped, so she would have to go straight for the goods.

"Is that right?" she mused. "Perhaps you might have more success with the program if you were to advertise it a little better. I could find nothing on your website about it, or anywhere else on the Internet for that matter." More sputtering from the weather station bank manager.

"And tell me, Mr. Bradley, is it customary for your bank to neglect to inform their customers in advance who their appointed mentor is *before* that person turns up on their shop's doorstep? Or better yet, that they are involved in a mentorship program at all?"

She could barely keep from laughing as she watched Bradley's pallor whiten further. It afforded her far more gratification than it should have.

"There really is no such thing as the mentorship program, is there, Mr. Bradley?" Frankie felt that she had waited for the truth long enough.

It seemed that Bradley was reluctant to comply at first, until she saw the sag in his shoulders that signaled surrender.

"You are correct, Ms. MacSweeney," he said finally, his voice closer to a whisper. "There is no mentoring program. I'm terribly sorry for the deception. But I hope you can understand that it was all done with the best of intentions."

Isn't it always, she thought as she carefully considered her response.

"What do you know about Henry Robert Fitz?"

It wasn't exactly the most graceful move, but she had heard enough 'I'm sorry's' to last a lifetime. This time, however, she gained none of her earlier satisfaction at watching the blood drain yet again from Bradley's face.

"Why…why would you ask?" His voice faltered, holding the faintest hint of a tremor.

"Because that was who showed up at my shop while I was in the midst of renovating, explaining that he'd been sent by the bank as part of the mentoring program. He even said that he was surprised that you, Mr. Bradley, hadn't mentioned it to me. And then he helped me paint."

She thought that Bradley was going to fall off his chair or worse, suffer a coronary right then and there. After much gaping and a little wheezing, he pulled it together enough to speak again. And by speak, Frankie felt that it was more like a verbal tap had been turned on.

"When Mr. Fitz came in that day and insisted that my assistant interrupt our meeting, I was so confounded by what he was asking me to do that I didn't really think about the reason or any possible implications," Bradley's words were coming out so fast he barely paused to catch a breath, "I simply did as I was told. The Fitz family have been loyal Lloyd's clients for generations; otherwise there would have been no way I'd have done it. But I didn't feel at the time, and for the record, I still don't, that any ill will was meant by the gesture. I hope that I was correct in that assumption?"

He cast a worried glance in Frankie's direction as he waited for her response. She could only nod in agreement because, as far as Bradley and the bank were concerned, there wasn't. And at least she'd got him talking. He continued with little sign of abating.

"He actually came back the following day to better explain the situation, even apologised for having been so cryptic. He told me that he'd been looking to invest in a local business, and that when he'd heard about your chocolate shop he knew he'd found the right one."

Bradley seemed sincere in his ignorance as he went on

with his explanation.

"Now that I think about it, it makes sense that he would show take such an interest in seeing a business like yours succeed. I'm not sure how well you know your history, Ms. MacSweeney, but Chadwick's was once Fitz and Company, which was considered to be England's first confectionary. I will admit, I'm rather shocked to hear that he came by for a personal visit. He gave me the impression that it would be a more of a discreet angel investor-type of arrangement. Why, the day he came in was the first time I'd ever even met him myself."

Mr. Bradley's colouring had returned to something resembling normal, and he appeared to be so genuinely mystified by the situation that it left little doubt as to whether or not he was being honest with her. Frankie wondered what else she could get him to divulge.

"And where is he usually? Mr. Fitz, that is." Although she figured she already knew what the answer would be – Switzerland – she was curious as to what Bradley's response would be.

"I believe he's all over the map; a bit of a nomad, really. From what I understand he's involved in a number of investments that span the globe, from America to Japan so he moves around a lot. But then again, I'm just a manager. I don't usually have much interaction with that calibre of client," he smiled weakly. Frankie smiled back, in spite of herself.

"I really am very s—" She cut Bradley off again quickly before he could say the 's' word again. The very sound of it was beginning to grate on her nerves.

"It's not your fault, Mr. Bradley. You just got caught in the middle, trying to do your job." And she was being honest. He seemed as much in the dark as she was about all of it.

Bradley smiled in gratitude before he stood up and came round the front of his desk, assuming everything had been cleared up. *Hmm, not quite.* He frowned when he noticed that Frankie remained in her seat.

"Was there something else I could help you with today, Ms. MacSweeney?"

She took a deep breath, almost unable to believe what she was about to say next.

"Um, yes, Mr. Bradley. I think there is."

Frankie had returned to the shop after her meeting at the bank, a little shaken by what had just transpired but also exhilarated from what she had somehow mustered the courage to do. A good thing, too, since she would be relying on that rush of energy to carry her through all the long nights of furious candy-making that lay ahead if she was planning to be ready for the opening which, at that point, was in less than a fortnight. Because, although she had thought that she had left Louise with more than enough stock, she could see the shelves remained almost half empty.

"Well, how were you supposed to know how much to make?" Louise had offered in an attempt to cheer her up. "It's not like you've ever had to stock your own store before, right?"

Louise bit her lip anxiously as she waited for Frankie to react. On any other day she would not be so quick to disappoint her, flying into a flurry of F words and whirling around the kitchen like an out-of-control carousel. But that day, she had simply put her handbag down and took off her jacket, rolling up her sleeves as she headed to the kitchen.

"Looks like I've still got a bit of work ahead of me, then," she said thoughtfully as Louise eyed her with suspicion.

"Are you all right?" Louise had followed her and launched herself onto the counter across from where Frankie would be working. She continued to watch Frankie, almost nervously, as she was rummaging through cabinets to get all of her tools ready.

"Frankie, did you hear me?" Louise repeated the question in a somewhat worried tone when she didn't respond.

"Oh, what? Yeah, I'm fine," Frankie smiled in apology. "Why do you ask?"

"Well, for starters, you would normally be running round swearing your fool head off instead of calmly crafting little marzipan fruits to go with your chocolate madeleines display. So, here's a thought: care to tell me the hell is going on? Where did you go today, anyway?"

Louise was becoming more hysterical by the second, her voice rising to a nearly inaudible squeak. Although directed at her, Frankie found it rather entertaining. But before her friend could throttle her, she decided she had better speak up. Not like she could ever hope to hide anything from Louise for any length of time.

"I went to the bank, to talk to the manager," she replied, and proceeded to tell Louise the whole story from start to finish.

She began with the emails from James that had reminded her of some key questions she'd forgotten to ask Henry, and ended with the conversation she had just had with Bradley who confirmed what Frankie had begun to suspect.

"So, wait, Henry made the whole mentorship program up?" Louise was shaking her head in amazement. "Now that's serious dedication. He must have really had it bad for you."

"It's not about me, Lou. It never was. He's just trying to take over your father's company. I think I was just a bit of fun along the way."

Louise opened her mouth in rebuttal before deciding against it. Employing one of Frankie's own patented moves, she changed the subject.

"You must have been seriously pissed. What did you do?"

Frankie took a deep breath as Louise took a sip of the specialty coffee she'd brought her.

"I told Bradley I didn't want his money." Louise almost choked on her latte.

"What the -- Have you gone *completely mad*?" She sputtered, struggling to recover so that she could continue to lay into her.

"Is your stupid pride *really* worth losing the shop? I mean it, Frannie. Look at all the work you've put into this. Why the hell would you throw it all away?"

Frankie waited patiently for Louise to finish her tirade. She had known that in spite of being her best friend in the world, she couldn't understand.

"I'm not going to lose the shop, Lou. There are a few other more legitimate government programs that, as it luck would have it, I *do* actually qualify for. And it gives me enough to keep things going. I mean, it's nothing like what the bank-- well, what *Henry* had given me initially, but it'll do for a start..." Frankie trailed off, uncharacteristically uncertain if she should finish her thought or not. Her natural inability to keep quiet won out in the end.

"And for the record, if I'd kept that money – *his* money – for the sake of keeping the shop, it just wouldn't mean as much. The whole point to this is to *make it on my own*. If I'd kept on like nothing had happened and let him bankroll things that would, I dunno, cheapen it somehow."

Louise looked at her, dubious, shaking her head.

"Well, Frannie, this much I'll grant you: you're either incredibly brave or unbelievably stupid. I suppose only time will tell which it is."

* * *

As Frankie stood back to examine all that they had done in such a short period of time in preparation for the opening, her mind was forced back into the present. She was shocked when she realised that only a month had gone by since Louise's birthday party. It seemed more like a lifetime had transpired in those few short weeks, both inside the shop's pink walls and beyond them.

"I hate to admit it, Lou, but you're right," Frankie said. "The lights are perfect. I don't feel like I'm about to go blind anymore."

Louise shot Frankie a sour look before coming to stand beside her to take in another viewpoint of her handiwork.

"Not that I'm one to toot my own horn, but it *is* pretty perfect, isn't it?" Louise folded her arms over her chest in a subconscious gesture of self-satisfaction. And as reluctant as Frankie was to boost Louise's overinflated ego any further, perfect was the best way to describe it.

Louise had artfully arranged fairy lights so that they hanged from every conceivable surface: strung along the walls, around every door frame, criss-crossed in the front window, over top the gilded display cases and even circling the gleaming cherry table that sat in the middle of the shop floor. Frankie's initial concerns that it would be too much had been unfounded. Once the sun had gone down, the lights left the shop with a soft, inviting glow not unlike that of thousands of candles. It worked well with the white and pink ostrich feathers she had placed in tall square vases amongst the displays of boxed chocolate. Tomorrow, she planned to add in the fresh white orchids she had on order, scheduled to arrive just before the party. She had also blown up pink and chocolate-coloured balloons to place in clusters intermittently throughout the room. And although Frankie was worried that her products might become lost amidst all the decorations, again her fears were unwarranted. If anything, the way that Louise had placed the feathers and balloons only served to draw attention to the delectable sweets she had worked so hard to create, not detract from them.

"I can't believe the opening is tomorrow," Frankie mused aloud, swallowing a lump of panic that was building quickly in her chest.

Not that there was any need for it; everything was pretty much done or would be by the following morning. There was more chocolate in the kitchen resting, ready to be arranged onto tasting platters, but she could always box them up to fill any space that remained and make more.

"I can't believe you gave me carte blanche in planning it," Lou added playfully. "Hell, you even agreed to the masquerade theme *and* trusted me to put together your costume sight unseen. When has that happened?"

Frankie had been extremely wary when Louise first approached her with the idea of having a theme for the opening. Although approach may not have been the right choice of words; it was more Louise berating in that 'can't take no for an answer' way that only she seemed capable of getting away with. Frankie was reluctant to go with anything too extravagant that could possibly distract people from the pure pleasure to be had in simply tasting the chocolate but Louise had made an excellent point: in a town which sees shops open up as quickly as they shut down, she would need something to create maximum impact and leave a lasting impression.

And seeing the way it had all come together in the end, Frankie could not have imagined it any other way. The masquerade idea seemed to fit in seamlessly. Of course, she'd had to rein Louise in a bit, something she'd had to do so frequently over the years that it had become second nature.

"But didn't you almost name your shop after one of the most decorative periods in history? Your opening needs to live up to that and set the standard," Louise had initially argued after suggesting that they add powdered wigs and panier hoop frames to the masquerade ball motif. Frankie held her ground firmly.

"But MacSweet won out in the end, Lou, didn't it? And it was more a play on words than a literal interpretation. I've made the obligatory nod to my love of the Rococo period with the gilding and the shell-like edgings on the display cases." Louise harumphed in response.

"Besides," Frankie added. "We wouldn't be able to fit as many people in here if we factor hoop skirts into the mix. We simply don't have the floor space for it." That seemed to work.

Louise backed down, even going so far as to admit that she'd made a good point. They came to a compromise: an American Jazz Age-style masquerade, complete with Louis Armstrong, 'bathtub gin' and miles and miles of flapper fringe.

On second thought, she thought as Louise bounced around the shop clapping her hands gleefully as she hinted how sexy Frankie's ensemble would be, *maybe I should be nervous.*

FIFTEEN

October 13th

12:13am

It was past midnight by the time Frankie and Louise had finished with the final details at the shop and made their way back to the Chadwick estate, with Frankie unsure of how she would be capable of getting any sleep. Her stomach was alternating between doing somersaults and twisting itself inside out. As Louise swung the Bentley round the back of the main house toward the garage, Frankie noticed the brief glance her friend cast toward its darkened windows as she bit her bottom lip.

"You all right?" Frankie asked. Louise seemed to catch herself quickly, shaking her head and flashing one of her award-winning smiles.

"What? Oh yeah, of course I am, silly," she answered in a little too much of a hurry. Anyone else would have been easily fooled by the response, but Frankie knew better.

"You sure?"

Louise abruptly braked and parked the car in front of the garage, shooting her a venomous look before wrenching herself from her seat and slamming the car door behind her.

Perhaps I shouldn't have pushed, Frankie thought, wincing.

"Louise," she called as she got out and quietly closed her door behind her.

She wondered briefly why it seemed that the people she cared most about – Louise and more recently Henry – were also the moodiest. Was it a case of like attracting like? This Louise was no stranger to Frankie. The selfish part of her even missed it a little, given the major personality changes her friend had gone through over the past few weeks. At least she knew what to expect from this version of her friend.

She followed patiently a few paces back as Louise stomped away, lost in her own huff. Waiting, watching, until the strop began to lose steam. By the time Louise had opened the door to the carriage house and thrown her vintage Hermes bag on the kitchen counter, it had already started to loosen its grip.

Had Frankie begun to count backwards from ten, she would have reached five before Louise turned to face her.

"I mean, it's not like it's much different from any other time he's gone away," she said with tears in her eyes, threatening to spill over at any moment.

Frankie knew that she'd have to be careful, that it would be the wrong time to tell her that it was in fact vastly different than any other time her father had been away. Because everything had changed.

Henry had made good on yet another promise, just not one that he had made to Frankie. It was one that he had made to himself many years earlier. After what had taken years of careful planning and saint-like patience, lying in wait for exactly the right moment to set his plan into motion, he had finally succeeded in reclaiming what he considered rightfully his: the family business that had been lost under the tragic and possibly treacherous circumstances that surrounded the death of his father. Circumstances that he had blamed himself for, for most of the past century.

But in the end, he succeeded. Henry had taken over Chadwick's.

He'd been clever about it, which came as no surprise to Frankie. He had appealed to the company's workers, the company's majority shareholders, the very same group that had been so against the initial merger between Tompkin's Toffee and some American chocolate company called Nelson's. In one of the many of news reports that kept coming out on the subject, Frankie had discovered that Quinn Baker, one of Louise's many would-be suitors, had initially worked for this American company and that Chadwick's had already quietly completed a small takeover of it less than a year earlier. But that was another story entirely... *And the same could be said for Quinn himself,* thought Frankie.

Mergers and acquisitions had suddenly become hot gossip around town, from supermarket queues to barber chair fodder. As was Henry himself, of course. *At least the three had something in common,* she reasoned. They were all, Henry included, subjects that she knew next-to-nothing about. And despite her best efforts to keep him from her thoughts, thanks to this latest high profile move and the power of the Brighton press, his perfect face was everywhere she turned.

For Frankie, it felt like there was simply no escape from him. As she drove into the shop each day with the car radio on, there would be a report with the latest piece of news about the factory's changeover. Switching stations was no help; they all seemed to talk about the same thing. Whenever she happened to pass by a newspaper box as she was walking through the Lanes, Henry's face would be gracing the front page of every paper. If she turned on the television, there he would be again on the back telescreen as whatever network analyst or business expert busied themselves with dissecting the astounding deal he had managed to pull off and what it would mean in the long term for the nation's economy.

From what Frankie had gathered from these bits and pieces, Henry had done his research. Meticulously so. He had already known, for example, that the main reason for the shareholder rejection of the initial plan being forced through by Louise's father hinged upon concerns over potential redundancies and quality degradation. So Henry had positioned his takeover plan as more of an opportunity for a mutual partnership between the company's board, its management and the shareholders; one that would be equally beneficial for all parties involved.

He began simply, by offering his own vision for Chadwick's. That included an ironclad promise not to move any production from the original Brighton facilities. He had also made a commitment to using fair trade and sustainable sources for raw ingredients such as cacao beans and cane sugar, and disclosed that he had been in discussions with some of the area farmers and other local producers with regard to those other important components in chocolate-making: milk and butter. An article Frankie had read in the

Standard said that the significance of such promises were threefold: first, that it would ensure that the region would not lose a major source of revenue by retaining Chadwick's local production and second, it created further opportunity by employing even more local resources. Finally, it would also guarantee that quality control would in no way be compromised; if anything, it could become significantly improved. They were calling it a 'genius' move. The completion of the merger would also see the company undergo a complete rebranding, including a return to the original Fitz & Company name.

This was hailed by several news outlets as a 'victorious reclamation of a piece of the nation's lost chocolate history'.

Of course, all of the praise was a far cry from the initial features that came out when the story first broke. The English media are not generally known for their kindness toward foreign strangers and, at first, many of the news and blog sites referred to Henry as some 'pompous nouveau riche dilettante from the Continent'. When it was discovered that he was a 'distant relative' of the original Fitz family who had heard about the financial turmoil Chadwick's had been undergoing and decided it was time to step in and 'do the right thing', those same sites suddenly started welcoming him home as the prodigal son.

That was the public story Henry was feeding them, and it would seem that the press were sucking it up by the spoonful. Frankie wondered briefly what would happen if anyone ever discovered who or what Henry really was. That would surely generate a lot more questions than could be answered within the realm of reason, much less any media-savvy sound bytes.

She found herself deeply conflicted.

Kerri Thomson

On the one hand, Frankie was grateful to Henry for what he was offering the plant and its hundreds of employees, for most of whom Chadwick's was all they had. His was a far more generous proposal than the alternative that had been presented by their own board of directors, well-established men who had worked alongside these people for decades, making it appear all the more noble and impressive. But then, Frankie knew that his motives were not quite as altruistic as they seemed. That, however generous on its surface, it was coming from a sense of vengeance which had coloured her impression. She wanted to believe in her heart that what Henry had done for Chadwick's, or any of the other countless corporations he had taken over in the past century for that matter, was done more out of a sense of ethics and basic human decency rather than some longstanding animosity and the settling of very personal vendetta.

Maybe then I wouldn't feel so ashamed for loving him the way I do.

She supposed there was some comfort to be had in the knowledge that it was not only all's well that ends well for Chadwick's workers, but for its CEO as well. Daddy Chadwick was faring far better than one might think under such circumstances. For a hostile takeover, it went through without much by way of smut, scandal or any sizable fallout. No small task, from what Frankie had managed to glean listening to the way James had talked about some of the major deals his firm had brokered in the past, as if they were case studies he meant to follow to the letter. Louise's father may not have made the astronomical amount of money his original plan would have yielded, but that didn't seem to deter him. He was off to the South of France in search of a vineyard which would yield a perfect Bordeaux grape.

Frankie was relieved that none of the salacious reports she had come across on that Save Chadwick's website had come to light and added further insult to injury. For all she knew, the entire thing could have been a complete fabrication. She wouldn't know a legal affidavit if it came up and slapped her in the face, so it wasn't impossible. There would have been no better time to bring something like that out and kick a man who was already down. Why *wouldn't* someone with that kind of dirt take advantage of the opportunity?

No, Frankie thought, shaking herself back into the moment. The particular hissy fit Louise was having was purely a reaction to her father's sudden departure, not to the takeover or any damaging information that could have been revealed in its wake.

She was well aware that her friend had never adapted that well to change. She needed time to absorb things slowly, give herself an opportunity to adjust. Her grand lifestyle was in no way under threat. Daddy C had made a number of investments on her behalf over the years, and she could live quite comfortably on their dividends for the next thirty to forty years at least.

But it seemed that Louise had something else in mind.

"I think I could do this planning thing for a living, you know," she had mused one day, as they were reviewing the RSVP list one last time. When Frankie gaped at her in shock, she scowled.

"What? I'm really good at it!" she shot back defensively.

Contrary to what she thought, that was not the issue

Kerri Thomson

Frankie had with her sudden declaration. She was too busy wondering when it was exactly that the two of them had traded places.

In just a few short weeks, the Louise that she had always counted on to be a privileged, spoiled Daddy's girl with a heart of gold had become a grown-up woman possessed of empathy and a sense of independence, as well as an apparent plan for the future. Frankie, on the other hand, was feeling more and more as though she had devolved into a completely self-absorbed, boy-crazy shell of her former self, barely managing to keep it all together while desperately afraid that it would crumble beneath her just as her dream was within reach. *A little melodramatic, perhaps, but true nonetheless.*

Frankie's friendship with Louise had been built on her own long-established sense of moral superiority. If she didn't cut it out with the Mother Teresa crap soon, Frankie was afraid that drastic action would be in order. Something like getting Louise absolutely shit-faced on Stoli one night down the pub, then throwing her at some lads from the local university in order to restore balance and harmony to their relationship, perhaps. But the temper tantrum Frankie had just witnessed gave her pause. It meant that, deep down, she was still the same Louise after all.

"Frankie? Hello? Are you even listening to me??" Louise was waving her hand and snapping her fingers in front of her face, for how long Frankie could not say.

"Sorry…must've zoned out for the minute there. Haven't been getting a lot of sleep these days. What was that?" She faked a yawn and mimed a stretch for extra authenticity.

"I was *saying*," Louise continued in the annoyed tone she used whenever she had to repeat herself, "that Jared has offered to build me a web page, you know, to promote myself as an event planner. I think there might even be some evening courses I can take at one of the colleges in town to help me with the more technical side of things. But really, when it comes to planning a raging party, who can top me?"

She made a very valid point. Louise had been throwing massive parties at least three or four times a year for the past ten years or so, and bossing the coordinators of those parties around for at least the last five. If anyone knew the secret formula for the perfect party, it was her.

"So Jared's a web programmer now, is he? Ooh, is there anything that man of yours *can't* do?" Frankie couldn't resist the chance to tease, cooing and batting her eyelashes before Louise gave her a shove hard enough to send her flying off the sofa.

Despite the teasing, she was well aware of what Frankie thought of her newly grown-up relationship with Jared: she couldn't have designed a better man herself for Louise.

"For your information," Louise returned haughtily, "there happens to be *lots* of things Jared is good at." The naughty wink she added left little doubt as to what she was inferring. Out of habit, Frankie closed her eyes and shuddered.

"Right, you win. I'm done teasing. Just please, for the love of God, spare me the details? It's bad enough I have to live with the two of you."

Louise laughed and Frankie couldn't help but join her, almost forgetting how much of a relief it was. What with the shop and everything else she had been dealing with lately, it felt good to just laugh like a little kid every once in a while.

"How is Jared, anyway?" Frankie asked once they'd finished giggling.

Between her own late nights and his, Frankie felt like she never saw him anymore despite that they were sharing the same house. She supposed that it was bound to happen, what with his appointment to chief of research and development at the newly restructured Fitz & Company. Not a shock, really. She knew that Henry was no fool. That Jared was a bio-chemical genius with a work ethic that was hard to come by would not be lost on him. But what Frankie had found surprising was the news that Von Hoffstatler had managed to secure a position as well, as technical adviser.

"He's good, yeah," Louise replied, almost too quickly and cheerily as she made her way into the kitchen, "really busy. But I guess that comes naturally with a big promotion and everything that's going on with the factory."

She seemed uncharacteristically cagey in her response, pausing awkwardly in more places than could be considered coincidence. At first, Frankie thought it was because they were discussing the company her family used to own, but something in her expression told her there was more to it. She started digging.

"So he's happy, then, with his new position? And the way things have... turned out?"

Frankie watched Louise's reaction carefully, prepared to back off at even the slightest hint of rage or tears. But there was neither, just a nervous titter in her voice that sent her intuition into overdrive. She knew what that sound meant.

"What is it you're not telling me, Lou?"

Louise shrugged and busied herself with making the tea.

"Fancy a cuppa?" Louise refused to face her.

Frankie pushed a deeply annoyed breath out through pursed lips, and began to drum her fingers on the countertop. Two sounds, she had discovered long ago, that were guaranteed to drive Louise round the bend. This time, she was only looking to find out whatever it was that Louise was not so cleverly trying to conceal. She waited for the sound to set in and do its worst, using Louise's physical reaction as a barometer to determine just how long it would take for her to crack. Judging from the way her hands shook as she brought the teacups down from the cupboard, Frankie was willing to wager that she had about ten seconds left.

Louise took a moment to steady herself, her hands splayed stiffly on the counter, before turning to face her.

"I don't think I should say anything," she said quietly, not making eye contact as she chewed furiously on her lip.

Frankie knew what that meant: while she didn't think she *should* say anything, it was slowly killing her inside *not to*.

"C'mon, Lou. When has there ever been something you haven't been able to tell me? It's late, and I'm getting cranky, so just pour the tea and get on with it already."

After a few more moments of watching her wrestle with her conscience, Frankie couldn't help feeling somewhat vindicated as she caved.

"Jared told me that Henry's been asking about you," Louise blurted out before squeezing her eyes shut, as if to shield herself from the fallout.

Frankie found it hard to understand the way she felt as she heard Louise say those simple few words. The best she could come up with was based on a memory from her childhood. As a little girl at school, Frankie had once swung herself too high on the swing in the park and managed to become airborne. As she hit the ground, the air from her lungs was pushed out so violently that it had made her feel like she was going to pass out and vomit all at the same time. She lay on the ground, hearing the people that were gathered around but as if she were deep underwater and they were on the surface. When she tried to open her eyes, to tell them that she was all right, she couldn't see past the spinning stars.

Hearing that Henry had been asking about her was a little like that.

Once the stars finally stopped spinning and Frankie was able to find her voice again, she was relieved to discover that her rational mind had remained unscathed. For a moment there, she feared the worst.

"Well, he probably still thinks he has some sort of financial stake in the shop," Frankie answered at last, pleased that she was able to keep her voice so steady.

She could feel Louise staring at her before she seemed to click that Frankie was merely bluffing her way through. *Denial is more than just a river in Africa, isn't it?*

"No, Frannie, I don't think he was asking from a

business perspective," she replied softly. "But Jared said he did start by asking if he knew about your shop, if it would be opening soon. That's how he'd found out that you two know each other."

Frankie almost slapped herself in the forehead, confounded at her own ignorance. Because she had spoken so often to Louise and Jared about Henry, she assumed that they would know each other. It had never once occurred to her that Henry had not met any of her friends, and vice versa. But she knew he would know who they were. And because Henry never seemed to do anything without having an ulterior motive, she immediately became suspicious.

"So what sort of things did he ask Jared? About me."

Louise seemed to regret being such a lightweight when it came to keeping anything from Frankie, but a stern look was enough to keep her talking.

"He started out with asking about the shop, as if you would be a potential client for them. But then, Jared said that he would slip in little comments like 'she must be incredibly tenacious to be opening a chocolate shop in this economy... has she told you what compelled her to do such a thing?'" Once the floodgates had opened, Louise's words soon began to spill out over one another. She continued with a torrent of other examples of the kinds of questions Henry would ask before winding down.

"And then he says he'll ask completely random things like what do you do when you're not at the shop and how long Jared has known you. Personal things that have absolutely nothing to do with the business."

"Oh, well, that's just another way for him to keep tabs

on me," Frankie tried to reply casually with an indifferent wave of her hand. She hoped that it looked more convincing than it felt.

"He's probably just pissed that I'm not his little pawn anymore," she added for good measure, when Louise wasn't saying anything. "Although he doesn't need me anymore. He's done everything he's set out to do."

Louise looked at her for another long minute, and then shook her head sadly.

"You don't really believe that, do you?"

Frankie faked another stretch and pushed her half-finished cup of tea across the island.

"Yes, actually. I do," she answered quickly through a poor imitation of a yawn, "but it's late and I've got to get to sleep. See you in the morning." She was out of her seat and halfway up the stairs before Louise could respond.

Frankie heard her say goodnight faintly as she sprinted to her bedroom.

"Good night," she called back, smiling at the irony of it. It wasn't like she would have much hope of getting any sleep that night with the opening looming. And after what Louise had just told her, that Henry had been asking after her, only made an already sleepless situation that much worse.

Whenever Frankie's eyes would drift close, there Henry would be waiting. Sometimes he was at the far end of Louise's back garden, the moonlight illuminating the dove grey of his hat and setting off his lightly sun-kissed skin in a

324

way that should have been illegal. Other times, he would be waiting for her inside the shop after she'd unlocked the door, the sleeves of his flawless white Thomas Pink dress shirt rolled up, ready to set to work with his shirt only halfway buttoned. Still other scenarios placed him in the dark of her bedroom. She would walk in and nearly scream head off when she discovered someone in her bed. Things would quickly take a turn for the better, however, once she realised exactly who it was and that he was wearing little more than a sheet and a smile.

All things considered, she thought grimly as she tossed and turned, *to say restful sleep is elusive is like saying that the Pope is a Catholic.*

Not long after dawn broke, Frankie stumbled downstairs at an uncharacteristic half seven a.m., trying in vain to rub the lack of sleep from her eyes. She hoped that she would find some time to grab a nap later, or she would have to rely on a mixture of caffeine, chocolate and sheer nervous adrenalin to make it through that night.

She almost shrieked out loud when she rounded the corner and noticed someone sitting at the breakfast table in the kitchen, pounding away with vigour on a laptop keyboard.

"Lou? What the fuck are you doing up at this hour? Christ, you scared the shit out of me," Frankie gasped as she lurched toward the coffee machine where, mercifully, there was already a pot on the go.

"Oh sorry, I've been up since six. Wanted to get in some final touches so that tonight will come off like clockwork," she replied with neither a glance nor pause in her typing.

Her voice had an annoyingly chipper note to it, one that could not be tolerated so early in the morning. Frankie eyed her with more than a little contempt.

"This shit has got to stop," she grumbled into her coffee cup.

Louise looked at her sharply. She had forgotten how sensitive her friend's hearing could be when she felt like listening.

"What was that?"

"What? When I yawned just there? Yeah, didn't get much sleep last night, I guess," Frankie deflected quickly, before announcing she was going back upstairs to take a shower in hope of making herself feel human again.

"All right," Louise replied dismissively. "And when you're done, I can go over the guest list with you. Oh, and don't you dare wash your hair! If I'm going to put it in finger waves later, the last thing we need is for it to be clean."

Frankie rolled her eyes, faintly amused at the casual way Louise barked orders at her as if she were just another cog in her well-oiled party planning machine. But really, how could she have expected this to be different from any of the dozens of other parties she had seen her plan over the years? Except that this time, there were no minions for her to boss about as she pleased. *Nope, this time it's just her... and me. Guess I can kiss that nap idea goodbye.* Frankie sent up a silent prayer that she'd managed to remember to wash her hair yesterday, feeling privileged that Louise was even allowing her out of her sight.

She showered as quickly as she could, half-expecting

Louise to burst in at any moment, telling her to shift it and tapping at her wrist. Never mind that Frankie had never, ever known her to wear a watch the entire time they had been friends; it was just who Louise was. Back in her bedroom, she threw on whatever clothes she could find that were clean, not the easiest of tasks considering that the last thing on her mind of late had been the washing. Unlike Louise, Frankie refused to allow Mavis to do it, which meant that she was left with some ratty old grey flannel plaid shirt that might have at one point belonged to her father and a pair of dark trouser jeans, the only jeans she could find that weren't covered in chocolate or powdered sugar.

Down in the kitchen, she found Louise still typing away. Frankie pulled a chair around to sit beside her. Louise wrinkled her nose in distaste after giving her outfit a slow once-over.

"Nice," she said snottily. "Thank God I'm dressing you for this party tonight, since apparently this is what happens when you're left to your own devices." Frankie made a face and gave her the two finger salute as she sat down.

"Shut it, slut," she said sweetly. "Now why don't you just show me what you need to show me?"

Her demeanour shifted dramatically, her eyes lighting up in a way that was normally reserved for when she would discover that her favourite Chanel lipstick had a matching nail varnish or that she had scored a last minute booking with the magical hands of the finest skin therapist in town.

"Right, so I've separated the guest list into three separate tabs: one for family and friends, one for media, and one for local business owners or anyone else who might qualify as a potential contact or resource. Now, if you'll look at this column here, I've included some little notes for you about who they are and what they do. It will make conversation easier... I know what you're like in a room full of people. You'll probably want to study this before we leave."

Frankie shot a quick scowl in her direction.

"You didn't mention anything about studying," she countered. "Will there be a pop quiz later and all?"

Despite her ribbing and natural disinclination toward all things academic, Frankie had to admit that she was impressed with how much effort Louise had put in and how seriously she was taking this. As if it really were a business opportunity, and that she was a proper client instead of her best friend. Frankie noted that her spreadsheets were flawless and beautifully colour-coded, making it easy to precisely pick out any information she might need at a glance. It was one of the entries, however, that gave her pause.

"I see that James and Shaye are coming," Frankie said quietly.

Louise looked up at her sharply and with no small amount of concern on her face.

"Yeah, he practically begged for an invite. Told me he wanted to show his support. That's all right, isn't it? I didn't even think to ask..."

"Of course," Frankie replied. "It's a bit of a surprise, but it would be nice to see him again, actually."

And she was being completely truthful; she had only been surprised that James would want to go. Frankie was fairly certain that, for anyone else, having their ex-fiancé show up at their shop's grand opening party with the woman that he'd cheated with would be their worst nightmare. But she already knew that she wasn't like most people.

Louise was busy going over the particulars of various local media personalities that would be in attendance when they were interrupted by a tap at the kitchen's French windows. Mavis was standing there, vibrating with excitement, holding the largest arrangement of orange and pink roses Frankie had ever seen. Her heart skipped two or three beats.

Before she could move, Louise was up and squealing as she ran to help with the door. Mavis's arms were so full of the flowers she could never have managed herself. Louise swooped in on the card with the air of someone so well-versed in receiving flowers that she could have done it with her eyes closed.

"They're for you, Frannie," she announced finally, then added a short pause for dramatic effect.

Frankie's heartbeat was fluttering so fast she feared it might fail on her altogether. When she thought that the silence of what seemed to be the world record-holder in pauses would be the death of her, Louise spoke again.

"They're from Quinn. And Alex."

Hearing the two names together brought Frankie back to yet another major development from the past few weeks.

At one time, Louise had regarded Quinn Baker and Alex Tompkins as potential suitors, way ahead in the running over Jared who had eventually won her over with a genuine devotion and affection that remained unchanged even throughout one of her darker moments. At the time, Frankie had been rooting for Jared, so she didn't give a lick of thought as to what might have become of either Alex or Quinn after Louise's party.

Until one night, not so long ago, when Louise came shrieking into her bedroom. It was about quarter past one in the morning, and Frankie had just nicely drifted off to sleep after spending yet another sixteen hour day at the shop making chocolate.

"Wha— Lou? What the f... what's happened?"

Louise's face was ashen, immediately leading her to assume the worst. Had Jared gotten into an accident? Her father suffered a coronary? Was she going to say that she'd found more Fitz Cocoa Creams and had fallen off the wagon? With so many questions tumbling round in her sleep-addled brain, she was finding it difficult to focus.

However, nothing could have prepared her for what Louise was about to say.

"Alex and Quinn are gay." That was enough to get her attention.

"Wait, Alex and Quinn... what?"

As Frankie bolted upright in bed, trying to shake off the last dregs of the sleep that had only just claimed her, Louise had come to sit at the edge of the mattress. She looked as if she might have gone into shock.

Clutched in her trembling hands was one of the nation's many gossip rags, the kind that you leaf through as you waited in queue at the corner shop or grocery store, hoping no one you knew would catch you. It was opened up to the society section, and Frankie could see the bold headline emblazoned across the page that had thrown Louise into such a fit.

Caught with His Trousers Down!

Toffee Heir Out having a Gay Old Time

A quick scan of the article showed that it was based on some sketchy eye witness accounts and a collection of doctored photos that insinuated Alex and Quinn were together in *every* way. Typically she would have dismissed it as nothing more than tabloid nonsense, but there was one photo in particular that was enough to make her look twice.

This picture, a candid shot, didn't appear to have been a cut and paste job or tampered with in any way. It showed Quinn and Alex at a football game, with their arms round each other's shoulders much the same as most of the other lads there, but with one major point of difference. The look on Alex's face as he was laughing with Quinn was startlingly similar to the one Frankie had seen on Jared's face when she had first met him at Louise's birthday. The same one she surely must have worn herself at her first, and any other encounter with Henry. In a word: smitten.

"C'mon Lou," Frankie had said, in retrospect a little unconvincingly. "You of all people should know firsthand what kind of rubbish they print in these magazines. They make crap like this up all the time."

Louise's eyes narrowed as she stabbed viciously at the same picture that had stood out to Frankie from all the others.

"Look," she had nearly shrieked in reply. "Look at that face! They can't make that up. They don't even need to. It's *right there!*"

It was clear that nothing Frankie could say was going to help the situation. But, true to form, it wasn't like she had ever let that stop her before.

"Well, right… so what if *it is* true that Alex and Quinn are together? What does it matter? It's not like it makes a whit of difference to you; you have Jared. If they're happy, who the fuck cares if they're gay or straight?"

Frankie felt certain that Louise wasn't terribly fond of her in that moment.. But she also knew that a little perspective was exactly what was needed. To her amazement Louise sat there in silence, staring at the magazine in her hands. Usually she would have shrieked back defensively, having always been of the opinion that she could bring someone round to her way of thinking by sheer force of volume. But not this time.

"It just makes me feel…foolish, I guess," Louise said finally without looking up. Frankie waited wordlessly for her to continue.

"You know what I mean? I mean, I chased the both of them so shamelessly and publicly, and not once did it ever occur to me that they wouldn't be interested. *Not once.* Am I really that vain and clueless?"

Frankie bit her lip, unsure if the brutal honesty that had always been her trademark was the best approach in such a delicate situation. *When in doubt, toss it back.*

"Do you really want me to answer that?"

Louise made a face as she deftly tossed one of the throw pillows at her. Somehow Frankie managed to catch it and throw it back at her. She giggled and sank to the floor, clutching the pillow to her face and screaming into it.

"No, seriously. What does this say about me?" Louise had laid her head on the bed, thoughtfully tracing the baroque pattern at the bottom of the duvet cover. "I mean, am I really so thick not to even pick up on something like that? Because, that... That's a pretty big thing to miss. And not just with the one. I missed any sign of it with both of them."

"Well," again Frankie had to carefully choose her words and stifle the caustic remarks that seemed to come out so naturally for her, "I think maybe you just didn't want to see it. But if it's any consolation, I totally missed it on both counts as well. And I'm usually pretty good with the gay-dar, so they must have been hiding it fairly well. Besides, I was more worried about making sure you behaved yourself at your party despite your resistance, so I wasn't really paying much attention. You were quite determined to be a dirty whore."

Louise made another face at her, but made no attempt to deny it. It was one of the traits that Frankie admired most in her friend. She knew who she was, and made no apologies for it. She left the room that night without further comment, and the next day made a few phone calls which ultimately confirmed the story as truth.

Apparently after the birthday party, Alex and Quinn could conceal their feelings no longer and just gave in. They had tried to keep it quiet at first, since the proposed merger between Chadwick's and Tompkin's had already created such a tense environment that even the slightest hint of scandal might have been catastrophic. But once news of Henry's coup began to dominate the headlines, the new couple took it as an opportunity to let their guard down. Unfortunately in doing so, one of the many bottomfeeding tabloids made that opportunity their own to effectively out them in the pages of their magazine.

The whole story had exploded into a local media sensation, including a very public row between Alex and his father, but it died down just as quickly once the paparazzo who had been trailing the two lovers realised that they had actually done Quinn and Alex a massive favour. In exposing them so publicly, it forced them to be honest about their relationship, as much with the world as with each other. In the end, it ended up bringing them closer together. And since happiness didn't sell newspapers neary as well as scandals and heartbreak did, the media had no choice but to move on. Although there was no real need to, the new couple decided it was time for them to move on as well.

Quinn had persuaded Alex to go back with him to America for a taste of some California sunshine, and the last that Frankie had heard they were loving it up at his house in Malibu.

"They're sorry they can't make it, but are still insisting you cater the dessert bar after their wedding ceremony," Louise continued to read off the flower's card, refusing to pass it over to Frankie.

"Of course. Not like I'd have much choice in the matter anyway, considering you're the one planning it," Frankie replied without missing a beat, shaking herself out of her memories. It was becoming more of a pattern than she'd care to admit.

Growing impatient, she got out of her seat and wrenched the card from Louise's grasp to read it for herself.

"They're so lovely. I wish they were going to be there tonight. I could use some familiar faces seeing as you've invited more than half the city." Louise clucked at her in disapproval.

"Frankie, you want your shop to succeed, don't you? Think of your grand opening as kind of like a first impression: it's something you'll never get a second chance at, so you have no choice but to do it right. And that means being nice and talking to the very people you would normally go out of your way to avoid. Oh, and could you maybe try to avoid saying fuck every second word? If only just for tonight... Please?"

Frankie rolled her eyes and stuck her tongue out at Louise, but had to admit she made a valid point.

"All right, fine. I'll be on my best behaviour. And speaking of tonight, when do I get to see this outfit you've put together for me? I mean, I've got a ton of shit left to finish. I've got to go to the shop and—" Louise cut her off mid-rant with a wave of her hand.

"Frankie, please, I am your event planner. I told you, just leave everything to me, and I meant it. Now, if you'll look at this chart, I've got the entire day planned out for us. We'll go get things sorted at the shop first, grab a quick bite to eat around two, then take care of any last minute bits and bobs before heading back here for four to start getting ready. With hair and makeup for both of us, that should leave just enough time to be back at the shop for seven and prepare for the doors to open at eight."

Frankie was impressed. It would seem that Louise had left nothing to chance. She'd even factored in loo breaks; they were coded in yellow. *Cheeky bitch.*

"Right. Shall we get started then?" Frankie reached for the car keys, and they made the now-familiar drive into town.

11:49am

By the time they arrived at the shop to put together a few extra boxes of chocolate for display, Frankie was starting to get very nervous. Terrified, more like. There was no tangible reason for it; everything was moving like clockwork. In fact once they had settled in to work, Frankie quickly saw that there was almost nothing left to do.

The shelves were stacked with pretty boxes of pale pink, lavender, sherbet orange and baby blue, all tied with a glossy chocolate brown ribbon bearing the shop's name. The antique glass display cabinets had been fitted with temperature controls so that the chocolate inside would retain its structure, sheen, and quality regardless of any weather changes; they stood patiently waiting to be filled with the more delicate truffles and other sweets she'd placed in the bulk storage humidor until the party.

Frankie paused to lovingly stroke the dark cherry table that held court in the centre of the room, adorned with gleaming silver tiered serving platters that would soon provide the backdrop for the tasting chocolate.

The scene was exactly what she had envisioned that first night she stood there, when the shop was nothing more than an empty shell waiting for someone to come along and breathe some life into it. It was on an evening not long after that Henry had knocked on the door and walked into her life.

That was the night that changed her life inalterably, in more ways than one. And she knew that the evening ahead would mark the beginning of yet another new chapter, one where she would step up as a successful business woman capable of running her own shop.

One where she would finally, really and truly, become a Grown-Up.

"Well, I think that's it," Louise announced in triumph as she emerged from where she had been tidying in the kitchen and office. Not that anyone would be going back there for anything besides the washroom but still, it had to look spotless, she had explained. Frankie wasn't sure when she could expect to recover from the sight of her best friend on her knees, scrubbing the toilet with pink rubber gloves edged in fuchsia feathers.

She conducted a final sweep of the shop floor, checking as Frankie had that everything was in order.

"You've started the drinking chocolate, yeah?"

"Of course. Just remind me to turn it on again when we get back. That way it will be warmed up enough to serve when people start arriving at eight. I can't turn it on now or it will burn," Frankie replied as she glanced at the beautiful urn-style hot chocolate machine, a last-minute splurge. Imported from France, it was a stunningly ornate piece of sterling silver that dated back to the late 1700s, etched with vines and flowers that cascaded over the two handles down to the spout. It fit in perfectly among the rest of the shop décor, and made her dizzy with delight just to look at it. Then again, she mused, that could just be the memory of how much it had cost her.

After one last walkthrough of the shop, they were on their way to the next stop in Louise's carefully crafted itinerary: to grab a bit of lunch before heading home to get ready. Frankie's stomach was tying itself into such knots that she was sure she would be incapable of keeping anything down, but Louise insisted.

"I know what you're like: you're so nervous that you think you can't eat anything, but once the party starts you'll be drinking like a fish. Then before you know it, it will be your twenty-first birthday weekend all over again. Only this time, with much more public puking and a lot less weed."

Frankie winced at the memory. Or would have, except that she really had no memory of that night beyond the bits and pieces that had been told to her. The only thing she knew for certain was that they had gone to Amsterdam, where she had decided it would be a really good idea to crawl into one of the bordello windows and dance with the prostitutes showing off their wares. Louise had pulled her out of there before she could either be purchased or put in jail and how had Frankie thanked her? By throwing up all over her brand new Prada square toe pumps.

Louise would make mention of it whenever it would suit her purpose, and this happened to be just another one of those times. But her point came across loud and clear. Frankie took another bite of her club sandwich and tucked into the chips.

"So tell me, Lou. On a scale of one to ten, how much am I going to hate wearing what you've chosen for me tonight?"

Louise put down her salad fork mid-stab to give Frankie a solemn look.

"Frankie, that hurts. I know how much you hate to be the centre of attention, but tonight you're just going to have to suck it up and deal. You'll be the most beautiful thing in the room."

"That doesn't sound promising," Frankie grumbled, absent-mindedly picking at her food. Louise smiled and winked as she continued eating.

Frankie's stomach did a flip. She was well familiar with that look. Familiar enough to know that no good could possibly come of it.

After Louise signalled for the bill, they walked to her car without another word. Frankie sat in silence as Louise hummed and giggled to herself in the passenger seat as she drove, pausing occasionally to comment about a song on the radio or what the weather was going to be like later in the week. But not once did she even attempt to answer Frankie's initial question.

No, Frankie thought, her stomach flipping again. *This wasn't good at all.*

SIXTEEN

October 13th

3:37pm

Frankie was filled with an overwhelming sense of déjà vu as she stood in her skivvies in Louise's bedroom. She couldn't help but think back to the last time they had gotten ready together: the night of Louise's birthday.

The night when the madness that had become her life had first begun. She tried to shake it off and enjoy herself, live in the moment, but knew that wasn't something that would ever come easily to a chronic overthinker like. Even if there was nothing left to think about.

Louise was a born party girl, and Frankie understood that her career move as an event planner was inspired. She had always treated getting ready for the evening with as much care and attention as the main event itself. She knew how to keep the wine glasses full and choose the right music that would ultimately set the tone for the rest of the evening. That night was no exception: Louise had pulled out all the stops with a selection of Frankie's favourite New Romantic and synth-pop hits from the Eighties, topped off with a couple bottles of Bollinger champagne.

"All right, Lou," Frankie was a girl with simple tastes, but the one thing she lacked was patience. "No more stalling. Let's see it."

Louise whirled around to face her, still in the throes of dancing wildly to Adam Ant's 'Goody Two-shoes'.

"Why, whatever do you mean?" Her tone was teasing, full of mischief. Frankie huffed, exasperated, and pointed to the clock.

"We're running out of time. We have to start getting dressed."

But even as she said it, she knew that wasn't entirely true. Thanks to Louise's efficient planning, they were running ahead of schedule. And though Frankie could feel her nerves continuing to creep up on her, she was managing to remain relatively calm. *Guess I've got the Bolly to thank for that.*

Louise giggled and turned the music down.

"God, you are *so* easy to wind up," she laughed as Frankie glowered, searching for something to throw. Tossing one of her ubiquitous throw pillows lamely only made Louise laugh louder.

"Fine, Pissy-Pants: you win. I'll put you out of your misery," she said as she left the room, closing the door behind her.

After she had been gone for what felt like an eternity, Frankie was about to follow when she heard her stop just outside the door.

"Now I know that purple is your colour of choice," Louise began theatrically as she slowly made her entrance into the room, clutching a grey plastic garment bag, "but it would seem that it wasn't very popular for clothing in the Twenties. Then I found this, and while it isn't purple, I knew it was the one."

She stood in front of Frankie and went to unzip the bag, but paused.

"Oy you -- eyes closed! You know the rules."

Frankie squeezed her eyes shut, half-annoyed but equally as caught up in the moment. And she knew it was easier to humour Louise. She heard the zip of the bag being opened, then the soft rustling sound it made as it slid from the fabric it concealed and came to rest on the floor. She held her breath in an attempt to keep herself still as she awaited further instructions.

"Open your eyes," Louise whispered.

Frankie did, and gasped at what was in front of her. On its surface it could best be described as a flapper's shift, a dress typical of what one might find oneself in when doing the Charleston at a speakeasy during the Jazz Age. But the dress itself was anything but typical.

It was a complex combination of fringe, feathers and beading; an overlaying fringe of rich green interlaced with threads of black and gold that added contrast to a base of bright peacock blue silk. The low collar was made from peacock feathers braided with velvet of the same striking blue. Its overall effect was nothing short of breathtaking. And for the moment, simply looking at it made Frankie feel breathless.

Like a rare and exotic bird of paradise, it was the kind of dress she would expect to see on some genetically perfect model or classically beautiful actress. Someone with a name like Laetitia or Audrey or Cate. *Someone whose name was definitely not Frankie.*

"Louise, I can't possibly wear that," she managed to whisper. "Everyone's going to be staring at me."

"Hello? That's kind of the point," Louise shot back. "These colours against your skin are going to be beyond gorgeous. Please don't do this to me, Frannie. Not now. Just...just have another drink and try it on."

Frankie noted the panic in Louise's face and the borderline hysterical tone of her voice, and knew that to argue with her would be pointless. It was too late to do anything about it. There was no Plan B.

Part of her knew that Louise had to have fully anticipated this reaction, which was precisely the reason why she had waited until just hours before the party to reveal it. She knew that Frankie would never agree to wear something so ornate under any other circumstance, but would be left with no other option because of the time.

Louise wasn't about to give Frankie time to overthink the issue -- she was on her in a flash, unbuttoning her comfy yet deeply unflattering shirt and yanking it off. The two had been friends for so long that they felt more like sisters, and had moved far beyond any semblance of modesty. They were quite comfortable stripping down to their skivvies in front of one another. Besides, strictly by comparison, Frankie was painfully aware that she had nothing Louise hadn't seen before.

She would not have seen a chest this flat since public school, she thought.

"Step in," Louise ordered once she'd gotten Frankie's jeans off, holding the dress in front of her.

Gingerly, Frankie stepped into it and allowed Louise to pull it into place. The silk felt cool against her skin, which had become flushed in agitation. She closed her eyes, fearing the worst, as she felt Louise smoothing the fabric into place. She heard a gasp, and her eyes flew open.

"What? What's wrong?" Louise could only shake her head, her eyes welling in tears.

Oh fuck, Frankie thought, racing as quickly as she could in such a frock for the closest mirror. Once she stood gazing at her reflection in the full-length glass that hung just behind the door, she became aware that something amazing was happening.

The last dress that Frankie had worn, that purple Victorian gown from Louise's birthday, was beautiful but felt very much as if she were wearing a costume. It had turned her into a completely different person, a character who was stepping into someone else's well-heeled shoes for an evening. She felt more like an imposter than anything else.

However, wearing this fantastic dress was an entirely new experience. Despite the initial reservations she'd had over wearing something so flamboyant, once she got a good look at herself in it, for the first time in a long time Frankie felt like herself. Her slim physique, something she had always considered a burden, was made for the straight lines and dropped waist of the flapper-style dress. The silk of the bodice draped against her frame in all the right places, and the fringe that extended beyond a hemline that ended at the knee danced invitingly around her bare legs before coming to a stop mid-calf. It made her legs look a hundred miles long. The brilliant blue and deep green hues made her skin glow as if it had been lit from within. Her hazel eyes sparkled like freshly cut emeralds. Even her hair seemed to take on new life, shining like a Titian halo one might find on some angelic being from a Renaissance painting.

It was as if the dress, at its core nothing more than a brightly coloured scrap of fabric with some feathers and fringe, had awakened something inside of Frankie. Something that perhaps had always been there, just waiting for the right time to come out.

"It's just… it's…. It's magic," was all she could muster coherently. Louise was nodding enthusiastically in agreement.

"It really is. I mean, it looks as if it were made for you."

They both continued to admire Frankie's reflection for a few minutes longer when she remembered something else.

"What are you wearing, then?" she asked Louise with a sinking feeling. *If this is the dress she picked for me, what the hell did she get for herself?*

"Oh, I went for something a bit more low-key, demure even. Well, for me, anyways," Louise shrugged non-committedly.

Frankie wasn't sure that she had heard her correctly. It was quite unlike Louise to pass up an opportunity to dress to the nines for a party. Especially one where she would be playing hostess to a number of journalists, television personalities and other local celebrities.

She urged her to go get changed, knowing full well that Louise had her own definition of these terms, ones that were often quite different from everyone else. Demure for her could mean something that didn't have a slit all the way up to the crotch or a neckline cut to her waist. Low-key for Louise could mean just about anything. However, as she came back down the steps, Frankie had to admit that she was pleasantly surprised.

"It's your night, after all." Lately, Louise had developed the unsettling ability to read Frankie's mind. Even more than usual.

Louise's dress was a masterpiece of silk velvet drapery, a rich claret colour not unlike an Argentinian red wine, with some jet-beaded fringe that draped across the bodice and past the knee with a hem edged in scalloped black lace and yet more clusters of dark, shiny beads. It was much darker and far more substantial than her usual party-going attire, but it was a dress that was at once both understated and elegant.

Two words that Frankie had never, ever thought she would use when describing any outfit that Louise would be wearing.

"Lou," she couldn't help herself from gasping. "You look so... *classy*." Louise promptly responded with the classic two finger salute, blowing a raspberry for punctuation. *Ah yes, the girl is all class.*

"No, really," Frankie said once the giggling subsided. "You look really beautiful. Definitely demure and low-key."

Louise beamed at her, her face flushed with a look that Frankie wasn't accustomed to seeing on her best friend when she was so covered up. She could have sworn it was pride.

"So, where the hell did you find all this stuff?" she breathed in admiration, watching as Louise dug out a plethora of era-appropriate accessories to complete their respective attire. Feathered fascinators, suspender belts, silk stockings, garter flasks…everything. Louise flashed her a mischievous grin.

"I have my sources," she replied cryptically.

It was when she pulled out a Marcel waving iron, which was mercifully an electric version instead of an original that would need to be heated up over hot coals, that Frankie had to insist that she tell her. Louise was more concerned with explaining that using the iron would save them much-needed time as opposed to the finger waving.

"Oh, all right," Louise later sighed as she wound a sizable chunk of Frankie's hair around the iron. "Remember when I was in my first year at uni and I couldn't decide what I to study?"

Frankie nodded. She was certain that Louise's father would remember it as well, though perhaps not quite so fondly. As Frankie was busy busting her behind working double shifts in a Soho café and taking patisserie courses in London, Louise had spent her time bouncing from subject to subject at Oxford. At least, whenever her classes didn't interfere with an ever-growing schedule of parties, shopping, and campus activities.

"Well, I started hanging round the drama students, helping out with their shows, handing out flyers, snorting coke… you know, the usual. There was a boy, of course. Jamie, who I fancied the pants off of."

"Of course there was a boy. When is there not?"

Louise was refreshingly predictable in her motivations: it either involved men or fashion, sometimes both.

Louise tugged hard on Frankie's hair to shut her up as she continued.

"I couldn't figure out why he was the only one who had no interest in getting into my knickers, despite how hard I was trying to get into his. Of course, naïve as I was back then, I never thought that he could be gay. He couldn't come out until after his Nana died or he would lose his inheritance or something. Hmmm," Louise tapped her cheek thoughtfully with the edge of the comb she was using, artfully arranging the waves she had just created in Frankie's hair.

"That doesn't sound familiar at all, does it, Lou?" Frankie couldn't help but tease. It was a risk, particularly since she was holding a hot curling rod near her face, but fortunately Louise let it pass by without incident.

"Now that I think about," Louise exclaimed, eyes widening in understanding as she pointed the comb at Frankie, "it was a lot like what happened with Alex and me. Anyway, he found me on Facebook a couple years ago and we've been messaging back and forth ever since. He's up in London, working as wardrobe manager for one of the big West End theatres."

"This is all very interesting," Frankie was beginning to lose patience with the characteristically drawn-out nature of Louise's story, "but what does this little trip down memory lane have to do with anything?"

Louise thumped her on the back of the head with the comb.

"Oww! What the fu—" Frankie squealed as Louise shushed her.

"Patience, Frannie. I'm getting there. So there I was, wondering where I was going to find authentic flapper costumes, when I see an ad for the final run of Chicago -- at Jamie's theatre! I sent him a message asking what they did with all of the costumes when a show was finished its run. He told me that sometimes they donate them to other theatres or to museums like the V&A if they are putting together an exhibit or something, or else they just store them until the next production comes round so, long story short, I was able to work out a deal to get hold of these ones." She smiled in triumph, indicating her story was at an end.

"So all of this is on loan then, right?" One could never be too certain when it came to Louise and these kinds of things.

"The dresses are, yes, but," she pointed to the stockings and other sundries, "he threw in some of the extras for free since they had a ton of leftovers."

Again, Frankie had to hand it to her. Louise had a way of getting things done.

As Louise continued to shape her hair into a proper 1920's-esque bob, Frankie could feel the butterflies building up once more in her stomach. This time they were fluttering so hard she was worried that her insides might come bursting out.

"Tell me this is going to work, Lou," Frankie pleaded as she was lining her eyes in a deep, bottle green cream eye shadow.

"Of course it will," Louise replied without hesitation. "By lining your eyes with shadow instead of pencil, it tends to have much more staying power."

"Not the makeup," Frankie sighed, rolling her eyes. Or at least attempting to with Louise's fingers in the way. *"Tonight.* The party, the shop, the rest of my life... You know: the whole reason we're doing all of this in the first place?"

Louise stopped and moved to stand in front of her, cupping her face firmly in her hands.

"Yes, Frankie. Your grand opening will be a smashing success, and so will your shop," she said solemnly, then picked up her eyeliner brush and continued applying the makeup as if nothing had happened. If Frankie could have shaken her head, she would have.

"Well," Louise sighed as she took a step back. "I think this just might be my finest work yet. Go on -- have a look."

Frankie headed for the nearest mirror to see what Louise had been working on so diligently for the past hour. She had to look twice to be sure that she wasn't imagining what she was seeing. Or maybe it was three or four times. Louise wasn't wrong; this was her masterpiece.

The reflection that stared back at Frankie was a vixen and a vamp, or some other combination of every possible adjective for sexy and seductive that she would never normally use to describe herself. Louise had given her the classic flapper look, dark eyes and strong lips with a Marcel-waved faux bob. The green she had used around her eyes was flecked with gold, making them shine even brighter than they'd done with the dress alone. The dark ruby on her lips made Frankie's skin appear as flawless as a porcelain doll.

While usually she would detest the idea of wearing that much makeup, there was no denying that it completed the look. As if the dress weren't spectacular enough on its own, with her hair and makeup done Frankie looked like a starlet who had just walked off of a classic film set. And yet somehow, she still looked like herself.

"Wow," was all that would come out. Louise appeared in the reflection behind her, gloating with immodesty. "I don't even know what to say. Thanks, Lou."

"Pleasure," she replied as she skipped away. "Now I'm off to finish getting myself ready, then we'd better get moving. I forgot to get the masks out of the boot earlier."

"Masks?" Frankie was still distracted by her own reflection.

"Umm, yeah," Louise replied as if she were speaking to a five year old, "it's a masquerade party, so masks are kind of a necessity. And since I can't rely on everyone to remember to bring their own, despite what's on the invitation, I made sure to have extras." And with that, she was running out the door to the car, leaving Frankie to wonder if there was any detail left that Louise had not thought of.

"These masks are fantastic, Lou," Frankie whispered, sifting through the box Louise had brought back in. "More donations from London's West End?" There were masks made of velvet and feathers in almost every colour imaginable.

"Extras from Moulin Rouge," she affirmed, "and they were only too happy for me to take them off their hands, so I got the whole box for a song."

It suddenly occurred to Frankie that putting this party together must have cost Louise a small fortune, in spite of the many favours she had called in, and that she hadn't paid her a penny.

"Lou, you've really gone above and beyond with this; I really can't thank you enough," Frankie began, knowing that she would have to tread lightly when it came to the subject of money. "I really couldn't have done any of this without you. So, how much do I owe you?"

She had tried to slip that last part in subtly, hoping that Louise would just answer without paying much attention. But Frankie should have known better. Considering who she was dealing with, that move was never going to work.

"You owe me nothing," Louise brushed it off without so much as a perfunctory glance in Frankie's direction. "I'm considering it an investment in my career. Besides, once word gets out that this is the best party Brighton will have seen in years, that in itself will be payment enough."

And with that she disappeared upstairs, leaving Frankie to continue marveling at the masks, once more awestruck by her best friend. She knew that there would be no further discussion of the issue. Before she'd had the time to consider a counterattack, Louise was back, looking flawless and grabbing the box away from her to choose the ones that would best complement their outfits as she shooed her out the door.

With another heavy sigh, Frankie hurried as quickly as her gold buckled heels could carry her over the cobbled stones of Louise's driveway to the car.

7:10pm

As they approached the shop on foot, Frankie tried her best to put her personal bias aside and see it with a more subjective eye, the way others would as they passed by it every day. The newly-mounted pink sign extended overtop the door in its oval gilded frame above the street, hanging from antique brass hinges as if it had always been there. It enticed passersby from both directions inside to experience MacSweet Chocolaterie, written in an elegant metallic brown script that itself looked good enough to eat, as if the words had been dipped in chocolate themselves.

She paused in front of the window. The pink and brown brocade silk damask curtains were drawn closed to protect the display Frankie had been working on tirelessly over the past few days. The hidden treats waited, patiently she imagined, for their moment in the spotlight. It was then that she realised, once she'd put this evening behind her, she should maybe look into trying for a full eight hours of sleep. That attributing human characteristics to the chocolate she made wasn't the sign of a well-rested mind. *Waiting patiently? What the fuck?*

After stepping through the shop door, they made short work of the remaining party preparations. The humidor in the main display had reached the perfect temperature to store chocolate, about twenty degrees Celsius, so it was time to fill it with all of the liquor-infused truffles, pralines and cordials she had produced. A variety of candied peels, edged in rich dark chocolate, added a splash of citrus colour.

The silver gleam of the serving platters on the table was soon obscured by a careful selection of Frankie's very best offerings that looked almost *too* good to eat, including her latest creation. A reimagining of the Brighton Button, with two round wafers made from both white and dark chocolate infused with blood orange liqueur, sandwiched together with an apricot cream. Her test batch had even managed to win over the harshest of critics: Louise's housekeeper, Mavis, whose own family recipe had served as both inspiration and a starting point. If Mavis approved, assuming that it was a sign of approval when she had downed three of the treats in quick succession, that was more than enough for her.

Shortly after they had finished lighting the candles and plugged in the fairy lights, Frankie noticed that her palms were soaking wet and her vision was beginning to blur.

"Lou, I think I'm going to be sick," she whispered as she sprinted for the washroom. Louise hurried after her, shouting something about how Frankie had better not mess up her makeup.

"Stretch out your neck so you don't get anything on that dress," she barked as Frankie heaved her stomach contents into the toilet, "and don't squinch up your eyes. Your mascara will run and there isn't time to fix it."

She stared balefully in the mirror as Louise continued to shout instructions on how to vomit with style from the other side of the closed door.

"You'll be pleased to know that I did not mess up my makeup, nor did I get anything on my dress," Frankie announced with no small amount of disparagement as she opened the door.

"Well, that's a relief," Louise replied without looking at her. She was leaning on the opposite wall, compact in hand, doing what she did best: admiring her reflection. In this strange new world that Frankie found herself in, it was nice to know that there were some things that would never change.

"I'm fine, by the way!" She all but shouted back over her shoulder, making her way back to the shop floor. Again, no response. Louise sauntered after her in such a languid and casual manner it made Frankie want to ring her perfect little neck.

"You've just got a case of the jitters, Frannie, is all," Louise came up behind her, reaching up to sling an arm casually over her shoulder as she tried to force herself to calm down. She was shaking from nervous energy or fear; she hadn't quite decided which emotion was winning out.

"I don't think I can do this," she admitted finally. All of the confidence Frankie had felt earlier seemed to have completely abandoned her. Even the gorgeous dress she was wearing wasn't enough to save it.

Louise spun her round to face her, so fast that Frankie almost lost her breath. And what may have remained in her unsettled stomach.

"Now you listen to me," Louise commanded. "You can do this, and I'll tell you why. Because this is exactly what you've always wanted, what you've dreamed about since you were a kid. It's what you're meant to do, Frankie! And I'll be damned if I'm going to sit back and watch you fuck it up because of a little case of nerves. You've worked way too hard, and that dress is far too fantastic, to give up now." Louise spoke so passionately, in such a heartfelt manner, that it nearly brought tears to Frankie's eyes.

She had always found it amazing how quickly her best

friend could turn on a dime. One minute she was nonchalantly dismissing Frankie's hysterics as an overreaction, the next she was giving some impassioned speech about how invincible and phenomenal she was. It would make most people dizzy with how fast she could switch it on and off, but Frankie had more than enough time to adjust to the pace. Louise been this way for as long as she had known her.

Perhaps it was why she had always felt so at ease with Henry and his wild mood swings, from the years of training she'd experienced with Louise.

That thought had crept in quietly, the way all of the other thoughts Frankie had about Henry over the past few weeks did. Like a thief in the night. It was gone almost as soon as it appeared, but the damage was done.

"Don't. Don't you dare start crying on me, Frankie. Because then I'll start and then we'll both need to fix our faces." Louise paused. Then she smiled slightly.

Frankie looked at her, puzzled, before she understood what she had been smiling about. There it came again, a soft knock on the door.

"Looks like someone is early," Louise said as she turned toward the sound.

She motioned Frankie into the back room, presumably so that she could make her grand entrance later after more guests had arrived. In what seemed like one fluid motion, she drew aside the curtains to unveil the window display and unlocked the door.

"It's showtime," Frankie muttered to herself as she

tried to keep her knees from giving out beneath her.

SEVENTEEN

October 13th

8:19pm

The very notion of walking into a room full of strangers would normally have been enough to fill Frankie with dread, but by the time Louise felt that there were enough guests in attendance to warrant her presence and came back to fetch her, she felt like she was more than ready for it. It was as though Louise's earlier words of encouragement had cast some sort of spell over her, a magical incantation that seemed to take away all of Frankie's fears over the evening ahead. Because without warning, the trepidation she had been experiencing seemed to disappear, replaced with a feeling of euphoria quite unlike anything Frankie had felt before.

"Ladies and gentlemen," Louise announced as she led her into the middle of the shop floor, "it gives me great pleasure to introduce you to the talent behind the fantastic treats you're enjoying this evening: one Ms. Frankie MacSweeney!"

Thank Christ for the mask, Frankie thought as the crowd

burst into applause and whistles around her. She could feel her cheeks burning with self-consciousness. Had this been happening but a few short weeks earlier, she would have melted into a puddle of her own anti-social insecurities, having never been one to enjoy being the centre of attention.

But not tonight. *Tonight, I am graceful. I'm sophisticated. I am fucking exquisite. And they love me.*

She could admit that the crowd's adoration may have had more to do with the wine they'd been drinking, or the chocolate they'd been nibbling, or perhaps it was the fact that everyone was wearing masks. Whatever it was, Frankie didn't care, because it seemed to be working.

Louise stood by her side, whispering the names and rank of the people who milled about so that it would appear that Frankie had known all along who they were. So clever, it made her wonder if Louise had somehow coded the masks they were wearing. After about fifteen minutes of greeting strangers, she finally happened upon a familiar, if partially covered, face.

"James," Frankie felt it was a little odd that she should be so genuinely relieved to see her ex-boyfriend. "I'm pleased you could make it."

She gave him a quick hug before nodding a polite hello to his new girlfriend whose name escaped her at that moment. *Why would I waste energy on remembering the name of the slapper he cheated on me with?* There was such a thing as *too* forgiving, after all.

"Wow, Frankie... you look... wow. Amazing," James spoke as if in a trance, his eyes roving up and down her form. Hungry, would be the best word Frankie could think of to describe it. His girlfriend seemed a little less than pleased as she noticed, too, which only served to give Frankie a badly-needed boost of confidence.

"It's so great to see you, James," she practically purred as she took hold of his arm and leaned closer, in another completely uncharacteristic move for her.

Louise covered her mouth to stifle a smirk, knowing exactly what it was that Frankie was up to. It was something that had been stolen straight out of her own playbook. Maybe it had been the two glasses of champagne she had downed that was making her so bold, but she noticed that James seemed to be rather enjoying her attention. On the other hand, his girlfriend did not.

"It's exhausting having to make small talk with a bunch of people you don't know," Frankie continued more conversationally, easing up on the sex kitten act. She didn't think it was a good look for her. It smacked of insincerity. And James wasn't Henry.

"Well, they seem to love you. But then again, who wouldn't, eh?" James leaned in closer to whisper in her ear. He had never been one for subtlety.

Frankie had to put on the brakes and save him from himself as she had done countless times in the past. *Stupid ass*

"Well, I think it has more to do with the food than it does me. It's Shaye, isn't it," she responded quickly as she turned to the girl, by some miracle managing to conjure up her name from nothing. "Have you seen anything you like? I mean, if there were anyone here tonight who would *really* know their chocolate, it would be you."

Shaye looked as though she was about to pass out from the shock, first that Frankie was even acknowledging her without a hint of malevolence and then that she should mention her background so openly.

"Well," Shaye began warily, casting a confused glance at James who seemed equally as confused. "They all look really good, but I'd have to say that my favourite is those little sandwiches on the table over there. Those are adorable." She offered a timid smile, which to her own surprise Frankie returned rather easily.

This didn't have to be difficult, she decided; they were all adults. Perhaps, in the future, they might even become friends.

"Yes, I see those have been flying off the plates."

It was a gamble that appeared to be paying off, as Frankie had so fervently hoped it would. Her version of the beloved Brighton Buttons was going down a treat with the locals: the fact that she had cared enough to research something traditional and reinvent it in a way that would work with her own product line appeared to be creating the connection she had hoped for. After this small victory, Frankie felt as if she could do no wrong. At one point, she was afraid someone would soon be asking her for a speech. There wasn't enough champagne in the world to make that happen, despite how well Frankie had been doing with the crowd.

But then again, perhaps she had spoken too soon.

Frankie's mother emerged without warning from the crowd, like a graceful swan gliding across a pond, her father trailing close behind. As he had always done. Frankie felt her

361

throat begin to tighten and fought the urge to run in the opposite direction. It would be the first time in well over a year that she had seen her mother in person.

"Shit," was the only thing that would come out.

She looked around desperately for Louise, who was off canoodling with Jared in a corner, feeding him what appeared to be a dark chocolate Scotch truffle. It was too late to make a run for it; her mother had already seen her.

"Frances, hello," she drawled in her soft Edinburgh lilt.

She stopped a polite distance away as her father dashed past to scoop Frankie up into a fierce bear hug.

"Oh, Frankie my girl, you are but a sight for sore eyes," he crowed as he swung her around easily, as if she were still a little girl instead of her adult height of nearly six feet tall.

Tears came to Frankie's eyes as she was reminded of how warm and wonderful her father was.

"Hi Dad," she gave him a squeeze back. "But, um, could you maybe put me down now please? People are starting to stare." Reluctantly, he obliged.

"Well, if they're staring, it'd be only at you. You look bloody gorgeous, you do," he boomed in his broad Northern brogue, adding in a concerned fatherly manner. "But you might be a little on the thin side. Hope you aren't working so hard you're forgetting to feed yourself."

"Of course she is, Stewart," her mother interjected. "You know what she's like. It's just a miracle that she's not as big as a house, what with being surrounded by all this chocolate."

And suddenly, in those two simple sentences, Frankie was reliving her childhood all over again. *Can't allow her to get to me. Not this time, not tonight. This is* my *night.*

"So what do you think of the place, Dad?" Frankie directed the question at him, pointedly ignoring her mother's comment.

"Oh, it's grand, Frankie, right out of an old fairy story—" he began before Frankie's mother abruptly cut him off. As she was prone to doing.

"Well, it seems that you have done quite well with the place, Frances, and I must say I am impressed. But, why the masks?" Her nose wrinkled in disapproval, an expression with which Frankie was all too familiar. "I mean, how are you to know who it is you're dealing with? It might be the mayor or the stockboy, and you would never know the difference."

Ever true to form, rather than allow her the luxury of enjoying the closest thing to a compliment Frankie would have received from her in years, her mother had to find something to criticise.

"Well, Mother," she replied through gritted teeth. "That's sort of the point. Since you can't really be certain who anyone is, it forces you to treat everyone the same way. It evens out the playing field so everyone is equal."

To be truthful, Frankie hadn't really given it that much thought, but dealing with her mother always had brought out the socialist in her. *Socialism is the opposite of fascism, isn't it?*

"Indeed," her mother mused by way of response.

Even though she couldn't see past her red mask, Frankie could tell by her mother's tone that her eyebrows had shot up in that condescending way they always did whenever she thought Frankie was being overly sensitive. Or impractical. Or hysterical. Or otherwise ridiculous. In other words, it was her common response to most of the things that Frankie said.

Frankie decided to try another tactic by switching the topic to something more benign. The weather. The three of them chatted cordially about the inconsistencies of the Scottish summer and how her parents were looking forward to their holiday in the South of France that Christmas. Then her mother seemed to remember something important.

"Where's this fiancé of yours, then? Has he not come out as a show of support? Or is he too afraid to meet your parents?" She seemed a little too pleased with that last question, and Frankie mentally kicked herself for forgetting to send her parents a quick update on her recently single status so as to avoid such an awkward question.

"We're not together anymore," she said quickly and without emotion. It was a half-truth, to be sure, but a necessary one given the situation.

Again, she could hear the eyebrows raising behind her mother's mask, and fought the compulsion to scream.

"I can't really say that I'm surprised, my dear" her mother responded, casually inspecting her manicured nails. "It's actually a relief to know that some things never change. But there must be some interim replacement, yet another Mr. Right Now? Where is he?"

The urge to scream became almost too much to bear, and Frankie very nearly gave in to it. But she knew that she couldn't allow her mother the satisfaction. And as luck would have it, that feeling was stronger.

"Actually, Mother, I've been far too busy putting this shop together to even think about men," she replied coolly. Another half-truth, equally as necessary. "And I know that in the past I may have had some co-dependency issues with men, but I've been single now for almost a month and it's been really good for me."

Frankie wasn't sure what had compelled her to add something so personal in such a public place. Perhaps there was a part of her trying to reach out. She was, after all, her mother. But she should have known better than that. Frankie's haphazard yet heartfelt confession had fallen upon deaf ears as her mother began to laugh.

"A month?" She finally managed through fits of giggling. "Isn't that some sort of record for you?" And with that, Frankie was done.

"Always a pleasure, Mother," she smiled tightly, "but if you'll excuse me, it looks like I have some platters to fill."

As she passed by her father, she told him to find her before he was leaving so that she could say goodbye, a request that she knew he would understand applied solely to him.

She blinked back the tears on her way into the kitchen. Louise would have her head if she knew that Frankie was letting her mother ruin her makeup like this. But she wasn't so much upset with her mother as she was with herself. It was foolish of her to even think that she would care, though somewhere inside that small part that had reached out earlier must have thought that tonight would be different. That maybe, just maybe, after all these years Frankie might have finally done something her mother might be proud of.

Frankie heard a small sound, like a footstep and a clearing of the throat, from behind her as she pulled more chocolate from the humidor in the kitchen.

"Dad?" She almost dropped her tray as she turned to see who it was. "You startled me."

He apologised as he came over to take the tray from her hands, which were shaking.

"I'm sorry, Frankie," he whispered, taking hold of her hands as if he hoped that the gesture would keep them still. "You know what your mother is like. She has a bit of trouble showing her feelings, that's all."

She let out a bitter laugh in spite of herself.

"No, Dad, that's just it. She has no trouble at all. She has made it quite clear, in fact, that nothing I ever do will be good enough for her."

She began blinking more furiously as the tears threatened to spill over. Her father pulled her into another one of his infamous bear hugs. The man took his hugging very seriously.

"No, no, duck, that's where you're wrong," he said softly, lightly stroking her back, "she loves you very much. It's all she can talk about, in fact, you opening this shop. Why, even tonight when we came in and had a peek round, she got a little teary and said that she wished your Nan was here to see how far you've come."

Frankie had never known her father to lie, even if it were in an effort to spare her feelings, but she had trouble accepting what he was saying as the complete truth. It was as if he was talking about a completely different woman, some alternate reality version of her mother with whom she had yet to be acquainted.

"But, why can she not just come out and say that to me? Why does she have to be such a..." she needed to remember that it was her father she was speaking to and that she would have to choose her vocabulary carefully, "total cow all the time?"

Her father shrugged as he relaxed his death grip on her.

"I don't know. It's just her way. But I've seen different sides to her, ones that you haven't, so you're just going to have to take my word for it."

There was a question that Frankie had always wanted to ask, but could never work up the nerve. Until that moment, apparently.

"How can you stand it? All these years with her, I mean... How have you been able to stay?"

That was where her father surprised her, something she had previously thought him incapable of doing. He did not hesitate with his response.

"Because I love her," he said, with another small shrug. "And when you love someone, you take the good with the bad."

Frankie's father, in addition to being a serial hugger, was a man of few words. But those few words, when he did speak them, were often so chock full of meaning that they rendered all further discussion in the matter pointless. She gave him another quick squeeze and sent him back out to enjoy the party, before her mother could come looking for him and ruin this perfect moment. Just one moment where Frankie almost believed that she could really be proud of her, and maybe wasn't as evil as she had always believed her to be.

She had just finished putting the last of the cherry cordials and milk chocolate-covered Frangelico pralines on the tasting table and was about to step out of the way of the ensuing stampede when she heard the faint ringing of the front door bell. Wondering who else could possibly have been showing up, especially since it had appeared that most of Brighton was already in attendance, she turned toward the sound with curious expectation. And froze.

The tall lean figure in an elegant white tuxedo suit moved through the doorway and in her direction, his pale blonde hair slicked back and shining like polished silver beneath the fairy lights. A simple black mask obscured his features, but they were features she was too familiar with to be fooled by such a simple thing.

As if it were possible to mistake him for anyone else. As if Frankie had not had his face so firmly etched into memory it may as well have been stone. As if she did not already see him everywhere she turned anyways, regardless of whether her eyes were closed or not.

"Henry," his name escaped her lips without her knowledge.

He came to a stop in front of her, careful to maintain a

respectful, almost cautious distance. She thought she saw his hand shake slightly as it extended, palm open and facing up, in a gesture meant to bridge the gap. Like a peace offering.

"Frankie," he whispered softly.

As he said her name, Frankie felt it resonate throughout her entire body, from the top of her head all the way down to her toes. She almost hadn't noticed that he wasn't finished speaking.

"You look… Well, I don't think there has been a word yet invented for how completely exquisite you look. Even if I had a thousand words, that wouldn't be enough."

Frankie remained frozen, not daring to breathe, not willing to move lest this moment dissolve into nothing more than a waking dream and Henry would suddenly disappear. From the corner of her eye, she could see Louise and Jared moving toward them, which reminded her. Of everything.

"What are you doing here?" Frankie whispered finally.

She saw his eyes flicker in confusion before hardening slightly. His hand dropped lifelessly to his side.

"I gather that Louise didn't tell you," he answered, somewhat stiffly.

Frankie shook her head slightly, not quite that sure she had heard him correctly.

"No. As a matter of fact, she didn't… tell me anything at all, it would seem," she replied just as coldly.

Louise appeared beside her in a flurry of burgundy velvet and black lace fringe.

"Oh hi Henry, so glad you could make it! Frankie,

might I have a word? Jared, darling, won't you get Henry a drink? We'll be back in a tick."

Louise was tugging at her arm, but Frankie remained stubbornly fixed in place. Henry didn't appear to be terribly eager to follow Jared to the bar, either. He remained motionless, his eyes burning into hers. Frankie held her own, struggling to keep her trembling to a minimum, refusing to let him know how much seeing him was affecting her.

A small, elegantly coiffed woman in her mid-fifties drifted over, intentions clearly fixed on Henry.

"Mr. Fitz, isn't it," she intoned in a casual manner, extending her hand palm down as if she thought she were the Queen or something.

Henry's gaze shifted sharply in her direction at first, before automatically softening. She was, after all, a member of the very public whose favour he was still in the process of culling.

Frankie didn't bother hiding the roll of her eyes as he took her hand gently and kissed it with a small bow, almost gagging as the woman giggled like a teenager. It was too much for her to bear.

"Is it? Mr. Fitz, I mean. Is it really? Are you quite sure? Because I could have sworn that you were someone else entirely," Frankie blurted out in a nasty tone before she could stop herself.

Louise, still fervently tugging, managed to wrench her away before anything more could come out of Frankie's mouth. As she dragged her back toward the kitchen, Frankie could hear the woman introduce herself as a food critic from one of the local magazines, and ask him point-blank for an interview. For some reason, it made her all the more furious.

She hadn't even bothered to say a single word to her, the person she was supposed to have been there to see and talk to. Frankie had even witnessed her polish off half a plate of buttercreams dipped in dark chocolate singlehandedly without so much as a 'thanks, these are delicious'.

"What have you done," she hissed at Louise once they were safely enshrouded in the darkness of the kitchen.

"Look Frankie. I was going to tell you, really. But when I saw how you reacted when I told you Henry had asked about you – that was a test, by the way, which you failed – I knew I couldn't risk it. If I had told you that he might be here tonight, you would have freaked out and blown everything, and this is just too important. So, much as it killed me, I had to keep it to myself."

She sounded heartfelt enough.

"How did you invite him? Through Jared?"

"No, not exactly," she said, suddenly reluctant to continue. "That was how I had originally intended to do it, but then he just… He showed up at the house one night. With Jared, after work. To apologise, for the whole Cocoa Cream thing and all. He told me his story, the same as he'd told you, and about how he'd never intended for the chocolate to have that kind of effect on me. It was just meant to be a warning for my father. And he thought at first that it would be a good way to get to him, through me."

Louise was chewing nervously on her lip as she waited for Frankie to react, and with good reason. The only reason she hadn't exploded earlier was because she was too enraged to speak.

"So what, that's it?' Frankie hissed. "He's said he's sorry and you've just *accepted* it, no questions asked? I mean,

371

it's all well and good that he hadn't *meant* for any of that to happen to you, but that doesn't change anything. While you were never in any real danger, you were under an influence that wasn't your own. And that, in itself, is dangerous." Frankie was trying to keep her voice low, speaking in as hushed a tone as she could, mindful of not creating a scene. It felt more like a whispered scream.

"I think Henry is genuinely sorry for what he's done and he has been trying to make amends since then so yes, I have accepted his apology. And if you get the chance, I think you should do the same. Frannie, he's a good man, and he loves you. Don't push him away."

She couldn't believe what she was hearing. Had discovering true love with Jared turned Louise soft? Frankie decided to change her strategy.

"But what about everything he's done to your father?" she demanded, pitch rising again. "To your family's business? He's taken it all away from you." Louise had begun shaking her head before she had even finished speaking.

"No, Frankie," she said softly. "He set my father free. Daddy always hated that factory, only stuck in and did it because he was a Chadwick and that was what he was expected to do. And to be honest, the way I see it, Henry is only taking back something that rightfully belonged to him. Something that had been taken away from *his* family. And he's turning things around at the company brilliantly, because that's what he's always dreamed of doing. Like you, with this shop. Don't tell me you wouldn't do the same if someone tried to take this place away from you."

"What, take part in some ancient Mayan ritual that would grant me near eternal life so I could spend the next hundred years plotting and scheming to get my shop back, all while ruining an infinite number of lives along the way? I don't think so," Frankie shot back defensively, but had to admit that some of what Louise had said made sense. However, being stubborn by nature, she wasn't quite ready to abandon all of her preconceived notions just yet.

"I still can't believe you didn't tell me any of this before, Lou," she grumbled. "Aren't we supposed to tell each other everything?"

Frankie had always found guilt to be a brilliant weapon. Louise sighed heavily.

"I'm sorry for not telling you, Frannie. Really, truly sorry. But please believe that whatever I did, what I've kept from you, it was for your own good. How many times have you taken care of me in the past, eh? Isn't it about time I returned the favour?" She paused for a moment – possibly for dramatic effect, possibly to consider what to say next – before continuing.

"Maybe you need to recognise that you can't control everything all the time, and that every now and again it's okay to let people help you. But to go back to the real reason we're here: why is it that you think you are so unworthy of Henry's love?"

If Frankie could have been struck down from the force with which that final question hit its mark, she would have been laid out senseless and drooling on the floor.

"What the hell, Lou? Where did that come from?"

"Well, that's at the heart of all of this, isn't it?" Louise pressed on, determined.

"You are so convinced that you don't deserve someone like Henry that you go looking for any excuse you can find not to be with him. You're terrified that you aren't good enough."

Frankie was so flabbergasted, both at her friend's nerve as well as how disturbingly well she could read her that she couldn't find the words to respond. Fortunately, she didn't need to.

"Right, too much for one night? Let's get back to the party then, shall we? After a quick freshen up, of course," Louise said airily as she went to switch on the washroom lights and inspect herself in the mirror, both with and without the mask.

Instead of continuing to stand there gaping like a fish at how accurately she'd just been pinned, Frankie decided she had no other choice but to follow. Silently, she allowed Louise to fuss about, checking to ensure that her makeup had held up and her hair was still perfectly waved before pulling her back into the party.

In their absence, the evening had taken an unexpected turn. Either Frankie had been a bit too heavy-handed with the booze in the truffles, or the party mix Louise had made on her iPad was so good that people couldn't keep themselves from dancing.

As she glanced across the shop floor turned impromptu dancefloor, Frankie felt her heart begin to pound as she caught sight of Henry. It dropped to her feet when she noticed who he was speaking with.

James and Shaye.

Almost against Frankie's will, Louise tightened her grip and towed her toward them. Henry, who had seen them approaching long before the others had, offered Frankie a polite nod and tight smile as they drew closer. But his eyes, which had not strayed from hers since she had begun to cross the room, seemed to reflect so much more. Frankie studied James for any sign of apprehension in the presence of his possible captor, for want of a better term, but found nothing. If anything, it was quite the opposite. He looked relaxed and happy as he chatted away with Henry, with Shaye tucked close into his side. She only had eyes for James; it was obvious to Frankie that she adored him.

After crossing the room in what felt like a lifetime, James nearly floored Frankie by giving her a subtle nod and an elbow in Henry's direction, punctuated by a little wink. Once recovered from her initial shock, she decided it was time to screw up her courage and take action.

"Henry, would I be able to speak with you…in private? I think there are a few things we need to talk about," she said quietly, praying her knees wouldn't give way.

His gaze, tinged with something Frankie could not place, flickered slightly while he considered his answer.

"I agree. But first, would you grant me one request?" His eyes remained unreadable.

"What's that, then?"

"Dance with me," he said, his voice rough and eyes darkening as they threatened to drag Frankie under with the intensity.

"But we need to talk," she whispered, breathless but determined to hold her ground. Henry took hold of her hand and pulled her to the middle of the floor without further discussion.

"We can talk and dance at the same time," he replied, his voice once more as smooth as the chocolate she had spent the last few weeks tempering.

He put his arms around her, pulling her tight against him as she heard the opening strains of one of her favourite ballads from the Eighties begin to play. The timing was almost comedic. Frankie's head dropped forward against his chest, an automatic reflex over which she had no control. She hoped he wouldn't take it as a sign of defeat.

"You know," he said finally after they had danced for a few moments in silence. "I've been wanting to do this since the first night I saw you." Frankie looked up at him, puzzled.

"That night at the shop?"

"No, no. Not then," Henry laughed. She could feel it rumbling deep in his chest where her cheek rested, then felt the low hum of his voice as he continued.

"The night of Louise's party. I saw you there, on the terrace. You were leaning on the stone wall, wearing the most remarkable velvet gown – purple, if memory serves – and the moonlight on your face... In that moment I thought you were the most beautiful thing in the world. But I suppose now I stand corrected, because every time I see you, I seem to think exactly the same thing."

Frankie had barely noticed herself melting into him. It felt like the most natural thing for her to do. But she knew that she couldn't. She could not allow herself to be influenced by his charm, by the euphoria that coursed through her veins when he confirmed that he had seen her that night as well, just like she had felt that he had. She could not let herself entertain the possibility that maybe he had been thinking of her as much as she had about him. She had to switch subjects before it was too late.

"So I hear that you've been making some really

positive changes at the factory in the short time that you've been there," she stammered, trying desperately to appear nonchalant. It seemed enough to give him pause.

"I suppose I have, but there was nowhere to go but up, really. The most important thing in this business is to keep your workforce happy, so I made it my first priority."

"And Jared tells me you've hired Dr. Von Hoffstatler on as well," Frankie prattled on, becoming ever more intoxicated by the nearness of him.

"Well yes, that is true," Henry responded after a moment's pause. "The good doctor is an expert in his field, so it felt prudent given my... condition. Not to mention that he's the world's foremost expert in the blending of chocolate." His reply reminded Frankie of a question she had wanted to ask him earlier, but was too afraid of the answer.

"So what's the deal: are you alive or dead?" There was a longer pause this time, allowing her time to listen for his heartbeat. She couldn't hear anything beyond her own.

"I... I honestly...don't know," Henry replied unevenly.

They danced on in silence as yet another one of Frankie's favourite songs came on. She was beginning to wonder if maybe Louise had planned things a little *too* well.

"Well, as much as I'm enjoying holding you here in my arms, something tells me that when you said you wanted to speak with me privately, talking about the factory or my questionable state of being wasn't quite what you'd had in mind."

Frankie froze mid-step as she realised what was coming next.

"When we last spoke," he went on, "you had asked me to give you time and space to think about everything I had told you. I was hopeful that when Louise extended the invitation to me for tonight, it meant that you were ready to see me. From the look on your face when I came through that door, I knew that wasn't the case. And I apologise for getting upset earlier... I'm not angry at you. I'm angry with myself for allowing myself to believe that you were ready to move forward. Preferably, with me."

She remained silent. *How do I even begin to respond to that?* Beyond a rather random series of monosyllabic grunts coupled with some unattractive drooling, Frankie was drawing a blank. She decided that the safest thing to do was the very thing she seemed to be entirely incapable of: keep her big mouth shut.

"Okay, still nothing I see," Henry mused, "let's try a more direct approach then, shall we? I know that you have been rather busy these past few weeks, but I need to ask. Have you thought of me at all?"

She felt her heart drop to her toes once again for what felt like the umpteenth time that evening, her mind reeling with the implications of his question. *Was that the same as admitting that he thought about me?*

Frankie remained quiet, still unable to trust herself to speak. She could feel Henry's arms twitching slightly around her in what must have been agitation but she thought he was keeping his composure rather well. Had she been in his position, she doubted she would have been able to do the same.

"Hmmm," he said, his voice sounding slightly more strained, "and again, the lady does not speak. That's fine. I'm prepared to wait. I believe I've already established that I can be very patient should the situation call for it. And until Dr. Von Hoffstatler says otherwise, I have nothing but time." His last statement cut through the fog of emotions swirling around her brain.

"What does that mean?" she asked sharply.

Henry stopped moving to lean back and look down into her face, smiling wryly.

"Ahh, at last! Well, I can't really divulge any details just yet, but for the moment I will say that this living forever business is highly overrated. I'm exploring my options."

He smiled at her again, more gently this time, and Frankie felt all of the steely resolve she had spent so long building around her come crashing down. It was so sudden and unexpected that she felt her knees weaken and begin to buckle beneath her. Not surprisingly, Henry caught her. But Frankie couldn't let him disarm her by being charming. There were a few questions she had that were in need of answering first.

"What really brought you here, to Brighton? Was it your plan for Chadwick's or me?" She fired at him point-blank. Henry didn't even flinch.

"Both," he answered without hesitation. "I had seen a photograph of you that intrigued me and when James mentioned the party you were going to at Chadwick's, I couldn't resist the opportunity to catch a glimpse of you in person. You see, I thought you would be just like them: wealthy, entitled, bloated with your own self-importance. But when I saw you for the first time, standing alone so serenely, I wasn't so sure anymore. So I started to follow you."

Frankie looked up at him sharply.

"You what?" That added a much creepier edge to his story, one she wasn't sure that she liked the sound of.

"Well, not directly, of course. I found out where you were going to be doing your banking by making a few calls. As it turns out, yours was the only chocolate business in queue looking for financing. It's quite amazing what you can find out when you are looking to become an angel investor."

"I knew the mentorship program was too good to be true," she said flatly. To her surprise, the comment made him wince.

"I had to make sure I had some sort of leverage over you, since at that point I will admit that I was still thinking you might be useful in getting to Chadwick if going through Louise was unsuccessful. And I don't mean that in the repulsive way it sounds. I fully intended to use all of my power and connections to make your shop the most successful in the country by using other suppliers, therefore forcing Chadwick's hand somehow."

"So you were planning on using me to get to Chadwick but in a way that would only benefit me in the end?" Frankie surmised, trying hard not to let her temper get the better of her.

"When you say it out loud like that it still sounds horrible, but I suppose in a way that's correct. That was, in essence, exactly what I was planning to do. But in the end, I couldn't go through with it. When I met you that first night in your shop, with primer dust on your bottom and in your hair, I knew then that you were nothing like them. How could you be? No Chadwick would ever think of getting their hands dirty doing actual work. So it was then that I resolved to continue to help you, but keep you well away from anything related to my plans for taking over Chadwick's."

The way Henry spoke made it all seem less despicable than Frankie had already managed to convince herself it was. Of course he wasn't going to make it easy for her. She had to stay strong.

"But then I refused to take any more of your money. I went to see Mr. Bradley at the bank," she said, though she was certain he would have already known that.

Henry stopped and grasped her firmly by shoulders, bending down so that he could look into her eyes.

"I know," he replied. "And that just makes me love you more." Frankie stopped breathing, wanting to hold on to that moment for as long as she could, but Henry wasn't finished.

"Your independence, that ironclad sense of ethics, your utter inability to accept anyone's assistance despite how much benefit it could provide... I just find it fascinating. Infuriating and exasperating, that too, but mostly I'm fascinated. It makes me want to know what makes you tick."

They had stopped dancing, but not for want of music. If Frankie could have turned her attention away from Henry she would have seen Louise at the sound system behind the cash register, furiously reinventing her playlist to keep the two of them slow-dancing for as long as possible. But there was no need: Frankie knew by instinct that it was all her doing.

There is no such thing as coincidence.

Henry and Frankie began to move again, closer than before, as yet another slow song swelled through the surround sound. The crowd had thinned out considerably, with only a few couples left wrapped in each other's embrace. But none of that mattered. As far as Frankie was concerned, they could have been in the middle of a mosh pit with a bunch of Liberty spike-wielding punks slam-dancing around them, and it wouldn't have made the tiniest bit of difference. The only thing that mattered in that moment was the two of them.

"So what happens now?" Frankie wondered out loud. She could feel Henry's chest heave and collapse as he sighed.

"Well, you know where I stand. I love you, and I want to be with you. The rest...well, I'm afraid that's up to you." *If only it were that easy,* she thought ruefully. Her prolonged silence seemed to make him nervous.

"If you can forgive me for everything I've done, try to look past the fact that I'm not quite human but know that it's something I'm working on, I promise you – you will not regret it."

Frankie thought back to something her father had said earlier that evening: *When you love someone, you take the good with the bad.*

"I love you," Henry continued with a little more urgency to his voice. "And I know that there's at least some small part of you that loves me as well. You wouldn't be here right now if you didn't. So tell me, what is it that's stopping you?" *What indeed,* she thought.

Why is it that you think you are so unworthy of Henry's love? Louise's words came drifting back to her.

"I'm scared," she finally whispered. It was the truth.

Henry tilted Frankie's chin up to face him.

"It's okay," he whispered softly. "I'm a little scared myself."

His face lowered, and Frankie raised up on her toes expectantly to meet him halfway. And then she heard Louise's voice screeching through the speakers.

"All right, everyone, it's midnight. Masks off!"

Right. She had forgotten all about that particular jewel in the crown that was Louise's master plan. About a week ago she had gotten it into her head how great it would be if, provided the party was still going, at midnight all the guests removed their masks. She kept calling it 'The Cinderella Moment'. Frankie had thought that Louise was having a laugh. There would be no Prince Charming, she remembered saying. No one was going to lose a shoe.

I guess the laugh's on me.

Without a word, Henry pulled Frankie's mask gently up over her forehead and slipped it off. In turn, she stood on tiptoe and removed his mask, letting it fall to the ground.

Masks off, they remained motionless, neither one daring to move.

"I love you," he whispered.

"I love you too, Henry. So much, I can't even..." She wasn't allowed to finish her thought before Henry kissed her.

Their lips met with a delicious heat that Frankie could feel all the way past her toes. She could have stayed that way forever. But, of course, these things can never last.

Reality came crashing back in the form of a drunken Louise singing along to the lyrics of the song that was playing. Although she seemed to be changing the words to make up a new song of her own. It was when she heard '*and Frankie and Henry are gonna do it tonigghhht*' that she decided that Louise had to be stopped. She was slurring so badly that Frankie doubted that anyone would have been able to make out what she had been singing, and the only people who remained were a few friends and her parents.

My parents...uh oh.

"Good night, duck." Frankie's father came over to gather her up in one final, rib-crushing squeeze. She kissed his cheek, trying not to smile as he gave Henry a meaningful once-over. Henry nodded politely and offered his hand in a firm shake as he introduced himself.

"Frankie?" She turned round and, to her utter astonishment, stood face to face with her mother. Who had never, ever called her by her nickname.

Her mother stood just behind her father, looking uncertain and hesitant. Two things that Frankie would not normally have associated with her. She stepped forward and before Frankie knew what was happening, her arms were around her.

"Your Nan would be so proud," were the only words she said, and then the moment was over as quickly as it had began. Once Frankie had recovered, she was already out the door.

"What the hell was that about?" Louise garbled as she stumbled toward Frankie and Henry, with Jared close at her side for support.

"I have no idea."

Frankie's mother had never hugged her, at least not in recent memory, so it left her at a bit of a loss. Of course it had to have been her father's doing, she presumed, but then again perhaps this was her attempt at turning over a new leaf in their relationship. A fresh start, even?

There seemed to be a lot of that going around.

Once all of the guests had gone and the shop was empty, Frankie did a final check before locking up. Henry leaned against the wall beside the door, watching her.

"It's been about a hundred and forty years since I've been in any sort of relationship," he said, almost as if to himself. "I hope I can remember how it works."

"Well, if it helps," Frankie replied, "I've never been in a relationship with a man I've respected before, so I guess it'll be a learning curve for both of us." He smiled and laughed, shaking his head as he so often did with her.

Frankie reached over and grabbed his hand as they walked together through the darkened, cobbled streets of the Lanes. Henry raised their clasped hands to his lips. And that was when she knew.

She knew that she was exactly where she was meant to be. In Brighton, taking care of Louise, although because Jared was shaping up to be something of a permanent fixture it looked as if she would have some help with that. In The Lanes, with a little chocolate shop that she could finally call her own.

And perhaps best of all, Frankie thought, *I'm here with Henry*.

She knew in her heart that this man would be beside her as they headed toward a future teeming with wonder and infinite possibility. She had no idea what it might bring with it, what new adventures would be waiting for them around the bend. But for the first time in her life, she looked forward to whatever lay ahead in part because she knew that she would not have to face it alone. Henry would be there, and they would handle it, whatever it might be.

Together.

We seem to be drifting into unknown places and unknown ways.
I will not let you go into the unknown alone.

-- Bram Stoker, *Dracula*

ABOUT THE AUTHOR

Kerri Thomson started writing at a young age, on a wide variety of topics ranging from the journey of a pumpkin seed through the human digestive tract at the age of six, an illustrated account of the Canadian Constitution at eight, and the script for a Christmas pageant at thirteen. In her Grade 12 Creative Writing class, she earned the moniker 'Kerri King' for the often macabre tone of her stories.

In adulthood she all but abandoned the craft but not her creative streak, with job titles that included shop manager for a Gothic and Victorian fetish boutique, and makeup artist in London, England. These days when she's not writing, watching TV or Tweeting about watching TV, she can be found in a white lab coat testing people's vision and enjoying it more than she should when patients thinks she's the doctor.

She enjoys shoes, hair bands from the Eighties and the colour pink.

The Chocolate Is The Life is her first novel.